Piece of my Heart

A LESBIAN OF COLOUR ANTHOLOGY

ANTHOLOGIZED BY

Makeda Silvera

ISBN 0-920813-65-8

1992 Second Printing

The outreach and promotion for this book was made possible in part with support from: The Lesbian and Gay Community Appeal and Société/Sociedad KIMETA Society of Toronto.

Canadian Cataloguing in Publication Data
Main entry under title
Piece of my heart: Lesbian of colour anthology

ISBN 0-920813-65-8

1. Lesbian's writings, Canadian (English).*
2. Lesbian's writings.
3. Lesbianism - Literary collections.
4. Canadian literature (English) - Minority authors.*
I. Silvera, Makeda, 1955-

PS8235.L47P5 1991 C810.8'0353 C91-095003-2
PR9194.5.L47P5 1991

Cover Painting: © *Rachel Henriques*
Production & Design: *Stephanie Martin*
Typesetting: *Blackbird Design Collective*
Printed & bound in Canada by union labour

Published by **Sister Vision Press**
             P.O. Box 217
             Station E
             Toronto, Ontario
             Canada M6H 4E2

Piece of my Heart

A LESBIAN OF COLOUR ANTHOLOGY

ANTHOLOGIZED BY
Makeda Silvera

Sister Vision
Black Women and Women of Colour Press

Acknowledgements

I want to thank all those wonderful, strong, sexy, talented women for their support and work in proofreading and inputting the manuscript. Karen Augustine, Aylssa Beckman, Margie Bruun-Meyer, Annette Clough, Sharon Fernandez, Tamai Kobayashi, Hazelle Palmer, Tracey Pinder, Ann Shin, Shenaz Stri, Melanie Tanaka.

Tamai, a special thanks. Honest, without your shared commitment to the project, *Piece Of My Heart* might still have been just a dream. Deep thanks to Stephanie, for her patience, particularly during those very tense moments; for love and editorial suggestions; and for her skills that finally got the book to the printer. My two daughters, Keisha and Ayoola, for putting up with my erratic behaviour and outbursts when the pressure got a little too much. Much thanks to all the contributors, without whom a celebration and a book such as this would not have been possible.

Last, to those sister women who held my hands and loved me when the dawn took such a long time to come and the nights too long to be real.

For Audre Lorde — her strength and courage
and for all women of colour who struggle and
celebrate living as lesbians

Contents

We Will Not Be Invisible   **169**

Pain and Betrayal   **217**

The Wanting and the Passion

Coming Into Our Own Power

INTRODUCTION

The publication of this anthology *Piece Of My Heart,* marks an important political and cultural contribution to the growing body of literature on Lesbian lives. *Piece Of My Heart, A Lesbian of Colour Anthology,* takes its place among these works; standing, proud, firm and brave in its honesty and uncompromising stance.

This book has taken a long time to come together. Close to six years. The first call for submissions went out in 1985 to lesbians in Canada, and later to lesbians living in the United States. The response was less than enthusiastic. Several other calls went out, but the contributions we received, though important, were not enough to make a book. It was not until 1988 through 1990 that the project began to develop a momentum and it seemed as if an anthology by and about lesbians of colour was possible. The anthology was not conceived in a vacuum; there are, were, always have been lesbians of all colours, of all cultures, of all socio-economic and political persuasions. We have always existed.

So why then did the anthology take such a long time to shape itself, why did it take so long to come out?

Judging from the response, it appeared that the time was not right, the climate was hostile and we were not ready to put our lives on the line. Our voices were stifled, stilted. Collectively, they were not ready to come out, to leave family—leave home in search of another home and family. It was also a question of energy—my own energy. As co-founder and publisher of a small, independent, woman of colour press, it is / was often difficult to keep the intense pace needed to encourage women to come out and put their voices in print—many of whom had never written or been published before. Difficult to be singularly focused on one anthology, when there were so many other writers with significant work that begged to be published. The role of publishers—good ones—are very much that of 'nourisher', and because of the demand to help in the birthing process of other books, *Piece Of My Heart* at times had to be put on hold.

Still something must be said about those 'stilted' voices, those voices that would not come out many years ago. In times like these, I like to go back to the personal, to turn the question around, "what about you? Would you have readily answered the call to such a book if you were not the initiator?" I have to honestly answer no. I would have hungrily bought the book, to read about others like me, to find strength and comfort in their words, but I might not have readily contributed without some coaxing. Why? The very thing that Audre Lorde so eloquently speaks about, that fear, that silencing of our voices, of our lives as lesbians. I quote from Lorde's essay "The Transformation of Silence into Language and Action", a piece I go back to, every time that awful 'fear' takes a hold of me.

> "In the cause of silence, each of us draws the face of her own fear - fear of contempt, of censure, or some judgment, or recognition, of challenge, of annihilation. But most of all, I think, we fear the visibility without which we cannot truly live."...
> "Your silence will not protect you...Your silence will not protect you." *(pg. 42 Sister Outsider, Essays and Speeches by Audre Lorde,)*

This is strong, powerful advice. And many brave strong women, feminists/and or lesbians have done this for years. Refusing to keep silent, and yet for each one of us who take Lorde's advice, there are still many others who remain silent. Some of our sisters and brothers live in cities, communities and countries where gays are in small numbers and there is little visibility. Because there is no organized groups, because there is no political or emotional support, fear is overpowering. Fear suppresses.

Fear of the loss of family, fear of obliteration from a whole community, a whole culture. For often times it is not just the loss of blood family we fear but that entire cultural community, where we go for comfort, for music, for food; where we go to when our daughters and sons get jerked around by a system that is plain racist. A system that tells us we are nothing but a bunch of criminals—that we have no voice. A culture that tells us that gay/ lesbian, women who love women of any colour are to be scorned and ridiculed. Our community, our family, are no exception, they are often embarrassed, scandalized, ashamed and fearful of us—lesbians—oddities. This is frequently what silences us, because without that home, without family, we often have only that hostile white world.

But we can remain silent for only so long, because with each silent day, with every denial of who we are, we die a little.

It is a serious and brave act each time one of us comes out, because for some of us the danger is real. There is always that threat of physical violence depending on the community that we live in, and depending on our socio-economic condition. Always, we must be on guard because violence against us is lurking. We are women, we are lesbians, we have no race privilege. Audre Lorde states in the same essay "...that the very visibility which also renders us most vulnerable is that which also is the source of our greatest strength. Because the machine will try to grind you into dust anyway, whether or not we speak. We cannot sit in our corners mute for ever...."

Piece Of My Heart stands as a testimony to the ongoing process of breaking our silences, being mute no longer. The voices are loud, honest, angry, passionate and full of love. These are the voices of lesbians who have always spoken out, who have been politically active in Black and Third World issues. These are the voices of women who are just embracing lesbianism, as well as political activism.

There are a few firsts in this book. To my knowledge it is the first such liaison of North American lesbians of colour, women coming together across the borders of Canada and the United States of America. We are women of different cultural, racial and class backgrounds meeting in one place and talking about our lives as lesbians of colour. There are many first time writers in the book, and many, many women who are immigrants to North America. These women, have historically been silent in anthologies, particularly in naming themselves lesbians. As an Afro-Caribbean woman, I was proud of the number of contributions that came from Caribbean women living in the diaspora. In our community, as I am sure in many others of colour, there is always the cry from heterosexuals that 'this is a white thing', that lesbians and gays do not exist in their communities. That if we want to be active politically in the larger heterosexual community, we must hide our sexuality. This anthology says to our respective communities— we will be silent no longer. Our children will know who we are. You will hear our voices! You will not be able to ignore us.

The body of work presented in this anthology varies. The work of women who have never written before and the writing of those of our sisters who have inspired us for years, appear side by side. This was a conscious decision. We need to hear all our voices. I feel that anthologies are one of the few places where new writers can get support and validity; where they can show case their work along with the established sisters that we all love and respect. It seems to me that to some extent anthologies have that political responsibility to first time writers. We need to accommodate and help expand the voices of our artists, recounting both happiness and tragedy in our lives.

The contributions in this anthology present a range of lesbian experience from coming out stories; the joys of being lesbian; the pain, the passion and the power. The stories are raw and loving. The book tells of our similarities as women of colour and also our diversity, which is often obscured by the term 'of colour'; a term that is politically useful, but often problematic in defining who we are. African Canadian, Women of the First Nations, Japanese, Chinese, African American, South Asian, Indo Caribbean, Afro-Caribbean, Latina, Chicana, Samoan, Pacifica/Asian, Puerto Rican, Malayasian, Mexican, Filipina, Chinese-Caribbean, Sansei (third generation Japanese Canadian), Filipina-Spanish and women of mixed racial heritage.

We are also, mothers, daughters, sisters, cousins, aunts, lovers, workers, victims, fighters, warriors, feminists, artists, visionaries. We are lesbian people. We carry with us always our cultural hearts and fighting spirit.

The work within these pages represent a diversity of voices, often reflecting the lives we lead, our reality, and the places we have been as lesbians and as women of colour, living and struggling in a racist, woman hating world.

Piece of My Heart is offered in eight sections, it begins with a topic that is so often on our minds, one we battle with constantly, and no lesbian escapes it.

COMING OUT, FINDING HOME—Mona Oikawa's poem, "Coming Out at the Sushi Bar", opens this section.

"The Maguro is the colour of dawn
this day as I tell you
'I am a lesbian.' "

Powerful words. The act of defining one's self. The act of forever coming out, naming ourselves. Voicing those words to family and friends, who sometimes act deaf, who often pretend that we have not spoken, that they did not hear "I am a lesbian."

The section speaks of betrayal, loss, culture, community, identity, conflict, the tearing apart between old friends and family, the search for 'a new home', and finding that home in women, in the building of new communities. Coming home to a woman.

MEMORIES/EXILE speaks to that conscious/unconscious self. Raw and urgent in its vulnerability, it reflects on childhood, cultural memories and the loss of home that one feels as an immigrant in North America. Belonging and unbelonging. The lesbian as stranger. In her journal piece Nalini Singh moves back and forth between her present home - Canada - and the one she left behind - Guyana. She uncovers memories of the vicious colour of racism. "Foreigner..foreign tongue—whispers in the snow about the paki who can't talk right." She wants to tell her grandmother about her love for a woman but holds back. "My tongue is burning to tell her of the night I have come from."

SISTER TO SISTER represents one of the largest sections in this anthology. Sharing our lives, our diversity, sisters talking to each other. Audre Lorde's powerful piece, "I am Your Sister" is reprinted. It is a timely and refreshing piece, though written many years ago. She speaks eloquently about being Black, woman, lesbian and the barriers we come up on as lesbians organizing with our heterosexual sisters. This is one article that every heterosexual sister who picks up this book should read. Debbie Douglas' piece speaks of the anger between us as Black lesbians, the confusion, the feelings of betrayal when one of us crosses racial lines and loves a white woman.

WE WILL NOT BE INVISIBLE addresses those parts of us that refuse to be invisible. Cheryl Clarke's "Saying the Least Said, Telling

the Least Told: The Voices of Black Lesbian Writers" and Karin
Aguilar-San Juan's "Exploding Myths, Creating Conciousness: some
first steps toward Pan-Asian Unity", are thought provoking pieces
that speaks to issues of in/visibility. Raymina Mays story "In The
Trenches" speaks about that Black working class cleaning woman
who is lesbian, dispelling another myth, the lesbian as white,
middle class. "I hear a Black American sister speak.'...... we have no
time to talk about who you sleep with.... Lesbian is a white
woman's game. Third World women have no time to talk about
who some privileged American women sleep with.' .....I ain't hardly
white or privileged and I know it's a damn lie what she saying".
Connie Fife's haunting poem "Bonnie, Because They Never Told
You Why", speaks to us painfully about being "brown, indian,
lesbian woman" caught in the grip of the racism, homophobia,
sexism of the court system. Other women speak also about living in
two cultures and that struggle always to be visible.

PAIN AND BETRAYAL speak to that *Piece of my Heart* that knows
hurt and pain. Pain caused through intimate relations with lovers
and friends, or the pain caused by a culture that is homophobic.
Women speak through poems about betrayal and anger, charting
the vulnerability and anguish that loving women at times cause.

CRAVINGS, a section featuring poems and food, adds delight
and humour. Some excellent recipes to try out.

THE WANTING AND THE PASSION is lusty, sexy and simply
hot. We are reminded of that roller coaster of feelings, that passion
for women that keeps us going and makes it all o.k. in the end.
Chrystos, poem "Dream Lesbian Lover" is a world of warm,
wonderful fantasy...

   "Dreamy woman has a bed of lace & roses & home
   She could build a fire in the rain
   Could always fix my car for free...."

Tamai Kobayashi's poem, "memory, need and desire" is burning
"...her skin is brown, golden, for we are people of rice...I want to
move against her, heart bursting, back arched, to see her eyes widen
in surprise, pulled beyond, this magical beginning, to feel her

move, beyond herself".....What more can I say, except read this section when the world gets ugly.

COMING INTO OUR OWN POWER, the last section of the book is about just that, power, our own. Silent no longer. Again, poetry is the dominant feature in this section.

Throughout the anthology, a thread of humour is ever present, even in the stories, journals, essays that are painful. This book is about us. These are our stories. Coming full circle we acknowledge and celebrate our differences, and there is power in our similarities.

I want to acknowledge with all my heart, women who came out in print and in their lives before this anthology. Women who paved the way, who helped build respective lesbian communities to make us strong and to serve as examples. It was through such women, the editors and contributors to *This Bridge Called My Back, Writings by Radical Women of Colour* (1981) and *All the Women are White, All the Blacks are Men, But Some of Us Are Brave* (1982) that my own voice began to emerge.

To the women who are coming into print, and coming out for the first time—more power!

Finally, I would like to say, I am exhausted! Yet happy, this is a time for celebration. The birth of *Piece Of My Heart*. She enters the world, full with life. Crying many voices. With One Heart, One Spirit.

Thanks and praises!
Makeda Silvera
October, 1991
Toronto, Canada.

Coming
Out
Finding
Home

MONA OIKAWA

Coming Out at the Sushi Bar

The *maguro* is the colour of dawn
this day as I tell you
"I am a lesbian."

We had taken our places
at our regular table
nestled in the privacy
of white *shoji*
far from the men
at the sushi bar.

I had given you
the prepared preamble:
how you were selected
first of all our family
to know the truth.

The steam from the *udon*
fogs my glasses
as I tell you
I feel closest to you
and need someone to know
who I really am
in case...

In case of accident,
or hospitalization,
or death.

And you in a tone
masking emotion,
inherited from generations
of women whispering
with sisters about lovers,
reply, "Yeah. So what?"

I am relieved yet disappointed.
Is it time to change the subject?

"The *wasabi* is hotter today," you say.
And feeling the pressure
to analyze and rationalize
(as so many straight people do)
you add,

"I knew after you had been away —
Was it in 1977? —
that you came back different.
I figured something horrible
had happened to you.
You had changed so much."
"It was actually after
I'd gone away in 1980 that
I decided I was a lesbian,"
I reply.

A familiar frost
is forming in my mouth
down through my chest,
reducing rich words of
lesbian complexity to
these elementary explanations
of why and how.

For I really want
to tell you that
my relationship with
my lover is turning,
maybe ending.

I want someone who has
known me all my life
to see this pain,
to hear how my insides
are being ripped away
leaving me hollow.

But all I say is,
"For me it is not
something negative
to be a lesbian."

And you with your *hashi*
poised to attack the
last California *maki*,
smile nervously.
"As long as you are happy,
that's what's important."

That is all.
No more discussion.

Maybe next time
I will tell you
how loving women
did change my life —

then describe to you how
a woman's skin is soft,
and how only a woman's touch
can send me beyond
the grief in this world —

But not tonight...

After the table is cleared
and our shadows grow large
against the ivory paper screens,
we will pay our bill and
each take a pastel-coloured mint
for the road.

You will catch
the go-train
to your family
in the suburbs.

And I will return
to my home,
moving in the wind
of women's voices,
lesbian voices,
honouring our passionate
comings and goings
through these life-long
journeys of coming out.

maguro: tuna
shoji: paper screens/doors
udon: noodles
wasabi: horse radish served with sushi
hashi: chopsticks
maki: sushi rolls

CHRYSTOS

Alone

in the Queer bar with ice water that cost $1.50
twenty years & hundreds of girlfriends later
I still
don't know how to do this
Never will
So I enjoy the closely swaying women's bodies
flicker of simmering desire
in this one place where we can sort of be
ourselves
that in every town is always smoky, tacky & not quite
clean
where class & race dim somewhat in red spinning lights
a haze of booze
Sober
this is not my home
but there's no place else to go
in a strange city

CHRYSTOS

Mama Wants Me to Come

home for Christmas
Better Homes & Gardens says daughter is supposed
to show up smiling   Pretend it's not old cans
    bottles   yellow newspapers
I come to your vacant lot   put a teacup on my knee
    watch you try to drape my queerness in ruffles
    stare at the dried weeds of memory
We've nothing   in common
different views of the same demolishing crew
    Your words are rubble mama   broken bricks
glass shards   rats   dog shit
    I come home like a wino falls asleep in a doorway
I come like fitting in a space no one else wants
    Your vacant eyes are weeping
want me to say I love you & I do
but I've rented a room with no view
        I burn your letter
            to keep warm

ANNETTE CLOUGH

Leaving Home, Coming Home

S ometimes, on one of those rare days in Vancouver when the sun is strong enough to seem to penetrate my bones, and I'm on a beach with my eyes closed listening to the waves, I almost feel at home. Then I open my eyes and see the snow capped peaks and the cold ocean and the nostalgia for what was first home comes again.

If home means place of origin, then home is Jamaica. I was born there, I grew up there, I am the product of that history, that climate, that landscape, and twenty-five years in Canada does not change what that means to me. Now, I am legally a Canadian and emotionally a Jamaican. I am also a lesbian, and that means I won't be going home, not to that country, that place. To live in Jamaica now would mean isolation, ostracism and fear. Living openly as a lesbian in Canada has its risks and dangers, but to be as "out" in Jamaica as I am here would be virtually impossible. There would be no lesbian community for support; I would face the possibility of gossip, innuendo and threats of violence almost alone. Now that I have become used to the relative safety of being a lesbian in a large city in Canada, I choose not to accommodate a large part of who I am to a society which will deny and threaten my existence even more than this one. So I choose to stay here and carry inside me an empty space which little in this culture, climate and geography can fill. The many things I miss are the way Jamaican people move and talk and touch and show their feelings in their faces; the way old people and children dance; the year round warmth and colour; an ocean I can swim in; the soft blue mountains; the smell of the tropics; a majority of dark faces; the familiarity of it all.

How did Jamaica shape who I am today? In so many ways, my values, perspectives, my joys and sorrows, the way in which I both do and don't fit in here, are reflections of my origins. I am very aware that a middle class upbringing in Jamaica, with its focus on British and North American values and culture, prepared me for life in Canada and made it seem almost easy at first to fit in. So did light skin. To a nineteen year old, belonging is important: I didn't realize what I was denying in order to think that I was fitting in. Now, with a more mature perspective on growing up middle class and light skinned in an ex-colony, I am aware that I was brought up on many levels of denial: denial of my mixed race heritage, of the meaning of being the product of slavery and colonialism, of the significance of Africa in Jamaican culture, of the fact that there is such a thing as Jamaican culture. The more I understand about where I came from, the more I identify with that history and culture, the less I feel a part of this society. Being a lesbian puts me outside of the mainstream anyway. Perhaps unravelling the layers of denial which make up my personal history and "coming out" as a woman of colour in Canada have something to do with being able to come out as a lesbian. I don't know which came first; both are processes which keep unfolding. I do know that being outside of the mainstream as a woman of colour and a lesbian feels like the authentic place for me.

Did Jamaica have anything to do with my becoming a lesbian? I never heard the word 'lesbian' when I was growing up and going to an all girls school. But I remember the passionate crushes on school friends and young teachers, and the innocence in which we walked around school holding hands with our best friends. There was no shame in those touches, in the love letters and tête-à-têtes and days and even nights spent together, but, oh, the intensity of those tender friendships. We knew, at least in theory, what sexual behaviour entailed, and did not identify our feelings with anything that would happen later (we assumed) with men. We loved each other purely, and I know that my reliance on women for friendship and support started there.

In that rarefied atmosphere of the all girls school, we became used to a society of women, much as we railed against it. We saw women in positions of power who were competent in all fields. We were able to be much closer than if we had been competing for the attention of boys and we could excel academically without worrying about being threatening to boys.

I wonder now about those older unmarried teachers whose whole life seemed to be the school. Did they, in their manless world, find affection and support from each other? Did any of them practise the love which in those days certainly did not dare to

9

speak its name?

There were so many unmarried women of my mother's generation. Were they all pining for the men they never had? Or were they pining for each other? Finding each other and their own form of independence under the guise of genteel spinster companionship? Who really was the woman they called "Miss Joe" who wore slacks all the time and smoked at a time when ladies did not smoke? Even though I was supposed to pity their single state, I remember my somewhat ambivalent admiration for their apparent comfort with their own eccentricity. I am in debt to those whose non-collaboration with society's expectations hinted at unacknowledged possibilities. Their subtle form of rebellion would in time reinforce my own.

Coming to Canada, originally to go to college, fully expecting to return to Jamaica to live, was perhaps the first major step towards becoming my own person. Eventually I would choose to immigrate. Canada created many possibilities for me; I had the chance to redefine myself, away from the strictures of class and family name. I did not have to deal with expectations because I had a certain shade of skin, went to a certain high school, spoke a certain way and came from a certain family. I was able to choose how I lived, where I lived, what I did for a living, how I dressed and who my friends were without raising anyone's eyebrows. Freedom from those limitations allowed me to understand the limitations this society puts on women, people of colour and gays and lesbians. But here, there are many others who understand why I want freedom from these limits too. The women's movement gave me the context in which to come out without fear or ambivalence. Now lesbians of colour are becoming a presence in the women's movement and more of the threads of my life are coming together. Going back to Jamaica now would mean unravelling the fabric of the life which I have created here.

So now I no longer define home by geography and culture. Home is a new kind of community which this continent is spawning, a community struggling to build bridges of understanding and solidarity. Most of all, home is where the woman I love, my partner in life, is. Meeting her, knowing her, loving her was coming home - to women, to her, to myself.

CHRISTINA SPRINGER

Reaching Across the Void
to my mother

You always seemed so lost
in the work you did
and I so lost in avoiding
you.

Move myth with ease,
your creation of personal saviour
born Black and Female
gave birth to phoenix
without being burned.

You planted infertile seeds
bragging your own power
to limit life,
manipulate passing,
seize control
and gorge yourself on it.

You were the crystal
born of lead, sand and fire
shattering white light
colors uncaptured
limited to your glory.

Pursued these self induced rainbows
need thirsting want
for you, the best
for me, you thought.

11

Cleansed melting pot stories
blind to weeds
growing amongst
this unplanted garden
exploding womanhood.

Crowing at the sun,
cocky thoughts
I would become you.
Your impeccable foresight
to harvest before frost,
I would rake no garden of pain
like your foremothers.

Infertile seeds, in virgin soil
heavily composted, nurtured
unthinking, grow cluttered
peace gardens, ridden with dreams
evolve into fighters,
long roots, impossible to pluck.
Your disappointment astonishing
in the wisdom of planting
these seeds desiring no care,
but fertilization by example,
becomes a flimsy challenge.

I manifest choices you never included
on blueprints drafted before birth.
This tendency to gravitate towards
the orchid shaped in myself
was no genetic mutation but,
a flower formed in spite
of seeds destined to wither
or form passive decorative plants.

And then, you are not the fantasy
mother, I sketched.
I reach deep into your soil,
imagine a reality, I have accepted.

I force embraceable differences
weed this fall garden, plant bulbs
crank completion without thought
through winter months with promises
of Spring and Summer again
embed a crystal formed from salt of earth
into your garden, eliminating need
of false imitations.

The simplicity of leaning in to each other
tornado swept gladiolus
flaunting multitudes of individual blooms.
is my challenge to you,
not death defying,
as you would like it to be.

We will learn to come together,
reach across this void,
kiss without fear of jeopardy,
grow into each other
naturally becoming the other's sun.

We will blow expanded legacies
into heirloom.

MAKEDA SILVERA

Man Royals and Sodomites:
Some Thoughts on the Invisibility of
Afro-Caribbean Lesbians

I will begin with some personal images and voices about woman-loving. These have provided a ground for my search for cultural refections of my identity as a Black woman artist within the Afro-Caribbean community of Toronto. Although I focus here on my own experience (specifically, Jamaican), I am aware of similarities with the experience of other Third World women of colour whose history and culture has been subjected to colonisation and imperialism.

I spent the first thirteen years of my life in Jamaica among strong women. My great-grandmother, my grandmother and grand-aunts were major influences in my life. There are also men whom I remember with fondness - my grandmother's "man friend" G., my Uncle Bertie, his friend Paul, Mr. Minott, Uncle B. and Uncle Freddy. And there were men like Mr. Eden who terrified me because of stories about his "walking" fingers and his liking for girls under age fourteen.

I lived in a four-bedroom house with my grandmother, Uncle Bertie and two female tenants. On the same piece of land, my grandmother had other tenants, mostly women and lots of children. The big verandah of our house played a vital role in the social life of this community. It was on the verandah that I received my first education on "Black women's strength" - not only from their strength, but also from the daily humiliations they bore at work and in relationships. European experience coined the term "feminism", but the term "Black women's strength" reaches beyond Eurocentric definitions to describe what is the cultural continuity of my own struggles.

The verandah. My grandmother sat on the verandah in the evenings after all the chores were done to read the newspaper. People - mostly women - gathered there to discuss "life". Life covered every conceivable topic - economic, local, political, social and sexual: the high price of salt-fish, the scarcity of flour, the nice piece of yellow yam bought at Coronation market, Mr. Lam, the shopkeeper who was taking "liberty" with Miss Inez, the fights women had with their menfolk, work, suspicions of Miss Iris and Punsie carrying on something between them, the cost of school books...

My grandmother usually had lots of advice to pass on to the women on the verandah, all grounded in the Bible. Granny believed in Jesus, in good and evil and in repentance. She was also a practical and sociable woman. Her faith didn't interfere with her perception of what it meant to be a poor Black woman; neither did it interfere with our Friday night visits to my Aunt Marie's bar. I remember sitting outside on the piazza with my grandmother, two grand-aunts and three or four of their women friends. I liked their flashy smiles and I was fascinated by their independence, ease and their laughter. I loved their names - Cherry Rose, Blossom, Jonesie, Poinsietta, Ivory, Pearl, Iris, Bloom, Dahlia, Babes. Whenever the conversation came around to some "big 'oman talk" - who was sleeping with whom or whose daughter just got "fallen", I was sent off to get a glass of water for an adult, or a bottle of Kola champagne. Every Friday night I drank as much as half a dozen bottles of Kola champagne, but I still managed to hear snippets of words, tail ends of conversations about women together.

In Jamaica, the words used to describe many of these women would be "Man Royal" and/or "Sodomite". Dread words. So dread that women dare not use these words to name themselves. They were names given to women by men to describe aspects of our lives that men neither understood nor approved.

I heard "sodomite" whispered a lot during my primary school years, and tales of women secretly having sex, joining at the genitals, and being taken to the hospital to be "cut" apart were told in the school yard. Invariably, one of the women would die. Every five to ten years the same story would surface. At times, it would even be published in the newspapers. Such stories always generated much talking and speculation from "Bwoy dem kinda gal naasti sah!" to some wise old woman saying, "But dis caan happen, after two shutpan caan join" - meaning identical objects cannot go into the other. The act of loving someone of the same sex was sinful, abnormal - something to hide. Even today, it isn't unusual or uncommon to be asked, "So how do two 'omen do it?...what unnu use for a penis?...who is the man and who is the 'oman?" It's inconceivable that women can have intimate relationships that are whole, that are not lacking because of the absence of a man. It's assumed that women in such relationships must be imitating men.

The word "sodomite" derives from the Old Testament. Its common use to describe lesbians (or any strong independent woman) is peculiar to Jamaica - a culture historically and strongly grounded in the Bible. Although Christian values have dominated the world, their effect in slave colonies is particular. Our foreparents gained access to literacy through the Bible when they were being indoctrinated by missionaries. It provided powerful and ancient stories of strength, endurance and hope which reflected their own fight against oppression. This book has been so powerful that it continues to bind our lives with its racism and misogyny. Thus, the importance the Bible plays in Afro-Caribbean culture must be recognised in order to understand the historical and political context for the invisibility of lesbians. The wrath of God "rained down burning sulphur on Sodom and Gomorrah" *(Genesis 19:23)*. How could a Caribbean woman claim the name?

When, thousand of miles away and fifteen years after my school days, my grandmother was confronted with my love for a woman, her reaction was determined by her Christian faith and by this dread word sodomite - its meaning, its implication, its history.

And when, Bible in hand, my grandmother responded to my love by sitting me down, at the age of twenty-seven, to quote Genesis, it was within the context of this tradition, this politic. When she pointed out that "this was a white people ting", or "a ting only people with mixed blood was involved in" (to explain or include my love with a woman of mixed race), it was strong denial of many ordinary Black working-class women she knew.

It was finally through my conversations with my grandmother, my mother and my mother's friend five years later that I began to realise the scope of this denial which was intended to dissuade and protect me. She knew too well that any woman who took a woman lover was attempting to walk on fire - entering a "no man's land". I began to see how commonplace the act of loving women really was, particularly in working-class communities. I realised, too, just how heavily shame and silence weighed down this act.

A conversation with a friend of my mother:

Well, when I growing up we didn't hear much 'bout woman and woman. They weren't "suspect". There was much more talk about "batty man business" when I was a teenager in the 1950s.

I remember one story about a man who was "suspect" and that every night when he was coming home, a group of guys use to lay wait him and stone him so viciously that he had to run for his life. Dem time, he was safe only in the day.

Now with women, nobody really suspected. I grew up in the country and I grew up seeing women holding hands, hugging up, sleeping together in one bed and there was no question. Some of this was based purely on emotional friendship, but I also knew of cases where the women were dealing but no one really suspected. Close people around knew, but not everyone. It wasn't a thing that you would go out and broadcast. It would be something just between the two people.

Also one important thing is that the women who were involved carried on with life just the same, no big political statements were made. These women still went to church, still got baptised, still went on pilgrimage, and I am thinking about one particular woman name Aunt Vie, a very strong woman, strong-willed and everything, they use to call her "man-royal" behind her back, but no one ever dare to meddle with her.

Things are different now in Jamaica. Now all you have to do is not respond to a man's call to you and dem call you sodomite or lesbian. I guess it was different back then forty years ago because it was harder for anybody to really conceive of two woman sleeping and being sexual. But I do remember when you were "suspect", people would talk about you. You were definitely classed as "different", "not normal", a bit "crazy". But women never really got stoned like the men.

What I remember is that if you were a single woman alone or two single women living together and a few people suspected this...and when I say a few people I mean like a few guys,

17

sometimes other crimes were committed against the women. Some very violent, some very subtle. Battery was common, especially in Kingston. A group of men would suspect a woman or have it out for her because she was a "sodomite" or because she act "man-royal" and so the men would organise and gang rape whichever woman was "suspect". Sometimes it was reported in the newspapers, other times it wasn't - but when you live in a little community, you don't need a newspaper to tell you what's going on. You know by word of mouth and those stories were frequent. Sometimes you also knew the men who did the battery.

Other subtle forms of this was "scorning" the women. Meaning that you didn't eat anything from them, especially a cooked meal. It was almost as if those accused of being "man-royal" or "sodomite" could contaminate.

A conversation with my grandmother:

I am only telling you this so that you can understand that this is not a profession to be proud of and to get involved in. Everybody should be curious and I know you born with that, ever since you growing up as a child and I can't fight against that, because that is how everybody get to know what's in the world. I am only telling you this because when you were a teenager, you always say you want to experience everything and make up your mind on your own. You didn't like people telling you what was wrong and right. That always use to scare me.

Experience is good, yes. But it have to be balanced, you have to know when you have too much experience in one area. I am telling you this because I think you have enough experience in this to decide now to go back to the normal way. You have two children. Do you want them to grow up knowing this is the life you have taken? But this is for you to decide...

Yes, there was a lot of women involved with women in Jamaica. I knew a lot of them when I was growing up in the country in the 1920s. I didn't really associate with them. Mind you, I was not rude to them. My mother wouldn't stand for any rudeness from any of her children to adults.

I remember a woman we use to call Miss Bibi. She live next to us

- her husband was a fisherman, I think he drowned before I was born. She had a little wooden house that back onto the sea, the same as our house. She was quiet, always reading. That I remember about her because she use to go to the little public library at least four days out of the week. And she could talk. Anything you want to know, just ask Miss Bibi and she could tell you. She was a mulatto woman, but poor. Anytime I had any school work that I didn't understand, I use to ask her. The one thing I remember though, we wasn't allowed in her house by my mother, so I use to talk to her outside, but she didn't seem to mind that. Some people use to think she was mad because she spent so much time alone. But I didn't think that because anything she help me with, I got a good mark on it in school.

She was colourful in her own way, but quiet, always alone, except when her friend come and visit her once a year for two weeks. Them times I didn't see Miss Bibi much because my mother told me I couldn't go and visit her. Sometimes I would see her in the market exchanging and bartering fresh fish for vegetables and fruits. I use to see her friend too. She was a jet Black woman, always had her hair tied in bright coloured cloth and she always had on big gold earrings. People use to say she live on the other side of the island with her husband and children and she came to Port Maria once a year to visit Miss Bibi.

My mother and father were great storytellers and I learnt that from them, but is from Miss Bibi that I think I learnt to love reading so much as a child. It wasn't until I move to Kingston that I notice other women like Miss Bibi...

Let me tell you about Jones. Do you remember her? Well she was the woman who live the next yard over from us. She is the one who really turn me against people like that, why I fear so much for you to be involved in this ting. She was very loud. Very show-off. Always dressed in pants and man-shirt that she borrowed from her husband. Sometimes she use to invite me over to her house, but I didn't go. She always had her hair in a bob hair cut, always barefoot and tending to her garden and her fruit trees. She tried to get me involved in that kind of life, but I said no. At the time I remember I needed some money to borrow and she lent me, later she told me I didn't have to pay her back, but to come over to her house and see the thing she had that was sweeter than what any man could offer me. I told her no and eventually paid her back the money.

We still continued to talk. It was hard not to like Jonesie - that's what everybody called her. She was open and easy to talk to. But still there was a fear in me about her. To me it seem like she was in a dead end with nowhere to go. I don't want that for you.

I left my grandmother's house that day feeling anger and sadness for Miss Jones - maybe for myself, who knows. I was feeling boxed in. I had said nothing. I'd only listened quietly.

In bed that night, I thought about Miss Jones. I cried for her (for me) silently. I remember her, a mannish looking Indian woman, with flashy gold teeth, a Craven A cigarette always between them. She was always nice to me as a child. She had the sweetest, juiciest Julie, Bombay and East Indian mangoes on the street. She always gave me mangoes over the fence. I remember the dogs in her yard and the sign on her gate. "Beware of bad dogs". I never went into her house, though I was always curious.

I vaguely remember her pants and shirts, though I never thought anything of them until my grandmother pointed them out. Neither did I recall that dreaded word being used to describe her, although everyone on the street knew about her.

A conversation with my mother:

Yes I remember Miss Jones. She smoke a lot, drank a lot. In fact, she was an alcoholic. When I was in my teens she use to come over to our house - always on the verandah. I can't remember her sitting down - seems she was always standing up, smoking, drinking and reminiscing. She constantly talked about the past, about her life and it was always on the verandah. And it was always women: young women she knew when she was a young woman, the fun they had together and how good she would make love to a woman. She would say to whoever was listening on the verandah, "Dem girls I use to have sex with was shapely. You shoulda know me when I was younger, pretty and shapely just like the 'oman dem I use to have as my 'oman."

People use to tease her on the street, but not about being a lesbian or calling her sodomite. People use to tease her when she was drunk, because she would leave the rumshop and stagger down the avenue to her house.

I remember the women she use to carry home, usually in the daytime. A lot of women from downtown, higglers and fishwomen. She use to boast about knowing all kinds of women from Coronation market and her familiarity with them. She had a husband who lived with her and that served as her greatest protection against other men taking steps with her. Not that anybody could easily take advantage of Miss Jones, she could stand up for herself. But having a husband did help. He was a very quiet, insular man. He didn't talk to anyone on the street. He had no friends so it wasn't easy for anyone to come up to him and gossip about his wife.

No one could go to her house without being invited, but I wouldn't say she was a private person. She was a loner. She went to the rumshops alone, she drank alone, she staggered home alone. The only time I ever saw her with somebody were the times when she went off to the Coronation market or some other place downtown to find a woman and bring her home. The only times I remember her engaging in conversation with anybody was when she came over on the verandah to talk about her women and what they did in bed. That was all she let out about herself. There was nothing about how she was feeling, whether she was sad or depressed, lonely, happy. Nothing. She seemed to cover up all that with her loudness and her vulgarness and her constant threat - which was all it was - to beat up anybody who troubled her or teased her when she was coming home from the rumshop.

Now Cherry Rose - do you remember her? She was a good friend of Aunt Marie and of Mama's. She was also a sodomite. She was loud too, but different from Miss Jones. She was much more outgoing. She was a barmaid and had lots of friends - both men and women. She also had the kind of personality that attracted people - very vivacious, always laughing, talking and touching. She didn't have any children, but Gem did.

Do you remember Miss Gem? Well she had children and she was also a barmaid. She also had lots of friends. She also had a man friend name Mickey, but that didn't matter because some women had their men and still had women they carried on with. The men usually didn't know what was going on, and seeing as these men just come and go and usually on their own time, they weren't around every day and night.

Miss Pearl was another one that was in that kind of thing. She was a dressmaker, she use to sew really good. Where Gem was light complexion, she was a very black Black woman with deep dimples. Where Gem was a bit plump, Pearl was slim, but with big breast and a big bottom. They were both pretty women.

I don't remember hearing that word sodomite a lot about them. It was whispered sometimes behind their backs, but never in front of them. And they were so alive and talkative that people were always around them.

The one woman I almost forgot was Miss Opal, a very quiet woman. She use to be friends with Miss Olive and was always out at her bar sitting down. I can't remember much about her except she didn't drink like Miss Jones and she wasn't vulgar. She was soft spoken, a half-Chinese woman. Her mother was born in Hong Kong and her father was a Black man. She could really bake. She use to supply shops with cakes and other pastries.

So there were many of those kind of women around. But it wasn't broadcast.

I remembered them. Not as lesbians or sodomites or man royals, but as women that I liked. Women who I admired. Strong women, some colourful, some quiet.

I loved Cherry Rose's style. I loved her loudness, the way she challenged men in arguments, the bold way she laughed in their faces, the jingle of her gold bracelets. Her colourful and stylish way of dressing. She was full of wit; words came alive in her mouth.

Miss Gem: I remember her big double iron bed. That was where Paula and Lorraine (her daughters, my own age) and I spent a whole week together when we had chicken pox. My grandmother took me there to stay for the company. It was fun. Miss Gem lived right above her bar and so at any time we could look through the window and onto the piazza and street which was bursting with energy and life. She was a very warm woman, patient and caring. Every day she would make soup for us and tell us stories. Later on in the evening she would bring us Kola champagne.

Miss Pearl sewed dresses for me. She hardly ever used her tape measure - she could just take one look at you and make you a dress fit for a queen. What is she doing now, I asked myself? And Miss Opal, with her calm and quiet, where is she - still baking?

What stories could these lesbians have told us? I, an Afro-Caribbean woman living in Canada, come with this baggage - their silenced stories. My grandmother and mother know the truth, but silence still surrounds us. The truth remains a secret to the rest of the family and friends, and I must decide whether to continue to sew this cloth of denial or break free, creating and becoming the artist that I am, bring alive the voices and images of Cherry Rose, Miss Gem, Miss Jones, Opal, Pearl, and others...

There is more at risk for us than for white women. Through three hundred years of history we have carried memories and the scars of racism and violence with us. We are the sister, daughter, mothers of a people enslaved by colonialists and imperialists. Under slavery, production and reproduction were inextricably linked. Reproduction served not only to increase the labour force of slave owners but also, by "domesticating" the enslaved, facilitated the process of social conditions by focusing on those aspects of life in which they could express their own desires. Sex was an area in which to articulate one's humanity, but, because it was tied to attempts "to define oneself as human", gender roles, as well as the act of sex, became badges of status. To be male was to be the stud, the procreator; to be female was to be fecund, and one's femininity was measured by the ability to attract and hold a man, and to bear children. In this way, slavery and the post-emancipated colonial order defined the structures of patriarchy and heterosexuality as necessary for social mobility and acceptance.

Socio-economic conditions and the quest for a better life has seen steady migration from Jamaica and the rest of the Caribbean to the U.S., Britain and Canada. Upon my arrival, I became part of the so-called "visible minorities" encompassing Blacks, Asians and Native North Americans in Canada. I live with a legacy of continued racism and prejudice. We confront this daily, both as individuals and as organised political groups. Yet for those of us who are lesbians, there is another struggle: the struggle for acceptance and positive self-definition within our own communities. Too often, we have had to sacrifice our love for women in political meetings that have been dominated by the "we are the world" attitude of heterosexual ideology. We have had to hide too often that part of our identity which contributes profoundly to make up the whole.

Many lesbians have worked, like me, in the struggles of Black people since the 1960s. We have been on marches every time one of us gets murdered by the police. We have been at sit-ins and vigils. We have flyered, postered, we have cooked and baked for the struggle. We have tended to the youths. And we have all at one time or another given support to men in our community, all the time painfully holding onto, obscuring, our secret lives. When we do walk out of the closet (or are thrown out), the "ideologues" of the Black communities say "Yes, she was a radical sistren but, I don't know what happen, she just went the wrong way." What is implicit in this is that one cannot be a lesbian and continue to do political work, and not surprisingly, it follows that a Black lesbian/artist cannot create using the art forms of our culture. For example, when a heterosexual male friend came to my house, I put on a dub poetry tape. He asked, "Are you sure that sistren is a lesbian?"

"Why?" I ask.

"Because this poem sound wicked; it have lots of rhythm; it sounds cultural."

Another time, another man commented on my work, "That book you wrote on domestic workers is really a fine piece of work. I didn't know you were that informed about the economic politics of the Caribbean and Canada." What are we to assume from this? That Afro-Caribbean lesbians have no Caribbean culture? That they lose their community politics when they sleep with women? Or that Afro-Caribbean culture is a heterosexual commodity?

The presence of an "out" Afro-Caribbean lesbian in our community is dealt with by suspicion and fear from both men and our heterosexual Black sisters. It brings into question the assumption of heterosexuality as the only "normal" way. It forces them to acknowledge something that has always been covered up. It forces them to look at women differently and brings into question the traditional Black female role. Negative response from our heterosexual Black sister, though more painful, is, to a certain extent, understandable because we have no race privilege and very, very few of us have class privilege. The one privilege within our group is heterosexual. We have all suffered at the hands of this racist system at one time or another and to many heterosexual Black women it is inconceivable, almost frightening, that one could turn her back on credibility in our community and the society at large by being lesbian. These women are also afraid that they will be labelled "lesbian" by association. It is that fear, that homophobia, which keeps Black women isolated.

The Toronto Black community has not dealt with sexism. It has not been pushed to do so. Neither has it given a thought to its heterosexism. In 1988, my grandmother's fear is very real, very alive. One takes a chance when one writes about being an Afro-Caribbean lesbian. There is the fear that one might not live to write more. There is the danger of being physically "disciplined" for speaking as a woman-identified woman.

And what of our white lesbian sisters and their community? They have learnt well from the civil rights movement about organising, and with race and some class privilege, they have built a predominantly white lesbian (and gay) movement - a pre-condition for a significant body of work by a writer or artist. They have demanded and received recognition from politicians (no matter how little). But this recognition has not been extended to Third World lesbians of colour - neither from politicians nor from white lesbian (and gay) organisations. The white lesbian organisations/groups have barely (some not at all) begun to deal with or acknowledge their own racism, prejudice and biases - all learned from a system which feeds on their ignorance and grows stronger from its institutionalised racism. Too often white women focus only on their oppression as lesbians, ignoring the more complex oppression of non-white women who are also lesbians. We remain outsiders in these groups, without images or political voices that echo our own. We know too clearly that, as non-white lesbians in this country, we are politically and socially at the very bottom of the heap. Denial of such differences robs us of true visibility. We must identify and define these differences, and challenge the movements and groups that are not accessible to non-whites - challenge groups that are not accountable.

But where does this leave us as Afro-Caribbean lesbians, as part of this "visible minority" community? As Afro-Caribbean women we are still at the stage where we have to imagine and discover our existence, past and present. As lesbians, we are even more marginalised, less visible. The absence of a national Black lesbian and gay movement through which to begin to name ourselves is disheartening. We have no political organisation to support us and through which we could demand respect from our communities. We need such an organisation to represent our interests, both in coalition-building with other lesbian/gay organisations, and in the struggles which shape our future - through which we hope to transform the social, political and economic systems of oppression as they affect all peoples.

Though not yet on a large scale, lesbians and gays of Caribbean descent are beginning to seek each other out - are slowly organising. Younger lesbians and gays of colour are beginning to challenge and force their parents and the Black community to deal with their sexuality. They have formed groups, "Zami for Black and Caribbean gays and lesbians" and "Lesbians of Colour", to name two.

The need to make connections with other Caribbean and Third World people of colour who are lesbian and gay is urgent. This is where we can begin to build that other half of our community, to create wholeness through our art. This is where we will find the support and strength to struggle, to share our histories and to record these histories in books, documentaries, film, sound, and art. We will create a rhythm that is uniquely ours - proud, powerful and gay, naming ourselves, and taking our space within the larger history of Afro-Caribbean peoples.

LELETI TAMU

Casselberry Harvest

We embraced and your arms
slipped slowly around me like
the limbs and branches of the
casselberry tree,
that grows from the dark moist
earth of ashanti soil

Your locks brown and delicious
carries the fragrance from the
blossoms of that tree

In the language of our
foremothers, casselberry must
mean sun-kissed days, blanketing
a soft orchard, with the
indigo sweetness of you

I anticipate the familiar
flavour of your casselberry
harvest.

LELETI TAMU

Making Love on Canvas
for Grace Channer

Your hands calloused soft in places
brushes the canvas like a womyn
Black hands
reaches up to complete her face
Hands that know so well what we feel like
what we look like
Lesbian hands
in sequence with brushes on canvas
telling tales of dark full lips
large mellow thighs that
send electric waves through me
Your hands Gracie amazing
as they stroke colours of deep reds
blues, black, potions.
Making love on canvas

MARIA AMPARO JIMENEZ

Terquedad
A Lillian

Los caminos se han forjado
con cada paso se marca
nuestra historia.
El miedo nos paraliza
dejamos ir al amor
que tanto ansiamos.
Pasamos de frente
temiendo andar la misma ruta
recordando las espinas
el sabor agrio
El amor insiste...
Podemos hacer nuevos caminos
andar por ellos de la mano
forjar un mundo nuevo,
donde tú, seas tú
y,yo,
          sea yo,
uniéndonos al final
en un camino nuestro.

MARIA AMPARO JIMENEZ

Stubbornness
To Lillian

The paths have been forged
With each step
our story is written.
Fear paralyzes us
we let go of the love
we so desire.
We pass by
fearing to walk the same paths
remembering the thorns
the bitter taste, yet
Love insists...
We can make new paths
walk them hand in hand
discover each road,
forge a new world
where you,
           can be you
And I
can be me
uniting at the end
on a path that will be ours.

RITZ CHOW

coming out
for each of every Asian Lesbian of Toronto

what i can't say
i punch into clouds
& fallen petals
into night
music behind me

my breath
urgent as blood
rushing vessels
for colour

words as letters
rub my worn
finger-thoughts
from beneath nerves
& intermittent rawness

what i can't reveal
is this need
for your arms
like ropes
to contain these
escaping parts

no alphabet for this
as i stare past
your voice quickly
erasing numbers

whose seconds
restrain the pulse
of my unsure face

what i can't say
i spray upon mirrors
& other distortions

what i can't write
i retain in
photo-angles

what i can't love
i swallow
like a volcano its own
thick saliva

NICE RODRIGUEZ

Big Nipple of the North

Once upon a time, in the tropical village of Munoz, there lived a girl who never liked dresses. Folks said that even as a baby, the girl had refused to wear any style of female clothing.

Once when her mom dolled her up in a red polka dot dress, the baby cried all day and night. The infant ran no fever but her swollen eyes expressed an untold agony and her voice was hoarse from days of ceaseless crying. Her parents felt helpless and finally brought her to the village chiropractor.

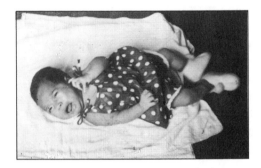

The doctor quickly put the exhausted infant on the bamboo floor and undressed her for examination. The baby sighed with relief as if he plucked a thorn from her heart, but as soon as he clothed her in the red dress, she resumed her wailing.

The chiropractor read the baby's pulse and aligned her supple spine. He tossed her front to back and checked her genitals for indeed she had female genitals. He found nothing wrong and certified her good health. The baby was wet and the doctor changed her diaper with his son's Pampers for boys. The infant girl giggled with delight and an aide rushed her out of the clinic wearing only a blue padded diaper.

The baby's face brightened when she recognized her parents, but when her mother appeared with the red polka dot dress, her hair stood on ends and her eyes widened with terror. She began to weep again as if begging for some intuitive understanding for she could only speak through tears.

They showed another dress - a yellow tube blouse but the baby howled two decibels louder than before. Next they tried to put the native dress on, a white saya adorned with stiff U-shaped sleeves, but she did not only scream but threw her arms and legs about.

Then from out of a bag, her daddy took out a blue athletic shirt and the baby stopped trembling. "Goo, goo, goo, goo," she babbled her first words. Her eyes twinkled with approval. The puzzled doctor watched all this unfold and prescribed boys' clothes and shoes for the infant. He said these were good for her spine but as soon as the family left, he scribbled some notes and filed the case under Ghosts and Other Strange Phenomena.

Word about the sick child spread throughout the village. One breezy afternoon, the elders met under the tamarind tree, concerned that the western settlers brought the virus which caused the ailment. A hunter said he had seen similar deviation among adults in far-flung and unconquered tribal towns. He added that the baby was merely an early freak and that it was not an epidemic. Nevertheless, they put her on a watch list.

The child performed well in the arts and garnered honours for her school. She was bright and well-mannered, and got into fits of melancholia only when required to wear a dress during formal occasions. Nevertheless, people still saw her as a freak, for now she was growing breasts but looked and acted like a boy.

Every Wednesday, the girl offered a peso to the saint of despair and attended a novena, praying that the village god would make her breasts stop their growth. At last, they stopped swelling, but she realized no prayer could flatten her chest again.

As she had with the pimples on her face, the girl learned to live with this pubescent burden. It seemed that her heart had swollen too, for one night in the cold month of December, she disappeared with her female math teacher.

The whole village talked about the incident for weeks. The school administration, although shocked, said they broke no rule since they probably just went away to work on a statistical project. The teacher, known about town for her frigidity, returned with an exotic aura of fulfilment. The girl, imbued with more confidence in life and algebra, headed on to a brighter path.

She attended the university. Yet when she graduated, there was no work for her. She passed all written tests but because she did not wear a dress nor a bra, flunked all the job interviews. She found odd jobs in journalism where there were other freaks slaving like her. She also settled down with a nice city girl.

When she walked the alleys of Munoz with her wife, men jeered at them. They scornfully asked what they did in bed. Their own bored wives wondered why the two women looked radiant.

She had tired of the villagers meddling looks but had learned to ignore them. Her own small world sustained her but she could not plan her future. She gained weight and grew depressed each day. Yet in her sleep, a voice told her to go to the Big Nipple of the North.

At first she thought it was a wild dream again about her busty ex-lover from Ilocos. The village seer said no - for that Big Nipple of the North was a place called Canada. A land with rich resources, it was like a nipple that had nursed many new settlers to lives of unimaginable prosperity.

The people in Canada had survived the land's extreme winters but beware, the seer warned, because many had perished in that cold land for it was cursed with big taxes. Go find your destiny and be as resilient as the bamboo that thrived in the outskirts of Munoz. Before she left, she asked the seer if breasts came in pairs, where was the other nipple? The seer said the Other Big Nipple of the North was a place called United States.

"But don't go there," he stressed, "for that one was infected with a malignant tumour which if unchecked, could quietly spread to the Canadian nipple."

Thus enlightened, she went to the Canadian embassy and applied for immigration. On the day of her interview, she wore a tailored suit but she looked like a man and knew she did not stand a chance.

They did not want masculine women in that underpopulated land. They needed baby makers for as much as Canadians loved to fuck they were not making enough babies. Her wife got mascara and lipstick and made her look like a baby maker. During her interview with the consul officer, she looked ovulating and fertile so she passed it.

Canada had strict immigration laws but even bugs could sift through a fine mosquito net. Some of her village's most notorious people were now refugees in Canada. Like the mayor's killer and the textile magnate who ran away with millions of debts, causing the fragile economy of Munoz to crumble. The witch who slaved her own children became a nanny there.

When the freak girl of Munoz arrive in Mississauga, she had fear in her heart but a vision overcame her when she saw the bi-coloured Canadian flag at the airport.

As the bright and blinding northern sun shone its rays through the flag, the red bars and maple leaf gradually merged with the white. The banner's colour changed to pink - the rallying colour of radical freaks! She smiled with relief for she knew she found a home. She sang and danced towards Church Street. And lived happily on welfare.

VICTORIA LENA MANYARROWS

bridge upon a rainbow

often i dream in colors
colors red with brown
green with blue
colors earthen and alive
softening the skies in my dreams
and the lands on fire

when i dream of the sunrise
and feel the first rays
the warmth keeps me from waking
enjoying such a dream

your touch i feel in my dreams
it is wet, it is soft
opening me and warming me and
filling me with all the colors of the rainbow

i'll dream some more tonight
colors filling my horizons
showing me more visions
building me a bridge upon a rainbow
over dangerous waters and sharp cliffs
guiding me on a path so sure
so strong
bringing me thru the night, the cold
to a place warm and safe
and next to you.

CHRISTINA SPRINGER

A Black Girl Thing

Blue light mind convertor
reverberates steady hum.
Perform the circle channel dance
cease performing flips,
settle to watch a mirror cracked.

Reach inside,
reach inside,

Empty spice rack on chicken,
simmer honey.

At the community potluck
serve up the single oddity,
burn sweetened tongues
like beauty parlour heads.

Sweep those floorboards
scattered with salt, in Florida Water.

Reach inside
the continent of your body.

Pull forth, birth
a solitary battalion.
puncture fiction.

Take the truth.

Archetype seeps
through floorboards
scattered with anisette
white candle burning
behind doors
next to bowls of fruit.
Voice flows
in thought
consoled by dead relatives
talking proud words.

Listen to this...
Listen to this...

It shakes an Earth.
It a Black girl thing.
It real.

It yours.

Jewelle L. Gomez and Barbara Smith

Taking the Home Out of Homophobia:
Black Lesbian Health

BARBARA: One of the things we've been asked to talk about is how homophobia affects Black women's mental health. I think that in addition to affecting lesbians' emotional health, homophobia also affects the mental health of heterosexual people. In other words, being homophobic is not a healthy state for people to be in.

JEWELLE: I'd like to hear more about that.

BARBARA: Well, it's just like being racist. I don't think that most Blacks or other people of color would vouch for the mental health of somebody who is a rabid and snarling racist. Because that's like dismissing a part of the human family. Particularly within the African-American community, when we are so embattled, it's just baloney to dismiss or say that a certain segment is expendable because of their sexual orientation. Anyone who would do that hasn't grown up, they're just not mature.

JEWELLE: I think it's even more dangerous for people of color to embrace homophobia than it is for whites to embrace racism, simply because we're embattled psychologically and economically as an ethnic group. We leave ourselves in a very weakened position if we allow the system to pit us against each other. I also think it renders Black people politically smug. That's the thing about homophobia, racism, anti-Semitism, any of the "isms" - once you embrace those you tend to become smug.

And once you take a position of smugness you lose your fighting edge. I think Afro-Americans who've taken the position of "we are the major victim" in this society and nobody else has suffered like we've suffered, lose their edge. They don't have the perspective that will allow us to fight through all the issues.

BARBARA: Right. From the time we get here, we are steeped in the knowledge that we are the victims of a really bigoted and racist

40

society. But we also have to acknowledge that there are ways that we can be oppressive to other groups whose identities we don't share. So I think that one of the challenges we face in trying to raise the issue of lesbian and gay identity within the Black community is to try to get our people to understand that they can indeed oppress someone after having spent a life of being oppressed. That's a very hard transition to make, but it's one we have to make if we want our whole community to be liberated.

JEWELLE: At this point, it seems almost impossible because the issue of sexism has become such a major stumbling block for the Black community. I think we saw the beginning of it in the 1970s with Ntozake Shange's play, *For Colored Girls Who Have Considered Suicide/ When the Rainbow is Enuf*. The play really prompted Black women to embrace the idea of independent thinking; to begin looking to each other for sustenance and to start appreciating and celebrating each other in ways that we've always done naturally. I think that the Black male community was so horrified to discover that they were not at the centre of Black women's thoughts, that they could only perceive the play as a negative attack upon them. I think that for the first time, that play made the Black community look at its sexism. And many people rejected Ntozake Shange and things having to do with feminism in a very cruel way. So years later, when we got the Central Park incident with the white woman being beaten and raped by a group of young Black males, all people could talk about was the role racism played in the attack.

BARBARA: I happened to be at a writers retreat in April 1989 when that incident occurred. It was a radicalized retreat run by a group of old lefties, so everybody there had to have a certain level of political consciousness. There was one woman there who had been involved in progressive politics for decades and she and I were discussing the Central Park rape. Her sole concern was whether these young Black and Latino men were going to get a fair trial. I couldn't believe what I was hearing. And I thought, this is why a Black feminist analysis is so important. It's important because my concern was that there was a woman lying up in the hospital almost dead. A woman who if she ever recovers physically, is likely to be profoundly psychologically damaged for the rest of her life. Black feminism is important because we can look at these issues from a holistic and principled perspective as opposed to a reductive one. There was an article in the Village Voice in which some Black women were asked what they thought about the Central Park rape and most of them came down very hard on sexual violence and sexism in the Black community. They indeed cited sexism as a cause of rape. This incident is not a mysterious fluke. It is part and parcel of what African-American women face on the streets and in their homes every day. There was a Black woman standing in a supermarket line right here in New York City and they were talking about the rape. There was a Black man behind her and he was apparently wondering why they had to beat the white woman, why they had to do her like that. And then he said, "Why didn't they just rape her?" As if that would have been okay. So you see, we have a lot to contend with.

JEWELLE: I think that the sexism continues to go unacknowledged and even praised as part of the Black community's survival technique. The subsequent acceptance of homophobia that falls naturally with that kind of thinking will be the thing that cripples the Black community. During the civil rights movement, it was a single focus on desegregation that gave us an impetus to move and hold onto our vision. But it is that same single focus that has left us with these half-assed solutions to our problems today. I mean a movement toward the middle-class is not a solution to the problems in the Black community. And I think it's just pathetic that the narrowness of vision in the Afro-American community has left us with that. Therefore, it's not surprising that homophobia is part of the fall-out. Nor should people be surprised about the anti-Semitism in the Black community. It's just one more of the "isms" that xenophobic oppressed groups justify themselves in taking on simply because they are oppressed groups.

BARBARA: Right.

JEWELLE: It's been said that people to whom evil has been done, will do evil in return.

BARBARA: Who said that?

JEWELLE: W.H. Auden. So I don't think we should be surprised about homophobia. It sneaks up in a very subtle and destructive way, even though homosexuality has always been an intrinsic part of the Black community.

BARBARA: Absolutely.

JEWELLE: When I was growing up, everyone always knew who was gay. When the guys came to my father's bar, I knew which ones were gay, it was clear as day. For instance, there was Miss Kay who was a big queen and Maurice. These were people that everybody knew. They came and went in my father's bar just like everybody else. This was a so-called lower-class community - the working poor in Boston. It was a community in which people did not talk about who was gay, but I knew who the lesbians were. It was always unspoken and I think that there's something about leaving it unspoken that leaves us unprepared.

BARBARA: That's the breakpoint for this part of the twentieth century as far as I'm concerned. There've been lesbian and gay men, Black ones, as long as there've been African people. So that's not even a question. You know how they say that the human race was supposed to have been started by a Black woman. Well, since she had so many children, some of them were undoubtedly queer. (Laughter.) Writer Ann Allen Shockley has a wonderful line about that which I use often. "Play it, but don't say it." That's the sentiment that capsulizes the general stance of the Black community on sexual identity and orientation. If you're a lesbian, you can have as many women as you want. If you're a gay man, you can have all the men you want. But just don't say anything about it or make it political. The difference today is that the lesbian and gay movement prides itself on being out, verbalizing one's identity and organizing around our oppression. With the advent of this movement, the African-American community has really been confronted with some stuff that they've never had to deal with before.

I grew up in Cleveland in a community very similar to the one you described. Today the issue is not whether gay people have been here since forever. It's that we are telling our community that it has to deal with us differently than before. That's what contemporary Black gay and lesbian activists are doing.

JEWELLE: I was thinking, as you were saying that, that if one embraces the principles of liberation, gay liberation and feminism, then you have to assault the sexual stereotype that young Black girls have been forced to live out in the African-American community. The stereotype that mandates that you develop into the well-groomed girl who pursues a profession and a husband.

BARBARA: High achiever.

JEWELLE: Or the snappy baby machine. You tend to go one way or the other. You're either fast or you're well-groomed. I think that for so many young Black women, the idea of finding their place in society has been defined by having a man or a baby. So if you begin to espouse a proud lesbian growth, you find yourself going against the grain. That makes embracing your lesbianism doubly frightening, because you then have to discard the mythology that's been developed around what it means to be a young Black woman.

BARBARA: And that you gotta have a man. The urgency of which probably can't even be conveyed on the printed page. (Laughter.) I was just going to talk about when I was younger and meeting people who would want to know about me. Not so much about my sexual orientation, because they weren't even dealing with the fact that somebody could be a lesbian. But I always noticed they were more surprised to find out I didn't have children than that I wasn't married. Marriage was not the operative thing. It was like, "Why don't you have any children?" That really made them curious.

JEWELLE: Right. They had no understanding at all that you could reach a certain age and not have any children.

BARBARA: And not having children doesn't mean we're selfish. It means we're self-referenced. Many Black lesbians and gay men have children. Those of us who don't may not have had the opportunity. Or we may have made the conscious choice not to have children. One of the things about being a Black lesbian is that we're very conscious. At least those of us who are politicized about what we will and will not have in our lives. Coming out is such a conscious choice that the process manifests itself in other areas of our lives.

JEWELLE: Yes, it's healthy. Having grown up with a lot of Black women who had children at an early age, I've noticed a contradictory element in that that's the way of many of them come into their own. I have younger cousins who have two, three, four children and are not married and will probably never be married. It seems that the moment they have the baby is when they come into their own and their identity after that becomes the "long-suffering Black mother." I think it recreates a cycle of victimization because a lot of these young women carry the burden of being on a road that wasn't really a conscious choice. On the other hand, when I look at Black lesbian mothers, I see that yes, many of them are struggling with their children. But there is also a sense of real choice because they've made a conscious decision to be out and have children. They are not long-suffering victims. They are not women who have been abandoned by their men. They are lesbian mothers who have made a place in the world that is not a victim's place. Now that doesn't necessarily mean that things are any easier or simpler for them. But there is a psychological difference because most Black lesbian mothers have made a choice and have a community they can look to for support.

BARBARA: In talking about choice, another thing we've been asked to address is why do people become lesbians, or why did we become lesbians, or why do we think there is such a thing as lesbianism?

JEWELLE: It was all those vegetables. Eating too much spinach. (Laughter.)

BARBARA: Well, I was a notorious non-vegetable eater all my life. Maybe it was the candy bars in my case. Seriously, I don't know why people are lesbians. All I want to say is that I think the reason women become lesbians is because they are deeply attracted - sexually - to other women. To me, that's the bottom line. There was a notion during the early women's movement, in which I was involved, that you could choose to be a lesbian. But I think the important point is whether you choose to be out, or to act on your lesbian feelings. Those of us who were coming out before there was a women's or lesbian and gay movement, understand this a little bit better. I teach students who are in their early twenties and they really perceive their coming out as say, a political choice because they are doing it in such a supportive context. Those of us who were coming out just before Stonewall[1] knew that we had feelings, passion, and lust for other women. We didn't necessarily have a place for our feelings that felt safe. But we knew intuitively - not because we read it in a book somewhere - that gay was good. Today people have women's studies courses, out lesbian teachers, all kinds of stuff that we didn't have. So they can indeed perceive their coming out as following in the footsteps of a role model.

JEWELLE: I grew up in a bar community and I knew I was a lesbian when I was quite young. But the only available role models weren't anything like who I thought I was going to be when I grew up. I knew I wasn't going to be sitting up in a bar all day, or hustling on the streets. So what was I going to be? There were no other role models.

BARBARA: That was the complete terror. Talking about how being a lesbian and homophobia affect one's mental health - I lived my adolescence and young adulthood in terror. I knew I was a lesbian, too. But likewise, I saw no way to act on it and stay on the path. This was a path that I had not necessarily chosen for myself, but that my family had worked very hard to give me the option of choosing, I'd think, How the hell can I excel in school, go to college, graduate school - and then become low-life by sleeping with women? I mean it just didn't jibe. Some people think that when I came out during the women's movement it was an easy thing. But I'd just like to say right here for the record, that from puberty on, I had screaming nightmares because I was having dreams of being sexual with women. I would wake up and my grandmother would be standing looking over me and I thought she knew what I was dreaming. She knew that I was disturbed about something, even though I never revealed to her what it was. So, I was really terrified.

I think that conscious lesbianism lived in the context of community is a positive thing. It can be a really affirming choice for women. The connection to sexism is deep, though. Homophobia is a logical extension of sexual oppression because sexual oppression is about roles - one gender does this, the other does that. One's on top, the other is on the bottom.

JEWELLE: I think the interconnection of racism and sexism has been so profound that we don't even know how the homophobia is going to be difficult for us as Black women. I've just recently begun to separate them out. I didn't really come out through the women's movement. For me, my sexuality didn't have a political context until later. I always had a sexual identity that I tried to sift out, but I was most concerned about how I was going to fit it in with being a Black Catholic, which was very difficult. Once I realized that one of them had to go - sexuality or Catholicism - it took me about five or ten minutes to drop Catholicism. (Laughter.) Then I focused on racism, to the exclusion of homophobia and everything else. That left me unprepared. I had a woman lover very early. Then I slept with men until my mid-twenties. They were kind of like the entertainment until I found another girlfriend and got my bearings. I didn't have the political context to deal with what it meant to want to sleep with both men and women. I skipped past the feminism until much later. So homophobia came as a total shock to me because I had never experienced it. Nobody seemed to be homophobic in my community, because no one ever talked about it. I hadn't experienced it because I wasn't out. I didn't know that I wasn't out. But I wasn't.

BARBARA: Because you weren't out, you weren't really experiencing homophobia consciously.

JEWELLE: Right. I thought it was an aberration. I didn't quite understand what it meant. It reminded me of the first time I heard about child abuse. That happened when I was a teenager and I thought child abuse could only have happened once or twice in the history of the world because it was so appalling to me and beyond my comprehension. And of course as I read more and realized it was...

BARBARA: Pandemic.

JEWELLE: Yes. I had to withdraw for a little bit to figure it out. It seemed as if someone had just stabbed me in my heart. I think I felt the same way when I understood there was such a thing a homophobia. A couple of years ago, I had an eye-opening experience while looking for an apartment in Jersey City. Now, I had experienced racism in Manhattan. In fact, someone had told me that when I called for an apartment not to reveal my last name because Manhattan landlords would think I was Puerto Rican.

BARBARA: This is America.

JEWELLE: So I'd just say that my name was Jewelle and show up at the apartment. This was in the early 1970s and it seemed that back then, being Black was a little bit more acceptable than being Puerto Rican, so they would rent to me. And also because I worked for television at that time, the landlords somehow took that to mean that I was okay, that I was better than just the average "Joe Blackperson" off the streets.

But looking for an apartment in Jersey City with my then lover, who was Black, was very different. Frequently, we'd be dealing with people who had two-family homes and were looking to rent one of the units. I remember we called this one place, and I was in stark terror. In my mind, I was thinking about a white couple looking at us and seeing two Black people that they were going to potentially bring into their home. It terrified me because I could see them insulting us or even possibly slamming the door in our face. And then just as we were about to get out of the car, it occurred to me that this white couple would also look at us and see two lesbians. (Laughter.) I was literally shaking. I had been so focused on them seeing two Black women, that it hadn't occurred to me that they would also see two lesbians. They'd see the quintessential butch-femme couple, both of us going into our forties.

BARBARA: Yes. Well beyond the college roommate stage.

JEWELLE: It terrified me. But as it turns out, they would have rented to us if we had decided to take the place, which we didn't. But the anxiety I suffered during those minutes before we rang the doorbell was devastating and definitely scarred me internally.

BARBARA: Of course. It's deep. This is one of the permutations of how homophobia and heterosexism overshadow our lives. One of the things that I'm very happy about now is that I live in Albany, New York. And they did allow me to buy a house there. I don't know how many Chase Manhattans I would have had to rob down here in New York City in order to get enough money to buy a house. (Laughter.) My house is in the heart of Albany's Black community. And one of the really nice things about it is that I know that nobody can put me out of my house because of what I have on my walls, who I bring in there, or whatever. That's very refreshing. Of course, it's the first time I've ever felt that way. What I'd always done before, because of homophobia and racism, was to be pretty low-key wherever I lived. I just felt that around my house, I had to try to be very cautious, even though I'm known to be a very out lesbian, both politically and in print. I didn't want anybody following me into my house who thought that bulldaggers shouldn't be allowed to live.

JEWELLE: I know. When the plumber is coming to my Brooklyn apartment to fix something, all of my lesbian things get put away.

BARBARA: Because he knows where you live and may even have a key to the apartment.

JEWELLE: Yes. I have no desire to wake up and discover the plumber and his helper standing over me.

BARBARA: That's right. That's real. This gets into an area that is very important for all people, especially Black people in this country to understand. And that is that we pay a heavy toll for being who we are and living with integrity. Being out means you are doing what your grandmother told you to do, which is not to lie. Black lesbians and gays who are out are not lying. But we pay high prices for our integrity. People really need to understand that there is entrenched violence against lesbians and gay men that is much like and parallel to the racial violence that has characterized Black people's lives since we've been in this country. When we then say that we are concerned about fighting homophobia, and heterosexism, and changing attitudes, we're not talking about people being pleasant to us. We're talking about ensuring that the plumber and his assistant aren't standing over our beds with their damn wrenches or knives. Everyone should have safety and freedom of choice. We have the right not to be intimidated in our homes or on the streets because we're Black, or on welfare, or gay.

JEWELLE: Right. My lover and I went camping in New Mexico recently. One day we camped on the Rio Grande in a fairly isolated area. We put up our tent and went away for while. When we returned, there were these guys fishing nearby and it made us really nervous. In fact, we had a long, serious discussion about our mutual terror of being a lesbian couple in an isolated area with these men nearby. I was especially conscious of us being an interracial couple and how much that might enrage some people.

BARBARA: Oh yes, absolutely. Speaking from experience, I think it's easier for two Black women who are lovers to be together publicly than it is for a mixed couple. To me, that's a dead give-away because this is such a completely segregated society. Whenever I had a lover of a different race, I felt that it was like having a sign or a billboard over my head that said - "These are dykes. Right here." Because you don't usually see people of different races together in this country, it was almost by definition telling the world that we were lesbians. I think the same is true for interracial gay male couples. So, you see, the terror you were feeling was based on fact. Just recently a lesbian was murdered while she and her lover were on the Appalachian trail in Pennsylvania. This is what colors and affects our lives in addition to Howard Beach and Bernhard Goetz[2].

JEWELLE: The guy who murdered the lesbian on the Appalachian trail claimed his defense was that he had been enraged by seeing their blatant lesbianism. He believed he had a right to shoot them because he had been disturbed by their behavior.

BARBARA: What is that defense called? The homophobic panic?

JEWELLE: To me, it's equivalent to the Twinkie defense[3].

BARBARA: Yes. There's a term of defense they try to trot out that suggests that the mere existence of gay people is so enraging to some that they are then justified in committing homicide.

JEWELLE: It's the sort of like saying that because you are scared of the color black you are justified in running over Black people in Howard Beach.

BARBARA: Right. We as a race of people would generally find that kind of thinking ludicrous. Yet there are Black people who would say that those murdered lesbians got what they deserved. I think that some Black men abhor Black lesbians because we are, by definition, women they are never going to control. I think something snaps in their psyche when they realize that Black lesbians are saying "No way. I'm with women and that's that."

JEWELLE: I think it's a psychological thing. Black women are perceived as property and they are the means by which Black men define themselves. It's another way they are like white men. They use female flesh to define themselves. They try to consume us to prove themselves as men because they're afraid to look inside themselves. The final note about our terror in New Mexico was that it was both a positive and negative thing. It was positive because we refused to give up ground. We decided to stay where we were because we liked the spot. Of course, it meant that I slept with a large rock in my hands and she with her knife open. But I'll tell you, I slept very well and she did too.

51

BARBARA: I'm glad you said that about not giving up ground because as out Black lesbians we have to live and do live with an incredible amount of courage. I've always felt that if anybody tried to physically violate me, that I would do my best to kill them. That's just fact. I'm taller than average. I'm as tall as most men and I don't slouch. When they're looking for people to harass, I feel like they skip me. (Laughs.)

JEWELLE: I've frequently felt that way too because I'm big. But I think that one of the things that's happening now with the homophobic backlash is that our size and presence enrage them too.

BARBARA: That's why self-defense is so important. As people of color, as lesbians and gay men, we live with potential or actual danger. Back to the point about courage, I attended a conference several years ago for women organizing around poverty and economic issues in the deep South. The Black women who came to the conference were wonderful and they treated me gloriously. As usual, I was out as a lesbian at this conference. Homophobia was the one issue they had not considered as a barrier to women's leadership. Funny thing, they skipped that. (Laughter.) But there was a little quorum of white and Black lesbians and we raised the issue. We got up on the stage and read a statement about homophobia. Then we invited other lesbians and people in solidarity with us to stand up. Almost everybody in the room stood up. Later we were talking about the incident in our small groups and a woman said something I'll never forget. She said that what we'd done had taken a lot of courage. And I have never forgotten those words because they came from a woman who was in a position to know the meaning of courage. She knew what it meant because she had been hounded by white bigots all her life. For her to recognize our being out as courage meant a lot to me.

JEWELLE: That's a very important point. I think that for those of us in Manhattan, Brooklyn, Albany, we have a certain leeway in being out. We have a diverse women's community that supports us in our efforts to be honest about being lesbians. I find it sad that there is a larger proportion of Black lesbians in small, rural communities who won't and can't come out because they don't have this support. I think they suffer an isolation and even a kind of perversion of their own desires. That's one of the things that Ann Allen Shockley writes about so well - the Black lesbian who is isolated and psychically destroyed because she doesn't have a positive reflection of herself. These are the stories that aren't often told. Such Black lesbians don't get many opportunities to share what is going on for them.

BARBARA: Yes. Class is a factor, too.

JEWELLE: Certainly. Your whole view about what it means to be lesbian is colored by whether you were able to get an education - to read different things about the experience.

BARBARA: Another point I want to make is that the people who are not out and have the privilege of good education and jobs need to be more accountable. It really bothers me that there are closeted people who are perceived as leaders within the Black community. This is something I find very annoying, because I think they are skating. If they were out on the job or in the community, they would automatically bring together issues that have been counterposed to each other for too long.

JEWELLE: Yes. They are skating on our efforts and devotion. It happens all the time. Another thing we need to talk about is religion in the Black community and how it has been such a sustainer in our lives. I find it despicable and a desecration that our spiritual beliefs are perverted and used against Black gay people. Anyone who understands what the spirit of Christianity is supposed to be would never use it against gays.

BARBARA: Love thy neighbor as thyself.

JEWELLE: Right. Christianity does not say pick and choose which neighbors you're going to love. And any of those biblical quotes that are used against Black gays need to be looked at in the context that that self-same Bible has been used to depict Blacks as inhuman.

Racists use Christianity against Black people and then Black people turn around and use Christianity against gays. It doesn't make any sense to me.

BARBARA: We also need to discuss some of the young Black men who are so prominent today in the Hollywood movie and television industry. People like Arsenio Hall, Eddie Murphy, etc. I think they are homophobic to their hearts.

JEWELLE: And sexist. I think it's telling that Spike Lee, the most popular Black filmmaker in the country today, includes the rape of a Black woman in his films. Sexism is so pervasive in our community that we don't even think of this as awful. Imagine what it feels like to sit in a movie theatre watching his film *School Daze* in which a Black woman is raped. The so-called Black brothers in the movie are saying, "Yeah, bone her. Bone her." And the Black women in the audience are giggling.

BARBARA: They were probably giggling because they knew they had to go back home with those kind of guys. This gets back to the Central Park rape that obsessed and terrorized me so much. The question I was raising at that time is: Do men understand that they can kill a woman by raping her? Do they understand that rape is torture and terror for us?

JEWELLE: I think that as Black lesbians, in some ways, we are very fortunate. This is because we are in a community that supports us in growing past racism, sexism, and homophobia. But as you've said, our heterosexual sisters have to go home with these guys.

BARBARA: We have to acknowledge that there are heterosexual Black females who are not putting up with that stuff. There are definitely Black heterosexual feminists who are saying - "No way. I'm not taking that kind of abuse, negation or suppression." And as more Black women become feminists, the men are going to have to change. My impression is that there used to be more cooperation between Black men and Black women. Back when lynching was a daily American pastime and the crazed white man was our common enemy, we were not as inclined to lash out against each other as we are today.

For instance, there was an article recently in Publishers Weekly about Black writers. The thrust of the piece was that Black male writers are suffering because Black women writers are getting lots of attention. This kind of thinking is based on the scarcity model that says there is only so much approval for Black writers within the mainstream white publishing industry. And that may be true. But there should be infinite approval within a Black context. Everybody who wants to write should write so we can all keep moving on up a little higher.

JEWELLE: Can you believe we've had this whole discussion without mentioning *The Color Purple*? To me, the criticism of the book and the film was very much like what happened to Ntozake Shange. People couldn't handle seeing Black women bond, even if it was only on celluloid. So it prompted unbelievable scenarios like grown men sitting at conferences debating whether Alice Walker should have been allowed to write *The Color Purple*.

BARBARA: What does that say about where we are? And as I've said at exactly those kinds of discussions - if people think *The Color Purple* is an exaggeration of Black women's lives, they should go to any emergency room, battered women's shelter or rape crisis centre in this country. If they did that, they would see that *The Colour Purple* is mild, bland and minimal compared to what is actually happening to women and children in this society.

JEWELLE: I'd like to close by saying that homophobia is particularly dangerous for Black lesbians because it is so insidious. There have always been acceptable places for gay Black men to retreat and escape from the danger, i.e. the "choir queen" or the Black gay man who embraces the white gay male community. But as Black gay women, we haven't been interested in removing ourselves from our families or communities because we understand the importance of that connection. The insidiousness of the homophobia lies in the fact that we've been forced to find ways to balance our contact with the community with our need to continue to grow as Black lesbians. We straddle the fence that says we cannot be the uplifters of the race and lesbians at the same time - that's what makes it so dangerous for our emotional health as Black lesbians. But you know, I think that our ability to see the need to keep the family intact is what is going to be our saviour and help preserve the Black community. As lesbians, we have so much to teach the Black community about survival.

BARBARA: I'm very glad that you said that about family. One of the myths that's put out about Black lesbians and gay men is that we go into the white gay community and forsake our racial roots. People say that to be lesbian or gay is to be somehow racially denatured. I have real problems with that because that's never been where I was coming from. And that's not the place that the Black lesbians and gays I love, respect and work with are coming from either. We are as Black as anybody ever thought about being. Just because we are committed to passionate and ongoing relationships with members or our own gender, does not mean that we are not Black. In fact, the cultural and political leadership of the Black community has always had a very high percentage of lesbian and gay men. Although closeted in many cases, Black lesbians and gays have been central in building our freedom.

JEWELLE: I think the political code has always been that you don't bring people out who don't want to come out - you don't force anyone out of the closet. But I think that's changing.

BARBARA: (Laughs.) I'm delighted, very delighted.

JEWELLE: With the way the media works now it's almost impossible to stay closeted. And I don't think people who are out feel as morally obligated to protect the ones who stay in the closet.

BARBARA: Especially now that there's AIDS. The ideology that you can just sit back and let a part of your community die off because of homophobia is untenable at this time. There won't be anybody here.

56

JEWELLE: Yes. It's very important that all our voices be heard. Everyone asks why do we have to talk about homophobia? Why can't we be quiet about it? The fact that we have to talk about it means that a lot of people don't want to hear it. And as soon as there's something they don't want to hear, it's very important that we say it. I learned that as a Black person.

BARBARA: I'd like to challenge all the non-lesbians to think about what they can do to improve the chances that we'll all be free and sisters.

Footnotes

1. In response to repeated police harassment, a group of gays rioted at the Stonewall Inn bar in New York in June 1969. The rebellion is heralded as the start of gay liberation.

2. In December 1984, Bernhard Goetz gunned down four Black youths on a Manhattan subway after alleging they had tried to rob him. In 1987, a gang of white New York teenagers attacked several Black men who had stopped in their Howard Beach neighborhood for pizza. One Black youth was killed by a car as he fled.

3. A defense used by San Francisco Supervisor Dan White in is 1979 trial for the slaying of the city's mayor and a politically powerful and openly gay city supervisor. White's attorney argued that his client's consumption of junk food contributed to his state of diminished capacity.

DIONNE BRAND

Hard Against the Soul

IV

you can hardly hear my voice now, woman,
but I heard you in my ear for many years to come
the pink tongue of a great shell murmuring and
yawning, muttering tea, wood, bread, she, blue,
stroking these simple names of habit, sweeter
and as common as night crumbling black flakes
of conversation to a sleep, repetitious as noons
and she up north, the hoarse and throaty, I told you,
no milk, clean up....

you can hardly hear my voice but I heard you
in my sleep big as waves reciting their prayers
so hourly the heart rocks to its real meaning,
saying, we must make a sense here to living,
this allegiance is as flesh to bone but older
and look, love, there are no poems to this only
triangles, scraps, prisons of purpled cloth,
time begins with these gestures, this
sudden silence needs words instead of whispering.

you can hardly hear my voice by now but woman
I felt your breath against my cheek in years to come
as losing my sight in night's black pause, I trace
the pearl of your sweat to morning, turning as you
turn, breasts to breasts mute prose we arc a leaping,
and no more may have passed here except
also the map to coming home, the tough geography
of trenches, quarrels, placards, barricades.

Memories...
Distances...
Exile...

CONNIE FIFE

Distances

last night
deep in the
womb of
mother earth
my prayers
for you
whispered to
my grandmothers
were
answered.
on this night
the spirits
will protect
you
in ways
i
cannot.
pull those blankets
closer
to
your
woman's skin,
wrap yourself
in blankets
of snow
under
skies of
woman's color

and once,
only once,
acknowledge the
spirits
who will
watch over you

in ways i
cannot while
so many miles
away.
know they
are strong
and willing
to protect
you
in this
your most
vulnerable state.
on this
night
touch my
hair
as i too,
wrap myself
in blankets
of snow

VASHTI PERSAD

Untitled - Journal Entry

Here finally. Exhausted, sticky, sad and happy. After Bermuda, Antigua and a stop, Guadeloupe, Grenada, Barbados. I see the mountain range of Trinidad's north coast. How beautiful. How full, rich and hot. This is my home. This was my home. The colours are familiar. So are the houses, roads, cars, bush fires and the memories. Home? Familiar yet distant. Under me now, a land I come to openly - but I have to remind myself it's not always safe. I leave part of myself in Toronto when I come here. It's the "safe thing" to do. And yet I come here to rest and make my soul strong again.

Right now I feel a kinship to the land I see beneath me. The memories of crossing this range on a Saturday morning to get to the best and roughest beach on the island. It was mine and I still defend its temper with mine. Maracus - brings thoughts of sitting on a car bonnet burning my young legs to get my picture taken by my Dad, the best photographer in my world; thoughts of finding a bush to wee-wee behind and then making sure the world was not looking at a six year old pee; thoughts of swimming in the sand because the water frightened me and then having my Dad pick me up and take me to what seemed like the middle of the sea just to be ducked under a wave; thoughts of bottles of rum, pots of rice and chicken and cars of relatives. Maracus, my childhood. The roads were steep, the cliffs were frightening and our little Hillman always won the challenge.

Two days ago, I turned twenty-nine. Two days ago, I was touching a woman whom I never wanted to leave. One day ago, I hugged a woman whom I will always love.

Now I just had a seven hour flight with a man next to me whom I did not know except for his rum breath and his elbow which kept nudging me and waking me up; and it wasn't even his assigned seat. Yes, I spent seven hours being possessive about a seat

I did not pay for. In addition to having to put up with this intrusion, I was battling obsessive thoughts of a lover - or an ex-lover - or whatever she wants to call herself. Back and forth, like a pendulum. Walk away, forget it all, risk the pain, protect myself, give it all to her. It was driving me crazy.

Now we have landed.

I am here to calm myself, collect my thoughts, my emotion. I am here to strengthen my soul. I am at a crossroads, searching for calm.

Right at this moment, I can't wait to face the hot air as I walk off the plane. Thoughts of the beach, sweat and starry nights await me. Before I leave the plane I must say goodbye to those two beautiful women. Ooops, I thought I left that part of me in Toronto. Again I think, where is home?

$*$ $*$ $*$

It is a week since I have been in Trinidad. There is comfort in being one of the many.

I am at the beach.

I am here for three days - my aunt, one of my mothers.

I look at the waves coming to the shore. The tide is low. The sea is calm except for that one wave which crashes to the sand. I am that wave - coming to these shores only to leave again - collecting what there is to keep, leaving what is heavy on my soul.

Strangely, I come here to free myself of chains I build in Toronto. Sitting here I can create a peaceful detachment. The things, and events and circumstances which brought me pain seem small and manageable. The pain of lost loves find a meaning. I find peace. I find a part of myself.

Ironically, finding peace has very little to do with my passion. My peaceful existence accepts my passions, but does not bring them to life. As I sit here and look at the sea and this one wave, I also picture one woman. I remember seduction. Just as the open sea pulls me deeper and deeper, and calls me to its depth, so I allowed myself to be called by a lover. The pull was magnetic. The force of this emotion was powerful. I look at the sea, and I dream of being surrounded, of being carried away, of giving in, of surrendering. Again, it is a search for home, for belonging. I am with the sea but my woman is not here.

Earlier this morning, after my eight a.m. swim, I attended a Hindu religious ceremony. I attend with respect but know that my knowledge of my heart takes me on a wider path. A little bit more, I find myself.

Reflecting now, I see myself being drawn into the life which my Trinidadian family respects. "Yes, I'll get married when the time is right", laughing when they all try to set me up with a young man.

Now sitting here watching the sea, I think to myself - where is the truth? How can I live my truth in this world? Yet finding peace has everything to do with finding truth.

This morning I was reading the BOMB, while the poojah was going on. It was a story about a man who found his wife in bed with another woman. The headline read, "The worst kind of horn: Donald is shocked: Darling, is that you?" Though appalled at the appearance of the story in the paper, I smiled. The husband described the women as being like "snakes intertwined holding each other". I was disgusted. I hated the imagery and I hated the article, yet in my mind the thought of these two women together brought a warmth and excitement through my body.

Yes, I am a lesbian.

I am a lesbian.

This is part of my truth.

I can only reveal this on these pages, however.

The world I know in Trinidad, which only includes my relatives, is not a safe place for this. I realize my limitations. I hear from friends about another world here. When I come here though I only become a part of my family's world - a world which warms me, strengthens me and cares for me; but in which I also feel caged. I can challenge it and I do, but I choose not to push the boundaries all the way. Political and spiritual boundaries are one thing - the boundaries of passion are something else.

So, I make my choices out of a need for this world. I want it. When I come, I come to hold and be held by my grandmother, to show her I love her. I come to retrieve my history from the hearts of my people and the words and vibrations of the island. I cannot lose this. There is lots of me on this island. When I find myself trapped and tortured by the weak links of love, by the isolation, the anger, the blindness, I need to run back here to nurse my soul. I will leave here in one week, wanting to get back to Toronto where my silent parts can begin to speak. I will go back stronger, calmer, more patient and more at peace. I will carry the love of my home country, my grandmother, my aunts, my relatives and the Trinidadian people. I will return to Toronto, longing to connect with my friends who give me a different sense of belonging and empowerment. I will recapture what I left behind.

✳   ✳   ✳

Tonight I am saying goodbye to this solitude as the sun sets slowly over the ocean. As I stare in amazement at the orange sky, I say to myself, my land, the beginning of my heartbeat. I feel proud to be of this land. I feel sad to leave it. Yet I am ready to go. It's strange. There is a pull to keep me here on this beach in seclusion, yet there is something calling me away.

It is a nice dilemma. A young man who lives here calls it magic.

He tells me to stay. His brother mentions marriage. Now I feel I am at that door. It opens widely every time I come to Trinidad, inviting me to come in. I see the tunnel it leads into. As my heart feels out the door, I realize how dangerous the desire to "fit in and be a part" can be. The pressure is extreme. And one more time I hear "it's lonely, you need a husband, you can't live alone, it's not safe." They all mean well. It seems over the years I have learned to accept this without much rebellion. At seventeen, at twenty-one and at twenty-four, I used to put up a fight, and I always threw the argument at them that I had to get an education and work a while. It always worked to keep the pressure off. Now these phrases are overused. I'm twenty-nine and almost past the "catching a boy" years of a girl's life. It's downhill from here. What will I do for the rest of my life if I do not take advantage now and "get a man".

I joke about this but a sadness comes into me. What about my truth? My love?

When I love a woman it's one of the most selfless and beautiful experiences I can have, and when I lose a woman's love, it's the worst pain I can feel. Yet I cannot share it with these people whom I love.

*   *   *

Last night, I slept with a woman I had spent a summer making love to when we were both 17 years old. She touched me, played with my hair, caressed me. I returned the tenderness. Her husband and children lay sleeping in the "master bedroom". I was a guest for the night.

The memories were strong. We reminisced. It meant the same for us at seventeen - yet our love went in different directions. We are both twenty-nine and the passion of twelve years ago easily comes back. The love was here. Commitment elsewhere.

So what does this say to me? Three days before I leave the island and after one and a half weeks of reflecting on the silencing of my sexuality, I find a night which is familiar. She was desirable and I sensed a passion within her. A little part of my love was getting a voice. Only I understood and I followed it softly and gently. When we were not reminiscing she was telling me about her husband, children and in-laws.

It is now morning and I am laughing to myself. I feel like I have completed this circle. I enjoyed the night, lying in her arms, knowing that I would be moving on.

*   *   *

I am treasuring my last three days and nights. I am spending my time close to my grandmother and my aunt. I am sad. I cannot make my Ma understand that she is one of the strongest women I know. She feels inadequate, somehow a failure, because her four children, her four daughters all live alone. It does not matter if they have re-married or if they live with someone. To her they are alone, all living in their separate houses. I tell her that she should be proud because she has brought up her daughters to be independent and strong. "They are survivors, just like you, Ma," I tell her. I am surrounded by strong, wise women, not only on my Mother's side but also on my Father's side. No wonder I am who I am. If only my Ma could feel this good. She is growing weak. She is afraid to leave. We argue. I try to understand. I lose my understanding. I get angry. She cries. I hug her. She hugs me, and talks to me like a little child. We carry on. I rub her head. She offers me food. It is always obvious that the energies between us are strong and stems from love.

As I look at my Aunt, my Ma's eldest daughter, she looks at me. As I think of something to say, she says it. As I find myself questioning, she gives me the answers. We talk without talking. There is a peace I experience in her presence. She is also one of the reasons why I come here. A rejuvenation of sorts. I am learning to understand. Everything seems to have a cause. Everyone seems to have a reason. I feel in control of myself. I am broadening my vision and I am excited. These words don't quite say it. It's hard to explain. I feel it. I am beginning to know it. *IT* being who I am. *Who I am* being my home. Home having little to do with geography.

*   *   *

Tomorrow I am leaving my Island. Tonight as I rub my Ma's head, shoulders and back, tears come easily. She was having a mild heart attack. I froze as I thought of losing her and I knew deep inside of me that I would carry her within me.

I stare out the back window of her house, mesmerized by the countless stars in the black sky and comforted by the warm night air, the breeze through the coconut trees and the smell of curry and rain.

I breathe in deeply to capture that energy within myself but realize that it is already inside of me.

DORIS L. HARRIS

Issada

Issada is my aberration,
cool as the first breeze of Spring
dry as dreams, that go unfulfilled

Issada, goes nowhere without her bangles
bracelets that jangle a response
to her every move, her every mood
Issada does nothing without her bangles
whenever she feels threatened, happy, angry
arrogant, or sexy those bangles that she so
proudly wears, announces her emotions
for miles around

rows and rows of multi-colored brass,

copper, silver, wood, and elephant's hair
(she swears) adorn her wrists, encasing her arms
protecting her

Whenever she is asked the origin of a bracelet or
the reason she always wears them
she just smiles and states
they are from the city of Babylon, of course
and my reason, my reason for wearing them is the same
reason the sun has for needing to shine

Issada, has taught me to love my reflection
in spite of myself
my full lips, nappy hair, big hips
Issada is as tough as these times have been
for poor black women
she is as fragile as a promise made to a child

one day, as she slept
I removed her bangles, lied to myself
that I needed to penetrate her defenses
one by one by one,
her tiny wrists were covered with an intricate mosaic
design, a roadmap with the most
delicate thin lines, healed over slashes
from a private time of terror

The only sound in the room, was my shame
spilling onto the floor, I lightly kissed the scars
replaced the bangles, respecting their power
I now know where Babylon is, it's where I've been
so often... before Issada

NALINI SINGH

pieces of mind: 1985-1986

I'm curved along the windowsill, lazy lizard sunning, saying phrases slick as sunlight. One eye open with my ears to the ground.

Little jewelled animals sitting on the back stairs, jumping off into bean vines. Child at play. Daddy's little turkey and growing up with the sounds of women washing dishes and cooking in the background.

Some have dreams of a palace in the country, marbled entrances, handlaid oak floors, expansive lawns, goldfish somewhere, maybe, swimming in an ornamental pond.

Vacuum sucks up everything, morals, integrity, everything, leaving empty space where not even air molecules venture to intrude.

Happiness, he calls it.

Put on your black velvet gold-patterned blinkers, breathe in and expand, belly large and turgid like a hairy watermelon. See only the future for the past can creep up and cloud your illusions of respectability.

How to Speak Confidently, Part I. Diplomas are gathering dust next to ancient photographs of flat land and smiling children with teeth that orthodontists have not yet touched.

As simple a thing as a tomato. Taken between teeth and tongue and enunciated. Laughter. Pointed fingers. Foreigner...foreign tongue...whispers in the snow about the paki who can't talk right. But she can do other things like work from next year's textbooks. A browner. Pinched noses guard against my imaginary smell, hoods over the eyes to guard against my imaginary intellect.

Subversive speech? Pardon me, my ears are plugged with wax. Glandular dysfunction. Excuse me, I don't mean to be impolite.

How To Speak Confidently, Part II. Classes are small, enrolment cheap. Swinging from the chandeliers, I can see, I can see small red spiders.

He's old and mellow now, intent on edging his way closer to the side of his god, armed with confident speech. Fists and sticks and razorladen words are now invalid forms of communication, and, not incidentally, there's no one left to listen.

Blending into a small rural stream in northern Ontario, she lies scattered, grey pebbles untouched by age. The end. Full stop there, period here. Summertime milkmaids grown old. The cow is dry, a flesh sac full of empty promises. You worship her on altars, in the pot of sacred fire, with fragrant oils and holy flowers. *Shanti, Shanti, Om.*

And we are the third generation, growing up in the promised land of Overseas, unlike my cousins who, left behind, barricade their houses at night because they do not wish to die in a sleep in which they dream impossibly of here. Eleven-year-old memory.

Palaces require nobility, so we are groomed for the professions, carefully trained to be twice as good as anyone else, for society demands this from its darker members. A fact of life, nothing more, like opposable thumbs and body hair. Who ever heard of dark cream?

To drink meaning out of broken cups. To wander through the walled pathways of order of which I am part, knowing they are not my routes.

Windshield wipers of cross-country cars meeting walls on which the writing is written. Voiceless. Authorless. And through the rear window mirror, understanding.

Time in its liquid crawl up the veins of your thighs. Her age is ended. No diplomas there. She left me some recipes, a sewing machine, her love. Perhaps she knew that my parents threatened me with her fate. I ran.

Sitting at the dinner table with a plastic bag between the legs. Into it, shovelling starch. Walking into the mirror, seeing oozing flesh everywhere, splitting its silvery sides. Also in the mirror, hiding from perception, where bones, rearing their sharp and lovely edges under skin shining soft, brown, warm. At a party, someone came up to her. "What's happened to you?" they asked. "You no longer have an ass!" She took this to be a compliment and promised to exceed herself next week.

Running far away from images of a fat, comfortable old woman who wears bitterness like a shroud. Grey sweater syndrome. Post-anorexic stability. Cover up and hide. Lumpy flies banging down the school hallways after last bell rings. Running away from all the women.

Who is talking here? Not I, not I, said the spider with the red glass eye. Not I, not I.

Not I watches undercover. Watches uncovered bodies once a week in claustrophobic change rooms and in a flash of clarity realizes that there does exist THE LESBIAN. Forgetting though, is as quick. It was not I who dreamt of shadowed women who leapt out of windows before I could touch them. Running out of breath. Trying to find places of rest, like this one: there are white lesbians and there are black lesbians, but I am neither and therefore not.

All the different lenses we wear. Sometimes focussing is in the realms of the mythical.

...floating voices from somewhere else...boats from the backdam laden with plantains, with old bone-thin women plying the oars, tattoos of spidery Hindi like blue lace down the length of their arms...

Remember where you come from. Voices. Her voice telling me stories of when they all lived in a shack whose walls were papered with month-old news. And how she would sew shirts for my father, pedalling late into the night, then getting up with the sun and working some more. And the scrounging and the hiding of money from the husband's thirsty fingers. She struggles and copes and the sons are eventually successful.

Midnight madness. Rum punch. Jump up. One-shot Caribbean vacation and it's all yours. Steel drums. Pretty island girls. Sun and sea. The other side. Seamy. Seedy. Rum-soaked. Poverty is the same in all colours.

But look now. Midnight parties under the tropical moon. Drunken people could stamp them foot on the wooden dance floor my parents had put down on the lawn for the weekend.

Back in the countryside, Derek, drunk every night at the rum shop, would come home sometimes to be thrown into the middlewalk canal by his wife's brothers. Brawling 'til two in the morning. She would close the lace-curtained windows and draw us into her protective arms. Watching is sometimes allowed, but we're told never to play with the village pickneys. Piccaninny.

I visit her in an antiseptic cubicle now. Massaging flaps of skin hanging over bones that hide death inside the marrow. Those warm and comforting arms that were tangible expression, matching the shine of love in her beautiful eyes, are like brittle sticks. She tells me more stories.

True stories. Tears and sweat. Her version of memories held onto over the years. She must speak and I must listen to her legacies. Or some other reason.

Never marry until you have an independent self, she says, and when you do, always keep your money separate. Helpful hints on how to handle the childishness of men.

Half listening. I've heard some of this before and sometimes things change with the retelling. Drifting into last night's hazy details of liquid labia and dancing nipples under my tongue. Curve of breast and hip and different kinds of tears and sweat. I have no words she will understand.

Photograph: Ida's head is on her shoulder and her hand rests on Ida's thigh. Both women smile at the camera, but not for the man behind it, my grandfather, the new student.

They met in a shopping mall just as Ida dreamt it, even down to the initial of her first name and after that they called each other D. S. - dream sister. Her other friend whom she cared for until death and told me about once, not thinking to hide the admiration and pride in her voice, told me of her pact of sexlessness with her husband.

Maybe she will understand? Questions and doubt and fear bounce back and forth and fall into a chasm of silence. No words to reassure me about other fears which I know to be all tied up with her.

Four in the morning last-minute essay writing. Snow outside. Everyone asleep. Uncontrollably it starts. Look at the clock imagine her dying there a year ago today with no one there but uniforms. A year ago this minute. Can't breathe grey flakes from the open window dying on my face, shaking deep yawning hole of panic and reality shifts its perspective on me. Terror like steel hands around my throat and I am her, dying alone and crazy. Howling grief tornado in my head spinning falling into somewhere with no sides and no bottom.

Shivering, I call for help but a strange voice thick and twisted, a distortion I refuse to recognize, speaks quiet words of abuse. Hysterical now blinded with my worst fear which is being alone with craziness and grief and no one there at all. This is how I have sometimes imagined Basiran. She-asleep in the water now-and I-running out of breath.

On the westbound midnight Queen streetcar, the woman driver
surreptitiously gives a free ride to a woman wearing nothing but
blue pyjamas. No underwear, no shoes, no coat. She rides to the
donut shop a few stops from the monolithic mental health centre
where she got on, and the waitress shakes her head. They both
shake their heads. I see her in women like these, only her craziness
was contained, hidden in the world of sons and grandchildren,
secrets of a lifetime locked away in her serving hands.

And who am I to transcribe their words? Someone who watches.
Elephants have photographic memories and they have always
remembered the original zookeeper.

how to speak confidently, part iii. What's he going to do with the
rest of those fucking diplomas?

She, on the other hand, embroidered more pillowcases than there
were ever heads for, cooked food and stored it away in a
multitude of plastic containers, hand-decorated elaborately
framed "oms" for her walls, made scatter rugs out of materials she
saved over the years.

Waiting for the days of deprivation and maybe too busy to notice
their ready presence around her. I slept on her pillowcases, ate her
food and retreated when she went on her rampages of destruction
or wove herself deep into tangled masses of deceit and paranoia.

Maybe. This is only conjecture. I am reconstructing, embroidering
the details of her life together with my own, for she is my archive,
my reflection, my history, and so many other things that change
and flow as I do.

And the writing. God, she must have had twenty notebooks at least,
of all different sizes, going all at once, into which she would scribble
famous sayings, religious parables, songs of worship, recipes from
the neighbours, old recitals from early interrupted schooldays —
Tennyson, Byron, all the British poetry boys.

All the points of connection. Knowing that she felt as I sometimes denied, that my life continues on from hers, anchored together by those places.

In a recent dream, my lover and I travel to Guyana to see her. Sitting outside the house is my grandfather, old, shrivelled, and rotting away from the inside. He says, "It's not me that should be dying, it should be her!"

As we walk away from him, he disappears and we wander around the backyard, my lover's face blossoming in delight because she recognizes everything without ever having been here. And then my grandmother comes out of her house, welcoming us with food and open arms, in the sunlight of her garden.

CAROL CAMPER

The Window

It is the year of my great depression; though I don't know it yet. I am on the inside looking out. Inside I peer from window to window. Inside this damp and musty old manse. Inside this tiny, Southern Ontario village where I don't belong.

Each time we moved we thought things were getting better, looking up. The Church would move us, my husband the latest candidate in a long family line of ministerial candidates. At first I liked this place. Lots of room, stained glass, a gleaming art deco diningroom suite. The back garden has a grape arbour and an asparagus patch. But, like all the other places, once you live in it for awhile, you come to know the inherent flaws.

My husband is not here. He is a theology student in Toronto and I see him only on weekends. I am alone. I am 23 and my children are both under 4 years of age. I have the car, true, but so little money that I don't bother to go out. I have the groceries delivered. I remain inside.

In my window are the best and brightest of things. Argentia, tradescantia, Saint Paulia burgeon on glass shelves. Treasured Danish crystal bud vases coax roots out of furry greyish leaves. A roar of engine takes my glance beyond my kitchen jungle. Alma is cutting the grass on the neighbouring church lawns.

It is a sultry September day - no surprise for a Southern Ontario autumn. Alma rides the John Deere back and forth across the grass, cutting swaths that fall just short of the manse. The church fathers pay her to cut the grass. I don't know why they don't have her cut our grass too, since it is all church property. I don't know why I am so drawn to Alma.

In this whiter-than-white Southern Ontario town, me and the Lebanese family who own the variety store are the only non-whites. Everyone else is white-white; the kind of white you get in small

Southern Ontario towns - or small prairie towns - or small Maritime towns. I wonder where Alma comes from. Alma of the quiet, brooding, black-eyed gaze. Thick lashes, heavy brows, coarse, shingled black hair.

In Sunday church service, where I sit firmly ensconced as the minister's wife in the choir stall, Alma wears pastel dresses, poorly fitting and an inward, otherworldly expression. She does not belong. She is guarded by a family phalanx - two quiet children, grey-haired mother, barrel-chested husband.

On Monday as she cuts the grass, strong, square shoulders and a sinewy back show above her strapless bikini top. Farming people, even white ones, have deep-browned skin. Alma is not like this. On her, there is no hint of the red that shows the skin was burnt first; no line of paleness to show she ever works with a shirt on. Her skin is burnished walnut brown.

Alma cuts another swath, her long, polished legs astride the mower. Her slender, muscled arms guide it. On this hot September day even the simple task of riding the John Deere makes Alma glisten, her sweat dampening the bikini top where it sticks between her small breasts. She does not belong and I follow her with my questing eyes asking a question I do not know.

Where do you come from, Alma? How did you spring up, a mahogany tree in this field of milkweed? Alma, bird of paradise, Green Mansions' Rima. I fancied you some noble, peasant woman; before I knew what a peasant woman was; before I knew who I was. We do not belong.

Twelve years later, I have come out from behind the windows. I have some inkling of who I am and I do not regret that I did not belong.

LANUOLA ASIASIGA

Untitled

Do you know what it's like
To have to try and make love
With someone you care about
Someone you really love
And in the middle of it all
You hate her
Hate her to death
For reminding you
For triggering the memories
You've buried so deep

NICE RODRIGUEZ

Innocent Lust

On the day before I migrated to Canada, I knew there was something else I had to do. I had packed my bags, two nylon suitcases weighing 35 kilos each, containing a little of everything I owned for 30 years. I could not bring more in excess baggage for I only had $400 to live on until I found a job in Toronto.

I spent the past days figuring out what to bring and not. What I could live without and what not. In the end, I realized it was my lover whom I wanted to pack with me to Canada.

In the Philippines, it was difficult to leave for abroad. Most embassies would not issue a travelling visa to any Filipino until they were sure he would return home. Many sought the greener pastures abroad, refusing to come back to a country of poverty, crime, violence and injustice. Ironically, many escapees also became willing victims to the same atrocities in another land.

My lover had applied as an independent immigrant to Canada, but she could not get through. I was just lucky and tomorrow I must depart. Although her heart would weep, I knew she would send me off warmly. A Filipino never grieved for another one who must go away to escape the political turmoil in our country. No explanation was necessary. It was a common suffering which many of us sought to get away from someday. Tomorrow, it would be my turn.

My lover and I had lived together for three years, but I knew she must selflessly let me go. There was no other option. We both wanted to see the world that our parents and ancestors never saw, and earn the dollars they never made in their lifetimes. My mother and brother pooled their resources together for my fare and pocket money. My father offered beer for my *despedida,* a farewell party. Friends embraced and kissed me like they would never see me again. I felt like a tourist trapped in an immigrant's body. I just wanted a holiday but everybody was driving me away. It became clear they did not want me back and that my mission was to clear the way for them when their own departure came.

My immigration papers were ready. I had to say goodbye to more friends. I had had devastating affairs with two straight women before and both separations had been disheartening. I could not call them up for they would not care. Besides, if my lover found out, she would think I was being silly. I had been faithful to her all these years and I did not want her to worry now that I was going away. I crossed out their names.

There was one person to call on my list. She had not been a lover and we were never intimate. Thinking about her still sparks an arousal in me. I never knew what she felt about me. At that time, only my eyes revealed my lesbian spirit and very few people could read eyes.

We went to a Catholic high school in Manila that believed in the segregation of boys and girls. The nuns handled us girls. At that time, I felt more like a boy but had to go through lessons on crocheting, embroidery, needlework and weaving. I brought my projects home for my mom to finish. I wished the nuns would let me work in the boys' room - woodworking, drafting, mechanics and leatherwork.

But segregation was the rule. We could not even mix with the boys who came in the afternoons. Just before they arrived, we must be out of the classrooms which we occupied in the mornings. Before they started classes, we girls must hurry down the stairs. Some wore shorts underneath our pleated blue skirts, fearing the boys who peeped through the slits between the stairs below would see our panties. My classmates never knew that sometimes I also sneaked a look at their underskirts. Well, there was really not much to see. Mainly legs and dark crotches.

Gigi, the person I wanted to call, joined our class late in high school. The other girls and I had been classmates for almost a decade now, some since our kindergarten days. Suddenly, a beautiful stranger appeared in our class. Nobody gave a damn except me.

The wide open windows brought cool air but I perspired profusely. She freshened the air with an enchanting aroma I had never breathed before. Her nearness made me shiver.

She came from an elite Catholic girls' school. She was slightly older, just a year or two maybe.

Each time I looked at her, I felt a surge of innocent lust. She had skinny arms but had a fully-developed figure. We wore thin polyester white blouses and the nuns wanted us to wear chemises over our bras. Gigi was not wearing a chemise. Just a bra which I wanted to unhook at that time. Suddenly, this intruder filled the fantasies I had vented on my female teachers.

In the classrooms, the teachers grouped us alphabetically, but outdoors we lined up by height. I was almost as tall as she was so she was never far from me.

Soon I was telling her jokes which she liked a lot. It was not hard for I was a natural clown. With her, however, I always felt I was running out of gags. I did not call her Gigi but I christened her Kiki, which in Filipino meant vagina. She endeared herself to me and I called her Ki. Soon others called her the same name but she did not mind being called Vagina. She had a game soul.

Her thick-black hair had a natural curl which I liked to roll around my young lesbian finger. She often enticed me with her round brown eyes and I would turn to stone. Her cheeks had a pinkish glow, and her lips were full and inviting. I wanted to kiss her but I was afraid.

I felt her force inside me. She was in my mind at school and at home. Not since her arrival had I worn such flawlessly shining shoes. I mended the holes in my socks and put elastics on them so they would not drop to my ankles for I thought that one day I might remove my shoes, maybe my clothes, in her presence. I saved money and went to the salon for haircuts. I asked my cousin to check my hair for dandruff and lice which I might have picked up last summer. The more I thought about her, the more I felt inadequate.

Sometimes, I called Ki over the phone for all the wrong reasons - assignments, projects, boys, but never about what I felt for her. Soon I became her confidante.

She told me her parents were separated. In the Philippines, there was no divorce. Kids who were illegitimate and came from broken homes bore stigmas on them. It was easier to say that her dad had died but she told me her mother was living with someone else. I liked her candour.

I wanted to bang down the phone whenever she spoke of boys. We had given code names to most of the senior boys in school. She was in love with Milky Way. I knew her before Milky Way even courted her but he was a boy, and so had the right to say his feelings. I kept my lesbian yearnings to myself. At night, I caressed my pillow and cried her name.

I felt bad but Ki would still find time for me. We would do silly things like walk to Quirino Avenue where Milky Way lived just to look at his house where Ki said she would live someday. Below the mercury street lamps, we waited for a jeepney to board home. It was rush hour and it was night time before we got a ride.

"If I got a car someday, would you ride with me?" I asked her wistfully. Only the rich had cars back home and we were not rich. Milky Way had a car.

"Of course," she said. "Fetch me."

"Yes, I will," I said.

Sometimes Ki would come so close to me, brushing a breast on my elbow. It was hard to say if it was a signal since my other classmates also did the same. There were just too many breasts in the classroom, 112 of them since we were 56 girls cramped in a class. Since it was our lone intimate contact, I taught my elbows to be tender with Ki's breasts. Maybe she liked it too, I thought.

Other times, pretending to study, she would put my head between her thighs while she sat on the wooden school chair.

"Come here," she called me. "Come to Mama."

I never knew what she meant but I came to her. Her legs were warm and I lay my head on her crotch. She touched my hair as she read her own book. I wanted to bury my head deeper into her.

The wooden chairs in the classrooms harboured bed bugs and at times Ki, would raise her skirt and show me the bite marks under her thighs. Sometimes, she lifted her skirt higher and I would blush. She never wore shorts. I blushed easily in her presence and she once wondered why I would get so red. I told her it could be a Vitamin B deficiency.

Until graduation day, I waited for the day Ki would stop talking about boys but she never did. If she had I would have dared confess my feelings even if it meant being expelled from school if the nuns found out. After a long wait, I figured out we were not meant for each other.

Besides, I was a neophyte. Even if I told Ki I loved her, I would not know what to do next.

How do lesbians make love? Honestly, at 15, I did not know. All the fiery sex manuals I read were about heterosexual exploits. What about same-sex erotica? There was none I could check back home. A Catholic country, these kind of books were probably set afire by religious groups. Maybe the priests and nuns kept it for their own reference. I was a scholarly nerd back then. Every answer I needed I sought in books.

As I got older, I learned it was mainly instinct - that when confronted with a nude female, I naturally knew what to do next. It was only in Canada, at age 30, that I got to read lesbian erotica. As an adolescent, I read heterosexual books and so fantasized about having a cock and a hard-on. The illusion was so strong I even dreamed about having a sex transplant someday.

There were only two sexes in the Philippines. No institution ever recognized the third sex. Since I could not be myself, I must believe I was a man. I told friends that I would save lots of money to get myself the biggest cock transplant ever.

Ki and I parted ways. In my graduation dress, I looked more queer than ever. Ki was radiant and the boys adored her. Soon she was dating the commanding officer of the school's military unit.

Two years later, she visited me at home. She was still a joy to behold with her easy laughter. She asked me to help her with her term paper. She said her boyfriend showed her his penis. She took my pen and paper and drew a cock for me.

"You forgot the veins," I said wryly. Ki made varicose details on her artwork. I had enough of her but could never turn her away. I told her to come back the next day for her term paper.

I saw her again after three years. At that time, I had moved out of the city to an east end suburb. I was then living with a lady from my newspaper's advertising department, who had a five-year-old son. I had a family. I saw Ki in my basement apartment in the city which I kept for convenience. The place was dusty and in disarray. Ki remembered my birthday and gave me a man's cologne.

Every object she touched would send dust off into the air and soon our hands and faces were smudged with dirt. It was hardly romantic. We laughed. She had flunked the government tests that I had passed the year before and we laughed again at her misfortune.

"I have done many things with men," she confessed, "but I'm still a virgin."

"You see, I have never done it with a man," I smiled. "I've done many silly things with women and I'm still a virgin."

We laughed even more. That was the last time I saw her.

Several years passed and now that I was leaving, I remembered her again. I called up Ki at the local beer company where she worked.

"Ki, I'm going to Canada," I told her. "I wanted to say goodbye."

"But you can't go without seeing me," she demanded.

"I'm leaving tomòrrow," I said. "Silly that I should call only now but I've got no time."

"I'm married now. I have a kid."

"Finally found someone," I said. "Well, I just wanted to tell you I was leaving."

"Okay," she said. "I will write. Take care."

And so I left. When I arrived in Toronto, I wrote Ki. It was the distance that gave me the courage to reveal what had long been unsaid.

> Dear Ki,
> I wanted you to know I loved you back then. Not in years had I found anything like it. I loved you more than Milky Way could ever have. I was afraid to ask - afraid for both of us.
> Love, N

The holidays approached and she mailed me a card.

> Dear N,
> I knew. Merry Christmas.
> Love, Ki, married with 2 kids.

It was a strange reply but I sighed with relief. After 15 years, I could not believe I finally told Ki what I thought I could keep forever. She knew at last and I eventually put my lesbian longing to rest.

MILAGROS PAREDES

Return from silk dreams

Slide billowing silk
between my heart and me
move where the wind
takes to kindness
and wraps soft silk sounds
round me

a moment's flight
to tenderness and beauty
to love that feeds nor breeds
no pain

sail into silk dreams

I feel the pulling in my belly
sucking my breath away.

She is holding on
running
round and round in circles
to keep from slipping
falling
burning
off her edge
she forgets about me
cannot live without me
but she fights her fury
against believing it
And I pull

Wrap your silk beauty around
me too
will you remember me?
will you take me in your arms
and remember me?

You want to draw me dry
your brown eyes plead, bleed
your heart's lonely pain
I feel you breaking inside me
I hear your rage so high and loud
I starve
to bargain for your silence
devour words from books
to quell your whispers
keep them from rising
high

And I escape
wrap around me silk.
I fear I cannot feed
your hunger
your pulling takes my breath away
you are too wild
and too strong
I am afraid of your telling.

Just give me your beauty
wrap your arms around me
cradle me and
remember me
I am yours and you
listen to my stories
my telling will not break
you.

C. ALLYSON LEE

Letter to my Mother

I lost my mother six years ago and still feel the tremendous loss very deeply. I wrote this letter for my mother while sitting on the beach on a grey, cold and lonely day in winter. I wanted to write down all the things I'd wanted to tell her but couldn't while she was alive.

Dear Mum:

There isn't a day that goes by without my thinking of you. Every day there is something, some place that reminds me of you, of your loving warmth and tenderness.

So many times I have wanted to share something with you, a funny story, a profound thought, the way we used to so many years ago. There is always a pain in my heart when I realize I can't turn around and call you to tell you what I saw today, who I talked to, or what I did. So many times I've wanted to bounce ideas off you, knowing you would understand.

There is no way I could ever understand how you've felt all these years living under repression, oppression, and unfulfillment. Knowing you had the wherewithal to have enjoyed a brilliant career, but was prevented from doing so because of family, obligation, and tradition. All I know is that it angered me so much when I'd try to interest you in taking a course here and there, and you'd feign disinterest and apathy. I knew you stayed home because you thought you should and because Dad demanded it. Even right up until the end, your mind was sharper and brighter than mine will ever be.

You were witness to the part of my life that was full of misery, self-deprecation, and insecurity. During those years I know I must have hurt you terribly being as irascible, stubborn, and hot-tempered as I could manage to be. I know you intimated to some of my friends that you wished I wasn't "so headstrong". But you know what? I'm glad I was and glad that I still am. I drew a lot of strength and courage from you, first and foremost as a person in your own right, and secondly as my mother. Of course we had our moments when we clashed and couldn't see eye to eye, but I always knew you loved me. You didn't know I never wanted to hurt you.

You never saw me help myself out of the darkness, and force myself to barrel through the mud and grime I allowed to build up around me. You never knew I had built a fortress of bitterness and hatred inside myself. It took me a lot of determination to take a cannonball to it all. You never knew that a lot of my resentment came from watching you being held down, kept down, and torn down by Dad, watching you not even try to defend yourself or stand up for yourself. But what I did know was that you were tired of it all, weary of arguing, and just resigned to what you thought was your fate in life.

You had vowed never to let yourself be treated like Po Po was by Grandpa, getting yelled at and ordered around constantly. But you did let that happen to yourself, and you knew it. I too vow never to be treated like that, especially by any man. But I have an advantage over you - I've been fighting ever since I was four years old and I've had lots of practice. You taught me something very valuable, not to let myself end up with anyone who needed me more than I would ever need them.

You will never get to see me overcome a lot of years of pain and wounds, and above all, you will never see me happy as I am now. It hurts me that I cannot introduce you to Mary and watch proudly as you meet and get to know each other, blending two very soft spots in my heart. I am saddened you will never see her smile or laugh, or know that she brings so much joy to my life; I am saddened she cannot meet the strong, clever woman who gave me life.

It hurts that I cannot tell you that the tenderest places in my heart are occupied by women. They will always be the most cherished and intimate parts of my life. How can I tell you that I feel so deeply and strongly for them, both as friends and as lovers, in a way that I could never feel for a man? I think that deep down, after all the intellectualizing and analyzing, you would begin to understand in your quiet way. I know you would finally see that this is what makes me strong, makes me happy, makes me feel like myself. And I know you'd want me to be happy above all else. Because of you I learned women can have a quiet strength.

Up until now, I've not done anything I've been especially proud of, and that's probably because of my lack of self-esteem and self-confidence. I know I felt intimidated and inadequate because of your anxiousness for me to do well. I always wanted to make you proud of me. I've been stuck in neutral all this time. I'm only beginning to go into drive and conduct my life down the road to recovery. Along each step of the way, each of my little successes I attribute to you and no one else.

I wish you could be here to revel in new joy with me, to celebrate and share in my moment.

Good night, Mum. I love you and miss you so much that sometimes I hear the wind whisper your name.

Sister to Sister

AUDRE LORDE

I Am Your Sister:
Black Women Organizing Across Sexualities

Whenever I come to Medgar Evers College I always feel a thrill of anticipation and delight because it feels like coming home, like talking to family, having a chance to speak about things that are very important to me with people who matter the most. And this is particularly true whenever I talk at the Women's Centre. But, as with all families, we sometimes find it difficult to deal constructively with the genuine differences between us and to recognize that unity does not require that we be identical to each other. Black women are not one great vat of homogenized chocolate milk. We have many different faces, and we do not have to become each other in order to work together.

It is not easy for me to speak here with you as a Black Lesbian feminist, recognizing that some of the ways in which I identify myself make it difficult for you to hear me. But meeting across difference always requires mutual stretching, and until you can hear me as a Black Lesbian feminist, our strengths will not be truly available to each other as Black women.

Because I feel it is urgent that we not waste each other's resources, that we recognize each sister on her own terms so that we may better work together toward our mutual survival, I speak here about heterosexism and homophobia, two grave barriers to organizing among Black women. And so that we have a common language between us, I would like to define some of the terms I use: *Heterosexism* – a belief in the inherent superiority of one form of loving over all others and thereby the right to dominance; *Homophobia* – a terror surrounding feelings of love for members of the same sex and thereby a hatred of those feelings in others.

In the 1960s, when liberal white people decided that they didn't want to appear racist, they wore dashikis, and danced Black, and ate Black, and even married Black, but they did not want to feel Black or think Black, so they never even questioned the textures of their daily living (why should flesh colored bandaids always be pink?) and then they wondered, "Why are those Black folks always taking

94

offense so easily at the least thing? Some of our best friends are Black..."

Well, it is not necessary for some of your best friends to be Lesbian, although some of them probably are, no doubt. But it is necessary for you to stop oppressing me through false judgement. I do not want you to ignore my identity, nor do I want you to make it an insurmountable barrier between our sharing of strengths. When I say I am a Black feminist, I mean I recognize that my power as well as my primary oppressions come as a result of my Blackness as well as my womanness, and therefore my struggles on both these fronts are inseparable.

When I say I am a Black Lesbian, I mean I am a woman whose primary focus of loving, physical as well as emotional, is directed to women. It does not mean I hate men. Far from it. The harshest attacks I have ever heard against Black men come from those women who are intimately bound to them and cannot free themselves from a subservient and silent position. I would never presume to speak about Black men the way I have heard some of my straight sisters talk about the men they are attached to. And of course that concerns me, because it reflects a situation of noncommunication in the heterosexual Black community that is far more truly threatening than the existence of Black Lesbians. What does this have to do with Black women organizing?

I have heard it said – usually behind my back – that Black Lesbians are not normal. But what is normal in this deranged society by which we are all trapped? I remember, and so do many of you, when being Black was considered not normal, when they talked about us in whispers, tried to paint us, lynch us, bleach us, ignore us, pretend we did not exist. We called that racism.

I have heard it said that Black Lesbians are a threat to the Black family. But when 50 percent of children born to Black women are born out of wedlock, and 30 percent of all Black families are headed by women without husbands, we need to broaden and redefine what we mean by family.

I have heard it said that Black Lesbians will mean the death of the race. Yet Black Lesbians bear children in exactly the same way other women bear children, and a Lesbian household is simply another kind of family. Ask my son and daughter.

95

The terror of Black Lesbians is buried in that deep inner place where we have been taught to fear all difference – to kill it or ignore it. Be assured: loving women is not a communicable disease. You don't catch it like the common cold. Yet the one accusation that seems to render even the most vocal straight Black woman totally silent and ineffective is the suggestion that she might be a Black Lesbian.

If someone says you're Russian and you know you're not, you don't collapse into stunned silence. Even if someone calls you a bigamist, or a childbeater, and you know you're not, you don't crumble into bits. You say it's not true and keep on printing the posters. But let anyone, particularly a Black man, accuse a straight Black woman of being a Black Lesbian, and right away that sister becomes immobilized, as if that is the most horrible thing she could be, and must at all costs be proven false. That is homophobia. It is a waste of woman energy, and it puts a terrible weapon into the hands of your enemies to be used against you to silence you, to keep you docile and in line. It also serves to keep us isolated and apart.

I have heard it said that Black Lesbians are not political, that we have not been and are not involved in the struggles of Black people. But when I taught Black and Puerto Rican students writing at City College in the SEEK program in the sixties I was a Black Lesbian. I was a Black Lesbian when I helped organize and fight for the Black Studies Department of John Jay College. And because I was fifteen years younger then and less sure of myself, at one crucial moment I yielded to pressures that said I should step back for a Black man even though I knew him to be a serious error of choice, and I did, and he was. But I was a Black Lesbian then.

When my girlfriends and I went out in the car one July 4th night after fireworks with cans of white spray paint and our kids asleep in the back seat, one of us staying behind to keep the motor running and watch the kids while the other two worked our way down the suburban New Jersey street spraying white paint over the Black jockey statues, and their little red jackets, too, we were Black Lesbians.

When I drove through the Mississippi delta to Jackson in 1968 with a group of Black students from Tougaloo, another car full of redneck kids trying to bump us off the road all the way back into town, I was a Black Lesbian.

When I weaned my daughter in 1963 to go to Washington in August to work in the coffee tents along with Lena Horne, making coffee for the marshalls because that was what most Black women did in the 1963 March on Washington, I was a Black Lesbian.

When I taught a poetry workshop at Tougaloo, a small Black college in Mississippi, where white rowdies shot up the edge of campus every night, and I felt the joy of seeing young Black poets find their voices and power through words in our mutual growth, I was a Black Lesbian. And there are strong Black poets today who date their growth and awareness from those workshops.

When Yoli and I cooked curried chicken and beans and rice and took our extra blankets and pillows up the hill to the striking students occupying buildings at City College in 1969, demanding open admissions and the right to an education, I was a Black Lesbian. When I walked through the midnight hallways of Lehman College that same year, carrying Midol and Kotex pads for the young Black radical women taking part in the action, and we tried to persuade them that their place in the revolution was not ten paces behind Black men, that spreading their legs to the guys on the tables in the cafeteria was not a revolutionary act no matter what the brothers said, I was a Black Lesbian. When I picketed for Welfare Mothers' Rights, and against the enforced sterilization of young Black girls, when I fought institutionalized racism in New York City schools, I was a Black Lesbian.

But you did not know it because we did not identify ourselves, so now you can say that Black Lesbians and Gay men have nothing to do with the struggles of the Black Nation.

And I am not alone.

When you read the words of Langston Hughes you are reading the words of a Black Gay man. When you read the words of Alice Dunbar-Nelson and Angelina Weld Grimke, poets of the Harlem Renaissance, you are reading the words of Black Lesbians. When you listen to the life-affirming voices of Bessie Smith and Ma Rainey, you are hearing Black Lesbian women. When you see the plays and read the words of Lorraine Hansberry, you are reading the words of a woman who loved women deeply.

Today, Lesbians and Gay men are some of the most active and engaged members of Art Against Apartheid, a group which is making visible and immediate our cultural responsibilities against the tragedy of South Africa. We have organizations such as the National Coalition of Black Lesbians and Gays, Dykes Against Racism Everywhere, and Men of All Colors Together, all of which are committed to and engaged in antiracist activity.

Homophobia and heterosexism mean you allow yourselves to be robbed of the sisterhood and strength of Black Lesbian women because you are afraid of being called a Lesbian yourself. Yet we share so many concerns as Black women, so much work to be done. The urgency of the destruction of our Black children and the theft of young Black minds are joint urgencies. Black children shot down or doped up on the streets of our cities are priorities for all of us. The fact of Black women's blood flowing with grim regularity in the streets and living rooms of Black communities is not a Black Lesbian rumor. It is sad statistical truth. The fact that there is widening and dangerous lack of communication around our differences between Black women and men is not a Black Lesbian plot. It is a reality that is starkly clarified as we see our young people becoming more and more uncaring of each other. Young Black boys believing that they can define their manhood between a sixth-grade girls legs, growing up believing that Black women and girls are the fitting target for their justifiable furies rather than the racist structures grinding us all into dust, these are not Black Lesbian myths. These are sad realities of Black communities today and of immediate concern to us all. We cannot afford to waste each other's energies in our common battles.

What does homophobia mean? It means that high-powered Black women are told it is not safe to attend a Conference on the Status of Women in Nairobi simply because we are Lesbians. It means that in a political action, you rob yourselves of the vital insight and energies of political women such as Betty Powell and Barbara Smith and Gwendolyn Rogers and Raymina Mays and Robin Christian and Yvonne Flowers. It means another instance of the divide-and-conquer routine.

How do we organize around our differences, neither denying them nor blowing them up out of proportion?

The first step is an effort of will on your part. Try to remember to keep certain facts in mind. Black Lesbians are not apolitical. We have been a part of every freedom struggle within this country. Black Lesbians are not a threat to the Black family. Many of us have families of our own. We are not white, and we are not a disease. We are women who love women. This does not mean we are going to assault your daughters in an alley on Nostrand Avenue. It does not mean we are about to attack you if we pay you a compliment on your dress. It does not mean we only think about sex, any more than you think about sex.

Even if you *do* believe any of these stereotypes about Black Lesbians, begin to practice *acting* like you don't believe them. Just as racist stereotypes are the problem of the white people who believe them, so also are homophobic stereotypes the problem of the heterosexuals who believe them. In other words, those stereotypes are yours to solve, not mine, and they are a terrible and wasteful barrier to our working together. I am not your enemy. We do not have to become each other's unique experiences and insights in order to share what we have learned through our particular battles for survival as Black women...

There was a poster in the 1960s that was very popular: HE'S NOT BLACK, HE'S MY BROTHER! It used to infuriate me because it implied that the two were mutually exclusive – he couldn't be both brother and Black. Well, I do not want to be tolerated, nor misnamed. I want to be recognized.

I am a Black Lesbian, and I *am* your sister.

JOANNA KADI

A Lesbian Love Letter

This is the letter I wish someone had written for me when I was a young woman.

Dear Sister,

There are stories I must tell you. Stories with knowledge and words and feelings that must be passed on. Because so many times, our stories to each other have not been shared as they were meant to be but rather they have been cut short, interrupted in the flow of one generation to another. What does it mean to be a lesbian of colour? what are the stories around this improbable/probable happening? Improbable because in a sexist, racist and heterosexist society, it is not likely we would find our way through the maze of external and internal oppression to come home[1] to this. Probable because it is oh so likely we would love each other/ourselves this much. I hold the improbability and the probability together as I reflect on these stories. As I reflect on the lack of stories offered to me as I grew up. And so I want to write this letter to a young woman of colour and to reach backward in time to offer it to myself. Because this is the letter I wish someone had written for me when I was a young woman.

There are stories I must tell you. Stories with knowledge and words and feelings that must be passed on. I can only pass on what I know as an Arab-Canadian, working-class lesbian feminist. And while my personal stories intersect with a larger framework, it is crucial to remember I speak only for myself. The unforgivable act of assuming a writer is speaking for whole groups of people is one I do not wish to repeat.

What story about knowledge shall I pass on? I must choose deliberately, understanding that knowledge of simple facts is power.

Here are some simple facts about lesbians of colour generally. Lesbians of colour exist. Lesbians of colour have always existed, and we will always exist. By virtue of our existence, we make a radical political statement against racism, sexism and heterosexism.

Here are some simple facts about the lesbians of colour I know. Lesbians of colour do not exist for the narrow purpose of engaging in genital sexual activity with other women. We exist broadly, as women whose primary emotional, psychological, spiritual, sexual and political connections are with women. We exist broadly, as lovers of women, of community, of self. We exist broadly, as activists who fight against every oppression and work/play toward global liberation. We exist broadly and we connect broadly, for we have left the isolation of oppression behind and moved into community. We exist broadly and we love broadly:

> I have never loved
> like this I have never seen
> my own forces so taken up and shared
> and given back...²

We exist broadly and we dream broadly. We refuse to have our dreams cut off at the roots and turned into paltry wishes for meagre reforms; we dream wildly and passionately and freely about a wild and passionate and free future.

What story about words shall I pass on? I realize I cannot talk about the words without first talking about the silences that must not be passed on. Because you see, my words had been stopped dead in their tracks by oppressive forces far greater than I, isolated and without a political analysis, could withstand. This meant whole stories stayed inside of me. They weighed me down and became burdens to be carried. It was a complete reversal of what was meant to happen because of course stories exist only for one reason – to be shared with others.

But when I came out as a lesbian both pairs of lips opened. My words inched their way forward, causing the stories to stir within me and begin to move outside of me. It was a fulfilment of what was meant to happen because of course stories exist only for one reason – to be shared with others.

It was a very slow process. To write that sentence now does not and can never capture the unbelievable slowness of the process. It started six years ago when I began to share words. First with my abusive husband (who did not notice when I went for days without speaking), but mostly with other women. I shared words about what it meant to be a lesbian feminist, the excitement, the wonder. I talked about the possibilities of women working together and creating something new, about women's culture, about feeling like I had come home, about a love I felt for all women, about women in Nicaragua, Palestine, Lebanon, South Africa, India, Korea, China, about a global sisterhood. I felt this love for all of us and I began to talk.

And because this is the letter I wish someone had written for me when I was a young woman, I must tell the whole truth and not gloss over the pain-full parts. I must share other words about the stark reality of racism and classism. I thought being a lesbian feminist meant something and now there are days when I wonder what it means. Because there are lesbian feminists who know nothing about working-class oppression and choose not to learn, who know nothing about Arab peoples and choose not to learn, who whitewash me and have the sheer weighty arrogance to presume they are doing me a favour and I wish I could say lesbians of colour never do this, never exclude Arab from the list when they say African Latina Native Asian, never profess to complete and utter ignorance about the Middle East. I wish I could say that but I cannot. And because when I came out as a lesbian both pairs of lips opened, I am able to share words about these pain-full things and about these wonder-full things.

This is the letter I wish someone had written for me when I was a young woman.

What story about feelings shall I pass on? Let me begin with a profound statement by Audre Lorde. "The white fathers told us: I think therefore I am. The Black mother within each of us – the poet – whispers in our dreams: I feel, therefore, I can be free."[3]

I feel, therefore, I can be free. When I first read this sentence, it grabbed at me with an urgent force and I understood (part of) its meaning immediately. Because when I came out I began to feel alive and in love for the first time. Not in love with one woman, one person, but with all women, and with my people. These feelings were new and different because prior to this I rarely felt. I had no time for feelings, because survival claimed my time.

My feelings were rudely interrupted by feminism, which is for me inseparable from lesbianism. It was anti-pornography work which pulled me into anger, grief, and critical feminist analysis. It was anti-pornography work which pulled me toward a passionate love of women and a desire to make my life with women. It was anti-pornography work which pulled me away from a six-year, abusive marriage to a white, middle-class man.

And it would not do to touch only lightly on the pain of those first repressed feelings that rushed to greet me once feminism tore the lid off. Such intense depressions, such bouts of sadness and grief, such paroxysms of self-hatred. All of the residue from years of sexist, racist and classist oppression had to be felt before different feelings could move in. And this makes sense. How could I truly love the Arab-Canadian/Arab-American communities and the Lebanese and Palestinian peoples without feeling, comprehending and letting go of the self-hatred forced on me by my oppressors who taught me that I and all Arabs are dirty? How could I truly love women without feeling, comprehending and letting go of the self-hatred forced on me by my oppressors who taught me that I and all women are only good for one thing? How could I truly love working-class people without feeling, comprehending and letting go of the self-hatred forced on me by my oppressors who taught me that I and all working-class people are stupid? (thisistheletterIwish someonehadwrittenformewhenIwasayoungwoman.) How could I fervently desire justice for poor and working-class people, the liberation of Palestine and Lebanon, my lover Jan? It was my coming-out process that allowed me to feel these desires and loves and to know they spring from the same passionate source.

These are some of the stories I must tell you, stories with knowledge and words and feelings that must be passed on. They are part of the larger framework of stories now being offered up so they can be shared as they were meant to be, so they are not cut short but rather flow from one generation to another. This will cause many things to happen. One is to help ensure that young women of colour know a simple and powerful fact: lesbians of colour exist. I was alone for many years and had no knowledge of this phenomenon called lesbianism. And some people think it only happened years ago, and that I am too young to have experienced this, and I say no, for a girl who grew up in a working-class Lebanese extended family in a factory city, I was not too young. I was 22 when I discovered lesbians exist, 25 when I came out to myself. It was highly improbable that I would have learned this earlier, and it was highly probable that once that simple and powerful fact presented itself I would rush forward to embrace lesbianism. How can we not love each other/ourselves this much? This is the letter I wish someone had written for me when I was a young woman.

1. Hoagland, Sarah Lucia. "Coming Home." *The Coming Out Stories*. Edited by Julia Penelope Stanley and Susan J. Wolfe. Watertown, MA: Persephone Press, 1980, page 146-148.

2. Riche, Adrienne. "Phantasia for Elvira Shatayev." *The Dream of a Common Language*. New York: Norton, 1978, page 5.

3. Lorde, Audre. "Poetry is Not a Luxury." *Sister Outsider*. Trumansburg, NY: The Crossing Press, 1984, page 38.

SKYE WARD

Meditation on LOC Sisterhood

As Colored girls, sometimes our minds give out on us.
We go crazy – we be crazy Colored girls.
We be bitter/angry/heartbroken/delirious/with pain...
We sing blues songs, build walls, stock jagged teeth
piranhas in moats surrounding our hearts.
We lock our pussy down or lace it with translucent
sweet tasting poison.
We bite/we cuss/we scream/we say get out my face bitch!
We say hold me pleeze baaby.

Hearts bleed...

Hemorrhaging unable to get a grip,
our brains turn to dust.
We go out of our minds – living off vapors
that used to be solid mind.
Fumes swirling empty cranial cavities,
essence of rationality searching for molecules
of wisdom to attach and bond to.

Yeah, we used to be whole.

Anthologist's note: When the call went out for submissions to A Piece of My Heart, *many, many pieces came in during the development of the book. There were just as many withdrawals and re-submissions. This letter represents one such piece. It touched me because of its honesty and simplicity. I asked the sister for permission to reprint and share it with other sisters.*

Dear Sisters:

A few months ago, I submitted several poems to be considered for the upcoming anthology by Black lesbians. I am writing now to withdraw some of those poems. Some of them no longer reflect who I want to be, what I want to write about, or who I want to love. I cannot, therefore, take the chance they may be accepted and published.

I began this letter more than two months ago, but have only now collected my thoughts together and summoned my courage to complete this process. So please, read my reasons for wanting to withdraw my poems before dismissing me as some strange and temperamental writer. In some ways, I believe you might recognize my dilemma as one which you have encountered in yourself or in other Black writers or editors.

The poems I submitted were written two to three years ago. I submitted them because they were among the few pieces I was no longer revising, and although I was uneasy with some of my own images, I liked the style and writing I demonstrated in them. Only after sending the poems to you did I closely examine why I had stopped working on these pieces. They are poems of naivete from my paler lesbian days. They reflect a period in my life when I stayed hidden in my own writing and instead lauded the "beauty" of my White lovers. I had an uncomfortable habit of writing myself into invisibility in my own poetry.

I have finally begun to examine why I have written about White women so much. Some of the answers to my inquiry include the discoveries that I do not know me enough to love me, to love my blackness, and to love other Black lesbians.

Other answers to my inquiry include the fact that I am among many Black women who write and translate our feelings into this English language as we weave our way through its profanities. I know there are words this language does not have for what I feel. I know also there are words I cannot remember from my first language which I could use to fill these mental gaps.

I heard Beth Brant, the writer, say at a talk, "Writing is an act of courage and an act of love." For me that means I am trying to move away from being an object of my own writing to being a subject in it.

With these discoveries have come a sense of responsibility to myself and to other Black lesbians. I want my words to be Black positive even as I strive to shape my own consciousness Black, strong, and hard. The images of Black and White women together in some of my poetry troubles me even though it reflects my reality. I do not want these poems, with White women in them, and me hidden in them, to possibly end up in an anthology for Black women. I hope someday to publish these older paler poems alongside my newer darker poetry so that the contrast between them will be obvious to all who read them.

Judy Nicholson

PATRICE LEUNG

On Iconography

I have fucked mostly white women.
It occurred to me the other day while I was brooding about life,
that each of these women was the fulfilment of my Marcia
Brady fantasy.

Marcia Brady, of course, was the eldest of the three Aryan vixens
on "The Brady Bunch", a show I watched with religious
abandonment every Friday at 8 pm precisely, on ABC.
My physical yearning for Marcia Brady was the realization of my
parents' dream for me.

We emigrated from Trinidad when I was six and as Chinese
immigrant parents, my mother and father wanted desperately to
protect me with the middle class stability that they had from time
to time found fleetingly.

Belonging to the middle class meant assimilation...

Yes, I was to aspire to at the very least middle class things: waffle
irons, clothes from the chubby section at Sears, and a God-fearing
husband.

And yes, I was to be proud of my genes: ancient, civilized,
highly creative and intelligent, superior in fact to those of other
races.

But I was not, under any circumstances, to make waves; to make
a spectacle of myself; to do anything that would anger the gracious
white hosts who had allowed us into their country.

In other words, the only protection I had against deportation
and racism was the cloak of middle class invisibility.

And so, I was surrounded and eventually absorbed by things white:

white toys – thank goodness for Malibu Barbie
white teachers – Mrs. Ujimoto was my grade nine math teacher/
her husband was Japanese
white religion – forced to pledge allegiance to a hairy man with
holes in his hands
white languages – je parle francais un peu mais je ne sais pas

parler chinois
white theories – I must ask my mother how to say penis envy in Chinese
white media – male & yankee influenced
white boys – BORING
white sales – ????
white girls – said a red-haired friend, "You know, I never think of you as Chinese"
white women – the lusty Marcia was replaced by Olivia Newton-John, Dorothy Hamill, Candice Bergen, Hanna Schygulla, and my blonde psych professor

An ex-lover was responsible for pointing out the internalized idiocy of my erotic patterns and for that I am grateful and embarrassed. It took a white woman to educate me in a matter of my own race.

I am pissed.

I don't want Connie Chung, Fu Manchu, or Charlie Chan representing my culture.

I don't want O-lan, the heroine of *The Good Earth*, portrayed by a white woman with taped back eyes.

I don't want Steven Spielberg to direct the film adaptation of *The Woman Warrior* or *China Men*.

I don't want Japanese actors cast as Chinese characters because we all look alike.

I don't want superficial images of Chinese because the CBC, NFB, and Telefilm have multicultural mandates to fulfil.

I don't want it assumed that I am meek, exotic, subservient, or heterosexual.

I want women of colour and lesbians of colour to control and celebrate our own iconography. WE are our own best icons. Until I made love with another woman I didn't know there were homosexuals of the Chinese persuasion. We need to let each other know who we are, for support, for inspiration, and of course, for dates.

Our visibility will challenge the male white-wash that perpetuates Marcia Brady and insists we not love ourselves.

We're too damn good.

We know it.

Let's show it.

Maria Amparo Jimenez

Cuentame Tu Historia
A mi Madre

Cuentame tu historia, Lea
que,
a traves de ti
conocere la de ella.
Rompe el silencio, Lea
guardado por tantos anos
dentro de su cuerpo inerte
que no recuerda el pasado.
Cuentame tu historia,
de esas noches sin descanso,
de hombres desconocidos,
de la lucha de tu alma
entre tu verdad
y la de ellos.
Rompe el silencio, Lea
de las companeras de establo;
sirve de voz
a ese silencio explotado.
Cuentame tu historia, Lea
de las noches sin trabajo
en que anorabas la cama,
y los brazos de tu amada.
Rompe el silencio,
para que yo comprenda
que su prostitucion
era mi supervivencia.
Cuentame tu historia Lea
que

a traves de ti
pondre perdonarla a ella.

Maria Amparo Jimenez

Tell Me Your Story
To my Mother

Tell me your story, Lea
through you,
I will know hers.
Break the silence, Lea
kept for so long
in her inert body
that does not remember the past.
Tell me your story,
of the restless nights,
unknown men,
The internal struggle
between your truth
and the accepted.
Break the silence, Lea
of your stable sisters.
Be the voice
of such exploited silence.
Tell me your story,
of the nights off
when you longed for the bed
shared with the woman you loved.
Break the silence,
so that I understand
that her prostitution
was my survival.

Tell me your story, Lea
so
through you
I can forgive her.

COLECTIVO PALABRAS ATREVIDAS:
MARIA CORA
KARLA ROSALES
SABRINA D. HERNANDEZ

Somos / Images of Myself

Somos

You are the guide in the distance
dancing along the razors edge
with your thick hair flying
skin the color of rich coffee
dark full lips never hesitating to part
for the sharp tongue
that slices away at obstacles
planted in our path
revealing the truth with which we steady ourselves
along the way

Yo soy tu imagen y tu la mia

No me tengas miedo
yo te entiendo
En tus capaces manos
pongo toda mi confianza
Solo a tus dedos permito el toque intimo
que me estremece
A tus brazos voy
a renacer, a crecer
y cuando me toque, a morir

Somos

Me recononozco en tu mirada y se la rabia
que sientes porque es las misma que siento yo
And I would scream
but my voice is plugged with fear
fear that you will not see me
perhaps you might hear me

Somos

Compartimos esa mirada
valiente y directa
de ojo a ojo
Sabemos lo que siente el corazon
cuando late bajo un pezon erguido
Cuando el mundo no te quiere
ni comprender ni aceptar
el dolor es tambien mio

Somos

C. ALLYSON LEE

An Asian Lesbian's Struggle

By virtue of the shape of my eyes and the colour of my hair, I am considered by Canadian society to have membership in a "visible" minority, and am also called a "woman of colour". This means that I could never "pass" for white, even if I tried. It has long been regarded as a privilege, to be able to be thought of as white, to have no physical characteristics which could set one apart for looking different. After all, in Canada, a white person can walk down any street and not be called a "jap", "chink" or "nigger" and not be asked "where do you come from – originally?" or "where were you born?"

Aside from the obvious racism generated from external sources, many people of colour often suffer from a more concealed form of oppression: internalized racism. This could be described as fear or hatred of one's own ethnic heritage or prejudice against one own race. For myself, it has taken decades to get to the point of claiming ownership of such feelings. For most of my life, I belonged to the "Don't Wanna Be" tribe, being ashamed and embarrassed of my Asian background, turning my back on it and rejecting it. I did not want to be associated with, let alone belong to a group which was stereotyped by whites as being noisy, slanty-eyed rice gobblers, "gooks" or chinks.

In spite of my being born and raised on the prairies, in a predominantly white neighbourhood with all white friends, my father tried his best (albeit unsuccessfully) to jam "Chineseness" down my throat. He kept telling me that I should be playing with Chinese kids – there were none in our neighbourhood. He chastised me for not being able to speak Chinese – by the time I entered Grade One public school, I was fluent in both English and Chinese, but my parents, worried that I may not develop good English skills, stopped conversing with me in Chinese. And my father warned me ominously, "You'd better marry a Chinese. If you marry a white, we'll cut you out of our will." All of this succeeded in driving me further away from my roots, leading me to believe that if I acted white enough, i.e. not chatter noisily in Chinese and not hang around in groups, I would actually not look Chinese.

Throughout my home life it was unacceptable for me to embrace my father's traditional Chinese culture and values unconditionally, because, in my mind, I would be accused by others of "sticking to my own kind" and would therefore be set apart from whites. But along with my father's wish for my awareness of cultural identity came along his expectation that I grow up to be a "nice Chinese girl". This meant that I should be a ladylike, submissive, obedient, morally impeccable puppet who would spend the rest of her life deferring to and selflessly appeasing her husband. He wanted me to become all that was against my nature, and so I rebelled with a fury, rejecting and denying everything remotely associated with Chinese culture.

When I moved away from the prairies to the West Coast, I remained somewhat colourless and blind. Still denying any association with my ethnic background, I often voiced, along with others, utter contempt for Hong Kong immigrants who were, in our minds, nothing but repugnant, obnoxious, spoiled rich kids. And it was in this city that I first experienced being called chink and gook on the street.

The connection between my sinophobia (fear or hatred of anything or anyone Chinese) and rebellion against my father did not become obvious to me until years later. Moving into another province meant that there was no longer daily contact with my father, the object of my defiance. I was becoming a little less resistant to Chinese culture, as I busied myself with the task of forming a new life in the city. Seeing new places, meeting new people and taking in new experiences left me a little less time to practice this form of self-hate.

Becoming a lesbian challenged everything in my upbringing and confirmed the fact that I was not a nice, ladylike pamperer of men. Somehow I must have known from an early age that I would never fit into this conformation. My friendships with women had always been more satisfying and intense than those with men. I had grown up with a secret morbid fear of marriage, and I did not know why until I became involved with a woman.

By coincidence, my first lover was a woman of colour, someone

116

who was proud of her own heritage. She became interested in mine, and through her support and love, I began to look more positively at my culture and see that it did hold a few interesting qualities. Her heritage and mine, although distinct and separate, had some notable and fascinating similarities. Both celebrated yearly festivals. And both cherished the importance of higher education and the formation of a solid family structure. She helped me see that it could be fun to explore the various aspects of my culture, but at this point I still did not claim it as my own.

Years later, white woman lovers came into my life, teasing me and calling me a "fake" Chinese because, after all, I did not even speak the language. This helped to bring back the old feelings of sinophobia again, and it did not occur to me then that certain white people would seek me out and be attracted to me because of my ethnic background. I had heard of "rice queens", white men who go after Chinese men. But there was no such term for white women who felt a strong affinity towards Chinese women. It would be much later that I would coin the phrase "Asianophile", my own description of such women.

Another woman entered my life, and by another coincidence, she was Chinese, born in Canada, and proud of her heritage. This I found to be both mystifying and affirming at the same time. She had not developed an attitude of sinophobia in her childhood, and as a result never felt contempt or derision for her background or her association with it. It felt like a bonus to be able to talk with her without having to explain little idiosyncrasies of our common culture and language. I no longer felt ashamed of it. She was starting to help me reclaim a heritage I had previously denied.

I felt certain that we were the only two Chinese lesbians in the world, until I began to meet others from different Asian backgrounds. At an Asian lesbian conference in California, I learned that there were indeed others who shared similar stories of struggles against externalized and internalized racism. Meeting Asian lesbians in my own city was like taking a course in Anti-Racism 101, which helped to raise my political awareness. These special women made me realize that it was fine to get upset over injustice and oppression, great to speak out about it, and necessary to fight against it. Gradually my awareness of my background was no longer the source of my shame, but the beginning of my empowerment.

My attempts at conquering my sinophobia continues to be an uphill struggle, as I deliberately seek out to meet other Asian lesbians and maintain friendships with them. Years ago I would have shunned them, or at best, ignored them. There is still a sense of discomfort, however, when I go out socially with a group of Asian women (and I find myself looking around the room hoping not to catch contemptuous racist stares from white patrons), or when my white friends tell me that they feel left out or uncomfortable around a large group of my Asian women friends.

As I go through this struggle, however, there are many bonuses in my life. I am enriched by the company of some very supportive and loving friends: Asian women, other women of colour, white women and men. I have reached a point of understanding about the origins of my previous self-hate and how it has pervaded my life and magnified the dysfunctional relationship with my father. And there is always that private joy in knowing that my father (who doesn't even know it) won't have to worry about my marrying a white boy.

DEBBIE DOUGLAS

A Time

Asha watched the heavy traffic flowing across Bloor Street as she waited for the light to turn to green. She shifted the plastic bag she carried from her right to her left hand. It was becoming heavier. She had stopped off at Spadina and taken the overcrowded bus south to Kensington, where she stood sweating, feeling faint from the strong stench of Babe and Brute which emanated from the stringy hair couple sitting beside her. She had rushed off the bus and across the street not waiting for the lights, afraid she would miss the fish market. It was almost six o'clock and she knew that the men and women who came to work at six in the morning would not spend a minute past closing time if they could help it. She walked in as the old man was preparing to close. From there she walked down Kensington street to the West Indian market owned by the aged, white Guyanese fellah who often went out of his way to take something off the bill of the older Black women who came into his store. Many remembered him as the young boy whose clothes they washed when he was still a child in the colour conscious Caribbean of the late sixties, early seventies.

The helper in the shop was an old African-Guyanese woman who had a bit of advice to pass on to every Black woman who entered the store. It was because of her that Asha chose this shop above all the rest; this grandmother who brought a bit of the Caribbean with her when she emigrated – the feeling of Yard, of community. Asha placed her attache case and the small bag with the fish she was carrying in front of the door. She stood in the middle of the shop mentally ticking away the things she had to get. She liked this store. The smells of too ripe bananas, aging mangoes, thyme and the rough dusty smell of ground provisions – yams, dasheens, cocoa, mingled to create a scent that invaded her nostrils and tickled her memories.

Asha walked around picking things up. First some pepper for the flavour, lime, thyme, a half pound of rice, oil, a small bag of flour, onions, scallion, and a hand of half-ripe plantains; not because she

119

needed it for the special meal she had planned but because she could not resist this perfect shaped sister to the banana. "That's all dear?" Asha did not respond. She was deep in thought, wondering whether or not to purchase the juicy over-ripe mangoes. Her thoughts went back to the Caribbean mango season. A time when the children woke at four in the morning armed with flour bags to pick up the beefy and starchy mangoes that had fallen the night before. It would be nice to have a bellyful of a Julie for dessert, to sink strong white teeth into pale yellowish flesh, juice running down chin, giggles as she offers to lick the... "Ma'am?" The wizened old face looked expectantly. Asha realized the woman was still waiting for a response. "Yes. I think so. That'll be all. And I'll take two of these," she said placing the two ripest mangoes on the small heap she had made on the counter. As the old woman tallied up the balance on a scrap of wrapping paper, Asha's mind returned to her plans for the evening. "That will be sixteen twenty-seven please," the voice said cutting into her reverie. Asha opened her wallet and pulled out a twenty dollar bill. Good, she said to herself. I have eight dollars left. Enough for a good bottle of white wine to go with the fish. She picked up her plastic bag with the fish and opened the door. "Look like you plan a good dinner, eh?" Asha smiled at the face that could be her grandmother's, "Yea. Stew fish and rice." She closed the door behind her holding the bloody bag away from her white linen skirt, a part of the outfit she called her organizational clothes.

Asha crossed the street quickly, cursing the driver making a left turn after the light had changed, barely missing her. She liked this neighbourhood, Dovercourt and Bloor. Walking slowly, she took in the loud reggae music coming from the record shop. Right next door was a West Indian shop, its doorway decorated with the bright red, green, and gold tams and wraps worn by the Rasta brothers and sisters lounging around, taking in the passing scene. She admired the many different types of locks, thick locks falling as rope or thick twine in some cases over shoulders. She self-consciously touched her own locks, glad that she had washed and oiled it only that morning, and now it hung black and shiny almost touching her shoulders, delicately held back from her face with a knitted red and black scarf. She felt a spiritual connection with the people she passed, glad that she was part of the great, colourful African diaspora.

As she neared the house, she reached into the pocket of her beige spring jacket for the key Mica had given her only the week before. Her thoughts turned to Mica and the long journey it had been.

Mica was Sicilian with pale olive skin, long thick dark hair and large brown eyes. She was a filmmaker, whose creativity followed her into the bedroom. A picture of thighs, opened, flashed before Asha's eyes and she felt a dampening in the black bikini briefs she wore.

She and Mica had ended up together by accident....

They were both friends of Akila whose party they had attended in Pickering three months before. They had both stayed after the party, neither wanting to make the long trip back to Toronto at three-thirty in the morning. They had shared a bed for the few hours left before the dawning of the new day. Both were still high with energy generated by being at a party with thirty women and the insistence of the drums that wrapped everyone in a passionate ritual of dance. Dawn found them, legs entangled, bodies glistening with sweat and that sweet stuff many of us women could die for. Mica had called her a week later and they had met for dinner. There was the same sexual spark – the kind that caused Asha's panties to dampen, the spark that makes you smile as if you've just been given the best compliment in your life. The spark that refused to be controlled by the rational or anything cerebral. Asha had opened up sexually to Mica in a way she never had before. She had been wet and open that first night, begging Mica to take her, filling her with hands made gentle by the look of caring in her eyes.

The sex was great.

Mica was a great conversationalist too, forcing political discussion at the oddest times, often quoting from Paulo Friere or bell hooks or Audre Lorde. She had little time for white feminist theorists with the exception of Adrienne Rich, whom she felt was one of the few who articulated through her political analysis that revolution by definition means the recognition of privilege. Mica often challenged her white friends and acquaintances alike "lets talk when you recognize your vested interest in the system and what role you as a white middle class woman can play to bring about the transformation." She was real clear about her place of privilege in society and never fell into the "Italian/Sicilian stereotype" as oppression excuse.

It was her intelligence and intensity which first struck Asha. That and the fact that whenever Mica began on one of her political passions Asha was often surprised for it would strike her at different times that Mica was white-skinned but the thoughts she expressed were quite similar to those of Asha's. The affair had gone on for a few weeks when Asha spoke to Akila about her fascination with Mica, the trust she felt, the safety. "Go for it," was Akila's response, "that girl is fine. One of her sisters may burst her head one of these days for the things she says about white feminism, but she has sense. And good looking to boot," she chuckled.

"But she isn't Black," Asha wailed.

"You've just noticed?" Akila came back refusing to turn this into the problem of the month. "And since when is skin colour the basis for political or sex-ual" (the last word she dragged out, mimicking Asha's mother who always stressed the sexual when saying homosexual), "compatibility? Come on Ash."

"I know, Aki, but you know how people talk. Especially now that we as Black Lesbian feminists are beginning to recognize the need to develop our own politic."

"Has spending time with Mica prevented you from fully participating in what you often call your community?"

"I can't honestly say that it has. I mean I feel self-conscious about the fact that the woman I'm becoming involved with is caucasian, and I know this is because of the reaction in THE group. I don't believe that everyone there disapproves, but you know how easy it is to develop a `collective stance' when the leaders of the group strongly believe something."

"Yea, I know. Communal lies, my friend Stewart calls it. But since when have you cared what other people thought or said about you?" asked Akila.

"I don't really. But it does get to me when it is implied that the colour of my bed partner somehow takes away from my political credibility or commitment. Half of these women just discovered that a Black community existed, that a political Black community was here and has been here for a long time. All of a sudden they're self-appointed speakers for the whole lot of us wanting to decide how we should think, dress eat, and whom we should sleep with. Frankly, I'm fed up. "

"There's so much to be done, even within our own community around homophobia and sexism, don't even mention poverty, and these women are concerned with the colour of my lover's cunt and not with her political analyses and where she has located herself in liberation movements."

"What do you really care though, Asha?" Akila paused and gets a drink of sour sop juice from her fridge. She continued. "People who really count know. Your friends know who you are and if any should question your commitment to the Black liberation struggle, my dear, just kindly tell them to kiss your black ass. After all what does it really matter in the end when we're all fighting for the same things. At least we say we are..."

Asha was still laughing at the kiss the ass part, doubled up she wiped tears from her eyes. "You know, Akila, that's why I love you. You put things in perspective."

She continued to smile imagining the shock on the faces of her group members if she told them all to kiss her ass the next time they made sly remarks about the undesirability of a dreadlocks woman in a relationship with a white woman. They would call her language abusive and probably expel her from the group.

She had noticed lately a new rigidity in the collective. Come to think of it, the women whom she really liked in the group were not coming as regularly, maybe she too should look at resigning from the Collective. She dreaded the meetings because of all the personal questions and she really wasn't clear about the political goals of the group. She wasn't even sure if there was a basis for the group other than they were all Black lesbians, most from Caribbean backgrounds.

"I have to get going, Aki. Thanks for the ear and the tea. I'll think about what you said. You do put things in perspective for me.

Whew! I feel much better. I should call Mica and let her know that I'm o.k. I've been avoiding her for the last couple of days, too freaked out by inter-racialism."

"Are you going to tell her that, when you see her."

"Probably. We seem to be able to talk about these things fairly easily. But I'm sure she's already heard what the reaction of my sisters have been to our relationship. She's probably freaked out too."

"You two will get through it. Just don't let those people get to you." Asha smiled and hugged Akila, liking the closeness they shared. She was the big sister Asha always wanted. Funny that in all these years they had never once attempted a sexual relationship. It just didn't seem to come up. Probably for the best, Asha thought, she didn't exactly have a great track record as far as romance went, and she valued Akila's friendship far more than most lovers she'd had. If they had been lovers chances are it would not have lasted. Asha thought about her record of short relationships. Maybe she just wasn't cut out to have long lasting sexual relationships. She sighed. Maybe this one is it, a little voice said in the back of her head. She was thrilled at the thought and quickly picked up the phone hoping to cover the embarrassed smile that came to her face. "It's ringing," she said to Akila and the joy in her voice was unmistakable.

Asha smiled as she entered Mica's apartment with her bag of food, her body tingling with the anticipation of the night ahead.

Sharon Lim-Hing

Superdyke, the Banana Metaphor and the Triply Oppressed Object

Characters:

DOROTHY – intellectual

FRANCIS – butch

LAN – punk

RACHEL – bisexual

SHEEMA – femme

All five characters must be played by Asian (should be of various ethnic origins, including South Asian) or half-Asian actresses. Their individual characters (i.e., intellectual, butch, etc.) can be indicated by dress.

*   *   *

One side of the stage represents DOROTHY's kitchen or dining room. The other side when lit represents the street. When the curtain opens, DOROTHY, FRANCIS, LAN, RACHEL and SHEEMA are sitting around a table in DOROTHY's apartment, having just finished dinner. LAN is slouched over, perhaps smoking a cigarette. DOROTHY is wearing glasses and reading a book. FRANCIS sits with her legs spread widely apart and arms folded or her hands firmly on her knees. SHEEMA sits in a femme-y position and checks her makeup in a compact mirror. After a few seconds pause for the audience to observe the characters, RACHEL gets up.

RACHEL: I'm so full I just have to get up and move around.

SHEEMA: Next time we'll have to remember: Asian lesbian potluck, not Mongolian feast.

DOROTHY: Delicious matar paneer. I never realized that chianti classico could complement Korean, Indian, Chinese, Vietnamese and Japanese food – all in the same meal.

LAN: Rules are made to be broken.

SHEEMA: I think I've just done my garlic quotient for the next two weeks.

FRANCIS: Garlic and rice – keeps that hair black and silky!

LAN: Speaking of lots of black, silky hair, that was a great Asian Lesbian and Gay Association party last night. Music sucked, though.

FRANCIS: At least you can dance to it. Unlike some of your favorites.

LAN: You can dance to Lydia Lunch. You just have to have the right pair of shoes. Don't you get sick of listening to the same stupid messages all the time? *(Lan stands up)* Pump up the jam, pump it up, DJ spin that wheel...

Dorothy stands up.

DOROTHY: I rather enjoy the mindlessness of contemporary North American disco-derived music. One could do a fascinating study on the abject cynicism regarding heterosexual relationships, particularly when transposed onto the schema of a gay dance floor.

LAN: Well, it makes me want to vomit.

SHEEMA: Please don't! You might splatter my skirt. Anyways, it rots your enamel.

RACHEL: And you're forgetting the most important thing – it's so danceable.

Rachel does some quick vogueing.

FRANCIS: Hey, who was that woman Michelle was with?

RACHEL: That's the fourth white woman I've seen her with...

DOROTHY: In as many weeks.

RACHEL: She's a bonafide North Pole female monarch.

Sheema stands up.

SHEEMA: Girl, she's the queen of snow queens.

LAN: She's the snow queen and potato duchess all in one!

Francis stands up.

FRANCIS: So! I don't see why you have to be so judgemental. It's Michelle's business who

she goes out with. Anyway, we all have
our own little things that we go for.
Michelle just happens to like sickly pale
skin.

RACHEL: I wonder what your "thing" is, Francis.

Rachel looks at Francis who looks away.

LAN: *(As if to herself)* Sticky rice.

SHEEMA: It would be her business if she were only
going out with these women. But when
she's sleeping with them, then it's our
business too.

FRANCIS: To gossip about, you mean.

SHEEMA: Think of us as the friendly neighbourhood crime watch committee.

DOROTHY: I do believe it was you, Francis, who asked
the question, and I quote, "Hey, who was
that woman Michelle was with?"

SHEEMA: Whoever she was or is, her eyeshadow
was just a tad overstated, don't you think?

FRANCIS: I can't believe anyone would wear
eyeshadow. To a party. For fun. I mean,
it's the 90's. Get with it!

SHEEMA: *(Looking at Francis' clothes)* Exactly,
Francis.

RACHEL: Not everyone has mastered the dubious
skill of being a girlie-girl like you, Sheema.

DOROTHY: Yes, I imagine there are so many different aspects of societally determined female appearance to remember. But there are so many other truly intellectually engaging questions to ponder. Say, who was that cutie with the bolo tie?

LAN: You mean the bolo tie in the form of a massive labrys? Or the one with the giant pink crystal labia?

DOROTHY: I mean the cutie-pie.

RACHEL: I think they were both cute. The women, not the ties.

FRANCIS: You think anything in pants looks cute.

RACHEL: As a former lesbian, coming out as a bisexual, I resent that. You know people call bisexuals fence sitters. Well, it feels pretty good sittin' on that fence. I'd like to launch a new term: Bi-envy. *(Turns to Dorothy)* Are you saying that the pudgy one was not cute? Do I smell some fat oppression here?

DOROTHY: What I'm saying is the "pudgy" one lit a campfire in my panties. Get it? "Pudgy?!" *(Mimics Rachel)* Do I smell some fat oppressive language here?

SHEEMA: Jeez! Let me out of the P.C. squadroom. *(Checks her watch)* The Goddess of Swatch Watches be praised! It's time for me to eclipse. I have a late rendez-vous.

LAN: With who?

129

SHEEMA: With someone you all don't know so you can't gossip about.

FRANCIS: Sheema, will you be safe walking to the subway? There's been a lot of gay-bashing around here lately.

SHEEMA: Do I look gay? Rape is my primary worry, not gay-bashing.

LAN: Don't worry, next year Asian-bashing will be back in style.

RACHEL: Aren't you afraid if you had to run in those heels you couldn't?

SHEEMA: No, 'cause these heels make great eye-poker-outers. And between Model Mugging and kung fu classes, I'm ready. *(Goes into a fighting stance)* In fact, I'm praying they'll try. *(Makes a savage jab)* Watch out for that flying, dismembered penis!

RACHEL: It's ricocheting! Everyone duck!

Everyone ducks.

SHEEMA: *(Dusting her hands together as if after a hard job)* That's another rehabilitated rapist.

DOROTHY: It's a bird, it's a plane, it's Superdyke! But how come she's not white like Superman, Batman and Robin?

SHEEMA: *(Indignant)* Dyke? Don't call me a dyke.

RACHEL: *(Teasing)* Hey, there's a hair on your leg.

SHEEMA: *(Shocked)* Where?

RACHEL: Nope, guess it's just a run in your hose.

FRANCIS: *(To Sheema)* So do you shave your armpits too?

SHEEMA: Bien sur. Even though I get razor burn. My skin turns red and if I sweat within two hours after shaving it feels like I'm rubbing salt in my wounds.

FRANCIS: That's insane! Why do you bother!

SHEEMA: You did say, "No pain, no gain."

FRANCIS: Yes, but I was talking about my quads and lats, not my armpit hairs! Armpit hairs are sexy. I love summer, wearing shortsleeve shirts, flexing, taking a swig of beer. *(Pantomimes her words.)*

RACHEL: *(Staring at Francis' armpits)* I used to have an armpit hair fetish, but I'm in recovery now. I don't shave either.

Rachel shows her armpits. She and Francis look at each other's armpits, then glance up simultaneously to meet each other's gaze. Sound of a triangle is heard. They look away quickly.

SHEEMA: Sorry I can't join in the bulldagger session, but I've got to go. *(Glibly)* Fifteen minutes keeps the suspense wet, thirty is fashionable, but forty-five and she won't let me in.

Exchange of goodnights. Exit Sheema.

FRANCIS: I can't believe that kid. Dorothy, remember the good old days, when jeans and a checked flannel shirt were just fine for every occasion.

DOROTHY: I don't remember what I wore. I just remember my eighth grade teacher, Mrs. Hutcheson. *(A dreamy look on her face)* She said my logarithms were perfect. I thought her kneecaps were perfect. She always wore long skirts, so I could only see her knees when her skirt would occasionally get hitched up on the chalk holder. I even loved her funny nervous twitch when all the kids laughed at her and she didn't know why...

LAN: How pathetic!

RACHEL: I'm a little worried about Sheema. This extreme femme-y-ness. And, I think she has a lot of unresolved banana issues.

DOROTHY: Banana issues?

RACHEL: You know, banana. Yellow on the outside and white on the inside. Can't face up to her Asian identity.

LAN: Oh, I thought that's what we called gay Asians who don't want to join the Asian Lesbian and Gay Association.

FRANCIS: Don't we all have "unresolved banana issues"?

DOROTHY: I believe some of her behaviour is due to the fact that her parents want her to

132

finish her studies so she can go home and marry the man of their choice.

LAN: Can't she just say no? That's what I did, and my family never bothers me anymore. In fact, we don't have any contact whatsoever.

FRANCIS: It's more complex than that... There's got to be a better metaphor than banana.

LAN: How about a hard boiled egg? Brown on the outside, white on the inside, but with a heart of gold on the inside.

DOROTHY: Summer squash? That's still a bit elongated, though.

RACHEL: Lemons? Grapefruit are yellow on the outside and pink on the inside. *(Looks at Francis)* Certain sensuous melons? *(Pause)* By the way, Francis, would you like to help me organize next month's rap?

DOROTHY: What's to organize? You simply choose a topic then let everyone know about it. *(Lan kicks Dorothy)* Ouch!

FRANCIS: Sure, I'll help. Why don't I walk you home? I mean, I was going to visit my friend George and... he lives near your street, I think.

RACHEL: *(Smiles)* You've never been to my house. How do you know where I live?

FRANCIS: I... must have seen your address on the mailing list.

DOROTHY: It's almost one in the morning and you're
                  going to visit your friend. I thought you
                  said you had soccer practice at nine A.M.
                  tomorrow. *(Lan kicks Dorothy again)* Ow!
                  Why do you persist in inflicting bodily
                  harm on others with those steel-
                  reinforced toes?

LAN: Well, it's late. *(Yawns exaggeratedly)* You
                  guys better be on your way.

*Exchange of goodnights. Francis and Rachel go out Dorothy's imagined
front door. Stage lights go out, except on Francis and Rachel, to represent
street.*

RACHEL: *(Stretches)* Ah, the wide open spaces of
                  Somerville.

They walk in silence for a minute or two.

FRANCIS: So, Rachel, is it true that... bisexual
                  women will leave a woman for a man?

RACHEL: That's a bit like asking if a lesbian will
                  leave a woman for another woman.
                  Depends on a lot of different things.

FRANCIS: Guess you're right.

RACHEL: Francis, is it true what they say: butch on
                  the streets, femme in the sheets?

FRANCIS: *(Laughs)* That's something you just have
                  to find out for yourself.

RACHEL: Hmm, sounds challenging... Here's my
                  house. That's my bedroom window.

Points and holds Francis by the shoulder, as if to better show her the right window.

FRANCIS: So, what would we discuss at the next Asian Lesbian and Gay Association rap?

RACHEL: Monogamy?

FRANCIS: Non-monogamy.

RACHEL: Taking the initiative in a new relationship!

FRANCIS: Unrequited love.

RACHEL: Sexual fantasies.

FRANCIS: Sexual rejection.

RACHEL: Throwing caution to the winds!

FRANCIS: Shyness.

RACHEL: Kissing?

FRANCIS: Kissing.

They kiss.

FRANCIS: Think it's safe for us to kiss on the sidewalk?

RACHEL: *(Dreamily)* No. I think I'm in danger of spontaneous combustion.

FRANCIS: Rachel, I don't feel comfortable standing outside here. Why don't we go inside?

RACHEL: Okay.

Rachel makes motions of opening her front door. Before Francis goes in and closes the door, she looks at audience and winks. Exit Rachel and Francis. Lights back on at the dinner table part of stage.

DOROTHY: Did you hear that laughing? Hey, what was all that rap organizing business about?

LAN: Dorothy, you may be writing your thesis on the incidence of sapphic activity among bovines of the jersey breed on free-running farms, but at times you can be a bit spacey. Two dykes conniving to converge into a seething compound of slippery female organs – without seeming too obvious or too eager... neither too much the sex addict nor too much the co-dependent.

DOROTHY: You mean... oh, I get it! Hope it works out for them. You know, since Jean and I broke up a year ago, I just can't imagine having a serious relationship. Though I would consider a quickie affair with Lily Tomlin.

LAN: Have you asked her to check her schedule?

DOROTHY: How about you, Lan? Any woman on the horizon?

LAN: Oh, lots of women! But that's where they stay – far away on the horizon. Anyway, you know I'm celibate. I don't know what came first, no lovers or validating my

state by a declaration of celibacy.
Sometimes I don't know why I even
bother to wear this button. *(Indicates pink
triangle pinned to her pants crotch)* Guess
I'm just a lesbian in theory. And in
practice I'm chronically horny.

DOROTHY: Look on the bright side. Celibacy is as safe
as you can get.

LAN: Thanks. Sometimes your utter optimism
just dumbfounds me. People like you
remind me why I decided to be celibate.
So what're you doing tomorrow, Dorrie?

DOROTHY: Workshop on racism for the Gay and
Lesbian Political Action Association.

LAN: Ugh! I can't believe you're still running
around trying to educate white, gay
liberals. It's not your job to educate them,
it's their responsibility to educate
themselves.

DOROTHY: Well, they're trying, and I want to help
them. It is frustrating at times, though,
the same assumptions, the same veneer of
understanding. But we are part of the gay
community, are we not?

LAN: I think I am, but no matter how
obnoxious I may act, Asians are invisible
in the "gay community", as you call it. To
hell with educating whites. They'll never
see you or me as a person. To them you're
a triply oppressed object, or a politically
correct icon. I'm just me, I don't represent
all Asian lesbians. And sometimes I just

	want to have fun, waste time, ogle girls, like everybody else.
DOROTHY:	Life isn't all fun, Lan.
LAN:	Ha! Don't I know it. But you can try to squeeze in some fun between the angst and the agony.

Pause.

LAN:	Been to the new women's bar?
DOROTHY:	You mean Closets? No.
LAN:	Music sucks. But people are friendly... enough.
DOROTHY:	Well, why don't we pop in. It's only one o'clock. *(Puts her arm around Lan in a friendly way)* I'll buy you a ginger ale.
LAN:	You're on.

Dorothy and Lan walk off together. Lights fade.

THE END

CHRISTINA SPRINGER

Ancestor Song

Soft sister / mother
dance between continents
shaped in rape

and I

Imitate your water dance of ease,
test for warmth.

Laugh imperious
fierce Siberian tigers
place tails between legs,

tamed then ignored
you roar
fierce and calm.

and I
I / YOU

and I

rolled in violets
wrapped in tye-dye cotton
hearing soft sister / mother words.

Shape the color of dawn
to my own liking.
Write letters to the Moon.
Walk her light dark vision.

Your clearing.

VICTORIA LENA MANYARROWS

the drum beats

far away and in the night
      a drum beats
life begins again
as we gather in circles
      completing a sacred order
spirits filling us with presence
      and the smell of sage and sweetgrass
making us whole and wise

together we send ourselves
from these lands to other lands
      and into the skies
the world between the clouds
where memory is eternal
and forgiveness is without limit

sister, i am calling you
from distant lands, i am calling you
sending you strength
      for your survival
holding you without touching you
wanting you without expecting you

sending you strength
      for your survival.

INDIGO SOM

The Queer Kitchen

context is everything. here is mine: i was born in san francisco, a cancer in the year of the horse. my spirituality is deeply rooted in this place, the bay area, which is my home in every possible sense of the word, from santa cruz in the south to point reyes and the beginning of the wine country in the north. my parents are both architects, originally from hong kong and canton. i grew up in marin county (one scarlet bridge north of san francisco), which is notorious for being rich, cocaine – rich, and just as white – and attended an exclusive, oppressive private prep school there.
i left to go to college in rhode island, where i figured out that i was not a white male, my upper middle class background notwithstanding. having made this discovery, i returned to the bay area for art school and eventually graduated from uc berkeley in ethnic studies. i am a writer, an artist ("in recovery from art school"), radical, and bisexual. i also happen to be vegetarian (although i sometimes eat seafood if it's fed to me), a deadhead (in moderation), and a hippie in general. i am happiest in mixed groups of queer women of color, especially if they are creatively oriented. i have no disabilities that i know of (yet). i dream a lot, always in color. i am in my mid-twenties, living in the east bay for five years now and plan to stay here for a very long time, probably forever.

Lesbians like to ask me if I am a lesbian-identified bisexual, but I refuse to identify as anything other than what/who I really am, so I call myself a bisexual-identified bisexual. (Not that different from being a woman-of-colour identified woman of color, right, sisters?) This assertion usually causes serious conceptual problems, until people can get beyond the rigid duality that hangs us up in our society: hetero/homo, male/female, good/evil, white/black. Being neither white not black, & often invisible because of it, I learned early that this simplistic kind of categorizing system just does not work. Let's face it, folks, the world is a little more complex than that. Complex & wonderful. Of course it hasn't always been wonderful for me. For a long time I was in a sort of coming-out stagnation. Being bi was not something to be happy about; it was a problem. I only felt the oppression. I thought it would be so much easier if I were either straight or lesbian. If I were not attracted to men, if only I didn't have such great sex with them, then I could go running into the open cosy arms of the lesbian community and live happily ever after. I never really thought that if only I didn't find women so attractive, I wouldn't have a problem either; trying to be a straight feminist (womanist, actually) caused me no end of internal conflict, only some of which can be attributed to my coming-out process.

So there I was, 20, 21, then 22 years old and knowing the whole time that there were some incredibly fine women around who I would love to at least kiss or hug or maybe – just maybe – undress. (I was afraid to think about what I might do once I got past the clothes. Years of living in a homophobic world can cramp your style considerably.) However, as a supposedly straight womanist, I had been in enough contact with the lesbian community to know that I would get infinitely more shit from many lesbians for being bi than I was getting from my mostly straight, feminist radical circle of friends. Actually, I got a lot of support and encouragement from my straight friends, so for a long time I couldn't see why I should bother to try getting involved in the dyke community at all. I was very into being single and was content to have occasional flings or one-night stands with men. Just a couple of little things seemed out of place.

For one thing, and this should be obvious, I was isolated as a queer. No commonalities or validation or role models or any of that stuff that it takes to figure out what it really means to be queer. Supportive straight friends can't do all that for you. The other thing was that I was in love with a woman. Very minor detail. Both of us were in absolute, complete denial about it. I think her being haole[1] put me even more in denial about my feelings for her. We were incredibly close friends and always overjoyed to see each other. We sometimes flirted. I even had sexual dreams about her, but I wrote them off as being random coming-out dreams, having nothing really to do with her. A few times we even tried making out, laughing uproariously the whole time from sheer nervousness.

Once I kissed her and she fled shrieking and giggling into the kitchen, where my lesbian housemate took one look at us and said, "Why don't you guys just go *do* it." We almost died laughing.

This "friendship" of ours survived numerous long-distance separations while we each jumped from school to school trying to finish our undergrad degrees. I still have piles of her letters, and the phone bills are better forgotten. Eventually we both graduated. She came back to the East Bay and moved into the apartment I shared with "my other best friend", a very heterosexual Pilipina American woman who was away in the Philippines at the time. Everything fell to pieces. Put into my colored context, living in my colored home, this would-be girlfriend suddenly seemed uncomfortably white to me. She was seeing a haole guy who also seemed awkwardly out of place among my friends of color. Somehow they had a stiffness, a rigidity, something missing in their humor; they had those qualities that I always associated with other haoles, not my friends.

I was experiencing a time-earthquake. (This "earthquake consciousness theory" of mine comes from growing up in earthquake country. Things – plates of the earth, or your own personal growth – are moving past each other all the time, but you aren't aware of the movement, the change, until the edges of the plates snap past each other to produce an earthquake, and the landscape readjusts to its new reality.) While my friend was still in Rhode Island, I was in the Bay Area getting heavily into Ethnic Studies and the community of people of color around it. I had grown to expect a highly developed consciousness around issues of race and ethnicity. Haoles who didn't have that kind of understanding and commitment couldn't be my friends. This woman, my best friend, who I used to think was "the coolest white person" I knew, suddenly seemed not to understand the first thing about living in a multicultural community, didn't know anything about people of color beyond theory. I asked her to move out. She did. We tried to talk, but didn't get anywhere.

In the fall, my housemate returned from the Philippines, impossibly more man-crazy than she had been before. Or else I was just more aware of it. She resumed her dysfunctional relationship with her arrogant boyfriend, and they began to have awful fights.

144

Meanwhile her self-righteously "radical", sexist older brother was homeless and crashing in our living room with his girlfriend. They fought constantly as well. It all kept deteriorating until I moved out several months later in total disgust.

In the middle of all this pain and chaos (which included a real earthquake in October), I realized that something just wasn't working. Out of sheer instinct, I think, I made a new year's resolution to go to a support group of queer Asian women, most of whom were lesbian but turned out to be at least bi-friendly enough for me to feel accepted, if not completely understood.

While I was getting used to being in that community, organizers were planning the first national bisexual conference for June. I joined the people of color caucus and for the first time felt that there was something really wonderful about being bisexual. Finally there were people like me! People who understood me exactly as myself, instead of trying to relate to only a fragmented part of me. At last I was allowed to indulge in my bisexual point of view, instead of feeling like I had to squeeze into the lesbian community's margins. The actual conference itself (although a little too white for my taste) strengthened my pride even more.

Not long afterwards, I fell in love for the first time in years. My lover is a wonderful woman, a Japanese American musician who is the most bi-friendly lesbian I have ever met. She likes to tell people that it doesn't matter if she's sleeping with a lesbian or a bisexual woman, as long as it's a woman! She is attracted to a gender, not an orientation. It makes so much sense to me. I, on the other hand, am attracted to qualities other than gender, although I am not gender-blind by any means. Far from it. I appreciate different things about women and men, whether I sleep with them or not, just as I appreciate different things about different cultures: Chinese chow mein, Afro-Cuban drums, Navajo weaving... I only demand integrity, a creative spirit, radical understanding and an open-minded willingness to struggle.

Bi is beautiful! I no longer accept falsely imposed limitations from either the straight mainstream or from lesbians and gay men. I can't be monosexual any more than I can be monocultural. The lesbian and gay community needs to see that we are not a threat, we are not confused, that we should be included as a visible part of the movement, and that such inclusion can only strengthen us all. *We have always been here in the community. Bisexuals are queer too,* and like all other queers, we must fight heterosexism every day of our lives. "You can't have your cake & eat it too," they tell me. Well, sure I can, if I learn to bake myself. Then I can not only eat cake forever, but I can have all different kinds. I can even have bread. Bisexual inclusion can only make the queer community more rich and nourishing – more powerful. My beloved sisters of color, welcome to the queer kitchen!

1. haole: Hawaiin term for European/white people, literally meaning "outsider" or "without land". This word gradually seems to be creeping into common usage among mainland Asian Americans.

INDIGO SOM

fall/
equinox

sudden squall
you tip me
& i feel
things
             falling out
tumbling from the
holes in me
                    saucers sliding
over each other
    handles breaking off
                         from their mugs
    & flowerz   squashed under
                    neath   books

you tip me over
         i am falling
spilled/ like alice   down
    a rabbit hole/ into some weirder wonder
land/ falling
         outta yr armz

         fall   like the end of summer
                      stumbling
    trippin into rain   puddles
    i always said
    summers are for women
    in the fall   i go back
    to men/ unless
    you cd let me

fall
into yr armz/   unless   we cd
put the typewriter   back
up on the table
& the records
into their sleeves

if you cd let
there be
summer/   in the
                                    fall

INTERVIEWED BY TERRI JEWELL

MISS RUTH

Ruth Ellis is a 90-year old Black Lesbian presently living in Detroit, Michigan. Conversations were held with her on April 23, 1989 in Lansing, Michigan and on February 10, 1990 in Detroit.

RUTH ELLIS: My life has been nothing special. I am a quiet person who came from a very ordinary, middle-class Negro family. I was born July 23, 1899 in Springfield, Illinois. My Dad's name was Charles, Sr. He was a stately-looking man, like what I would call a Black Colonel. I favor him. My Daddy was a well-built man and black-skinned, very proud. I don't think he had much schooling, but he knew what it was all about. I didn't appreciate him when I was younger like I think I could now. I sort of feared him. He was so strict, you know. And I shied away from him. I clung to my mother. Her name was Carrie Farrell. She was very smooth, just a kind person. I was crazy about her. My mother was medium-brown, a nice looking woman. I was a "Momma's girl." I have my birth certificate...

TERRI JEWELL: Your mother was 35 years old when you were born and she was from Tennessee as was your father. He was 38 when you were born. She was a housewife and he was a mail carrier.

ELLIS: I do remember my mother saying something about being born in ... she'd just say, "in '65". I think she must have been in her 40's when she died. She had a massive stroke and I was around 11 or 12 years old. My daddy raised us children.

I had three brothers. Wellington was the youngest brother, Harry was the middle one, and Charles, Jr., the oldest. I was the baby and had a twin who died as a baby. All my brothers were World War I veterans; Harry and Charles, Jr. went overseas, but not Wellington. He eventually got married. Now, my oldest brother never married. I think Charles, Jr. was gay because he used to like having male office boys. He never talked about it or anything like that. Harry never married, but became a boxer.

We had quite a bit of music in our family. My daddy used to sing in the choir at Saint Paul AME in Springfield and my brother played the pipe organ. The oldest brother could play the violin, the middle brother played mandolin and could play piano by ear, but I didn't get very far with any of it. I like the better class of music – orchestra music and the old-fashioned religious music like Marian Anderson sings. And we played jazz and dance music. I love to dance. I don't know too much about this modern music at all. I don't listen to it at all except when I go dancing. But I don't like the records I hear these days. I don't like vulgarity.

We lived in an integrated neighbourhood in Springfield. There was a riot there when I was about 8 years old. The whites rioted because they found out a Black man had a white wife. White people were told to put sheets up in their windows so the rioters would burn out only Black families. The only weapon my Daddy had was a sword from the Knights of Pithias. Troops came in and took all the weapons away from the colored People but not the whites. The wrong Black man was hung... I didn't even know what a riot was.

I do remember one friend I used to have. She was a white girl named Esther Black. My mother would let me go down the block to play with Esther for a half-hour. And Mrs. Black would let Esther come over to my house to play, too. When we started school, though, we couldn't play together anymore. When children are left alone, they don't care about all the foolishness that the parents worry over. Children get all that hate from their parents.

I didn't learn too much when I was in school. If I were going to school now, I would be in what you would call "special classes" because I was a slow learner. I went to a white school. They didn't pay attention to colored kids then. I had no one to take a real interest in my schoolwork. My brothers, I guess, were busy studying for themselves. My Daddy was crazy about schooling. We had a little library and he had the works of Shakespeare, a set of encyclopedia and law books.

We could go into the theatres, but we had to sit in what they called "Pigeon Heaven" – way up in the balcony. We couldn't go in the restaurants. We couldn't go to the "Y" where young white kids could learn how to swim. We had to go to the river to learn how to swim. But Daddy wouldn't let us go everyday because too many children got drowned.

But the teachers didn't teach me anything, you know? Now if I had been raised in the South as a kid, I would have been taught to work. I was a loner in school. I didn't mix very well with the white girls. Or they didn't mix with me. In gym class, the teacher would have to hold my hand because some of the girls didn't want to hold hands with someone Black.

When I went to high school, I fell in love with my gym teacher. She was a Portuguese woman named Grace L., and it didn't matter to her what color anyone was. I didn't get through Springfield High School.

JEWELL: Were you gay before you were 21 years old?

ELLIS: Yes. I used to fool around with girls and have them stay all night. One morning, my Daddy said, "Next time ya'll make that much noise, I'm going to put you BOTH out."

JEWELL: You mean to tell me you were in your Daddy's house?!

ELLIS: Sure! That's where I lived! I think he was kind of glad I had a woman instead of a man because he was afraid I'd come up with a baby. If you had a baby in those days, you'd have to leave home. And he wanted me home.

I've had one intimate boyfriend. He took me to Decatur to a

151

dance and that was something! Then, all of a sudden, I never saw him again. And I know what happened. The people he stayed with knew I was gay. "You with a bulldagger..." And I never saw that fellow again. He has passed now.

My people have been dead so long, so long. Daddy was the first colored man to be at the post office in Springfield, Illinois. A man insulted him once and Daddy got fired. He never got a good job after that.

JEWELL: What kinds of jobs have you worked?

ELLIS: Just printing. After the war, my oldest brother, Charles, came to Detroit. I left Springfield when I was 37 and moved to Detroit because Charles was here. Now, when I first started to work in Springfield, I made $3.00 a week taking care of a baby and I stayed on the place. I was a woman past the age of 21. But the top wage then was $10.00 a week. If you were a cook, you got top wages. But look at what you could get with $10.00, with $3.00. You could buy 2 cents worth of potatoes, a steak for fifteen cents., a loaf of bread for a nickel. You could buy a penny's worth of candy, your insurance would be 5 cents a week... a "5 cent policy". When I moved to Detroit, I got a job making $7.00 a week. In the meantime, on Thursdays, I'd look for a printing job. I finally found one and stayed there about 10 years.

JEWELL: But how did you get interested in printing?

ELLIS: Well, I kind of fell into it. After high school in Springfield, a neighbourhood man taught me how to set type and run his presses. I stayed with him for quite awhile. When I moved to Detroit, I worked for a printer named Waterfield for awhile, then decided to have a shop of my own.

I had one real girlfriend. Her name was Ceciline. We called her Babe. She was the only person I had ever lived with. Babe was from Springfield and she once told me, "If you ever leave Springfield, I'll come where you are." So, when I came to Detroit, she came here, too, but later. We lived together for 30 years. Babe was 10 years younger than I, weighed about 250 pounds and stood under 5'5".

And she was medium-brown. She could cook! That she could do. And she always wore a dress.

When I decided to have a shop of my own, my girlfriend and I bought a home. It was a two-family flat at 10335 Oakland Avenue in Detroit. There were 5 rooms downstairs and I took the front room for my shop. I printed anything small, not books or things like that where it had to be linotyped. I did all printing by hand. The largest printing I did was 11" x 14". I called it "Ellis and Franklin Printing Company". I didn't have any help, either. That's why I refused a lot of jobs because it was too much for me. I wasn't going to have it run me crazy. I would just take in the walk-in trade.

There were quite a few churches in my neighbourhood and I used to do a lot of their work. Coin envelopes and raffle tickets... I made enough money to live off of. I didn't save too much, but I could pay my bills and eat what I wanted. Babe worked as a cook in a restaurant. I also taught myself photography by reading books. There weren't always color films, so I hand-colored my own prints. I had my own dark room and had it set up in a coal bin.

Our house was noted for being the "gay spot". There weren't very many places in Detroit you could go back in 1937, 1940. We rented out the back 4 rooms of the downstairs to a gay fellow. When we had a party, we would open up the whole house. People used to come from every place. They'd be all out in the yard, upstairs and downstairs. Sometimes, people would bring their own bottle. They would get so drunk, everybody would get to fighting. I'd be looking on because I don't know how to fight. Next morning, I'd be sweeping up hair from the women fighting. And the boys would fight out in the yard. Now, I wasn't a drinker. If I drank anything, I'd put it in the little cap of the bottle. That would be my portion. Put ginger ale or Coca-cola in that, sip on it. But my girlfriend could drink!

Babe and I were two different types of people. She liked to go a lot, gamble and drink, but I didn't take that up at all. I was the stay-at-home type. But we made it pretty well. I learned to accept her faults. A lot of people would ask me, "Why don't you leave her?" That was my home, so I just stayed. I had hobbies of my own like my photography to take up my time and we had a couple of dogs. Whenever she'd leave the house she knew the dogs would be taken care of because I'd be there. I liked my home. We had a nice place and a big yard. Babe remodelled our place, you know. She could knock the plaster off the wall, put in a doorway, do all that kind of stuff. But she never wore pants or anything.

JEWELL: Did you ever cross-dress?

ELLIS: The only time I did that was on Halloween night. I'd put on my brother's trousers.

JEWELL: Is your house still standing?

ELLIS: No, the city had it torn down during Urban Renewal. Babe and I separated then because I wanted to live downtown since I had no car. Babe had a car and wanted to live up near where she worked, so she moved out to Southfield. I had a key to her place and I could come and go as I wanted, but she couldn't have a key to my place. Where I lived, they wouldn't let a resident have 2 keys. I lived at the Wolverine Senior Citizen moved housing complex for 16 years in downtown Detroit. Then, I moved to my present address, still in downtown Detroit, and I've been here for 3 years.

Babe had a child when she was 17, before she got out of school. Her daughter got mixed up in dope, then broke herself of the dope habit. But she got on a whiskey habit and then she wouldn't eat anything. She became dehydrated and had to be put on a respirator. The daughter had 4 children and they were scattered around at different people's houses, but now they're doing very well for themselves. I never see them, though. Babe died in 1973. Her daughter passed about a month afterwards. Babe's daughter never knew that her mother had died...

Now, is this a story? To me it's nothing. Some people have all their life mixed-up. There's so much happening in their life. Not mine. My life is ordinary, calm. I love to dance, bowl and go to classical music recitals. I have many young friends who treat me wonderfully. They make me feel young! I'm having a lot of fun for a 90-year-old woman!!!

Mona Oikawa

Safer Sex in Santa Cruz

"**M**icrowavable Saran Wrap is thicker than ordinary plastic wrap," explained Alex, her playful tone easing the tension in the room. "It does the same trick as a dental dam but can be more versatile since it can be cut to size."

There were a dozen of us in the safer sex workshop. Twelve women out of 175 who were attending the First National Asian/Pacifica Lesbian Network retreat in Santa Cruz, California. I was not aware of any safer sex workshops being conducted for lesbians of colour – let alone Asian lesbians – in Toronto. I thought more women would be here for this. It's so important.

Alex was responding to a question raised by the woman from the Asian Aids Project in San Francisco. "It's true that microwavable Saran Wrap has not been tested for efficacy, but it is impermeable and I still recommend it as a barrier to the HIV virus during oral sex. Of course, condoms can also be cut to serve the same purpose." Mila, the co-facilitator, was rummaging through a nondescript cardboard carton of safer sex paraphernalia. A bright yellow box with crimson swirls magically appeared from its depths and was passed from woman to woman in a steady rhythm. We each tore our microwavable pieces against the silver teeth, pulling the plastic taut between our hands.

My neighbour snapped her sample enthusiastically. The sound echoed through me to thoughts of my mother cooking in her kitchen deep in northern Toronto. So much time had passed since that New Year's o-shogatsu dinner where she had shown my lover how to wrap sushi carefully in plastic wrap to prevent it from drying out.

What would Mom think if she knew that the box neatly beside the aluminum foil in my Rubbermaid dispenser could be used for this new purpose as well as for the maki sushi? And how will she take the news that the woman she had taught to roll nori around rice, firmly, tightly, was gone forever from my life?

Mila was handing out another plaything. The lilac-coloured dildo was greeted by giggles from the women on the other side of the room. As I watched it being grasped by anxious and gentle hands, I wondered why I had come to this workshop. I was really too self-absorbed to concentrate or relax. Maybe I should have gone to the beach with Toshi. I could have been enjoying the last of the summer sun.

But political commitment must prevail even in times of personal turmoil, I assured myself. This opportunity must be seized to help me carry out my project at the Toronto Women's Bookstore. This month, I was determined to start dispensing dental dams and safer sex information at cost. I must stay for the entire workshop. After all, I was doing it for the women of Toronto, not myself.

The object of our scrutiny had made its way to my hands. "Dildoes and other sex toys should be cleaned with bleach or alcohol before they are shared," Mila explained. "But don't forget to rinse them with water." "Aren't silicon dildoes warm and soft?" Alex added, smiling in my direction. Blushing, I quickly passed my sample behind me.

Mila and Alex tried to cushion the technical sound of their words with comfortable laughter. Alex, who routinely gave safer sex workshops in San Francisco, showed her expertise in unfolding a condom onto a dildo. She offered this as a convenient option to bleach or alcohol.

I found out later that the two facilitators were lovers. They did seem to fit lovingly together in their open and caring interchange. Nevertheless, it was hard to relax even in their warm presence. AIDS is a terrifying reality, and it is difficult enough to talk about sex with lovers and friends, let alone women I don't even know.

It was time to examine the turquoise dental dam draped casually over my knee. This colour had always looked good on my ex-lover. Not that we had ever worn dental dams or any other safer sex gear. Eight years of monogamy had wrapped us in a cocoon of security, safe from sexually transmitted disease. This history, however, did not protect us from a severe erosion of love and commitment.

Just weeks before the retreat, in one of our final separation discussions, the reality of AIDS had entered my life in a new way. I

had watched my lover sitting stiffly, her hair lightened by two
months under the Greek sky. Despite myself, I had wanted to take
the strands falling across her face and, in a motion bred from years
of loving, stroke them away. I held myself back from the desire to
touch and the need to speak a lifetime of thoughts in the moments
closing fast. All I could utter was, "Please practise safe sex."

Alex raised her hand now covered in a latex glove. Nothing new
about gloves. But finger cots, those were interesting items. "Can
more than one finger fit into a finger cot?" asked Suniti, the martial
arts expert from Washington, D.C. Alex handed her the glove
saying use this for more than one finger.

"This is great information," I whispered to Jin beside me. "I may
even expand to finger cots at the bookstore."

Mila had launched into a discussion of the importance of
negotiating safer sex. She emphasized the need to have the
equipment readily available. Only with the latex close at hand
should we even begin to negotiate.

"Lick your dental dams and Saran Wrap before you use them
with a partner. Experiment with the toys, have fun with yourself.
Then you'll be prepared for that next special encounter."

Such good advice. These were the physicalities of safer sex. But
how do you prepare yourself emotionally? How do you have sex –
and safe sex – with someone else after having loved one woman for
eight years?

My ex-lover seemed to have no trouble with this question.
Sleeping with someone else was her way of leaving me, a final
stroke of power brushing away the years of caring that had held us
together.

Many women in my life were now giving me advice on how
long I should wait before sleeping with someone. This ranged from
the two weeks recommended by Carmen, my hair sculptor, to the
year advised by Trish, my older (by a month) and wiser co-worker.
Sylvie, my friend from Montreal's new path of long-term celibacy
for healing her ten year relationship was fading fast as an
alternative for me. How could one think seriously about celibacy
when surrounded by 175 lesbians?

But at home, I was hearing very little about safe sex. Are other
women doing it safe and just not talking about it? Had eight years

of monogamy made me too complacent, restricting my vision of AIDS to an exterior political world, rather than a deeply personal issue lived daily?

A sudden stillness in the room hurled me back to Santa Cruz. "We must dispel two myths: One, Asians don't get AIDS; Two, lesbians don't get AIDS. Although they are only one percent of the total reported cases, the incidence of Asians contracting AIDS rose 71 percent over the previous year. This was the most significant increase of all ethnic groups in the United States."

Alex continued, her voice quietly passionate. "There have been four documented cases of women contracting AIDS from sexual contact with women. But the recording agencies have not kept very good statistics on women and AIDS. Once again, women's, and specifically, lesbians' existence is being rendered invisible."

For the first time there was no laughter in the room. These numbers in real terms represent our sisters and our brothers. I looked around at the eleven beautiful women. In our own way, we are each trying to fight this killing epidemic. There is something powerful in this moment and the many moments during the retreat where we have come together to share our knowledge and our lives.

Our strength is visible in the ways we are forever coming out to the straight world and to each other as lesbians, Asian women, singles, couples, monogamous, non-monogamous, and safer sex practitioners. Daily, we peel back these layer, making ourselves vulnerable in a world where there are people who hate us because we are Asian and we choose to love women. But neither their misinformed hatred nor the fear of AIDS will stop our loving and our pleasure.

Now I know what to do to have safer sex. The larger question for me is how do we make our relationships safe and nurturing places, where mutual respect marks our beginnings and our endings? Meeting these women in Santa Cruz has helped me deal with the end of my relationship and my grieving moments of self-doubt. But not even the combined wisdom of 175 Asian/Pacifica lesbians can give me the answer to my question. Somehow, I think I must find it within myself.

Mila's gentle goodbyes reminded me that it was time to leave for dinner. I made a note to call Maria at the AIDS Committee of Toronto. She has the address of the dental dam supply store in Scarborough. Maybe we could also discuss the possibility of doing a safer sex workshop for Asian Lesbians of Toronto.

I threw my borrowed dental dam into the box beside Mila. Alex stopped me and handed me a safer sex kit. "Have fun," she smiled. "I think I will," I answered.

I slowly stepped out of the building. The sun was still brilliant overhead. I placed my zip-locked kit into my backpack. This was just one of the special gifts I was to receive that weekend in Santa Cruz.

Author's note: This story does not attempt to give complete safer sex information. It is merely fragments from one workshop. For current information on safer sex, contact your local AIDS community group.

Lesbians of Colour: Loving And Struggling
A Conversation Between Three Lesbians of Colour
1983 Toronto, Canada

> *Anthologist's note: This taped discussion took place one ordinary winter night on the third floor of a small house in downtown Toronto, in 1983 with three lesbians of colour. Times and circumstances have changed since that night. These three lesbians have been 'out' many years since this discussion and are politically active in the lesbian of colour community and also their respective cultural/racial group.*
>
> *This taped discussion is an important document for us to remember how it was and how it still is for others in communities and societies where there are few of 'us'. And also, this is for younger lesbians of the 90's who sometimes forget that some folks before them helped pave the way.*

JOANNE: Why don't we want to use our real names?

PRAMILA: It's all so complicated.

ANU: I haven't come out to anybody except my closest friends. And I don't plan on coming out at this time to my community (East Indian) or to my family. I think that if my parents found out, or my siblings, they would reject me and I would be isolated. Until recently, my family was the only place of refuge, of comfort, of love that I have had in Canada. We have a shared experience and understanding. When we first came to Canada from Guyana we felt very much alone in Canadian society. You see, we came to Toronto before the racist immigration policies were changed and more East Indians were allowed into the country. Wherever we went, we were the first of our people. My bothers and sisters were the first East Indians in the schools where we lived, we were the first East indians to move into the neighbourhood. At that time, there were no community organizations so we were very much on our own.

There are moments when I think that my family would support me if I told them I was a lesbian. They have a very strong belief in family, they also know that we live in a place where we are isolated (in so many ways) and that "we only have each other," as they keep reminding me. So maybe they *would* support me..?

JOANNE: If you do tell them, let me know. I would be interested in knowing what happens.

ANU: I know this is a rhetorical question, but why don't you want to use your real name?

JOANNE: I work for the government in one of the social service departments and most of my co-workers are white and fairly open about sexuality. So a few of them know that I am a lesbian. But you see, most of my work is done in the Black community and I know that if they found out it would be hard for me. I could easily be ostracised within the Black community, I don't believe clients would respect my work. It's really unbelievable how rampant homophobia is within the Black community. Sometimes I feel like I live in two worlds. With my friends who I'm 'out' to I feel comfortable. I have no fears. With certain sections of the Black community and my family, I feel really uptight - wondering when they will find out.

Another reason why I'm so hesitant to come out is because of my twelve year old daughter. I want to talk about my sexual preference with her before I come out to the world. You see, lesbianism is something relatively new for me, like I didn't know when I was fourteen or sixteen years old that I would be woman-identified or that I would want to spend my life with women. So for me it's like something new and I really want to spend the time to work out my feelings and be comfortable with the choice I've made before I'm exposed to the coldness of the larger society. It's really important for me to work it out, to give myself a chance with the person that I'm involved with and to work with my daughter. It's really such a crucial age for her too, she has reached adolescence and she has her own little world to deal with. At this point, I don't want to confuse her and I don't want her to be hostile towards me.

JOANNE: What about your community Pramila, do they know?

PRAMILA: There are some women that know. I used to be part of a women's group in the community and some of the women in that group knew. All my sisters and cousins know, but my parents and older relatives don't know.

JOANNE: Do you think you would be isolated if they found out? I mean by both your family and the Indian community?

PRAMILA: Most definitely, and I do feel isolated. One, because I'm a lesbian and two because the woman I'm involved with is white. In our community there's a whole way of relating with friends and extended families, you know, friends become like family. And I feel a lot of reluctance from the woman I'm involved with to be any part of that. On the one hand she feels that she wants to be - but I feel that because she is so unclear about how much of my life she wants to be a part of, that it makes things difficult. If I have a social event to go to, she will be reluctant to come because she might be the only white person there, and it becomes a real hassle to be always pulling her around with me, especially when she herself is so up and down about it, and so totally insecure about relating to a whole other culture. But then, they never think what it's like for us. We have to spend all our lives in a white culture. So, you know, sometimes I really feel isolated...and because of my lifestyle I could never live in an Indian neighbourhood. Because I feel that I could not live as a lesbian there. There would be too many restrictions and who needs more hassles.

I really value the sort of work I do, which is working with my community. I'm really committed to my community, and I feel that if they found out it could create problems. So, in a sense, I really have no place where I sort of touch base in any way.

JOANNE: It's really quite sad, you know. I mean, we are isolated from our communities because of our sexual preference. And the support we need we often don't get from the white feminist/lesbian community. We experience so much racism from within the women's community.

ANU: Yes, and another thing we have to deal with is our invisibility, which is part of their racism; they usually don't see us as lesbians. I remember I was applying for a job a few summers ago within a feminist organization and I was competing for the job with a white lesbian. I was hired over her. Later on, I heard that I was hired because they "already had enough lesbians," and so they didn't need any more, but what they did need was a woman of colour because they had no contacts in those communities. They hadn't even asked me in the interview if I was involved in my community or in any other women of colour communities. They were buying themselves a ready-made full-fledged woman of colour to make contact with the women of colour communities.

JOANNE: That's very interesting and so typical.

ANU: When they hired me their underlying assumption was that a woman of colour could not be a lesbian. In their minds, these two things were mutually exclusive. They just assumed that I was straight and they never checked it out with me. During the interview one woman asked me if I would have problems working with lesbians. Even after I started working with the women as a group they overlooked every instance that could point to the fact that I was woman-identified. I live with a woman and they know that, but they haven't made the connection yet.

I've decided not to identify myself as a lesbian with white women anymore. When I do tell white lesbians/straights that I am a lesbian, I am met with curious disbelief. Or they begin to regard me in a sexually racist way—I'm exotic, a novelty, a toy....

I think one of the other reasons that the women that I work with don't see me as a lesbian is because they can't see through the myth and that myth is: women of colour are male-identified. I remember that summer a lot of the women saw me around town with a very good male friend of mine (we were from the same community), and I can see how that possibly has fed into their myths about male-identification.

PRAMILA: And the way we dress also feeds into their idea of us as heterosexual women. There are a lot of unspoken and unwritten laws in the lesbian society of how to dress and how to look. I think that most of us are not able to fit in a very clean-cut way into those categories: of having short hair, being white, you know, plaid shirts and boots. And if you are not conforming, if you don't fit into those laws and those definitions of how to dress and behave, then you are not so easily identified as lesbian.

ANU: I'm never going to cut my hair again...

PRAMILA: When we look at who we are and what our culture is, and how we dress, most of us are not going to fit in. And I think that puts us even farther apart. But I'm sure that if you, Anu were to cut your hair and dress up like the norm dictates, you know , very butch and all that, you would be considered lesbian. I think the problem is that, for example, women in saris and salwar kameez would never be seen as lesbians. One night I was taking a feminist from India to a number of gay bars in Toronto and she was wearing Indian clothes and I was wearing Indian clothes and we were with a Japanese woman...

ANU:..and they figured you walked into the wrong bar, right? (laughter)

$$* \quad * \quad *$$

JOANNE: Anu, earlier on you had started talking about something that is very interesting and very popular in the white women's community: the concept of women of colour being male-identified.

ANU: I feel that so strongly, that that is what they think....

PRAMILA: What do you mean male-identified? You don't mean heterosexual?

ANU: That we are always thinking about men.

JOANNNE: Always thinking about *our* men, not white men. Always protecting *our* men.

PRAMILA: Against white women?

JOANNE: Against white people.

ANU: I've been in lots of situations where women have said to me, "Why are you always talking about yourself as a group?" I guess it's that notion that Shulamith Firestone, and a number of other feminist writers and theoreticians have put out, that sexism is more of a fundamental problem than racism, and I guess that goes very deep into white women's consciousness, they're raised to believe that.

JOANNE: Yeah, and the books really put that out, and also the Women's Studies courses..so it's really easy for them to say, "ignore the race business." Their history is just so completely different from ours that they can afford to separate themselves form their men, and I support them, but we can't afford to...

PRAMILA: I think that one of the reasons that they can separate themselves from their men is that most of them live in exclusive small lesbian sub-cultures. Most of us also live in the lesbian sub-culture, but we also live in a whole other mainstream society and we are people of colour and so it makes absolutely no sense to only function on the premise that you work only with women or that you only address women's problems.

JOANNE: No, how can we be separate when we have a history of oppression and exploitation as a *people?* When the Ku Klux Klan attacks, or any other right-wingers for that matter, they don't just attack women of colour, they attack our men and children.

PRAMILA: There's an incident that happened to me that I'd like to share with you. It's to do with this male friend of mine. We spend quite a bit of time together. Well, this white woman I know, said to me one day that, "Oh, so I see that you are taking care of_____." She said it like a put down. That here I was, a woman, getting sucked into looking after this man. And isn't that what women end up doing all the time, anyway. Meaning that I

165

was playing the traditional role of women.

What she fails to see is that we both care for each other and that maybe I want to put out to him. And that maybe he also puts out to me. Also , if I had a similar relationship with a woman it would never be questioned. I think this example typifies the problem of men between women of colour and white women.

*   *   *

JOANNE: How hard is it to come out to each other as lesbians, and also to come out in our own community?

ANU: I don't think people, in general, understand what it's like to be a lesbian of colour in this society and how difficult it is to come out. I am not negating the fact that it is difficult for all lesbians to come out, but for women of colour, I think that there are some special problems that we face.

What I would like to stress the most is that women of colour, lesbians of colour, have essentially, a smaller community of people that we can expect support from, so to us it is a big risk to jeopardize that community. For if all that we have left is the lesbian community, then we are in big trouble. No matter how much they would like to believe otherwise, the lesbian community is still a representation of the larger society, infected with the same sorts of diseases: racism, classism.

I would like to relate an experience of mine to you. I went to a conference not too long ago on Third World Women and Feminism. A white woman approached me and started to tell me about her relationship with an East Indian woman who now lives in Toronto.

She told me about how she felt the woman was cowardly for not "coming out," for not choosing to live a "lesbian lifestyle." I became really angry with this woman and took her to task for her racism, her non-understanding, and her non-supportiveness of what a lesbian of colour's experiences and reality is in a society that is racist, classist, and of course, homophobic. This woman wanted her lover to follow the politically correct line as to how to live her life, as set down largely by white middle class lesbians.

166

This woman then went on to ask me what it was like to be a lesbian in Toronto. She did not ask me what it was like to be an East Indian lesbian in Toronto. Obviously race is not an issue with her. She assumes that as lesbians we all experience the same sort of problems. She was oblivious as to how race can be an issue....

JOANNE: I know, the whole thing is really totally fucked. I mean it's even hard for us to come out to each other for fear of the consequences. I remember one night I went to this gay club in Toronto and there were a few black women in there and I really wanted to go up and speak to them. And it was really difficult. The first thing that came to my mind was: I wonder if they want to be invisible? I mean, do they want me to talk to them? Do they want to be recognised as lesbians by another black woman/lesbian?

PRAMILA: I think that it's okay in a bar - it's a safe environment. But if you were to meet them on the street another time, or in a restaurant they would probably be a lot more reluctant to talk to you.

JOANNE: But I still think that even in a club or bar there is some fear. You know, like the fear of what might happen if they saw me on the street the next day and I was, say, walking with someone who didn't know I was gay?...

PRAMILA: I think maybe that some of that tension is a factor of age? My sense is that younger women in this society, in this day and age, are a lot more comfortable, a lot more secure about their sexuality and that maybe it's the older women who feel insecure? That's the sort of impression I get from talking to women in the bars.

But, what I think is even more threatening in all of this is that there is a lot of sexual tension when women of the same race meet each other, because I feel it reminds them that they live in so much of a white world and that many of them are involved with lovers who are white, and most times that means that they are culturally separated. But I think that lesbians, period, are all paranoid to some extent or level. Unless they are really out there in the world, only

167

their close friends and community know and support them.

JOANNE: Which is something we as women of colour don't have—that community support. It's something that we have to begin working on. I don't know how we are going to do it, but I know that I get tired of being invisible to people I work with, within the Black community. I know that I'm good in my work and my sexual preference shouldn't be a strike against me.

PRAMILA: We have to begin a dialogue with other heterosexual women of colour. We have to cross that bridge to create a "new" community.

We Will Not
Be Invisible

VICTORIA LENA MANYARROWS

today we will not be invisible

today
we will not be invisible nor silent
as the pilgrims of yesterday continue their war of
attrition
forever trying, but never succeeding
　　in their battle to rid the americas of us
convincing other and ourselves
　　that we have been assimilated & eliminated,

　　　　but we remember who we are

we are the spirit of endurance that lives
in the cities and reservations of north america
and in the barrios and countryside of Nicaragua, Chile
Guatemala, El Salvador

and in all the earth and rivers of the americas

CHERYL CLARKE

Saying the Least Said, Telling the Least Told: The Voices of Black Lesbian Writers

The struggle for identity/ies:

> Why should the world be over-wise
> In counting all our tears and sighs?
> Nay let them only see us, while
> We wear the mask.
>   *(Dunbar, 1913)*

The struggle to be an "out" lesbian writer is simultaneous with the struggle to be a conscious, black identified (and anti-racist) black person. As a result of the female-oriented upbringing - with emphases on self-sufficiency and self-determination - and an undergraduate education at a historically black institution during the black consciousness era of the sixties, I found myself in pursuit of a "non-traditional" life and "non-traditional" relationships as well as in pursuit of role models - in life and in literature. I had taken up writing poetry as a way of entering into political dialogue with my peers, because other priorities prevented me from being a campus activist. After Baldwin, who I'd first read in 1963, the new black poets of the Black Arts Movement became my first literary role models. This protracted search first led me to graduate school in a very competitive program where there were few resources, no mentors, and little support for black women, especially those of us interested in things black.

During this time, 1970, I was thrown back upon my own devices and, so, I began to teach myself historic and contemporary black male literature. Baldwin was followed by Wright, Ellison, McKay, Hughes, and strange Jean Toomer. It was not until 1971 that I discovered the tradition of black women writers, when I saw *One Jump at the Sun*, a stage adaptation by black director Glenda Dickerson of Hurston's *Their eyes were Watching God*, in Washington, D.C. I rushed to find a copy of the novel, engaged myself in reading it, and began to teach myself the literature of black women novelists, whom I have read and been inspired by for the last nineteen years to the virtual exclusion of every other kind of writer, except for an occasional reading of a vintage black male writer. It is black women writers who became my primary literary role models. And I tried to write essays, criticism, and fiction as a way to enter into dialogue with those writers. These exercises in prose were as futile as the exercise in graduate school. I gave both up in 1974, a year after I had come out as a lesbian. I'd satisfied part of my quest. Choosing lesbianism was a process of affirming women and my love for women and of rejecting traditional and compulsory heterosexuality.

The struggle against silence and invisibility:

> I know that in writing the following pages I'm divulging the great secret of my life, the secret which for some years I have guarded far more carefully than any of my earthly possessions.
> *(Johnson, 1912)*

If one were asked what "great secret" the narrator of James Weldon Johnson's *Autobiography of an Ex-Colored Man*, a novel not without homoeroticism, is referring to in the above passage, the answer would probably be "homosexuality". The act or necessity of "passing for white" is almost unheard of today. However, the act of "passing" as heterosexual, in a hostile, homophobic, and heterosexist world, still reflects much of gay and lesbian life. Not that racism has ended, but that whiteness is not as compelling an ideal as it once was nor are the penalties for being black as all-encompassing, severe, or life-threatening as they once were. The consequences of divulging one's gayness are, in many cases, still severe, punitive, and in many cases life-threatening. In either case, passing as "straight": or passing for white, the "passing" person must accept the twin albatross of silence and invisibility. Invisibility may be defined as the ability or will of the power group not to acknowledge the presence or influence of the "other". Being invisible as a black person runs the gamut from the daily experiences of entering a room full of white people and not being

172

noticed to the other extreme of erasure from history. Where would Mick Jagger or David Bowie (or James Brown and Michael Jackson for that matter) be without Little Richard? (No matter how much he recants, Little Richard is still gay.) Silence may be defined as the act of subordinating the expression of the other's needs to the will of the power group. Sometimes the silence is strategic, as in the case of Walter White, field secretary for the NAACP during the 1920's who passed for white while he travelled through the South compiling statistics on lynchings; and sometimes it is a suppression of one's beliefs to accommodate what one has been told is the "greater good", as in the case of Bayard Rustin, socialist, black civil rights activist, and architect of the 1963 March on Washington, who was not allowed to assume visible leadership in the movement because he was homosexual.

Silence and invisibility, according to writer Toni Cade Bambara, are two of the greatest metaphors Afro-Americans have contributed to art in the western world - realistically and figuratively. But perhaps gays and women have contributed those metaphors also, perhaps all disenfranchised peoples have turned those metaphors into paradoxes and created ways for us and the world to understand our oppression. Thus, my sonnet:

> We are everywhere and white people
>   still do not see us.
> They force us from sidewalks.
> Mistake us for me.
> Expect us to give up our seats to them
>   on the bus.
> Challenge us with their faces.
> Are afraid of us in groups.
> Thus the brutal one on one.
> Like a t.v. news script, every
>   transaction frustrates
> rage. Hand in hand with me
> you admonish
> not to let them come between us

> not to let them come between us on
>   the street.
> We are struck by war crazy men
> recording their gunfire on stereo
> cassette decks.
>   *(Living as a Lesbian, 1986)*

The challenge and difficulty have been in entering into dialogue with the black literary community and the white feminist literary community, who are willing, without irony, to impose silence and invisibility on black lesbian writers - either actively or unconsciously. Thus, a vigilance must be assumed to counter the sexism and racism of heterosexist black and feminist intellectuals and critics, who come between me and my audiences, who ignore and consign me to special interest categories - like the Gay and Lesbian Caucus of the MLA - and exclude me from traditions that have nourished me. Make no mistake, I am here because you are here. And I thank you, again, for asking me to speak. But our voices have to be heard in the general body of sessions.

Barbara Smith's groundbreaking essay, "Towards A Black Feminist Criticism", is a model of vigilance for all lesbian writers. Thus, I have used the essay for political expression and critical vigilance regarding issues of heterosexism and racism by commission and omission. The essay, "Lesbianism: An Act of Resistance", in *This Bridge Called My Back: Writings by Radical Women of Color* (1981) was a way to enter into dialogue with other lesbian writers of color. This essay is used in many Women's Studies courses. Also my essay, "The Failure to Transform: Homophobia in the Black Community", in *Home Girls: A Black Feminist Anthology* (1983) was a way to enter into dialogue with many of the black literati who historically and currently exclude black lesbian and gay male writers, concerns, and perspectives from their black world view. I consider essay writing a political responsibility, not a labor of love, rather a labor of labor. I became an active participant in the production of feminist and lesbian literature in 1981. I self-published my first book of poems, *Narratives: poems in the tradition of black women* in 1982, and what an immense lesson that was, because I was very involved in the mental and physical acts of production. Producing a book is something I can always do, given certain resources. Also, I was invited to join the *Conditions* Magazine Collective, which is committed to new writing by women with an emphasis on writing by lesbians.

Understanding how books are made, understanding aspects of production, the politics of publishing and distribution, I came to see more clearly how much of an audience there is for lesbian writing, how committed women are to publishing women, and how many women are committed to telling women's stories. Joining feminist publishing, I also came to know the work of other lesbians of color: *She Had Some Horses, Zami, Abeng, Cuentos, A Gathering of Spirit*, as well as works written by my colleagues here today, Becky Birtha and Luz Maria Umpierre.

The feminist writing and publishing community, characterized by lesbian leadership, has enabled me not to be silent or invisible. Visibility and vigilance are integral to my everyday, nonwriting lesbian life.

So, as a writer, I have more than "moments of inspiration", I have whole movements of inspiration.

Poetry:

> poets are among the first witches
> so suffer none to live
> or suffer none to be heard
> and watch them burn before your eyes
> less they recant and speak their verse
> in latin
>
> i'm a poet.
> i speaks in piglatin.
> i eats pigs feet- a shonuff sign of
>   satan
> to those whose ears are trained to
> dactyls and iambs
> who resolve all conflicts in couplets...
>   *(Living as a Lesbian)*

I find the choices I have made re my identity are made more complex by my choice of poetry as my expressive art. This is a prose-oriented culture - commercially and in the scholarly realms. Certainly most of the critical paradigms have been constructed for the novel. What are the uses of poetry? I find, certainly, within the recent history of Afro-Americans, the Black Arts Movement is my mentoring movement. Yet, also, so was the black literary movement of the 1920's, which was propelled by poets. I find my life full of unconscious responses to traditions. Afro-American literary history begins with women poets, Lucy Terry and Phyllis Wheatley. For black people, poetry has been the great teacher of consciousness, of history, of self-love as well as duplicitousness, as expressed in Dunbar's poem, "We Wear the Mask", with which I began this talk. And so has poetry been these things for women as an oppressed people and culture and no less for lesbians. I find my choice to be a poet consonant with this search-turned-journey I am engaged in for my life; it is consonant with choosing to be a lesbian, which is poetry, for both always were and neither have a beginning, middle, or end; it is also consonant with being African, which is the first become last.

My first book, *Narratives:poems in the tradition of black women*, was a self-published effort and served to tell some of the suppressed stories of black women re sexuality, age, empowerment, incest, development. All kinds of traditions helped me form these stories into poems: the prose poems of Toomer's *Cane*, the legends I grew up with in my family of origin, the early fiction of Alice Walker and Toni Morrison, the black lyric voice of Langston Hughes, and the telling irony of the blues:

> If you got a good woman,
> better tie her to your side.
> Said, if you got a good woman,
> better tie her to your side.
> Cuz if she flag my train,
> I'm sure gonna let her ride
> *(Narratives: poems in the tradition of black women,* 1982)

176

Living as a Lesbian, my second book of poetry, served to advance a lesbian aesthetic and perspective - politically, lyrically, and unequivocally. I plainly wanted to advance Audre Lorde's thesis in her piece, "Uses of the Erotic", by promoting the concept of lesbian sex, which itself is poetry - it is and without beginning, middle, and end. It is the improvisational clarity of jazz that drove this book, and that, too, is lesbianism:

> the promises
> the absurdity
> the histrionics
> the loss of pride
> the bargaining
> the sadness after.
>
> in wakefulness wanting
> in wakefulness waiting.
> *(Living as a Lesbian)*

And *Humid Pitch* (1989), my new book of poems, returns me to the tradition of storytelling to once again unearth the untold or not told-enough tales of women of color, triumphant lesbians, ambivalent men, slave women, and the children who survive childhood, still moving language to the rhythms of black music, exploring my themes of love, sex, lesbianism, loss, and the open road:

> I'm a mean woman
> and don't need a man.
> I make my bed soft
> and take my lovin hard
> drink my whiskey straight
> and like my coffee sweet
> *(Humid Pitch)*

Crossing the boundaries:

> She dreamed of life beyond its
> > crumbling perimeters
> and memorized the rarefied space
> between lines of poetry.
> Moby-Dick and the Bible whispered
> > their passages to her as she rode
> > the train downtown squeezed
> > between
> Philistines.
> She was a solitary dolphin.
> Ilona of Hickory
> ....
> Ilona translated the language of
> > women,
> did not fear men disguised in their
> > inventions.
> She bonded with them both,
> sometimes both at the same time.
> > *(Humid Pitch)*

I attempt to cross sexual boundaries, gender boundaries, and racial boundaries as a lesbian of color writer who is Afro-American. (I take issue with the term, "Minority Writer".) Persons in academia have to begin to do this, if only in theory - i.e., use their imaginations, read between the lines, break the codes. Inclusiveness of writing by lesbians and gay men and lesbians and gay men of color, greater support of small and women's press books and journals in which much of our material appears, and more willingness to take risks with students are critical.

I want personally to thank all of you who have supported the work of gay and lesbian writers, especially those of us who publish in the small and feminist presses - because that is where most of us are thriving - in the small presses. You have bought our books, ordered them for your classes, included us in your bibliographies, made reference to us in your scholarship. Yet, you -, we - cannot do it all. Your straight colleagues must now become "encouraged" to give more than tacit support to lesbian and gay studies. They have to do what you have done, take some risks. They must be more supportive of you, help create a safer environment for you to do your work as lesbian and gay scholars, take some stands.

As a black lesbian writer, my advice to myself, academicians, and other lesbian writers is: say the least said and tell the least told.

CONNIE FIFE

Bonnie, Because They Never Told You Why

twenty eight years old
at an age where
to be told
is to understand
yet on this dark
night you are
stopped by the police
questioned by men
whose minds are
locked in a
vice grip of racism
condemned by a court
system that leaves
rooms taking its
small barred cells
to the streets where
white men prowl
like starving dogs

not finding a guilty party
they settle
for the innocent
stopped
you question
their investigation
and
receive only their
special looks saved
for indians who believe
we never lost

the war of the west that
they are sure they
are still fighting

until our total annihilation
not one of us
is above suspicion

this time it
is you
who is taken to
their station and
enclosed behind steel
obstructions released
early the following day
you are finally entitled
to knowledge of your crime
you are guilty of being
brown indian lesbian woman
you are criminal in
your nature because
you do not
believe in your guilt
like they do
will sign no confession
instead swearing to fight
back against a system
that wishes for your silence
and eventual death
though as long as you
do die they will
allow you to scream

you dare to walk down
sidewalks of cold concrete
alone deep into the night
in the belief that you
are entitled to be
anywhere on this continent
left to you by your
grandmothers and grandfathers
worse than this attitude
you travel where and
when you want

your skin is not white
and you say you are
proud to be
indian
prouder still of your
love for women
so you carry your head
raised always to the sun
back straight
you break all laws
by not lowering your
eyes to the stares of
white people
by not cowering in dark corners
meant for rats and alcoholics
safe in their drunken stupors

you are charged with
two counts of assault
and one of robbery
but not until you
have been hurled

against the police car
handcuffed
while they try to
steal your dignity
still you say you
will
fight back

MARIA AMPARO JIMENEZ

Diosa

Soy esa mujer comprometida
Vulnerable
Escarnecida
Soy tu
Soy ella.
Soy aquella.
Soy la que fui
la que eres
...soy yo,
caminando por las calles de la vida
soy la historia, aun no escrita,
de toda mujer que resucita.

Goddess

I am that compromised woman
Vulnerable.
Scorned.
I'm you.
I'm her.
I'm them.
I am She who was
you who are,
I am Me
walking through the streets of life
I am the history,
though unwritten,
of all women
who are reborn.

KARIN AGUILAR-SAN JUAN

Exploding Myths, Creating Consciousness: Some First Steps Toward Pan-Asian Unity

The following essay is based on a keynote address I gave at the Tenth Anniversary of Asian American Awareness Month at Brown University (November 1990). I was asked to speak to the theme "A Collage of Expression: Recognizing Our Diversity." The student organizers wanted to hear something about the things that drive Asian people apart - nationality, immigration status, class, gender, and sexuality - as well as the necessity for building community across those differences.

As an activist, I felt the best way to address such a wide-ranging theme in an accessible way would be to talk about a few personal experiences. From each of those experiences, I have learned something critical about what it means to be Asian in this white society, and I believe that sharing those thoughts can spur greater race awareness among Asian people and broaden the discussion of racism in general - often cast only in black and white terms.

My comments begin with the conference on Asian American Women Writers held at Tufts University in October 1990. A couple of things that happened during the panel discussions illustrated to me that we need to be constantly vigilant of racism and homophobia. One of the first things we need to do is to examine the myth of the Asian Americans as the "model minority". We also need to challenge our own internalized racism.

As a Filipina, I have a particular perspective on the Asian American experience that is often overlooked by those who consider "Asian" to mean Chinese or Japanese. Filipinos carry a unique burden related to their specific history of coming from a former colony of the United States. In my visits to the Philippines and to Spain, I realized how our colonial past requires that we now "decolonize" our minds.

Finally, I speak to the invisibility of lesbian and gay men within the Asian American community. Our struggle to maintain our integrity, our wholeness, is often at odds with our desire to preserve our cultural heritage. Yet, as Asian lesbians and gay men, we are organizing ourselves so that more of us will be able to do both. In a way, coming out whole - against a society that refuses to see us as a powerful, unified people - is what the Asian American community must eventually accomplish.

As Asian and Asian American people, we are aware of our race *every day of the year.* November is not really different than any other month in that regard, except that this month we are highlighting and celebrating the special contributions we have made and keep on making to this society. We are also choosing to recognize the struggles we continually wage in order to preserve our culture and our heritage, indeed, to maintain our Asian sense of self.

We live in a racist society that lumps all of us together as "Asian", leaving us to bicker among ourselves about who is "Asian" and who is really "Asian American", as though being American were something we have reason to claim. The hyphenated term, Asian-American, draws distinctions on the basis of the intimacy - or distance - with which we relate to Asian life. Yet the term "Asian" is not one we've chosen for ourselves; we, or our ancestors, came from the Asian continent, but beyond that, our national and cultural identities are diverse. For example, as an American-born Filipina, I share very little with my Cambodian sister who recently arrived in this country as a refugee. Yet because we are marginalized in similar ways as *people of color,* we need to create a sense of shared identity among ourselves. Then, we will be better equipped to acknowledge - and appreciate - the richness of our cultures.

For me, each day poses a political and personal challenge. Each morning I ask myself, "What will I have to do today so that I will be heard, despite all the myths and stereotypes that this white society perpetuates to silence me?" After all, I am Asian, and I am a woman. When a white person sees an Asian woman walking down the street, they probably think of Suzy Wong or Yoko Ono or the little Korean girl just adopted by their yuppie neighbours next door. It is incredibly taxing to have to confront those racist and sexist images every day, and *no* place is free of them.

We desperately need to confront racism between and among ourselves. At the recent Tufts University Conference on Asian

American Women Writers (October 26), one of the panels included three Asian women and one white man. The mere sight of the panellists infuriated me, because I am aware of the multiplicity of opportunities that white men have in academia to show their stuff, and the very few such opportunities that are afforded to Asian women. Asian American courses have been part of the regular curriculum at Tufts for only six years; white men have been expounding on literature for at least 200 years. I wondered if the Tufts organizers thought that the participation of white academics would somehow boost the legitimacy of that gathering.

But what was truly a horror was to witness a student raise her hand after the talk so that she could *praise* Donald Goellnicht for "being a man, even a Caucasian man" who is trying to understand how a woman of color feels. My first reaction was dismay; after all, why should she thank him for studying her culture, instead of *expecting* or *demanding* that he do so? In the conference program, Goellnicht listed Asian American writing among his research interests, along with romantic poetry and literary theory. As far as I am aware, he risks nothing by becoming a so-called expert in this seemingly exotic body of literature - and can only gain credentials by doing so. Furthermore, this young man is building his career more or less *at his leisure:* no one is restricting his choice of academic terrain.

Goellnicht's candid reply hit the nail on the head. He said that as a white Canadian man his study of writing by Asian women is "fraught with problems of empire" - of colonialism and imperialism, of the need for white people to take over "once again". But his comment was a small consolation, similar to GI Joe gently suggesting to Suzy Wong that he's not giving her as good a deal as she thinks.

Given the fact that our political consciousness still reflects centuries of colonial domination by white imperialists, now is hardly the time to invite white people to speak to our experience as Asian people. The fact that white people can become recognized "experts" on our experience is evidence of the race privilege they wield. Significantly, later in the conference, up-and-coming novelist Gish Jen pointed out that Asians are seen as experts only when they speak about their own heritage. When white society invites Asian people to speak, they are asked to confine their comments to their own particular culture.

I cannot express the embarrassment I felt upon learning that the student who made this regrettable comment was of Filipino origin. Thinking of it, centuries of colonial domination fly before me. I would like to issue a disclaimer, but I know I can't; in a way, I am responsible for the fact that in 1990 Filipinos are still saying "Thank You" to their white colonizers, praising them for their generosity and benevolence for "allowing" the Philippines to make the transition from an outright colony to a semi-sovereign nation, for waging "only" ten bloody years of war against Filipino nationalists. In a way, I am responsible for the fact that Asian women still splay themselves at the feet of white men - having rejected Asian men as too effeminate - obliterating their own identities in the process. I can't claim to be free from racism and colonialism if the Filipinos around me are still kowtowing madly.

We urgently need to challenge the internalized racism that infects our consciousness. One of the first steps toward our politicization as Asian people is to address the myth that we are this nation's "model minority". According to this myth, we are no longer plagued by racism, and are now partaking of the wealth of this nation. They say that we boast higher incomes than African Americans and even whites because of our superior work ethic and our evidently genetic capacity to follow orders. In contrast to that myth, we know that higher household incomes among Asian families reflect the fact that more family members are working for pay than in families of other racial groups. Asian men still earn only a percentage of what white men do at the same jobs, and for some Asian groups the poverty rate due to these inequities is appalling.

Now that the United States is witnessing a period of imperial decline - mitigated momentarily by its current build-up to war in the Persian Gulf - and white people who are poor (as well as brown, yellow, and black people) are feeling the heat, the model minority myth serves to uphold a racist and exclusionary status quo. "Anyone can make it in America, if they try hard enough. Look at Johnny Woo. He's a computer engineer..." Never mind the fact that Johnny's options for success are confined to those occupations that are "reserved" for Asians. Never mind that many Asians who work hard will never "make it" in America. But as long as there are Asians to give life to that myth - Asians who follow the traditional roads to success without any sense of responsibility to the community that nourished them, who buy luxury cars and memberships to posh clubs, marry, have children, and praise Uncle Sam for treating them as if they were white - then that myth will continue to break us apart.

Over the last decade, the college campus has become the contest terrain between Asians and whites. Many of today's Asian under-graduates are the offspring of professionals who immigrated to the United States in the mid-1960s, bringing with them social and economic advantages to which African American and Latino students rarely have access. This disparity has helped perpetuate the model minority myth, and helped fuel a new wave of anti-Asian hostility. In his groundbreaking history of Asian America, *Strangers from a Distant Shore,* Ron Takaki chronicles a racist incident that occurred in my hometown only three years ago. A group of Asian students at the University of Connecticut in Storrs were on their way to a formal dance. On the bus, a bunch of white students vented their racial hostility by spitting at the women and jeering their boyfriends, "You want to make something out of this, you Oriental faggots?"

I grew up on that campus, and I can well imagine that racist and homophobic incident taking place, since I have endured similar ones. The truth is that as people of color, our skin is a constant, visible disruption of the status quo, affecting our daily lives in ways you can barely imagine if you are white. Growing up on the East Coast, where there are few large Asian communities, was not easy. In that context, finding common ground with other Asians and Third World people was, and continues to be, essential to my survival.

Going to the country of my parents' birth has been critical to that project. In 1986, I visited the Philippines to witness the current state of human rights. Strolling down Magsaysay Boulevard in Olongapo, the city neighbouring Subic Naval Base, I ruminated on the city's nickname, "City of Sin". I felt only a small accident of fate separated me from the dark-skinned women I passed on that street, women from the countryside who had packaged and painted themselves and were now desperately flagging down Navy boys to offer them a cheap night of fun; "Rest and Recreation" is what the Navy calls it.

On the street, a red-haired youth brushed by me - he couldn't have been more than seventeen years old - and bragged to his friend about all the "girls" he'd have while he was at port. Privately, I marvelled that he could have been my high-school classmate. While the seeds of militarism were probably sowed in him as a child, I felt saddened by the prospect of what the Navy would do to his mind, and how it would shape his perception of Filipina women just like me.

The effects of U.S. colonialism were vivid at Subic. I ran into the colonizer again last summer, when as a publisher, I attended the IV International Feminist Book Fair in Barcelona, Spain. I was staying at the Filipino Center, which is run by nuns. When they asked me to attend Mass with them one Sunday, I felt it was only fair to oblige. It happened to be the fourth anniversary of the first Filipino Mass held in Barcelona, so after the Filipino priest finished his sermon, the Spanish priest made a guest appearance. He urged Filipinos to put aside their anger at the Spaniards and focus on the bigger things in life, like God.

I found this advice a little insensitive, given my observation that many Spaniards treat Filipinos the way white bigots in this country treat African Americans. Then, to top it off, he told the Filipinos that they were welcome to worship at that church "not just for four years but for four *hundred* years." I don't know if he chose that number on purpose - the Philippines once endured 400 years of Spanish sword and cross - but, evidently, the Spanish clergy have had a hard time getting that number out of their minds.

My awareness as a Filipina has been rendered more sophisticated by experiences such as these. As a lesbian, parallel experiences have affected my consciousness and identity. At the Tufts conference on Asian American Women Writers, one of the panellists I know to be a lesbian made no public mention of that fact. For the most part, when we - lesbians and gay men - choose not to talk about our sexuality, that choice is not made freely but under duress: we risk losing our jobs, our homes, our children, our friends, our family. For those of us who are Asian, losing connections to our family represents one of our greatest fears, since in this white society, our cultural identity depends precisely on family links. Some of us are forced to conclude that coming out is simply not worth that price.

This woman's silence, though it represented a measure of safety for her, helped keep my experiences as an Asian American lesbian invisible. Her choice to remain in the closet is all the more ironic when I consider that Maxine Hong Kingston had opened the morning session of the conference by reading passages from her latest novel, *Tripmaster Monkey,* whose Chinese protagonist is named "Wittman" after Walt Whitman, the great North American poet. Kingston explained that the character Wittman came to her in a dream, that in her novel she intended to celebrate erotic life - as Whitman did - but with an Asian American twist. She neglected to mention that Walt Whitman was gay or that his homoerotic poetry is an important cultural landmark in gay male history. The passage she read described a heterosexual love scene, and when a woman in the audience later asked if Wittman encounters any lesbians or gay men, Kingston, clearly embarrassed by her own omission, responded, "I don't remember."

Kingston's novel is fairly brazen, even though the stuff she writes about is mild compared to the Free Love of the 1960s, a period she remembers with some amusement. We all know that sexuality, in any form, is difficult to talk about. I don't think Asian Americans have a corner on that problem. But it is important for Asians to recognize that lesbians and gay men suffer from a special kind of prejudice, and we are frequently pushed to disguise ourselves for the comfort of the heterosexual world.

I recall when Marie, a member of AMALGM (Boston's organization of Asian Lesbians and Gay Men), told us her mother had offered to cook her friends a traditional Filipino meal. We all drooled enthusiastically at the idea of *adobo* and *pancit*. But Marie's mother didn't know she was a lesbian, or that the friends she had invited to dinner were lesbians and gay men, so like dutiful Asian children who know when it's better to acquiesce to the demands of our parents (no matter how oppressive to our sense of self), once we entered the house, we arranged ourselves strategically around the living room - boy, girl, boy, girl. Looking back, passing for "straight" can be easy, but it's a game that always leaves a bitter taste.

I believe that Asian lesbians and gay men are a tremendous asset to the Asian American community. We challenge the silences around sexuality and personal life, and we are creating an Asian American language that can accommodate our experiences. As women, we offer positive models of independence in a society that denigrates self-sufficient women. Importantly, gay men offer a redefinition of masculinity so urgently needed given the so-called emasculation of the Asian male.

To have to choose between being gay and being Asian is an absurd and infuriating reality. Our coming out process - the process of acknowledging our lesbian and gay identities - is an important example of the personal risks we are taking in order to explode myths and create consciousness. Ours is an individual struggle to come out to our families and friends; Asian people as a community face a comparable challenge of coming out whole against a society that wants us to be divided, fragmented among ourselves.

The legacies we carry as Filipinos, Cambodians, Koreans, Asian Indians, Chinese, or Japanese make us separate and distinct. In our effort to build pan-Asian unity, we must not gloss over those important differences. Giving voice to those specific legacies and the way they shape our contemporary lives is key to our solidarity - and empowerment - as an Asian community.

MARIA CORA

Dos Culturas / Two Cultures

Soy la coyuntrua de dos culturas en lucha
Tengo por herencia ambas caras simbioticas del
coloniaje
He dejado anos, lagrimas,
esfuerzos y cantares de sobrevivencia
   en las arenas de Borinquen
   en el cemento de Yanquilandia

Hago la politica en mi ingles manipulador
Hago el amor en mi espanol apasionado

Como semillas al viento,
he presenciado en mi carne
el desparramiento de mi familia, mi gente, mi pueblo.
Es nuestra la dura cosecha
de desubicacion, enajenamiento y nostalgia.
Yo nomada involuntaria, nutrida de
   los planes del proximo viaje
   las llamadas telefonicas
   las cartas esperadas
   la separacion
   el sueno del volver eterno

Hubiera enloquecido de no haber tenido
la suerte de nacer negra.
Ahi se reconcilian mis conflictos existenciales
De lado y lado mis antepasadas
maldijeron su rapto de mi tierra santa Africana
Y derramaron sangre resistiendo
   violaciones

la venta de sus hijos
el ardor del carimbo
las condiciones inconcebibles
de sus abusadas vidas como esclavas.

Y continuaron recordando
que lo esencial es dar vida
y no dejarse vencer,
no dejar de sonar para el presente y el futuro

Y yo recuerdo con ellas.
Hoy lucho a diario,
resistiendo el legado del racismo
    a veces directo, otras veces sutil
    mas siempre nocivo
    lo mismo aca que alla

No me impresionan la gente rubia
ni me estiro mis pasas queridas.
Soy bruja Yoruba y sonera
que vocaliza pregones que saben a jazz y a rumba
en la marginal.
Yo no permito que me definan:
    lo mio lo defino yo.
Vengo como los huracanes
    como la muerte.
Seria un grave error para cualquiera
subestimar lo que soy y a donde voy.

Two Cultures

I am that place where two cultures struggle
I have inherited both interdependent sides of
colonialism
There, my years, my tears, my efforts and songs
there, I left them
    on Puerto Rican seashores
    on city pavements of Yankee Land.

I do politics in manipulative English
I make love in passionate Spanish

Like seeds in the wind
I have witnessed in my flesh
the scattering of my family, my people.
For us a bitter harvest
of displacement, alienation and nostalgia.
Unwilling nomad nourished on
    thoughts of the next visit
    telephone calls
    awaited letters
    separated
    forever dreaming of going home

I would have lost my mind
but that I am blessed to be black.
There all of my existential conflicts reconcile
On both sides those women, my ancestors
cursed their being abducted from our motherland Africa.

And they shed blood resisting against
    the raping
    the selling of their children

the burning of the brand
the inconceivable conditions of their abused lives in
slavery.

And they always remembered
that which is essential
to give life and not let yourself be beaten
to never stop dreaming for the present and the future.

And I remember with them.
I struggle day to day resisting this legacy of racism
   sometimes direct, other times subtle
   always deadly
both here and there.
Blondes do not impress me
I will not straighten my beloved naps.
I am a Yoruba sorceress and voice
whose verses taste of jazz and hot rumbas from the
side.

And I do not allow others to define me
That which is mine I define.
I am on my way
   like hurricanes
   like death.
It would be a grave mistake
for anyone to underestimate
who I am and where I am going.

SUSAN BEAVER

Gays and Lesbians of the First Nations

This article is dedicated to all those who have gone before us to the spirit world and to all our Grandmothers, without whom we would not be here physically or culturally.

Generations before the Europeans invaded Turtle Island our Grandmothers and Grandfathers, our ancestors, lived, breathed, held ceremonies and governed themselves according to the complex demands and gifts of the land, our Mother. It was, and continues to be, a life rooted in respect, spirituality and a little bit of humour.

Before the Europeans invaded Turtle Island there lived the Berdache, the cross-dressers and the two-spirited people, in a respected and vital place in the societies of the ancestors. "Two-spirited" is a positive, traditional term that we prefer to call ourselves. What heterosexual people achieve spiritually in marriage, the union of two beings, we achieve by simply being ourselves. Creator made all beings spiritual beings but Creator gifted some of us to carry two spirits - male and female. Before the invaders we were the healers or medicine people, the visionaries and the blessed. For 500 years the colonizers have been trying to stamp out the First Nations people. And we have survived. Our cultures, languages, land, governments and children have all been the subject of attack. One of the first things the Europeans used to justify our inherent inferiority to their ways, and subsequently most viciously attack, was the two-spirited people. And we have survived.

Today we come together after a long, hard road on which we still travel. Our strength lies in our collective heritage as First Nations people. Like First Nations people everywhere, we are still feeling the effects of colonization. Some of us can't speak our language, some were raised as Roman Catholics and others stolen outright from their people. We come together with our varying degrees of knowledge and hope both to learn as well as share. We learn what it is that makes us unique as Nations and as individuals.

197

We come together as social creatures (witness our tea and bannock get togethers) to forge stronger links. We learn of similarities as First Nations people and our differences as men and women. We come together as educators: GLFN's "Aboriginal Women and AIDS" community forum. We have gone out into our own communities and talked about what it is to be two-spirited, to be HIV+, to risk rejection by our family and community. We speak of acceptance and respect.

Like many communities, we have been infected and affected by AIDS. Our response has been that only Native people can talk to Native people about our sexuality, our lives and our futures with any understanding or success. This is very much in line with principles of self-determination for Aboriginal people. Our response has taken us to high school classrooms, reserves, to our own leaders and to nurses. We ask you, the reader, to take time at this point to honour and remember the ones already taken by AIDS.

As First Nations people and as two-spirited people we struggle to maintain our circle in a society that does not value the First People of this land. It is our intention as an organization to strengthen our cultures and reclaim our place in society. It is also our intention to laugh at ourselves and at life, the entire journey. Ny-weh/Meegwetch.

Midi Onodera

Untitled

It was of course Monday and it wasn't simply chance that her head ached from the drinking binge the night before. What an embarrassment. How could she face work at the collective this morning? She stared blankly at the crumpled mess of clothes scattered by her bed. At least she was alone. Those god damn buttons, badges on her faded jean jacket spewing out those tired slogans, "The Future is Female" ha! "Out of Pittsburgh Now"; "Pro-Choice: You say Tomato and I say Tomato"; "Reagan Drops Acid"; "No, No, No". Already her double women's symbol had tarnished.

Her thoughts drifted back to the unforgettable Saturday morning. She had been in a hurry from the moment the alarm went off. Still captured by her vivid dream of making love with that attractive Japanese woman from the Centre, she drifted toward the kitchen for her coffee ritual. She justified her dream by thinking that she wasn't seeking sexual gratification through "the other", after all she was also Japanese. It wasn't her fault that she had never made love with another Japanese woman.

Everything went wrong that morning, from the coffee maker running amuck, the clogged toilet, the mismatched socks, and that phone call from Roberta. After two years of not speaking she had picked that moment to call her and discuss "what really happened in their relationship." Apologizing as best as she could, she hung up the phone and grabbed her speech, stuffed it in her purse and ran to the appointed location of the Demo.

Right on time, the opening speeches had just finished and people were busily searching for the right banner to stand behind in anticipation of the march. The crowds and confusion were overwhelming, she didn't even have a hope in linking up with her contingent the Lesbians of Colour For The Elimination of Racism, Sexism, Capitalism, Theorism, and ism-ISM's. Instead she fell behind the Animal Rights For Self Government banner. It was strange that she even knew some of her fellow marchers, but of course not strange that they knew her.

Guilt had always been the reason why she never turned down a

speaking engagement, she was the "only choice", or so they told
her, the perfect oppressed spokesperson for every occasion. At first,
she tried to be logical and somewhat humble about her position,
but now, it seemed the process of justification had become
ritualized - there were so many reasons why she had to do it.

After the non-violent, non-meat-eating demonstration had
stopped the requisite number of cars and captured the necessary
number of pedestrians, they stopped to hear the allotted quota of
speeches, one of which was hers.

Still floating in an aura of self-importance and having been once
again seduced by the swarms of eager believers, she mounted the
stage. Theatrically unfolding her words of wisdom and taking the
customary sip of water, she launched into her attack.

Thinking back on the incident made her cringe and the heavy
burden of the episode made her body sink deeper into the bed. Her
head began to moan and the soles of her feet began to perspire. It
was the wrong speech. She had stuffed the wrong speech into her
bag that morning. But that wasn't the worst of it. She didn't even
know it until she had finished reading the entire thing. No one
stopped her. Everyone was in a state of shock. It was only after,
when listening to the absence of applause, did she realize
something was not right. One of the marshals helped her off the
stage.

Roberta was standing at the foot of the stairs and staring at her,
aghast.

"What the hell did you just read? Do you have a death wish
reading something like that to this crowd? You better leave, NOW!"
It was too late. The crowd had already turned into that well known
ugly mob. Placards and styrofoam cups were hurled in her
direction, angry, obscene faces, (the kind the press are so fond of
capturing) verbal abuse and in the end, insanity.

It was over with that cup of organic lemonade someone threw
on her. Before she knew what had happened, or could decide what
was politically correct to do, she began to feel this weird sensation
over her entire body, almost as if acid were eating away at her skin.
She could barely get out the words, "Help, I'm MELTTTTING!!!"

And after, all that was left, were those damn buttons with their
optimistic slogans and losing causes artfully composed on the

lemonade stained grass. The remains of someone she thought she was; that she, as much as they had created.

Although this story is obviously humorous fiction the situation is not so far fetched. "Wearing too many hats" or the "Circle of Confusion Syndrome" - as I call it, is something that both feminists and artists of colour are familiar with. Whether that means active participation in more groups than is humanly possible, or even more draining, being called upon to represent several viewpoints in one group.

As a Japanese Canadian lesbian artist filmmaker, I deal with several overlapping communities, often finding myself the only person of colour, as well as the only gay representative. Of course, one would like to believe that artists are selected to participate in shows, discussions, juries, etc. based on their abilities and contributions to their chosen field of work. But this is not always the case. Instead we are sometimes there to prove others' political correctness and if we represent more than one downtrodden minority, so much the better.

One could refuse to participate in any event in which one was in danger of being used as a token, or one could participate and try to ignore what is going on. After all, these people we are talking about are not raving bigots, they are men and women who do not share my experience and are therefore operating under certain assumptions we can't afford to let them keep. By accepting these invitations and trying to destroy rather than perpetuate stereotypes, we react against the token situations and hopefully assist in the creation of an environment open to constructive exchanges. We cannot afford to throw away any of the few platforms we have. As the gay community has long known, the stubborn refusal to live up to the expected stereotype can be most effective. The mere act of being yourself can be extremely threatening and the use of these occasions to speak out against oppression and omission is important. Through these means we gain control of what is potentially a very degrading situation. We gather strength from our support systems, strength which should be called upon on these occasions.

Another facet of being used as a token, is the frustration and awkwardness it causes the individual. Denial of the personal experience in favour of a "community experience" and the necessity of generalization, occurs as we are forced into a spokesperson position for the group. Although we may share the same oppression, the same skin colour or the same sexual orientation, we do not always want to be seen to be speaking for our community, but rather for ourselves, as individuals. One thing that is certain about the supposed role of a token, is that it has nothing to do with being an individual.

The media, as we all know, finds its own spokesperson for the many communities that exist and is forever quoting Authority X on this issue or that. However, they are frequently not the people whom the community would have chosen to represent them, but instead are people who will verify the assertions of the media. Even as we may deny that we stand for our communities and assert our individuality, we are also strongly tied to those communities. Furthermore, we worry that stands that we take may work against our communities. In the past I worked on a film which explored the cultural links between three generations of Japanese Canadian women. During that time, I faced numerous conflicts both in trying to sublimate my point of view and more dangerously, around areas of self-censorship.

Do I only present images in a positive light and white wash the negative? Do I closet my sexuality because I fear that both individuals and the community as a whole will reject me and the film? Or do I scrap the production altogether because it's too difficult to produce politically loaded independent films anyway, so I should concentrate on docudramas about the Prime Minister's interior decorator.

The answer of course, is that I continue to make the film, without denying my sexuality. I continue to accept invitations to events where I know I will be the token whatever...(Japanese Canadian, lesbian, experimental filmmaker, take your pick). But I no longer play the role of the expected stereotype. I think I try to do what most of us do in this situation, which is to make the best of it. Certainly it has taken a long time to reach the point where I have confidence to disagree with the majority view.

Often the hardest part of playing this game is the loneliness and the exhaustion. There have been times and there will continue to be occasions where one feels like they're speaking into a vacuum. But occasionally, one meets others who are in the same position and the feeling of isolation is lifted. Taking responsibility for our involvement and assisting in the creation of an environment open to participation by all, is a task which we should share equally. Each of us has a point of view and something to contribute. One group's struggle is not less important than another's; the differences and similarities should be valued, not used to pit one community against another.

As I sit and write this, I can't help but feel that what I have said has been said before, but perhaps we need to be occasionally reminded that we are not alone in our struggle. It has been long and will continue to be laborious, frustrating, painful and sometimes victorious. But if we share the load and support each other in our efforts, somehow I imagine a lighter burden for all of us.

Nice Rodriguez

Straight People, Wild Ducks, and Salmon

I came to Canada on a hot summer day during a heat wave. The weather was too hot even for someone like me who grew up in the tropics. It was a long trip half-way across the globe, north to a prosperous country I knew very little about.

I am a Filipino dyke, 32, married by lesbian standards. I left an anguishing wife in Manila. I landed alone in Vancouver declaring no goods nor wife to follow me later on. I finally settled in Toronto wondering if I could ever make a home or stand my first winter without her. She had been a friend for fifteen years, five glorious years as my wife.

She did not have an easy start on life. Yet despite her poverty, she made it to the university where we were both good students, finding ourselves like guinea pigs in a Third World cost-saving educational experiment. Both of us qualified in an accelerated accounting program that compressed four years schooling to three. It was a hectic student life but 95 per cent of us passed the government tests. Notwithstanding the success, the controversial program was eventually shelved. If it had not been for her, I might have quit the program.

I had artistic inclinations but because Third World realities dictated a more pragmatic decision, I became an accountant. I was the only girl in our brood and my sexual preference was common knowledge. My lesbian lifestyle, which at that time only meant dressing up like a man, disappointed my parents.

Back in high school, my mom said I was insane and I believed her. And it was not just her. An American institution had declared homosexuality a mental illness.

My sexual urges were potently forming a design of its own. I had no desire nor power to change its course and prepared myself to life in an asylum. I eagerly awaited the school's field trip to the mental institution. When I got there, I was relieved to find myself not like the inmates. They had given up on life while I was ready to embark on mine.

The Catholic school where I spent eleven years also condemned

204

homosexuality. Already alienated, I kept away from other butches afraid that my parents would accuse them of being a bad influence on me. I locked myself in my room most of the time, thinking only about what people might say about my parents, not about me. But I spent lots of time wondering if I was good-looking and smart enough to win a girl someday.

Those were trying times. If not for my innate lesbian strength, I would have conked out. It was only recently that I realized my life had been a constant struggle to prove that I was sane and normal. Yet the harm had been done. I suffered from an inferiority complex and my life remained an enduring battle to express my homosexual self.

It was this identity trap and financial woes that made me seek my lot in another country. My insecurities as a lesbian made me work harder in school and at work, which eventually earned me points as an independent immigrant to Canada. If I were a straight man, I could have tugged my wife along; unfortunately, in order for her to follow me, she had to make it herself as an independent immigrant. Those odds were hard to beat.

When I was leaving the Philippines, I was old enough to make a commitment. I was not sure I was ready for this but my wife was. She said she was not a piece of garbage I had picked up on the street to bring home....and to forget. Like marriages in our country, we arranged a meeting with both our parents. We told them of our plans to live together.

When her father arrived, I had cold feet the whole time. That night, I was relieved; because of his misery, he was dead drunk. Even so, I told him his daughter would live with me from now on. His words were mostly incoherent but he did make one request: that I would allow his daughter to return home if she wanted. He made me swear I would never harm her if that was what she decided.

In my country, the butches have earned a nasty reputation for not being able to let go when an affair is over. They do things like beat their wives, kill themselves or make scenes in public; wilder than any jilted man. They would even dare a man to a burly match or hire goons to teach him a lesson. All because of the macho syndrome that pervades our society.

Every night since my arrival, I face southeast Toronto, hopeful that my thoughts would link me further east to the Philippines where she awaits my return. Ironically, I was waiting in Toronto for her too. But I soon realized, that we could not go on dreaming any more. Some drastic action had to be taken.

That's when I finally thought about paying a man to marry her for convenience. I was never good at saving. The price could fetch $5, 000, I heard. No way could I raise that much money considering Toronto's high cost of living. I was underemployed too, working in a low-paying job that was below my qualifications.

There is some unwritten law here that immigrants must fund Canada's schools first before they can ever find good jobs; an irony because as independent immigrants, we were selected from many applicants mainly on the strength of our career and education.

Unable to save, I was also not good at asking. How could I ever approach an eligible man to marry my wife - my wife! When I attended gatherings, I tried to propose on her behalf when I spotted a bachelor, but I never able to do it. Just the thought gave me goose pimples. Could be my macho pride.

Macho? Yes. The butch among us Filipino lesbians really think of ourselves as men. The Philippines was under Hispanic rule for almost 400 years and so machismo has been a part of our social structure. I wasn't immune to that system.

Coming from a far-flung country. I was surprised to see feminists among the Asian dykes in Toronto. We, Filipino butches, were chauvinist pigs in every way. Like the men in our country, we had fits of superiority. We wished to be served, we wished to be right. Yet even with these hard rules, our women stayed.

If I declared myself a feminist in Manila, I would be the butt of jokes. Macho was my other name. I aped men - the thug type. I slouched to cover my breasts, swaggered when I walked and wore a mean countenance. By some strange will, I made my stomach swell to hide the curves in my hips and to achieve the male beer drinker's body. I wore briefs over my cockless loins. I was expected to be short in temper, bitter that I was a half-man, while my neighbours eagerly tallied the girls I brought home.

Men accused us of showering the girls with money and

pampering them with material goods. When a woman leaves a
man for another woman, Filipino men would use their poverty as
an excuse, never their impotency or callous ways with the women.
I was not in the best financial shape when my wife and I started to
live together. I wooed her with my green Converse canvas shoes.
She later found out it was my only pair.

I tried to rid myself of illegal thoughts. I raised my hopes and
asked my wife to persist in her independent immigration
application.

"Are we so desperate," I wrote her, "that we would need a man?
Let's see how things turn out. I love you."

Yet in my heart, I ached for justice. Why is a lesbian marriage
not categorized as a family class under Canadian immigration laws?

Why does a man have more rights that I have? Where would I
find a gay man in the same predicament, so that I might marry his
lover, and he mine? I was new in a strange land. My resources were
limited. I was losing hope.

It is foolish for law-makers to think that immigrants are always
straight, or that homosexuals cannot establish relationships. No
distance can immediately dissolve the emotional bonds when gay
or lesbian couples separate. If they become promiscuous, it is not by
choice.

Despondent, I would regale my wife with stories about my new
friends in the Toronto gay and lesbian community.

"We have our own bookstores, our own newspapers, our own
radio shows, our own awards nights, our own 519," I said ecstatic
during one of my overseas phone calls. In the Philippines, we had
no such thing; but we did have gay beauty contests.

"It would be so nice if we could live here together," I added.
"And yes, we have our own church too."

We used to date after church, not only on Sundays but novena
nights as well. Every Sunday, she volunteered for the lectern, always
making sure she pronounced the words of the epistles the right way
so people would understand God's words.

As a young Catholic teenager, it devastated me when the
Vatican released a condemnation of homosexual acts in 1975. At

about the same time, I stopped going to church. Many times, I went to church merely to fetch her.

In Manila, we had never heard about gay rights but it was something we never felt bad about. In a place where human rights were often breached, nobody ever gave a damn about gay or animal rights. We could not care less about the environment either. For in our lives, our minds and actions were consumed by thoughts of daily survival. Our struggle was for the most basic right - to live. And being gay or lesbian in a Third World setting, complicated your life even more.

I told my wife that I attend a monthly meeting of Toronto's Asian lesbians, a support group. They are articulate and aggressive, not like me, I told her. Even in my native tongue, I hardly spoke about my feelings. In my country, men seldom got emotional and neither did butches. My voice had trembled when I introduced myself to the group.

"I come from the Philippines. I left a wife in Manila," I felt a lump in my throat and my eyes got misty. "I miss her very much. I cry with envy whenever I see straight immigrants leaving for the airport to fetch their newly-arrived wives or husbands."

I stopped talking. I saw a vision of my wife in despair, abandoned in a poor unstable country. Why couldn't I just give her up?

There was no justice on earth, not even in Canada. I wished I had been born a fighter, but like most Filipinos, I am a fatalist. This was our destiny. No way could we alter what was in store for us. Maybe I should just head home to join her and we would eventually die together in an impoverished country. Forgotten lesbians born in the wrong place and time. Perhaps only straight people, wild ducks and salmon migrate.

Two years had passed since I have seen my darling wife. I can still remember her waving as I crossed the immigration line at Benigno Aquino International Airport. I turned my head as I paced the hall leading to the airport gates. I saw her small as a dot waving, waving until I saw none of her. Tears ran down my cheeks. As I realized the uncertainties that lay ahead, my face grimaced, my legs shook, my lips trembled. I tried to compose myself.

"I will get you," I wanted to say before we parted. "I will petition for you." I could not make her any promises. Nothing.

"We must always think that we will be together again. We must fight thoughts to the contrary," I told her in bed the night before I left. We were locked in a warm embrace all night, a warmth that I can still feel during long, wintry Canadian nights.

As poor lesbians, we had nothing but hopes and prayers. Our chances were nil but we prayed that an aberration would occur that would help us realize our dream of togetherness in a bountiful country. An aberration just like us - people of the third sex born in the Third World.

MARIA AMPARO JIMENEZ

Untitled

You're too white for the brown
too brown for the white
too mexi*can* for the ri*can*
to ameri*can*ized to be mexi*can*
-I'm latina...
Stick around child
you'll *understand*
what we have in common
is only the *can*
-Does that mean power or what?
-Stick around child,
    you'll *understand*
To be ameri*can* is power
to us it's just trash
It's the melting pot you're at
-Aren't we all...
-Stick around child,
you'll *understand*
It Chicago you're at.
can also means
where they put you away...
Like beans in a *can?*
-What would happen
if hand in hand
we all jumped out of the *can?*
-Stick around child
you'll *understand*
it's all about money
so they won't allow it -

everyone's fine
if they stay in their *can.*
-Time passes and I fail to grasp,
what I should *understand.*
I rather be gone than *understand*
  I won't stand under!
  Do you *under-stand?*

RAYMINA Y. MAYS

In the Trenches

I'll tell you why I was tired. I come to work at 'bout six-thirty-quarter-til-seven. I don't have to be at work proper 'til seven-thirty but if you know what I know you'd get here early. If you didn't like hairnets, like I don't like hairnets. If you hated white uniforms and wearing stockings in the summertime especially, but most times generally; if you had to get it together about how much shit you were not going to take short of losing your job; if you have to rag down (as my kids would say) in a bunch of nothing clothes that you wouldn't ordinarily be caught dead in, you'd get here early too. This is a known fact.

I'm telling you this to say that when you come to work this early, you need a break in the middle of the day. You take it when you can get it.

I'm tired like I said. We got 600 women come to the building I work in. Come from all over the world to work out things between them. Smart women. You can believe that. I watch a lot of these women come in and sign in at the desk. Every color you could imagine and dozens of pretty languages. From Chile, Egypt, India, Africa, Cuba, Iran, Puerto Rico, Mexico City, Asia, Native to America, Black Amerian. Sarees, three-piece suits, corduroys, sandals, boots and tennis shoes. Afros, braids, and straight hair, and....See what I'm saying? From all over the world.

I'm taking this in. Then I decide that for the rest of the day, I was going to be walking up and down halls and in and out of rooms so I could snatch bits and pieces of what was being said. This is to say, everything I ever learned come from another woman, you understand. This conference was on international perspectives.

Now you tell me. If you was in a building full of women that talked from a point of view you never heard, from a place in the world you could only wish you knew or read about, and you know at the same time everything you know (at least what you use to survive) come from women, wouldn't you walk the halls with open ears and hang in rooms long after you set up chairs or served the fresh water?

That's what I did. I hung around. Then weary from my work, you understand I hid out in a certain conference room. I sat down, listened, and tried to understand most of what was being said. Genital Mutilation. A mysterious disease of school girls where there was a war going on over homeland. I'm seeing women I been seeing all week long in the hallways. I wave at my friend the doctor from Egypt, who when these boys cornered her and asked her why she had on pants and tennis shoes, said, "I'm comfortable." She told the boys to get back. When they have wars, you know, the women and the children starve first, get cared for by the doctors last, get raped, get they arms torn off, get killed straight out.It really got to me how this country I live in got so much to do with whether people in another country will starve or eat, live or die. This country got his greedy paws in everybody's shit.

I'm getting a whole lot of notions about the work that's got to be done. My Latina sister stands up to make more talk about it. "Sex, Race, Class, Sexuality. I see these as all connected. As a lesbian...."

I hear a Black American sister speak."We have no time to talk about who you sleep with. There are starving women and children in the world. Lesbian is a white woman's game. Third World women have no time to talk about who some privileged American women sleep with."

Good thing I'm sitting down. I'm mad 'cause I ain't hardly white or privileged and I know it's a damn lie what she saying. Somebody gets up to make the point I'm making to you.

I'm tell you. Spit starts flying. Sister don't bit more want to hear the truth than the man on the moon does, that even in bad times the women have concern about love and affection and who they will get it from.

Sister and some others don't want to hear that sometimes the thing that takes you further is for somebody to hold you. Don't want to know that you can't hardly talk about those things they talk about if someone want to kill you because you in love with a woman. I don't give a shit where in the world you live. It's like they think if you was lesbian through and through, heart and soul, all you care about is pussy all the time. I like me some though. I like titties and elbows and kneecaps, too. And speaking for myself, I

213

ain't marched since that night when I nightmared about the dogs, and the firehoses and I remembered my girlfriend of the time catching it across the brain with a flying billy club and how I held her all night and how we was fifteen.

I wished these two women, Mayrine and Laura, who live across the way from me, was at this conference, so they could tell these queer-haters something. Mayrine and Laura could tell what happened when they went on that march against those fuckers in South Africa who step on our peoples necks. They can tell how when they come back from the march about this, the landlord inspected they apartment while they was gone, evidently inspected they bookshelf and they closet. When they got back in town all they shit was on the street. Clothes, books, everything was on the damn street.

Do you think those brothers and sisters that chartered that bus and marched with Mayrine and Laura jumped off and organized, made signs, marched or whatever it took, in they defence? Do you think brothers and sisters yelled and screamed,,"Forget this shit. Give these women back they apartment"or "Hell no, this shit has got to go"? Hell no, they didn't do this. First off, Laura and Mayrine can't even be out to these folks. Second,if they was, folks would be saying that they bought into some white folks' shit that was taking them away from the real stuggle.

I'm getting mad and thinking who the fuck did this woman think she was talking to, green martians? All the lesbians standing up was Third World and it seemed to me that they weren't the kind of women to buy into anybody's shit. Including the stuff coming from my sister.

Meanwhile, sister plagiarizing the Third World's business 'cause she scared of queers and two women in front of me are doing some serious comforting of each other and asking each other, "Whose country is she talking about where women don't talk about these things?"

My sister is so uptight. She is hot. If her words was fire, she'd burn the building down with all us in it. Brought to mind the man who wanted to bash my skull with a Coca-Cola bottle not too long ago because I made it plain that, no, he couldn't come in our house. My sister brought to mind him throwing Coca-Cola all over

me, and when I locked the bastard's thumb in the door and
threatened to call the police, brought to mind him
screaming,"DYKE SLUT BITCH. YOU NEED A DICK. I COULD KILL
YO' ASS AND THEY'D CALL IT A CRIME OF PASSION. THEY'D
COME SAYING YOU DESERVED IT. BULLDAGGER. SWING YOUR
BLACK ASS IN FRONT OF MY FACE. OPEN THIS DOOR, BITCH."

My sister is going on and saying, "I RESENT THE HELL OUT OF
ALL OF THIS. PEOPLE ARE STARVING. CHILDREN ARE STARVING.
THIS `WHO YOU SLEEP WITH' HAS NOTHING TO DO WITH
REAL OPPRESSION. I'M DAMNED ANGRY. A FEW PRIVILIGED
AMERICAN LESBIANS MONOPOLIZE THIS CONFERNCE."

Right now, my sister is water and I'm a sponge, just absorbing
this shit and not knowing exactly what to do with it. My first
inclination, when somebody is wishing I was dead with they words,
is to knock them out. Tell them there are two things I'm going to
love being for the rest of my life: queer and black. My second
inclination, if she be a queer hating sister, is to ask if anybody held
her in bad times, tittie to tittie, all arms, cheeks, whole body. Shit,
knee to knee, toes to toes. She'd be bound to say her mother or risk
being called an out and out liar. Then I'd ask "How did it feel?"
Then I'd be inclined to ask,"If we was in the trenches (and I know
we in the trenches from what I learned in this room), if we was in
the trenches, and this race, this class, this sex this economic that
she was talking about was pounding us in the ground, and we keep
trying to get up and out, and I'm having a hard time, would you
pull me up and hold me and tell me to keep on climbing? If I was
climbing with you, and a queer basher let you pass and put a boot
on my neck, took my children set fire to my belongings, would you
join with me in taking this foot off my neck, get my kids back, put
out the fire, like you'd do if they said I was the wrong color or class
or sex? Could we touch each other and comfort each other while
we was in the trenches?" That would be my question. Could we be
queer and hold each other hard and cry and fight on the way up?
Seems women don't do this nearly enough, I'd say. I could bet on
my life that even if sister wouldn't say no to my face, she'd be
thinking it.

Anyhow, like I say, I'm sitting in this room trying to rest up and
really thinking on this business of all sisters being sisters and how it

could be worked out international-wise and neighbor-wise, and my supervisor come tapping me on shoulder for me to turn around. And she was looking dead in my face, and you can believe hearing the word lesbian being used with not too much care and understanding.

Pain and
Betrayal

CONNIE FIFE

Twisted Tongues

this familiar language of yours
rings harshly against the silence of
this place changed now by your presence
and the words you have brought through
using an outsiders tongue

i have often wondered what it is
to be told to no longer speak
in the language of my origin was
not allowed to touch on the syllables
of my grandmothers i know only of
the meaning of loss and what it is
to crave for that which you never had

i twinge not out of being inadequate at
the english spouting from your lips
could match you word for word
i react out of not being able to
speak with those women who sat
with me in the sweat lodge on the
eve of my first return home
here i was surrounded by their
prayers for the healing of my wounds
the mending of my heart torn by
years of absence and forced assimilation

this class of yours bores me for i
do not desire to speak with the same
lack of meaning found in your words
i will sit patiently until the breeze
caused by your lecture has subsided and
the smell of your acidic breath leaves
this room i cannot respectfully
apologize for this desire in my
body to spit your words back where
they belong instead my silence and
lack of attention is all i am left with
following years of living on the
borders of your world.

RITZ CHOW

Is My Name

like my mother before me
i've killed a man
took his life
like a cent
and threw it where
it would land

closed my eyes
before the bang
and held my ears
to me

only 22
so much
these hands
would do
and nothing
left
to keep

nights of holding
forks and spoons

washing with
palmolive
but never
able to get clean

must be the mother
in me working
shoulders
to straighten the back
some sort of
walking arrangement
lost

this child
running
from her own
angry fists

like my mother
before me
and the child after
i'm folding
paper fans
and melting
plastic sins

JUDY NICHOLSON

From Space to Page

On Sunday mornings I play soft music and think. I think about racism, sexism and homophobia, each in turn. I think about my mother, my father, and my grandmother, each in turn. I think about my ex-lovers, each in turn. Then I sit and try to write my experiences of these things and people, from space to page, to create a memory of them.

I think about my need for safety because there is danger here. I think about the person in my neighbourhood who has been writing homophobic graffiti on every pole and wall.

lesbians corrupt unsuspecting straight women.
bitchy lesbians need a good beating. kill all lesbians.

I think about my need for revenge because there is danger here. I think about the person in my neighbourhood who has been writing racist messages on every pole and wall.

send the niggers back. milk isn't red - white is
purity - white nation now.

I think about my need to kill every man who reminds me of my uncle and his filthy hands his filthy penis his filthy mouth reaching for my small body.

Then I sit and try to write my anger, from space to page, to create a memory as though taking a picture to be used as legal evidence when I am put on trial for murdering these men.

I think about a time not long ago when I felt that I had already been tried and condemned. I think about leaving Toronto years ago in a frenzy of anger, fear, shame, and resentment. I think about my dear mother throwing me out for being who I am - a lesbian who is also her daughter.

come and get your things or i'll throw them
outside and burn them. all my suspicions
confirmed. i'll never have grandchildren.
what did i do wrong? i would have preferred
if you had come home pregnant. my god, my

god, this is a nightmare. when am i going
to wake up from this nightmare?

i remember the trip back to my once-home to
claim my material things. rummaging behind
a supermarket first to gather milk cartons
and boxes reeking of dog piss to pack my books,
my clothes, my shoes, my this, my that. A note
across my picture on the table: my daughter
died december 31, 1985.

I cannot survive another banishment of this magnitude.

I think of these experiences not as the blackest days of my life,
for I am just beginning to experience my deepest darkness.
I think about exchanging this sad Sunday morning music for an
album by Prince instead, so that I can listen to him croon his
creative songs and hear our black and blues foremothers and
forefathers in his smooth voice. Oh, but what a pig he can be
sometimes with a mere twist of his words. I think I would much
prefer to listen to a female artist's voice: lyrical, beautiful, and
provocative. I don't listen for Tracy Chapman songs on the radio
anymore. The white DJs piss me off by talking about how they
understand the need for a revolution, but they wonder "egzactly
whut kint of kar she meant in hur song, Fast Cars."
I try to write my frustration, from space to page. I think about
how I miss my hot birth island where the land, the air, and the
people are warm. I remember the love in my grandmother's
clouded eyes as she slowly moved her dark rough hands over my
face and neck and called me her beautiful black baby.

I think about how I tried to hide my darkness as I grew up in
this Canada. I think about the white wymyn I have liked and loved.
I think about our outrageous fights and wild laughter. I think about
how we made love, fucked, or didn't. I think about the relief I felt
when I left or the disappointment I bore when she left. I try to
remember the colour of each one's hair but fail because subtle
shades of blond and brown are indistinguishable to me. I think

about the one brown womon I have known intimately and how she lifted my spirits and challenged my ideas. With warm familiarity, I think of those who are still good friends, and I muse on the tensions I feel with those who are now near-enemies.

I think about myself as lover to myself and how my times of celibacy are the most peaceful and powerful moments. Sometimes I think I endure these relationships with other wymyn purely to feed my imagination for writing. I give my body's passion in exchange for the new words these wymyn inspire. But I often write about these wymyn when they are still here. I write about them with affection. I try to write them from space to page in anticipation of our parting.

> what is this inspiration
> you give me to write when i see you
> first i want to touch you
> then i want to write you
> from space to page
> using my eyes and fingers to translate you
> to preserve your voice and movements
> with my words and images
> so that i can read you
> from page into space
> when you are no longer here for me to hold
>
> i know you are going to leave me womon
> like the others before you
> i know soon i will be tearing up
> these pages i have written
> soon i will be writing of loss
> instead of lust or love

On Sunday mornings I sit and write my experiences of these things and people. I write them from space to page. I write to create a memory of my frustrations, my pain, my anger, my passion.

MARIA CORA

Single Embrace

It is like seeing you
out of the corner of my eye
The image, blurry with tears,
is residual
from another time and space.

You hover around the periphery of my world,
just out of reach
Making sudden unexplained appearances
in my dreams
Acting out of character and context.

Your voice lives inside my head
answering my every question,
making it seem like my accusations
do not fall on deaf ears.

Even though I hid all of your photos
from myself
your smile, your eyes, all of your gestures
waver in the candle light
as I watch.

They say you feel a phantom one
when you lose a limb
My heart still thinks you are
attached to my soul
My hands still feeling the contours of your body
in absentia.

I see you in every dreadlocked woman
   in every runner
   in every hardhat

All the love songs
somehow belong to you
even when they are new to me.

Elusive may be the best way
for you to be
This way
I keep company with all my
   could have beens
   should have beens
   would have beens the best love of all time
While you find new reasons daily
to stay away from me.

But know this,
I will be with you
   in every crowd and audience
   in every single embrace.

MARIA CORA

Fear

Lately I have let fear lodge in my bones
make a corrosive home for itself inside
deep within, out of reach
from where I could try and yank it out
roots and all

No, somehow it found the unprotected flank
the soft vulnerable spot within my psyche
and decided to stay.

Was it the crisp look of the young blonde
as she sped by in her red Mercedes,
not wanting anyone to cut in front of her
on the freeway of her life?

Or is it the invisibility,
the absence of any news of my people
my island
unless it is a major natural disaster
defined by them
which, of course, would not include
our slow dying?

I would never speak of my fear aloud
feeling the shame already
the judging eyes
the older voices
    "We have suffered so you could live
    will you dishonour us now with your fear,
    even as our ashes find no rest,

no home, no nightly fire to draw us
There is only your flickering candle?"

But to myself I cannot deny this fear
I hate so much
If you had only seen and heard as I have
    the stories of the children being tortured
    in Soweto cells
    the sound of Victor Jara's fingers and guitar
    being broken
    the white haired woman in Esquipulas
    telling how the contras cut the throats
    of her four sons
    all in one day.

This smell of fear would also
soak through your clothes
like the sweat of someone on their
deathbed.

I know of heartsick
is there such a thing as soulsick?
Can I get a witness or two?

The fear has begun to seep
out of the crack
between my two selves
the private and the public.
As I form words of encouragement
hope for a jaded world
trying to stir up revolution
and ward off despair,
There is a bitter taste in my mouth.

LANUOLA ASIASIGA

For Marilyn
In the Rose Garden

there is no wind
just the sound of the waterfall and the fountain
people murmur reverently
you and I walk slowly
eating our ice creams
Pele has found children
and is running excitedly round and round
I can feel myself unwinding
the days drain away
I am content to sit and absorb
Pele reads this as an excuse
to start digging up part of the garden
another dyke walks past
and smiles sympathetically
dogs and rose gardens don't always mix
we'll have to move, you say
we walk on
I don't mind what we do
so long as we stay
something inside of me is being released
and oozing down into the earth

we find a bench
you in the sun and me in the shade
Pele has found more children
I sense a slight unease in you
sitting beside me
a growing agitation

while the rose garden
has a calming effect on me
it is arousing an unsettling disquiet
in you
we leave

at the station
I can't leave
I know there is something
something unsaid
we chatter on
still I don't leave
you start to talk
really talk
about the work you've been doing
for you
and suddenly
there it is
the naming
your pain fills the car, spilling out
I am engulfed in it
you have waited so long for this naming
and at times I have watched you
feeling quite helpless
I look at you
and know the scars you wear
I want to tell you how brave you are
But the words don't come
all I can do is nod
and acknowledge your pain

when I get home
I am overwhelmed with sadness and anger
at the countless stories of sexual abuse

that women have shared with me
I want to scream it to the world
that this is not how things should be
yet after thousands of years of conditioning
we are primed up to be the victims
and even with our awakening
our pain silences us

in pain we whisper our stories to each other
in our pain we can't believe that another
human being could treat us so
we take that hatred that has been thrust into us
and we believe it
we feel shame that we have been abused
and often we believe that we deserved it

why the fuck
should you and I feel shame over a situation
where we were totally powerless

I cannot be silent any longer
don't let the pain silence you

when we allow ourselves to be silenced
we remain victims
we remain powerless

as more of us refuse to be silenced
we become a force to be reckoned with
we claim back our power

LANUOLA ASIASIGA

Answers to Questions I Am Constantly Asked

No, it isn't amazing that I speak English so well
No, I'm not an overstayer or a FOB
No, I'm not a night cleaner and I don't work at
Mitsubishi
No, I don't play the guitar, sing or dance the hula
No, I am not fluent in my "own" language

Yes, I am Samoan lesbian
No, I don't speak for the whole Samoan community
I don't speak for Samoan dykes
I speak only for me

Oh, so now you want to dismiss me
as not being the "real" thing
not being the genuine article
You think I'm not a real Samoan

You mean you were only interested in me
If I spoke with an accent and wore a lavalava
A genuine native artifact to be displayed to your friends
A "real" Third World PI woman

I don't get it
If I'm ESL and of a different culture
I'm classified disadvantaged, "less than"
(to be read as "less than Palagi")
Now I'm English-speaking, still of a different culture
But you're telling me I'm a "less than" Samoan

In your antiracism workshops
You say "differences" are important
and should be acknowledged
Well I'm a "different from your stereotype" Samoan
Acknowledge me

FOB: fresh off the boat
PI: Pacific Island
Palagi: White person

SHARON FERNANDEZ

Terimahkaseh

The room was almost totally dark but there was a thin yellow line where the curtains didn't meet. I'm glad she's gone to sleep. After all this time there is no pain. Pain for me would be a relief, an ability to cope, but I can't cope. At dinner she had touched the tip of her wine glass to mine, taking my hand, she had kissed it for all of the hetero world to see, saying "to us, to love, to growing old together." Now I dream of escape, of freedom. Tonight had been the worst night ever. All lines have been crossed long ago and the limits are anyone's guess. At times like these the tiny thing that is me disappears. She is screaming at me, calling me words that are not who I am. Maybe after all this time she doesn't know who I am. When the champagne bottle broke, my naivety grew large before my eyes and foolishness flooded my heart. But I believe in her. Does that mean I believe in her power not to hurt me?

I have come to some conclusions. Deep hurt is very solitary. It is another country which you visit. If I say I love you many times will you believe my repetition? If you say I love you many times am I supposed to cease thinking, wrapping those words around your reality like trees I can shelter under from its storm, wrapping those words around my reality like leaves, like something to hold on to because I can't hold on to you?

Why do I dream of freedom when my heart is wild with love for you?

She moves protectively, holding on to me in sleep. There are no boundaries between our psyches trying to find the meaning behind the confusion. All the divisions of physical existence, the inevitable separations, what kind of woman makes such a choice?

Tomorrow depression will set in. I listen to the night's sounds, couples leaving the bar, returning to their rooms, trees creaking in the wind. The only part of me that moves is my mind, running in the dark of this land that is our love.

I hear Tia's voice. She is my friend, beautiful in her integrity. What is obvious is not obscured to her caring heart. She questions my abstract privilege and tears overwhelm my desire to talk, to delve into the female landscape of denial, our capacity, our appetite. Who has given us the taste for this? From it I've painted canvas upon canvas, colour upon colour. Did it make me larger than my life? Who can I turn to when I have chosen to love you... you who have another love.

If you say I love you many times, do I stop listening to the beating of my own heart and move closer with my ears to yours? Is this what it means to love vicariously? My denial is sometimes light, it wears an intellectual mask, chanting words that keep me from going deeper into the craziness, following an ancient music the heart intuits but can't interpret. This country room, our clandestine home, outside it has started to rain gently. When I was a child I was only fearful of the supernatural, the grieving women spirits 'pontianaks' who had died in child-birth and lived in the large flowers of the banana groves in bloom and full of smell, especially when planted near graveyards or railroad tracks. Now at 30 I am afraid of love, of many of the words in this language that start with the letter L, liaisons, lies, liberal, love, lovers.

This room I chose with its pinewood, its sensual privacy, is another moment of hope, where the truth of our intimacy could shine like a star, however brief.

Outside the rain is gentle.

My thoughts move back, forth, over, under, longing to be free from male attitudes of love that strangle the soul in broad daylight. Her arms in deep sleep are afraid of losing me. My body is as still as the sunlight was on the lake today, reassuring her, willing her to sleep on, far from me in her own troubled land of terror.

There are limits to all endurance before we take our rage and stand up in it, solitary, single, able to face the world without our mothers, without our lovers, without.

The taste of this love spills from my skin irrational in its will to be, to surrender to what is sacred and known. What should I do? Leave the city, move away, start a new life?

Will I die of it? In the struggle what of me will I leave behind? Tonight has been an invasion from another land, a land where no birds fly, a land no secular reality comprehends.

The night has passed. The thin yellow line where the curtains didn't meet bursts into our room and she is awake holding me.

My being wants to fly, but I am passive on the edge of resistance. Words like dark earth fall warm from her soul to embalm the memories. They fall fertile with love, but my body is a wall. The words pile heavy over my heart.

I want to cry out, to scream as she has screamed.

This strange landscape of sound, the sound of love that has no solid shape, that has no face, that has no ability to appear and look you in the eye, or be held in the hand, an ideal love...

Not ours alone, a collective dis/ease blooming like a giant tree green with leaves. A subversive landscape of sound, the sound of love that is a memory.

She is nervous like a horse, skittish, wanting to make love, to affirm us. But there is nothing in me that can move to meet her.

She is as loving as only she can be, whispering in the silence close to my ear. She would like it to be easy, a new day. I would like it to be easy, a new life.

She doesn't understand that every little hurt is a key opening a door into the special darkness of a resentment that sits in me, like a woman waiting, growing hideous over the years.

Her lips move down, reaching for mine. I feel her hands mediating with my skin. I hear her voice from far away.

"I love you. I love you. I love you." Her body moves saying the same thing but my mind is still on the run.

The emptiness in me remembers the conversation I'd had with Tia last week. Tia smoking endless cigarettes, calm in her depression, overworked, burdened by the needs of lives devouring her own.

"Look," she says, "these kinds of relationships are only good for two things: idealism and bullshit."

"What about love?" I ask. "If it's strong can't we build new ways of relating?"

"Sweet girl, love demands concrete reality for expression, what is within needs to move outward toward creation to reflect itself; so you tell me how you're been able to do this, when the space is already taken?" Tia says. "If the conditions repress love's full expression then love lives in the shadow," she added.

"But Tia, can't we as lesbians revision relationships, move

toward radical positions of love that are more liberating?" I demanded. She looked at me shaking her head. "Do you know what my radical definition of love is? It's about not hurting the person you say you love, as simple as that. Is it asking too much to expect that conscious women balance their self expressions with their abilities to commit, if not what's new about it? A new mask?"

"Listen, girl," she continued, "The moment you are intimate with someone you are entering unpredictable territory, the boundaries get shifted and you are in the unknown."

"In every kind of relationship the seriousness of the commitment/or lack of has to be equal for it to endure or end without damaging those involved."

"Don't you think we can love more than one person at a time?" I ask.

"Sure," she says, "but that love extends in context of our abilities to fulfil our obligations to it and also in context of equality of power."

"Look," she says patiently, "intimate relations are always feudal relations. It is something that only the lips to the lips, the leg to the leg and the breast to the breast understands."

Terimahkaseh is the Malay word for Thank You. Its literal translation is I take with love.

MILAGROS PAREDES

Love in Echoes

How long will it take
before I walk to the
other side
and believe in your love?
Will it take time
and time
and time
or will it take a moment
to steal away from this lonely cave
of child-old echoings
telling me

You do not care
whether I live or die
stay or leave
You do not love
me

I am small.

In my fantasies
you offer me words of love
coated with
the warmth of your heart
I grow languid
in you liquid brown eyes
your arms embracing me.

You have told me
I may fall in love
I may love other women
You will tell me when this happens
we will talk
then.

This is the stuff of my fear.
I am waiting.

She holds tight
a sword and shield to protect herself
save herself
I cannot convince her to
lay her weapons down
Surrender

She is still
in the past of unloving.

I want to take her sword
carve a hole to my heart
let your love in.

My world would change
to be worthy of love
to be loved
whether or not
I pleased her
or her
or her.

I would be living in a different world
if I could lay down
my sword and shield
carve a hole to my heart
surrender.

SHENAZ L. STRI

untitled

i write because
i cannot talk.
my closed mouth.

my silence is agreement,
i'm told.
my silence is watching,
not trusting...
i say.
it's not understood.

my silence is agreement.
i disagree.
i write... i talk.
but i am not heard.

my silence is agreement.
it is insisted.
my silence is protection,
it's my right.
listen to me... my words...
myself...
my silence is listening,
i hear you
i don't know you.

my silence
my silence
my silence

silence...

i'm saying something
you don't hear me.
reassuring me that everything is okay, now.

i yell... scream... and rage
it's all inside.
i am terrified of my silence.
i agree...

my silence is a watchdog
always aware.

silence is not agreement
trust me.

i know.

Doris L. Harris

Image

Don't tell nobody
not a living soul

I save rose petals
in jars
bowls
boxes
I've got a dresser drawer full
pink, yellow, white, red and more
most have dried and cracked with time
but just like a woman,
their scent is still strong

Don't tell nobody

as a black woman
I'm suppose to be exotic
a warrior
queen of the Nile
a bottomless vessel of maternal wisdom
with a communal bosom
complete with martyrdom, understanding
and forgiveness
a warm place where the world
can lay its weary head
my shoulders must be made of a fortified steel
mere flesh and blood will never do
they must be strong and broad enough to carry
the weight of oppression,

racism, sexism, and poverty
without working up a sweat

Don't tell nobody

KIT YEE CHAN

Sometimes, Survival is Work

I manage to push this body
of mine
limp from days existence
into the streets, the bars
finding comfort by the droning beats and glaring lights

Its not that i like it
but i don't hate it
coz i need to do it

Sometimes, surviving means this
Sometimes, survival is work

Everyone uses the word (survivor) to mean different
things

In defining myself, and my occupation
I am an Asian Confusexual Survivor.

Do you know how much work i do?
not nine to five that's for sure

When sleep becomes my vacation
it is paid for with darkness and fear.

I fear sleep because i am helpless
when my eyes are shut
they shut as if to close doors
where images form.

like a shadow

when i close my eyes out here
i hold some kind of freedom
i can never have at home

at home
i can not wash the blood stains away

i have tried.
will i be forgiven - like everyone wants to?
will i forget - like you have?

my work is to remember
my work is to forget

Sometimes, surviving means this
Sometimes, survival is that

for me,
Surviving is work.

The more poison I swallow
The more I have to spit out.

A fist of shame
jams down my throat
because i have not had any water
for 2000 years.

A fist full of shame
jams down my throat
because i am Asian
all my life

A fist of shame
jams down my throat
because i figured out
where my genitals were (through other people)
when i was young.

A fist of shame
jams down my throat
and i bite the fingers off
like poisoned raw meat
spit it out
because i am a survivor.

DORIS L. HARRIS

Goodbye

Guarding your fidelity
has been exhausting
eavesdropping on your phone calls
has been all consuming,
the manual dexterity needed to juggle these awkward voids
of silence has made me weary
fending off unprovoked verbal barrages
so that you can justify your sudden need to leave
has wasted so much time
trying to live by your standards, only to find out too late
that you have no standards
has made me feel crazy
become a bad liar, a sneak, and a spy
accepting too much bullshit under the guise of love
was making me sadistic
evil
and a clown without the grease paint

BETH BRANT

Home Coming

She felt the thud before it registered in her mind that she had struck something in the road.

She braked the car, turned off the motor and sat. It couldn't have been a dog or a child, though god knows, she thought angrily, there are too many of those species on this god-damn island. The woman's mouth formed into a straight, bitter line. She pushed her dark, long hair over her shoulders and sat, staring out the front windshield at the full moon that seemed to be careening down on top of her. The Harvest Moon, the whites called it. She had forgotten the Indian words for this kind of moon. There was a lot to harvest around here, she thought - kids, dogs, booze, the occasional gunshot heard on a Friday or Saturday night; the plentiful yelling, screaming and fighting that came before the occasional gunshot.

The Harvest Moon.

Granny died today.

The woman unbuckled her seatbelt, irritated that she was so careful of herself inside a car, when she was never so careful inside her life. She opened the car door, listening for a sound that might identify what it was she had hit. There were no whimpering sounds like a child or dog would make. Or the screaming that rabbits make when dying.

The woman had a surge of memory of the first time Grampa had taken her out to shoot rabbits.

"You have to be fast," Grampa said.

"Rabbits freeze for a few seconds, but then they move real fast, so you only got that second to take good aim."

He demonstrated his technique four times - each time a true shot, each time an instantly dead rabbit. The girl carried the canvas sack filling with rabbits, the sack warm against her side. Grampa had wanted five rabbits that day. He had decided that was his quota. Grampa's quotas were never the same, and the woman never got to ask him how he came to his decisions. He had died before she remembered to ask

The fifth rabbit jumped in front of them. Taking aim, Grampa shot. The rabbit fell into a cover of weeds and the screaming began. The girl looked at her Grampa, hot tears beginning a course down her cheeks. Grampa ran to the weeds, pulled out the rabbit and wrung its neck. The rabbit was silenced.

"This is a bad thing, Granddaughter. I did not kill this rabbit proper. No animal should scream like that. I must be getting old if I make an animal scream like that."

Grampa had buried the rabbit, rather than putting it in the sack. He said it wouldn't be right to leave it for the crows, it had not died proper. He took her hand saying, "I am tired, Granddaughter. Take me home."

It occurred to the woman standing outside the car that Grampa had indeed become old that day. His face, a mass of lines and cracks, seemed to sag into itself on that day. He smiled at the girl holding his hand, but the smile was more a grimace than the sweet curve of mouth that was his usual expression. "I'm gettin' old, eh?"

She hadn't remembered to ask him about his system of rabbit quotas. It seemed important that she should have asked.

She heard a rustling on the right side of the car. As she cautiously walked around the car, the rustling became louder. She saw it. A Blue Heron. It was struggling to rise, to attempt a flight that even the woman, who did not fly, knew was impossible. She felt a scream pushing through her body.

"My first time back on this god-damn island in five years and I do this! I hate this place. Even the herons are cursed. They walk in front of cars and get killed. I hate this place! I didn't want to come back here. I didn't. I didn't."

This is a bad thing, Granddaughter.

The woman wept, her hands drawn into fists that she raised to the moon, as if to smash the golden light into splinters. But the moon's brightness remained steady, its face relentless on her powerless fists. Hundreds of tiny moons made a path down the woman's cheeks as the light reflected off each tear that came from her grey eyes. She walked toward the heron. It tried to rise, the long neck trying to unfold, the beak moving back and forth, back and forth with a jerky rhythm. The bird made no sound. The woman reached out, her long fingers wanting to touch the heron. She touched it. The heron's neck sprang forward, then receded. The bird became still, its opaque eyes on the woman. She put her arms around the bird and sat on the road. She could feel a heartbeat under her fingers.

Granny. Oh Granny. When Brother called me today, I knew what he was going to say. I tried to keep him from saying it.

"She's dead, Sister. Our Granny is dead. Please come to help me get her ready. She wants you to come and help me get her ready. Her last words were about you." His quiet voice went on in the familiar cadence, "I have missed you too. I have prayed that you would come back to us. At night, I would look over the river and try to see you and I would call to you. Did you ever hear me, Sister?" The woman wanted to scream into the phone, yes, I heard your voice, constantly at me, constantly in my dreams, always at me to come home to that island! Instead she replied, "No, Brother, I didn't hear you. You know I left it all behind." She could hear her brother sigh, "Will you come back this one time? To help with our Granny?" She made her own sigh, "Yes, I'll be there as soon as I can." Her older brother began to sob and the woman was stunned, then angry that her brother could cry over the wires, while she stood helpless in her apartment, holding on for dear life to the telephone, not shedding a tear.

I'm holding a dying bird. I'm sitting in the road like some crazy woman, talking to myself. But that's who I talk to - myself. Granny, you told me I was special, I was *Nishnawbe*, I was different from Mum. You said I wouldn't make the same mistakes she made. Oh, I made them, Granny. I made them. I hated you and Grampa, making excuses for her. The time I ran after her, begging her to come back in the house. "You care more about your friends than you do about us," I yelled at her. Mum kept on walking, looking for the booze, the party, the men. She didn't even look back at me! Granny, you and Grampa and Brother came to take my hands to pull me away from the night, from the picture of Mum walking down the road, not looking back at me. Granny, you said that Mum had forgotten how to be an Indian, that she would learn. She didn't, did she? But me and Brother learned plenty. How to live with a drunk for a mother. How many drinks it takes before you pass out. How to avoid your mother when she has a hang-over.

How to smooth things over so no one remembers anything. How to clean up after her. How to hope that maybe *this* night, your mother will stay home. Granny, my mother didn't forget how to be an Indian, she *was* being an Indian!

The heron fluttered, its feathers brushing against the woman's wet cheek. She inhaled the scent of the bird - the smell of marshwater, reeds and fish. The bird remained silent, an almost calm look in its eyes. Without wanting to, the woman remembered a day when their mother had washed and braided her and Brother's hair. Mum sang a song about *Fly me to the moon*. She said she had the most beautiful children and that their hair was the tenth wonder of the world. Brother and sister laughed in each other's faces and sang along with their mother.

The woman touched her hair, remembering the feel of her mother's hands as she drew the brush through the long mass of hair, then held the strands as she began the braids. Her mother's hair had been black, pulled into a ponytail or left falling down her back when she went out.

The smell of the bird reminded the woman of how she had loved it here as a child. Grampa taking her and Brother fishing, their lines getting tangled in the Pickerel Weed. Brother getting so excited he'd cry out - "Fish, fish, come and jump on my hook. I want to eat you!" The terns circling above them, their raucous voices begging for a piece of whatever the trio might catch. Marsh wrens clattering as they delicately flew from reed to cattail. Red-wings whistling and giving chase to anything that threatened their nests. Grampa paddling further into the channels where everything was quiet except for the startled croak of a heron or an egret. They would sit for hours, fishing and growing sleepy under the sun, Grampa's voice telling stories.

Brother never stopped loving it here. But he was different. Even from the start, Brother was marked in some way. His way of seeing, his dreams, the way he would listen, as if he heard something that no one else could hear. Oh yes, Granny, the special brother and the sister who was going to grow up to be like her mum. Isn't that the way it was? I've missed you so much, Granny. I would call you on the phone and hear your voice and want to rush back to you. But I couldn't come back here. Not here. I'm lonely, Granny. I have no children, I wouldn't have children. I was afraid to. I'm lonely. I go to my job, I come home, I eat, I watch tv, I go to sleep. I dream. You told me that when we dream our souls fly. My soul doesn't fly, Granny. It's a lead sinker that pulls me down till I can't breathe and I wake up crying and afraid. You told us lies, Granny. Standing at the cookstove, putting together the stew, you told us we were a proud people. Brother believed you. *He* stayed here to keep himself an Indian. As if living in a run-down shack on a god-forsaken island is something special, something the whites don't have, something that makes us better than them. What a joke. Proud people. Proud people! Drunks! What a lie, Granny. Isn't it?

The heron moved. Its eyes looked again into the woman's eyes. Its feathers rustled in her arms. The scent of the marsh brought another memory. Granny laughing as she mended some clothes and Mum sitting next to her making a pair of earrings for her daughter. There hadn't been enough red beads and Mum had to start all over again so the pattern would be consistent and perfect. The girl watched her mother patiently threading the beads, the kerosene lamp hanging over her mother's head, casting lights on her fingers as she slowly beaded the earrings and talked with Granny. Brother sat in the corner of the room reading books and, looking up from the page, he smiled at his sister.

"Come home."

The words hung in the air like the Harvest Moon. The woman stared into the eyes of the heron, seeing her reflection and something more. What was it? The bird stared back steadily and clearly.

What do I have to come home to? What happened, Granny? I never thought you'd die. I wished and wished for Mum to die when she was drunk. Then she did. I didn't mean it! I was always scared. Scared of the screaming and shouting when she got drunk. Scared of the men she hung around with. Scared to see her go out. Brother was scared too, but he would hold me and tell me I couldn't change her, couldn't make her different. I knew he was right, but I was a little kid and part of me thought that if I wished hard enough, she would stop drinking. Then I began to wish she would die. And that wish came true. Why couldn't the other one?! I'm afraid of death, Granny. I'm afraid of life. I look in the mirror and see my mother's face. I haven't touched a drop in five years, yet here I am holding Heron and wanting to feel the hot taste of whisky in my mouth. I'm scared without you, Granny. Even living in the city, I knew you were here for me. I could call you and hear your voice. You told me you were proud of me for not drinking. That you prayed for me. That you missed me, but you knew I was doing what I had to do. I am so scared! You held us when Mum couldn't. You talked to us when she couldn't. You yelled at her only once, when you told her she was making shame in the Creator's sight. She laughed at you, but then she cried. She pointed at me - "Don't let her be like me. Don't let Marie be like me!" Granny, I remember how you tried to pull her into your arms, but she ran out of the door, hair still matted from the night's sleep, her make-up smeared and dissolving. She ran out the door and came back dead. I didn't mean it!

"Come home."

The heron's heart was beating, erratic and small against Marie's fingers. She rubbed her wet face on the feathers and touched the beak. The bird shifted, its weight falling more on her. The eyes regarded her, the moon's reflection staring out at her. Her own face looking out at her. Her mother's face looking out at her.

"Come home."

I thought if I left this island I could save myself. But I gave up parts of me at the same time. I'm lonely, Granny. Lonely for the smell of the water, the way the sky looks when it's going to rain, the men setting trap lines in the fall, the way the water looks in the winter, hundreds of muskrat houses poking up through the marsh, the sound of Brother's laughter. You and Grampa. My mother. My mother who stares out of the mirror.

"Come home."

The words floated above Marie's head, above the heron's head. She could touch them, if she only reached for them. Heron's eyes held hers, almost like an embrace.

The last time I saw a heron was five years ago. I saw one sitting in a willow tree as I left the house and was driving towards the road that would take me over the bridge and into the city. I laughed when I saw it, it was so big and awkward perching on a willow branch. When I got closer, the heron squawked and flew out of the tree. I stopped the car and watched - the graceful legs floating behind its body, like strings across the sky. I watched until the blue wings disappeared over the marsh. I thought for a moment that you had sent the bird, Granny. I went away from here because I thought I wasn't strong enough to be like you. I thought I wasn't strong enough to stay. I ran away from you, from my mother. Forgive me, Granny. Forgive me, Mum.

"Come home."

The words became the heron's low croak. The bird shuddered in Marie's arms - the eyes, the powerful eyes, never leaving Marie's own. The bird's heart stopped beneath Marie's fingers. The moon's light intensified as it focused on the pair sitting in the road.

Marie lay the bird aside and went to open the trunk of the car. She got out the tire iron, the only thing she had to dig a grave. She fought the hard dirt, scooping and struggling to make a shallow hole. She picked up the bird, once again breathing in the smell of the island. She laid the heron into the earth and plucked a few of the feathers. She covered the grave with dirt and reeds. She touched the grave and looked at the moon. The moon looked back, its light caressing her face.

Six more miles to Granny, and to Brother, who would be holding out his hands to her, standing in the open doorway. Beyond him would be Granny, waiting to be washed and covered with sweetgrass. They would tend her together and sing for her. There would be food to prepare and drummers to call.

"I'm coming, Granny."

Clutching Heron's feathers in her hand, Marie put the car in gear and headed up the road.

CHRISTINA SPRINGER

Alana

(was lost to the destructive forces of homophobia, sexism and classism, her death, while noticed, went unpublicized and unaddressed)

I.

Hanging,
a small portion
of my performance artist career
       thought it art
       to string tampons
       from bushes.

Tampons, glorious brightly hued
TAMPONS!!!
dyed
myriad of unimaginable colors.

A tantalizing fabulous rainbow dance
rocking, swinging, dangling dance
in TAMPONS
alerting onlookers feminine protection
is a beautiful fact of life.

Each passing of sun and moon circling
I remember driving
past your body
some thinking
it was performance art
to hang large swinging objects
from trees,

We
    had habit
    of hanging
    all available objects
    from trees.

II.

Hanging out,
the *only* two lesbian couples
in married students apartments on campus
revelled in victory of recognition.

We
    hung out
    together as stained laundry
drinking gin and tonics
pretending to enjoy life
in an elaborate gay complex
Your child bride and I delightedly bourgeois
barbecuing with the other wives.

You were so bogged down with reality
        ever practical, scientific
        our imaginations
        irritating, impractical, artistic,
        uncovering Goddess
        in ourselves was fantasy.
        Science Fiction.

I wonder, perhaps
your analytical orderly mind
found it too good to be true for you.

Fantasy
Science Fiction
Love
Gin and Tonics

hanging
out.

III.

A prophet, I painted
    furiously, painfully
    three months of studies
    in cloaked woman
    and nooses.

A peculiar fascination
dramatic artistic statement
wildly mysterious subject
    empty nooses
    hanging
    from sleeping clawed trees
    against the drop
    of purple orange sunsets.

I remember driving
as any morning
past campus
to class
wondering what grandiose newly created spectacle
the people had gathered to see.
Savoring the notion of fantasy
spectacle
AND FREEDOM OF EXPRESSION!!!

We drove past your body
     hanging in a noose
     unknowingly savoring
     large swinging objects
The tantalizing,
  fabulous, rainbow dance
     rocking, swinging,
     dangling dance
     from trees
     performance art.

We didn't know.
We drove past your body
swinging from a noose
in a tree feet barely caressing the earth
devoid of anything that was you.

We thought you might be an installation piece
         hung
         for our viewing pleasure
         on the way to art class.

We didn't know
and savored the success of whomever's latest creation
unaware you had uncreated yourself
for our viewing pleasure
in a tree your feet barely touching.

IV.

I feel your essence
continuing to weigh this memory
of one we could not afford to lose.
Your tree has begun to die,

I wonder / if imagination ultimately more powerful.

This writing of you
not so easy as the cryptic notes
                   you typed
                            in a public library.

I lash out, confused
no comprehension of to where
              or to whom
              or the how
              I am to address my anger.

You, hung yourself.
Typed a note in a public library
with people passing by
searching the stacks for knowledge
watching your preparation
to leave no forwarding address.

Saying this
        bizarre western workaholic notion
        of not doing it
        if you can't do it right
        that lesbianism a classic example
        of not doing it right
Is angering me

for you not knowing the idea
is not to be taken literally
and have no recourse for debate.

I am left with a letter
I can not send.
I cut down your tree,
compost the note with your branches.

V.

The child of my body you do not know
holds tea parties on your tree.
Sitting with animals stuffed, sewn and dyed
has an interesting effect.

Dining on your death
                place
                is new life.

A branch pokes itself
out from the stump
I made you leave.

Imagination ultimately more powerful,
                we play happy games to alleviate
                this pain pushing out.

I do not sever this branch
growing from pain,
I invite rebirth unconditionally
praying on demands
to write no more letters
and leave it as we were.

MICHELE CHAI

I - Woman

when the woman
was a figment
she knew
nothing
except the thing
connecting
her mass
to that which
expelled her.
amidst noise
and light
a child,
taught in haste
differences:
black,
white,
and man
and man
and man
woman -
was the thing
she was.
yet less
and less
as she developed
breasts
and curves
and sensitive folds
of flesh -
pure sweet flesh

a girl
taught in haste
differentiate,
flaccid from
ERECT.
learned
hate
in haste that
the phallus
tasted
as sweet.
as she
(and this)
animal
frenzied against
her flesh
[FATHER]
[BROTHER]
[STRANGER]

no more,
no less,
her friend and
this pain
filled thing -
the accepted
good/evil
the act
her purpose.
VICTIMIZED
VIOLATED
cast into desolation
(that)
scourged

her innocence
drawing shame
filled
baggage
wept
without knowledge
desperate to
find to
end
suffering
and failing,
unearthed
courage
charged
bitter truths;
reinstated
the healing
the rebirth
to exile
the boys
the men:
that tortured
her sex
white washed
her reality,
that tainted sleep
her bruised vagina
stitched past _
present
to WOMAN
secure
in her existence
her sun
will warm
her brow

her trust -
the midnight storm
will pacify
silent hatred.
WOMAN
it has come
the time
and I -
WOMAN
STRENGTHENED
reclaiming
what is mine;
redeeming
PRIDE
on my terms.

KAREN AUGUSTINE

Lesbians Get A.I.D.S.

for Michael Smith 1957-1991

i watched it struggle with the hard choke/sink to the base on
the roughness of your tongue
when the pain became too much
when that contracting organ collapsed
did your eyes roll upwards
did your face sweat cold drips from resistance?
collapsing on the jade-green couch/sliding down on the worn
out carpet
spitting up blood caught in the vein/in the throat/in the mouth
in the very strength of our oppressive systems...chanting
up racism-sexism-homophobia
promoting fear-hatred-ignorance/providing special treatment
for those who live strongly
with difference

Organs grind
together
twist
veins
suffocate cells
in dark wine blood
This poison suckles at his rib cage
        squeezes moisture
out of tissues

Its sharp spit
scrapes the
bones to a fine powder

in canada a lot of a.i.d.s. information is not kept on
the basis of race, so even if we were being propor-
tionately hit, we do not have that information - and
so, one of the important things to do is to collect
that information and then make that data available

and here I am
beneath his bed in Wellesley Hospital
my skin against cold floor tiles/syringes/bedpans
reeking of ammonia

I get up and watch him
slim
clay-coloured skin
upon stale bedsheets
the room smelling like dirty
        urinals
and canine breath
this disease in his blood
damages cells
consumes internal moistness
into full-blown A.I.D.S.

I watch and
    listen
        to sickness
destroy organs, blood and bone

        52% of all womyn w/a.i.d.s.-related disease or +hiv
        status are black/a.i.d.s. is the leading cause of death
        for black womyn between the ages of 24 and 36

IT awakens him from sleep
slam dances
in the skull
increases its pressure
with its size
(wanting to get out through a pore for easier access to
kill)

I can only watch for so long

   black lesbians may have been involved w/ men
   because of community and cultural pressure and
   lack of support w/in the gay community

I think of him
white man
watches
black womon
cope with his sickness - with our infection - with A.I.D.S.

   lack of a.i.d.s. prevention programs in communities
   of colour, lack of primary health care and the virtual
   absence of social and emotional support for black
   womyn w/ a.i.d.s. have exacerbated the problem

lying beneath his bed
in Wellesley Hospital
I keep company a very strong friend

C. ALLYSON LEE

untitled

I feel such a hollowness
        right in the pit of my heart,
        and this wound
        cries out
for reassurance and love.

Like a piece of jagged glass,
        it hurts
        and hurts
in the same place always.

And I am bleeding
        from too much
        loss,
        pain
        and humiliation.

I need time now
to free myself.

Indigo Som

dream #90

you show up again
naturally/the way an old
friend does/after being gone so long
you are comfortable to be in my dreams again

we sit at different tables/with different
people/at the farthest point from each other
in some smoky blue jazz club
furnished with chinese banquet sized tables

our eyes meet and we point gun-shaped hands
at each other/playful
with secret knowing smiles/
when we pull our triggers
it feels more like a kiss

you cd see/straight into
where i hurt/the soft part
tender like an overripe cantaloupe
& i knew what you
were lookin at/cause
i had seen it myself/tasted
the grainy pale flesh
with all the sugar turned to starch

i'm not sure you didn't wink
as we shot
twin kisses/across
huge banquet tablecloths
in jazzclub dreamscape/across

four years of time/untold space

& that bullet/kiss
entered me/your eye
plunging through my tangled thorns
direct to the center/where pointy green
shoots push up now/like old
dried-out onions which sprout
in spite of themselves
from deep purpling skins

Jaisne Blue Sexton

untitled 2

you said:
"we belong only to ourselves"
yet
you stole something of me when you left
and the me that remained
covered her face
and wept.

untitled 3

let us not speak overmuch of grief
life is all too brief
and time, a master thief

untitled 4

I've never understood why I fell for you
whispering sweet nothings
you wove a magic spell
I was powerless to resist your summons
your eyes were quite enchanting
as you lured me straight to hell

untitled 5

early in the mornings
and late at night
echoes from a soul
lost in flight
come to haunt my dreams
trapped somewhere
floating in dream space
crying endlessly
and searching for its place.

JUDITH NICHOLSON

Until You Said

when we first kissed so soft i... now all i feel is this
    flaring new pain
so burgundy i can hardly grasp it into words
an unbearable disappointment seeks me and haunts me
    into writing

my friends will be asking many searching questions
i told them that i
had
fallen for you
now i've just simply fallen

how could i have been so stupid
not to see you seeking
my vulnerability in the colour of my skin

why was i so calm
is it because i like you enough to want to see if you will
    change
was my response so like a quiet evening breeze because i
    wanted
to hold you gently for just a little longer

what made you so sky-and-earth special to me
was it seeing the designs of your artistic hands with
    paint on fabric or
the results of how they expertly cradled a camera to
    capture the metaphors
of this septic passionate life or was it seeing those same
    white hands being

smooth and creative on my brown body and drawing
    sweet and artistic motions
in me that was so magical so deceiving

when will the cool numbness come to quell these hot
    pains inside that are
melting me down to ash nothingness

i did not write your wonderful blue-gray eyes and
    sunshine hair while i was touching you
i did not reveal how i secretly watched the dimple in
    your chin dance so with each easy laugh
i did not draw your capable hands and strong arms in
    rich melodic tones while they were playing with me
not a word did i write about how i loved moving my
    hands down your solid broad back following the
brown against white contrast to the taper of your
    slim waist and then to the rising and falling of your
    moon-round bum
nothing written about the way you started my rivers
    running warm
teasing and playing your long exciting fingers around
    my open cunt
holding my legs apart with your own wet muscular
    thighs
pulling me in with your erotic perfume of w-h-i-s-p-e-r-
    e-d words
not a word or phrase did i write
until you were no longer here

i trusted you until the day you said you could never go back
after having a black woman

CHRYSTOS

Ya Don Wanna Eat Pussy

that Chippewa said to that gay white man who never has
Ya don wanna eat pussy after eatin hot peppers   he laughed
I stared   in the white sink memorizing rust stains
He nodded in the general direction of the windows behind us
        Two Native women chopping onions & pickles
        to make tuna fish sandwiches
        for these six men helping to move
He said *Ya didn hear that did ya   Good*
She answered   *I chose to ignore it*
I muttered   *So did I*
Ya don wanna take offense at an Indian man's joke
        no matter how crude
in front of a white man
Close to my tribe   he probably guessed we're lesbians
said that   to see what we'd do
which was to keep on doin what we had been doin
That gay white man stopped talking about how much he loved
hot peppers
That Chippewa said   *Not too much for me   Don eat fish*
probably another joke we ignored   I said
The grocery was fresh out of buffalo & deer
Much later that gay white man called that Chippewa a drunk
        we both stared at a different floor
        in a different silence just as sharp
        & hot

CAROLINA PESQUEIRA

La Madre

Yo soy La Madre
la que vigila
la que espera.
Lloro, grito
Dolor todo el día.
Que importa...
Se mueran niños en mis brazos.
Se mueran niños lejos de aqui,
pedacitos de carne en un nido de la tierra;
el pensamiento un huevo enterrado
en lo hondo de la carne
en lo hondo del lodo.
En lo hondo de la garganta
de la vida
un llanto está esperando nacer,
un anhelo de ternura
una abundancia de calidez
anidado en mi pecho.
Yo soy La Madre
la que vigila
la que espera.
Lloro, grito
Dolor todo el día.
Que importa...

CAROLINA PESQUEIRA

The Mother

I am the Mother
who watches,
who waits.
I cry, I scream
pain all day.
So what.
Children die in my arms.
Children die far away,
pieces of flesh gathered in a nest of earth,
the egg of thought buried
deep in the flesh
deep in the dirt.
Deep in the throat
of life
a cry waits to be born
a longing for softness
a wealth of warmth
nestled in my breast.
I am the Mother
who watches,
who waits.
I cry, I scream
pain all day.
So what.

S. Renee Bess

Driving Alone To P-Town Is No Easy Thing

Solange checked her appointment calendar to make sure that she wasn't leaving anyone in a jam. No, everything was covered. The parent-school coalition workshops wouldn't begin until October first. Her staff of tutors could cover the September jitters that her overzealous parents would begin to experience by mid-month.

After one last glance at her schedule book, and a momentary pang of guilt about her abandoned-at-the-vet kitty, Solange was ready for the road. She put her suitcase and beach gear into the trunk, methodically arranged her toll money and maps, and settled in behind the steering wheel. It never entered her mind that she was running away when she phoned her favorite Provincetown bed and breakfast to request a week-long reservation. She was taking a much deserved vacation, that's all; her first since she started her consultation business two years ago, her first vacation away alone. But Alicejane, her running buddy, had certainly accused her of being on the run.

"Why drive all by yourself for eight long hours to a place where you'll only feel lonelier? I thought you were gonna relax at home. This trip is silly. You're just runnin' away, girl, and that won't solve your problem."

"I'm not running away, Alicejane. I'm just tired of things going wrong. After I broke up with Sarah, I was determined to stay single for a long time. I thought I had learned a lesson. She was bed-hopping with every new thing that came along, and I never knew it until it was too late. How could I have been so stupid to make that mistake twice? Darnelle must have seen me coming."

"You know what's gonna happen. You'll go to the bar and think about her, or you'll go for long walks and think about her. You'll see someone who reminds you of her, and you'll feel bad. You'll probably pack some of your tapes in the car, play them all the way there, and by the time you get to P-Town, you'll be missing her so much that you'll want to turn around and come right back and park on her doorstep."

"That, Alicejane, is ridiculous. Anyway, I've stopped missing her so much. After weeks and weeks, it doesn't hurt as much. There is something about spending time alone that is downright curative."

"Alone, just means lonely to me."

"Well, not to me. And if I get tired of being solo, maybe I'll have a wild fling. Who knows?"

"That doesn't sound like you, girl."

"Why not? It's for damn sure that Darnelle isn't mourning all by her lonesome."

"You don't know that, Solange. I heard...."

"I don't care what you heard, Alicejane Cooper. What counts is what I saw the last time I went to her office. I went to try to talk with her, to try to mend things. I felt like such a fool..."

Solange pulled away from her driveway at four a.m. An early departure, she figured, would get her to her destination by noon or shortly thereafter. The Pennsy Turnpike merged into Jersey's. She drove easily, and filled the car with the sounds of the radio talk-show stations. For the first two-and-a-quarter hours, she didn't give a thought to her business, to the other drivers, to the emerging dawn, nor to Darnelle.

Her first stop on the Garden State parkway gave her a chance to refill her coffee thermos. The prospect of the rest of the drive alone was empowering. Why had Alicejane been so sure that driving alone to P-Town was no easy thing? Solange went to the restroom where she splashed water on her face and smoothed her slacks and closely trimmed Afro. She left the rest stop with the beach and the dunes of P-Town on her mind.

Cruising into the last toll plaza on the Parkway, Solange was jarred by a memory, when a female toll collector's hand called attention to itself by pressing the change into Solange's. That anonymous pressure recalled Darnelle's hands, firm and gentle at the same time, a kind of giving as well as taking gentleness. Too bad, she scolded herself, that she had placed so much trust in those hands; that she had felt an instant confidence from their first meeting at the Community Health Center, where Solange had been hired to conduct a series of meetings for parents.

"I remember you. You're Darnelle Masters. We were in high school and college together, weren't we? But I don't think that I saw you at our reunion last year."

"I was there, though, and I saw you. Is it still Solange Thomas, or do you have a married name? I think I remember hearing that you got married."

"Yes and no. Yes, I was married very briefly, a stupid mistake. (Why am I telling her all of this?) When I divorced, I took back my maiden name."

"That's great. I admire women who do that. So how have you been since the reunion?"

"Fine. I've started a new line of work. I'm in the consulting business. That's why I'm here tonight, to do a workshop for parents on assertive skills."

"You're from Consult-to-Learn?"

"Yes, it's my company. I've left the school system, but I didn't leave teaching. What about you?"

"My colleagues and I here at the Health Center arranged this series of workshops."

"You're a physician?"

"Yes, I'm a pediatric surgeon. I'm part of a group practice. It keeps us all busy, but I love it."

"That's great. So, it's Dr. Masters."

"Yes, but it's still Darnelle to a former classmate. Listen, we're about ready to start. When tonight's meeting is over, we'll need to talk about the others in the series. There's a diner across the street. Let's go over there and compare notes."

"Fine, I skipped dinner, so coffee and sandwich would be great."

Darnelle, of the medium length afro, clear brown eyes and tea with lemon complexion, was born a take charge person. She was used to arranging consultations, examining people and problems, forming a diagnosis and deciding upon a protocol of treatment. But, take charge or not, she was unsettled by seeing Solange that evening. Although Darnelle's profession was her lover, she did remember Solange. In fact, she had gone to her class reunion with the sole purpose of seeing her, after a friend of a friend told her that they had a lot in common. Halfway through the evening, she spotted Solange from the vantage point of a crowded banquet table. As she watched her, Darnelle could see that Solange had not lost her persuasive smile and quiet manner. A womanly maturity allowed her to project her comfort with herself. When Darnelle freed herself from a conversation with two friends, it was too late. She couldn't find Solange.

Until that evening at the Health Center, Darnelle kept a fleeting memory-image of Solange tucked away behind her daily routines of office and hospital. But the instant that they met, the moment that she saw Solange's direct gaze, heard her voice as she answered the parents' questions, heard her laughter and felt her gentleness, Darnelle knew that she wanted to replace a vague memory with a beautiful reality. She knew why she hadn't forgotten Solange.

The highway swept past Solange as she moved through coastal Connecticut. Talk radio switched to a Motown oldies show: "Can I Get a Witness?", "Shotgun", "Since I Lost My memories"... Darnelle, cool and organized... athletically coordinated... well planned button-down oxford, taking achievement for granted.

Determined to drive memoryless, Solange fixed her attention on the traffic. Sailing through Westport, Groton, Mystic. Mystic, where she had phoned Darnelle a week after seeing her that first time at the Health Center.

"Darnelle, I'm glad that I got you at a free moment."
"Solange, it's good to hear your voice. Where are you?"
"In the lobby of the Mystic, Connecticut Hilton. We're taking a lunch break."
"How's the seminar going?"

"Great! It's given me some good ideas for the next two
meetings at the Health Center."

"Is that why you called me? I'm disappointed. I was
hoping you'd say that you enjoyed our late dinner last
week."

"I did enjoy the dinner, especially your company."

"I'm glad to hear that. How long will you be away?"

"I'll be back on Thursday afternoon."

"Why don't we have dinner Thursday night? I'm free
about eight, barring any emergencies, and I'd like to hear all
about your great ideas."

"Is that why you want to have dinner? I'm disappointed.
I was hoping you'd say that you'd enjoy our spending some
time together."

"Touché. You've just won yourself a dinner at my place."

"I'll see you on Thursday at eight, then."

"You bet. Have a good trip, Solange."

Solange came out of her reverie and made a pit stop in Westerly,
Rhode Island. Barely noticing what she ate, she leafed through the
stack of local attraction leaflets she had picked up at the restaurant's
entrance. Those, and a recalcitrant child seated at the table next to
her, claimed her attention. The little girl was obviously a champion
at playing and winning the "I'll-scream-and-embarrass-the-hell-out-
of-you-until-I-get-my-way" game. Sure enough, her parents
rewarded her with an ice cream cone. Solange mused about the
intelligence of kids. They're so smart, yet so underestimated by
adults. Even the youngest child who has been the victor in a power
duel with a parent becomes a master fencer....fencer.....

"Why are we fencing like this, Solange? We've been
seeing each other for weeks now, whenever we can both be
free. We talk and share and laugh. When we leave each
other, I can't wait until I see you again. But just as we're
feeling close, I see you retreating, pulling away from me. Can
you tell me why?"

"I don't know that I'm ready for anything more."

"Why?"

"I'm a little shy of relationships right now. My last one didn't turn out too well."

"But, Solange, I'm no Sarah. I'm not anything like Sarah."

Darnelle stretched her long legs and arms, and, in one movement, included Solange, pulling her within the borders of her arms.

"I don't intend to use and hurt you. You are special to me. And I want you."

Solange remained in Darnelle's arms as she slipped hers around Darnelle's waist. They gazed into each others' eyes and souls until neither could continue breathing without joining in a deep kiss. Solange moaned and touched Darnelle's face softly with the back of her fingers. With mutual and complete understanding, they lay down together. Quickly undressing herself, and then Solange, Darnelle began the love liturgy with light as a breath kisses to Solange's calves, to her knees, to the insides of her thighs. Solange kneaded Darnelle's shoulders, and encouraged the kisses to her stomach and breasts by calling Darnelle's name, softly but steadily. A sweet buzz arched the connection between her breasts and her love center. With the perception of all new lovers, Darnelle knew when to slip into Solange and whisper, moan and move her until they both rocked together and sang out their coming, joyfully.

Massachusetts was whizzing by. New Bedford, Fall River, the signs for the island ferries, Route 6. The music on the stronger signalled radio stations was annoying in its sameness. Time for a tape, any random tape from the glove compartment. Anita Baker, "Watch Your Step". Rain began to fall as Solange passed the Barnstable exit. She turned on the windshield wipers, and then had to turn up the tape's volume to compete with the rhythm across the windshield. The eleven o'clock traffic slowed to a crawl as a disabled motorist shrugged to the side of the road. That poor driver with a car emergency on a rainy road.....

"But you said you had an emergency, Darnelle. That's

why we couldn't meet."

"It was an emergency, Solange."

"It took all that time? What was the problem?"

"An appendectomy. We had to be sure there was a problem before we went into the o.r., and then we had to hurry because the boy's appendix had begun to rupture."

"Then what?"

"Then what? You really don't understand my job, do you? I can't just cut, yank something out, wash my hands and wave good-bye. I had to be sure that the little boy was stable. There were signs of infection because of the rupture.

"I understand your job, Darnelle. And I admire the kind of doctor you are, how you care for your patients. What I don't understand in this case is how much you're caring for this patient's mother. I don't understand why you waited for the patient to stabilize at the patient's mother's apartment. That's where your partner, Jerry, told me I could reach you."

Silence.

"Honey, I used to go out with Sheila some time ago. I knew that she was upset about her son, and it seemed like the right thing to do. Nothing happened."

"I need to know if there's any connection between Sheila and the last two evenings you've been unavailable."

"Yes, there is a connection. Could I explain?"

"Forget it. I've heard it all before."

Dennis, Orleans, Brewster, then Welfleet sloshed by under her tires as she decreased her normal speed on the rain-stained highway. Well into the eighth hour of her journey, she felt tired and stiff, as if her body would always be in the behind-the-wheel posture. Eyes gritty with forced concentration she plodded through Truro and decided to turn onto 6A, taking her into North Truro and Provincetown. Passing the privately owned cottages, she held her breath as she always did when approaching the last rise, the one which rewarded her with her first view of P-Town. Wet, calm and gray, the town spread itself in front of her, like an old friend.

"Oh, excuse me. I'm an old friend of Darnelle's."

Sheila quickly stepped away from an obvious embrace with Darnelle.

Solange achingly managed, "Yes, I know. But I'm the one who should be excused for intruding. Darnelle, I didn't realize that you weren't alone. The secretaries have all left. I wanted to discuss the next round of parenting work-shops. If I had known that you were busy, believe me, I wouldn't have come in. We have plenty of time yet to talk about the workshops."

"We can talk now, Solange. Sheila was just leaving."

"So am I. I'll be extremely busy in the next few weeks , so I'll phone you when my schedule permits."

Darnelle had no chance to explain the embrace of thanks for a fully recovered son. Solange left the office quickly, disappearing from Darnelle for the second time in their lives.

Bearing to the right, onto Bradford Street, Solange drove the last mile toward her lodging. She checked in and felt grateful for the familiarity of her favorite room and of her warm hostess. She showered, put on fresh clothes, found her rain slicker in the car trunk and decided to paddle the streets, her streets, until she reached the Pied and a Bloody Mary. There wouldn't be a crowd this time in the afternoon.

The bar always looked smaller in the daylight. Taking shelter from the rain, there were about a dozen women scattered throughout the room. The sliders leading to the deck were closed in deference to the gale outside. Solange ordered her drink, and toasted her safe arrival to her reflection in the mirror behind the bartender. The music, without bodies to absorb the volume, was very loud. Fingering an ad for a Lesbian Whale watch, Solange struck up a conversation with a bar-mate.

"I've heard that there are plenty of whales in these waters in the summer. Do you suppose they're still here now, in September?"

"Sure. That whale watch trip is great! I went on it last year, and we must've seen about fifteen different whales. They're beautiful. If you went, you'd enjoy yourself."

It never ceased to amaze Solange that she could start a bar conversation with a white woman without a second thought. She never, or almost never, considered it a pickup attempt. And surely, most white lesbians never considered her chatting with them a preamble to anything further. She had experienced that black lesbians were not always obvious to their white counterparts. And there was always a certain loneliness attached to being invisible to people with whom you shared so much, when those people preferred to share so little with you.

"How big is this boat? It doesn't look large enough to go ten miles out to sea."

"It's big enough. Are you worried about getting seasick? That won't happen, especially if the weather's good and the weather's calm."

Solange had been seasick once in her life, and once was more than enough.

"Have another Bloody Mary and keep my beer company."

"Thanks. And here's to the Lesbian Whale Watch! Do you think that means a trip especially for lesbians who want to watch whales, or are there lesbian whales out there?"

"That's pretty clever. Uh, are you here waiting for someone?"

The stranger, sensing far more than simply a drinking partner for the rainy night ahead, decreased the space between herself and Solange. A new arrival seated herself on the other side of Solange, and the beer drinker wanted to convey her claim of familiarity.

"They always have Dramamine on board, you know. You won't get sick. Listen, if you think you're gonna go, maybe I'll go too. It's more fun if you go with a friend, and I'd like to be a friend of yours. My name is Sandy."

Despite her post eight hour drive second drink, Solange sensed the music's increasing pulse and the closeness of the barmate's body to hers. She was on the verge of agreeing to more than a whale watching voyage, when she felt the slight pressure on her arm.

"You don't really want to go out watching whales, do you, Baby?"

Solange pulled herself back from the verge and turned her barstool half-way around in time to gaze directly into Darnelle's clear brown eyes. A flood of words, accusations, recriminations zoomed through her mind. But all she could say was, "Why did you have to cheat with Sheila? I trusted you."

"You weren't wrong for trusting me. But you didn't trust me as much as you thought you did. If you had, we would have talked. I won't deny what you saw, Solange. That would be wrong and stupid. But what you saw didn't mean what you thought."

"Then just what did it mean?"

"It meant absolutely nothing. I've tried every way I know how to contact you. Your answering machine is always on at home, and you never returned my messages. The one day I did get you on the phone at your office, you were so cold, all business."

"My staff was right there. What did you expect?"

"I didn't care about them. I wanted to explain. I didn't give a shit about the parenting workshop, nor about who was going to appear in your place. You never gave me a chance to explain."

"So now you're here, trying to screw up my vacation?"

"I'm not here to ruin your week. I'm here because I wanted to see you. Alicejane told me where you were."

"That's friendship for you."

"Solange, please, Baby, we need to talk."

"I'm surprised that you've taken the time to drive up here. Is Sheila back at your room in some motel?"

"Of course not. Anything more than a friendship with Sheila is pure fiction. Look, I can't take all this distance you've put between us. We had so much to build on, Solange. We still do. If you tell me no, today, I'll be back tomorrow. And if you refuse me then, I'll return the next day. I'm not going away. I'm not giving us up."

"And I'm not willing to sleep with you one night, and look over my shoulder for Sheila the next night."

"I missed two evenings with you because Sheila called me to look at her son. He wasn't feeling well, and her regular pediatrician couldn't find anything. He wasn't a textbook appendicitis case. I don't love Sheila. I love you."

"I want so much to believe you."

"Please do. I need you, Solange."

Solange drew Darnelle close to her, as Darnelle rested her arms on Solange's shoulders. They looked at each other for as much time as it took for some of the anger and hurt to begin falling away. Then, they kissed a kiss that felt like the first time. Solange eased off the barstool and slipped her hand into Darnelle's. Excusing themselves from the whale watch enthusiast, they left the bar.

Two rain-wrapped souls walked, arms entwined, back to the women's bed and breakfast, where they talked far into the night before powerfully loving away the memory of the eight hour lonely ride to P-Town.

Cravings

RITZ CHOW

thinking A.L.O.T.

thinking bread
one broken night

fingers deep
into dough
inside light
past grey carpet
in the thread of heat
above a brow

on the tip of teeth
sweeping
lips:

maybe you

yeast like pebbles
rolling
to water
to be persuaded
down
to time

yes then
maybe
the heat in
eyes
bakes
the rising
lashes

the breast
inside
the breast

comin' out
comin' round
to a table
to a cup
across a woman

brown loaves
and dawn

Sweet and Simple Surprise Loaf

2 eggs
1 cup milk
1 tablespoon melted butter
1/2 cup pure maple syrup, honey, or molasses

3 cups whole wheat flour, or a mixture of whole
wheat and white flour
2 teaspoons baking powder
1 teaspoon salt

Add your Lover's favourite fruit or nut.

Beat eggs, milk, butter, and syrup together.
Mix flour, baking powder, and salt and stir into the liquids.
Fold in fruit or nuts.
Pour into an oiled loaf pan. Bake at 350 for 1 hour. Cool on rack.

Brown Rolls

Makes: 4-5 dozen rolls
3 cups warm water
2 tablespoons dry yeast
1/4 cup unsulfured molasses
1/4 cup unrefined corn germ oil
1 egg, beaten
1 tablespoon sea salt

7 to 8 cups whole wheat flour

Have all ingredients at room temperature.
Stir the water, yeast, molasses, oil, egg, and salt until well blended.
Gradually add the flour and knead until smooth.
Place the dough in an oiled bowl. Turn to coat the dough. Cover
and let rise in a warm place until double in bulk. Punch down.
Shape the dough into desired rolls and place in oiled muffin tins.
Allow rolls to rise until double in size.
Bake for 40 minutes in a preheated oven at 275. Remove from the
oven. Let rolls cool in the tins for 20 minutes. Remove from tins
and cool to room temperature. Wrap in freezer plastic and place in
freezer.

These rolls will keep 1 week unrefrigerated, 2 weeks in the
refrigerator, and 3 months in the freezer.

Refrigerator Rolls: When ready to serve, unwrap and place on an
oiled cookie sheet. Bake 8 to 10 minutes at 400 or until brown.

Freezer Rolls: Unwrap frozen rolls and place on cookie sheet. Put
directly into the oven to brown without thawing first.

CHRYSTOS

I Just Picked the First Ripe

tomato from my garden cherishing her sensual cleft
gold freckles around stiff hairy sepals
Inhaling deeply her sharp smell   my nose pressed
to smooth bursting flesh   Kissing pure skin
planning to eat her like a peach
juice dripping down my neck
very slowly
because it's september after a rainy cool summer
The rest of the vine may stay green
have to be brought inside   carefully wrapped in paper
to eventually turn orange but not red hot
glowing with sun
as this
who could be
the only one

(especially for Janice Gould & Mimi Wheatwind)

Tomato Soup

1 lb fresh tomatoes
2 carrots
2 onions
1 oz sugar
salt and pepper to taste

1 cup milk
2 potatoes
bunch of mixed herbs
1 oz margarine
2 tablespoon flour

Fry the sliced onions lightly in half the margarine. Chop up the tomatoes and dice the potatoes and carrots. Add to the saucepan, place on lid and cook gently over a low heat for 15 minutes, shaking occasionally. Add mixed herbs, sugar, salt and pepper, cover vegetables with stock and simmer until quite tender. Rub through a sieve, rinse the pan and melt the remaining margarine in it. When hot, gradually stir in flour, then milk and add the sieved puree. Cook until rich and creamy.

Tomato Raita

1 lb ripe tomatoes
1 cup shredded coconut
2 Tbs minced green chilies
1/2 tsp salt
2 cups yogurt
1 Tbs vegetable oil
1 1/2 tsp whole mustard seeds
1/2 tsp crushed dried red pepper

Chop the tomatoes coarsely. If you have fresh-grated or pre-grated but unsweetened coconut, combine it with the tomatoes in a bowl. If as sometimes happens, you are only able to find the sweetened kind, soak it first in several rinses of water, then drain thoroughly and add to the tomatoes. Add the chilies, salt and yogurt as well and mix it all up.

Heat the oil in a small skillet and fry the mustard seeds and crushed pepper in it until the mustard seeds start to jump and snap. Pour this all into the yogurt mixture and stir it in quickly.

Chill the raita for several hours before serving.

Serves 6 to 8.

LING HUA CHEN

Papaya

Dreamlover
your cunt
is like the papaya
my grandma eats every morning
Long as her forearm
curved voluptuously
she slices it lengthwise
sets it on a white porcelain plate
and with her spoon scoops out
the rich sharp tangy creamy deep-red orange
flesh
sweet and a little bit salty
mellow
but it can burn your tongue

Small black seeds
fleck the top
shiny and slippery with juice

Soon all that will be left is
the thin deep-green skin
abandoned next to
a spoon
some tea still steaming
and my smiling
grandma

Papaya and Mango Punch

1 cup mango pulp
1 cup papaya pulp
1 cup fresh orange juice
1 teaspoon grated orange rind

1/4 cup lime juice
4 cups water
sugar to taste

Crush slices of mango and papaya to make pulp. Add other ingredients blending well. Sugar to taste and serve chilled or with cracked ice.

Papaya Chutney

Hot East Indian condiments of fruits and peppers, chutneys are
served as a relish, often with curries or cold meats. Some cooks
prefer to use very green, unripe papayas. A partially ripe papaya will
be green flecked with yellow and will feel hard to the touch. Raisins
can be added if desired.

4 cups diced, ripe papaya
1/4 cup sugar
2 chayote, peeled and diced
2 tablespoons ground ginger
1/2 cup vinegar
1 medium-size onion, finely chopped
2 teaspoons salt
2 large sweet green pepper, seeded and finely chopped
2 fresh hot peppers, seeded and chopped
2 1/2 cups water

Combine all the ingredients in a saucepan and simmer gently for
50 minutes, stirring constantly. Remove from the heat, cool, and
pour into a glass jar. Store for later use. Serve with curries or fish.

Note: To make mango chutney, substitute diced partially ripe
mango for papaya and proceed as above.

Makes about 6 cups.

MICHELLE MOHABEER

Starr-Apple

Ambrosia cream - fill
Luscious purple flesh
My lips full on your mound

My tongue probes and teases
You moan in ecstasy

As the wet and warm tongue
Fleetingly darts
From the centre
To the tip of your hot pulsing cunt

You moan... I suck...
I suck the sweet essence of you

Memories of your musky scent permeates my senses
And I am once again filled with desire for you.

Passion Fruit Punch

6 tablespoons passion fruit juice (combination of papaya, mango
and pineapple juice, or any of your favourite fruit juices)
2 tablespoons lime juice
3 tablespoons syrup
7 tablespoons white rum
Dash Angostura bitters
Crushed ice
Grated nutmeg

Place the passion fruit juice, lime juice, syrup, rum and Angostura
into a cocktail shaker. Shake vigorously. Pour over the crushed ice
in a glass. Serve with the grated nutmeg on top.

Serves 2.

MICHELE CHAI

For Karen Lopez

You
cocoa butter touch
lightly caressing
in-side
Salted
Sweet
ackee tongue
teasing teasing
testing
lips,
Engorged
like ripe mango
Smooth
like coconut jelly.
Passion -
fruit juices that escape
throats,
slide past
mouth corners
down cheeks.
You
sweat mauby-bark
bitter sweet
cool down
Pearls
forming
on breasts
sliding past
an arched

torso (then)
Pulsating
like guava pulp
Blended
(into the finest)
Caribbean Cocktails
Spilled -
into ocean spray
off-shore spasms.

Mango Affair

This tart is superb when served with a topping of whipped cream or vanilla ice cream.

4 to 5 ripe mangoes, peeled and thinly sliced
1 cup honey
1/2 cup water
1 teaspoon cornstarch
2 egg yolks, beaten
1 teaspoon ground cinnamon
2 tablespoons butter
9-inch shell

Combine the mango slices, honey and water in a saucepan and cook over medium heat for 15 minutes, stirring constantly. Mix the cornstarch with just enough water to form a paste and blend with the egg yolks. Add to the mango mixture and cook for another 5 minutes, or until it becomes thick and smooth. Stir in the cinnamon and butter.

Pour into the tart shell and bake in a preheated 350 F oven for 30 minutes, or until filling is well set and the top is golden brown. Cool and serve at room temperature.

Makes 8 servings.

Guava Nectar

ripe guavas
lime juice
granulated sugar
nutmeg

Crush some ripe guavas and to every cup of pulp use 1 cup sugar, one teaspoon lime juice and 1/8 teaspoon nutmeg. Mix pulp with sugar, stir and bring to the boil. Simmer for 25 minutes or longer until guava is cooked. Cool, add lime juice. Chill and serve with ice and grated nutmeg.

Mauby Cool Down

2 oz mauby bark
12 cups water
piece of mace
2 lbs brown sugar

large piece cinnamon (spice)
few cloves
piece dried orange peel

Boil mauby bark in water (about 4 cups) with spice, cloves, mace and orange peel until liquid is very bitter (about 1/2 hour). Strain it off, add the rest of water and sugar until very sweet. Bottle the cooled liquid, leaving neck of bottle unfilled for froth. Cover and leave for 3 days. Serve very cold.

CHRYSTOS

Poem for Lettuce

                    I know
you don't want to be eaten
anymore than a cow or a pig or a chicken does
but   they're the vicious vegetarians
& they say you do
Gobbling up the innocent green beings who gladden
any reasonable person's heart
        I'll tell you little lettuce
you'll see them in cowskin shoes & belts
        & nobody can make sense of that
Those virtuous vegetarians they'll look at you with prim distaste
        while you enjoy your bacon
                    Makes me want
to buy some cowboy movie blood capsules
        Imagine an introduction
I'd like you to meet Lily, she's a non-smoking non-drinking
vegetarian separatist Pisces with choco-phobia
& I smile
while secretly biting down on the capsules concealed in my cheeks
        then shake her hand   drooling blood
I whisper
Hi   I'm a flaming carnivorous double Scorpio who'll eat anything
& as she wilts in dismay   trembles with trepidation
hisses with disgust
Ah   then   little lettuces
        we'll have our moment of laughing revenge

    for Elizabeth Markell

306

Fish Soup

First clean the fish, if you have four medium
sized fish,
Cut your fish in four or five pieces.
Then put in pot to boil for one hour or less.
Put half water in cooking pot.
Then if you think your fish is done or cooked
take all the bones from the fish
Then smash it and put it in the pot.
The pot that you used to cook your fish in, of course,
and then you use the same water.
Let it boil for one hour more.
Then you mix a little flour into a mixing bowl.
Then water, and put this into the cooking pot to
thicken the soup.
This makes six or eight servings.
Of course you can put salt or pepper in if you wish.

Escovitch (Fish)

This is a development of the classic Spanish dish called Escabeche.

2 sweet peppers - 1 red, 1 green
1 teaspoon hot pepper, seeded and chopped
2 bay leaves
3 onions, sliced in thin half rings
1-1 1/2 tablespoons sea salt
2 cloves garlic, thinly sliced
6 blades chives, tied together
Black pepper, freshly ground
1/2 pint water
1/4 pint vinegar (preferably white)
3 fl ozs olive oil
2 1/2 lb red snapper, filleted
Juice of 1 lime

Put the sweet peppers, hot pepper, bay leaves, onions, salt, garlic, the bunch of chives and a little black pepper into a pot.
Pour in the water, vinegar and 3 tablespoons of oil, and bring to the boil. Turn down the heat, cover and simmer gently until the vegetables are tender but still fairly firm. In the meantime, pour the rest of the oil into a heavy frying pan and when hot fry the fish, a fillet or two at a time, until lightly brown on both sides.
Place the fried fillets into a large serving dish with some depth and pour the hot vinegar mixture over the fish. Discard the bay leaves and chives and add the lime juice. Serve hot or refrigerate to serve cold.

This is also excellent as a main dish.

Serves 6.

DENISE MARIE

Restaurant Talk

Conversation for a
food hunger.
Meant pleasure, talk.
Enjoyment spread on a
serving platter.
Smells of talking
about different tastes.
A walk to eat.
Table manners.
Edible orders.
Rules for a table, set
in placement.
Etiquette chosen instead
of home.
A casual meeting.

"Handi Snacks"

Treats of eats,
Food that is junk,
Munchies
Coffee, tea or soda
Chips, chocolate and
cake
A tasteful delight!
School-time finds,
after a study session.
Midnight hunger,
Making tracks,
Fridge raids,
Pleasant bitefuls.

Laura Irene Wayne

I Too Like to Eat Out

I too like to eat
to eat out
I like to eat among the brown, black brush
pushing, parting, letting
my tongue graze amongst the dew
searching, touching, tasting
the honey of the flower
I too like to eat
to eat out
massaging its petals into splendid form
watching its growth harden, flourish
watering, eating to fill my insatiable appetite
reaching in drinking its sweet wine
filling up on arousal, excitement
I too like to eat
to eat out
I relish
knowing my hunger will arise again
and I will find myself
among the brush
I too like to eat
to eat out

The Wanting and the Passion

TAMAI KOBAYASHI

memory, need and desire

memory

trying to remember the feel of her skin between warm sheets, body
smooth, skin brown from sun. she is taller than me
stronger too. she tells me of herself, old hurts, stories of
the refugee camp and journeys by sea, stories of old lovers.
her body is solid, her legs hold me up, her hips thrusting.
I remember running my teeth along her thighs, the tremor
of her body, the welcome of lips parted in wetness. I rub my
cheeks against her mound, pressing her thighs wider with my
tongue flecks tender flesh, outer lips, slowly circling
inward. I tease her lightly with my breath. she moans and
how she moans. my heart and clit are beating in tune and I
want to feel her come, to bury myself in her cunt.
my tongue slips between her lips, tasting her, knowing
her pleasure, building a rhythm in the wave of her hips, in
the pull of her thighs. sucking out her lips, my hands
squeeze and slowly release. I am drawing myself into her as
she begs. stroking her centre, I slip my fingers into her
as she comes, deeper with every thrust.
she rests.
I lie cradled on her belly, a smile and the taste of her
on my lips. she lifts me, rubbing her thighs against me,
sucking at my breasts, tongue darting with the edge of her
teeth. her hands are everywhere. she has pushed me back
onto the bed, thighs streaming with wetness. she kisses me,
hungry, hungry, but pulls away as I respond. her hands
stroke my body, fingers dancing fire. she slips lower, from
breast to belly and there, she's between my legs, teasing me
as I lift my hips to her. she takes them easily, strong as
she is. I don't know what she does but I'm crying, full of
her, tongue, hands, fingers dancing. I come flinging myself
into her and she takes me to her rest.

need

she is thirty years old. this I know. smile is kind,
hesitant. and beautiful. I think she thinks I am odd, an
angry youngster, raging against the world. I puzzle her as
she puzzles me.
she towers over me. yet she is uncertain, not knowing
where I am coming from. and I can only wonder about her.
is she or isn't she? what are her needs, her desires? will
she turn me away?
I dream about her, dreams of hot sex and crumpled sheets,
my lips on her soft breasts, along her strong thighs. I want
to hear her cry out, her fingers slipping along my back, her
tongue in my mouth, in my ears. I want and the wanting is
urgent, painful.
her skin is brown, golden, for we are people of rice,
fisherfolk and farmers, her arms strong, shoulders broad.
I long to stroke the length of her back, to sink into her
breasts, to fill my mouth with her nipples and roll my tongue,
stroke by stroke. I want to move against her, heart bursting, back
arched, to see her eyes widen in surprise, pulled beyond, to
this magical beginning, to feel her move, beyond herself, to
feel her in me, in this wetness of salted honey, body loose,
skin smooth, before everything I knew.

desire

I want to nibble on your ears fuck you like you've
never been fucked before suck your toes spread your thighs
I want to make you come woman wild shouting begging for more
I want to tongue your nipples trill on your clit rub the
juices on my lips and kiss you in that wetness
I want to fuck you woman like you've never been fucked before
I want to rub up against you on the dance floor unzip your
pants slip my hand inside in front of everyone I want them
to know who you're going to fuck tonight I want to rip off
your shirt rake my fingers down your back bite your thighs

I want to kiss you long and hard my hand in your pussy
fingers stroking your wetness I want to sit on your face and
feel my juices over your nose mouth cheeks chin
I want to cry out as your fingers fill me your mouth devouring
I want to come knees weak hips wild laughter soft in darkness
I want to hold you woman hold you and moan your name in my
coming

CHRYSTOS

Sestina for Ilene

Taking you my fist becomes a rose
opening into our journey where wings
move over deep water dark with my tongue curling
into your screaming joy your flushed red breasts
Trail of crimson petals I paint along your throat
Your thighs clench my head until I'm near the edge

of losing breath flying into this dawning edge
where our hearts pound one drum Our bed a rose
As I open my eyes drift slow your throat
flutters alive dancing hungry with bright wings
My free hand reaches to stroke your breast
My cheeks wet with your dark hair curling

I'm open to your scarlet openness curling
through my veins   Our bodies blurred no edge
to cut our tongues   My heart dark within my breast
Our fingers twine   My lips suckle your nipples rose
Air soft with songs of our flushed wings
as joy moves deeply red in my humming throat

You suck my toes dancing my throat
open   White water heats rushes through my curling
blood   My thighs tremble open Touch wings
of your tongue as you fling me into this edge
of silken red flowers blurring to rose
I gasp   Squeeze my dancing breasts

My mouth desperate hot to suck your breast
I find you deep growling in the dark your throat
painting inside my skin with roses
My eyes wet petals   My fingers curling
as you lift my ass & enter me edge
to edge so deep I find my hungry wings

soaring out my love clenches & rises wings
behind my back opening in my breast
reaching joy thick & drifting to an edge
of losing walls   All my cries pulsing open throated
Deep inside my hungry petals curling
around your hand which must be a rose

Our thighs rose   Wildly throbbing our throats
still sing our wet breasts   Our spirits curling
deep within our dancing edges where we are all wings

for Ilene Samowitz

CHRYSTOS

Dream Lesbian Lover

is there when I get home from work but allows me silence
to unravel or better yet   isn't there
but has left a note & a little surprise
She rubs my feet for hours
She wants to love me till I can't stand no more
& she rolls over to me so sweet
Dream lover cooks me hot meals & washes up after
Never arrives without flowers & only brings my favourites
Dream lover has long fingers   a patient playful tongue
& thrives on five hours sleep a night
She could play the harmonica   weave pine needle baskets
bead me a wedding sash   write me lust poems & love poems
Dream lover has eyes deep as the sky   feels herself in others
feels our connecting bones   Rises early in the morning
to make the best rich coffee
Aah she could bring you to your knees with a look
& does
Dreamy woman has a bed of lace & roses & home
She could build a fire in the rain
Could always fix my car for free
Could call the dentist to make my appointment
Iron my shirt when I'm in a hurry
Knows how to make chocolate mousse   chocolate silk pie
black bottom cupcakes   molasses cookies   sour cream cake
lemon pound cake & fresh mango ice cream
O such a creamy dreamy one
She's showing up tonight with a butch pout & a femme slink
a tough stance & a long knowing

Dream lover
she won't have any other girlfriends
but won't mind
if I do

a *Personals Ad* with tongue in cheek

Milagros Paredes

Christmas Eve Imaginings

last night as my family and i were driving along the linearly lit
mounding L.A. freeway to our friends' house to celebrate christmas
eve, i closed my eyes. My sister called my name, afraid i would fade
away, leaving her alone with the rest, during the long car ride.

I imaged your grand powerful woman body as i see it when
       I raise my eyes towards your rising breasts
       as i stroke my tongue,
       search lusciously
       along
       around your damp thick vulva.
       I pull myself away
       half reluctantly
—slowly brushing my searching face
            devouring your skin—
       and i bury my face
       with your rich breasts
—your flesh
   velvet
       envelops my face
       like ocean waves, salty, soft, deep sounds
       caressing my body
       my heart beats with love lust longing
       for you my love.

C. ALLYSON LEE

Untitled

Can you feel me tonight
holding you tightly
and warmly
all through the night
as you sleep at home
alone?

I am sending you
warm kisses
and love
to lift you up softly
through your dreams.

Feel my hand
clasping yours

assuredly
and affectionately
as you close your eyes
in comforted surrender.

Caridad Rodriguez

The Plan

The password was *Wasabi*.

Rosa had never forgotten it and thought about how long it had been since she'd eaten *sushi* as she stole into the hallway of Mari's flat. The air was crisp and the morning fog had left a damp cold film on her face. The darkened hall was warm with an undisturbed quiet. As she turned to close the door the light stung her eyes and she held back a yawn. She turned and walked through the unlit passage, tucking her hand into the left breast pocket of her jacket, and retrieved the single silver key buried there. A quick soundless roll of the wrist and the door opened like a treasure.

As she tiptoed past bright portraits and wooden masks, she thought about the silver key and Mari's eyes and the plan they had devised so long ago. The door to the bedroom was ajar, and she caught a glimpse of a single female body silhouetted by a white sheet which clung to her like a glove. Rosa took off her shoes and left them silently by the bedroom door. Mari didn't stir. For a long lingering moment Rosa let her gaze caress the outline of this woman who was both so familiar and so unknown.

It had been a crazy and wonderful plan. Over dinner they had made all the arrangements as they fed each other cool morsels of *sushi* dripping with soy sauce; the fiery hot *wasabi*, and the delicate fish flavors bursting inside their mouths. Rosa remembered the sweet delight of crimson pearls of roe exploding on her palate, releasing their salty presence. Mari called them "taste bud orgasms" as each jewel box of Japanese perfection closed behind their teeth. Their evening meal had lasted for hours and it was not until the last taste of spearmint and plum had left their mouths refreshed and clean that Mari had slipped her the single silver key and smiled.

Rosa unwound the electric blue scarf she had wrapped around her neck and tested the strength of the silk between her hands. She looked around Mari's bedroom for the first time. Slivers of light made rippling slices across the shadows on the bed and a vase of blooming irises rested on the dresser. She took a slow breath and with movements that were swift and sure, walked to the bed, grabbed Mari's head in her hands, cupped her mouth, and deftly wrapped the scarf around her eyes.

For the next few moments she held her struggling lover against her breast and felt Mari's heart pounding furiously against her own. Rosa was confident of her strength and her tenderness and waited quietly until Mari's panting sobs subsided. As she removed her hand from Mari's mouth she heard her lover plead softly, "No, please no." Rosa waited for a long moment and listened attentively to Mari's cries and then lay the full weight of her body over her desire, pushing Mari's face down deeper into the folds of the bed, muffling her words. As she pulled another silk band from her belt, she felt the emerald smoothness rub against her own skin. She pulled Mari's arms over her head and tied her hands, first together, and then to the piping of the brushed copper headboard. She had always had a talent for knots.

Only after she had secured her lover's arms, did Rosa pull the covers off Mari's body. She traced the curve of Mari's back, pressing her hands where the sheets had been. Her fingers began to dig deeper into her flesh as she moved down her body, opening her buttocks, and her thighs. Now, Rosa was at the foot of the bed holding Mari's legs apart and peering into the shadow of her sex. She tied first one leg and then the other. She wet her index finger and drew a line between the protruding mounds of Mari's buttocks. She stepped back and saw this unknown passion bound with blue and green and pink fuchsia strips of suspense. She leaned closer and smelled the sex and the fear emanating from Mari's writhing body. She pressed her face against the delicate seashell colored arch of Mari's foot and looking up, noticed the soft golden glow of the body that lay open before her.

Kissing and biting her way up the smooth and shapely legs, she gazed lovingly at the curve of Mari's behind. Wrapping her arms beneath the firm thighs, she lifted her hips to her face and kissed her tightly clenched opening. At once, she felt the weight of her lover's body plunge into the bed as she struggled to get away from the wet heat of Rosa's probing tongue. But Rosa's strength held her open and exposed, and her tongue licked the length of Mari's cleft over and over again, burning her sex.

Mari had never thought it would be like this, that the fear would be so consuming. The doubt. Was she surrendering? and to whom? In her fantasy, she had fought and been subdued, but now the fear had left her paralyzed and weak. She wanted it to stop, just for a moment. She needed to know for sure. Her helplessness collapsed upon her as she felt her vulva being filled and explored. A tongue pierced her anus and she felt naked and shy.

She had surrendered and for the next several hours, (or were they days?) she saw only a blue haze of light and felt her whole body disarmed. She was penetrated over and over again, never knowing where the next attack would come from. She would be moved and retied, forced to shift positions only to find herself more accessible to the stranger's probes. At times, the stranger would kiss her so lovingly, rubbing soft flesh over her belly or breasts. Other times she felt only hard groping hands, teeth biting into her nipples, and her sex. For moments that seemed endless, the hands and the Other would be gone and she could only hear the stranger's rhythmic breathing and sense the eyes that were piercing her skin.

Rosa took her lover again and again, never tiring of having her desire spread out before her. She never allowed Mari to reach her pleasure, always stopping short so she could watch her lover's agony as she squirmed in frustrated rapture. Hours passed and once again Rosa felt the heat of Mari's pearl swell between her lips. Her tongue was quick and knowing. She thought of her own wet and throbbing sex and rubbed her own protruding clitoris as she felt the tender swollen labia of her lover bloom under her tongue. She slipped her fingers between the wet succulent lips and pushed her hand deep into her lover's cave. At once, Mari's body shuddered and arched with contorted pleasure. Rosa felt the gush of her lover's orgasm as she pushed her fist deeper and deeper inside her. Mari's body rose and met each lunge with her own, she screamed out in ecstasy and pain. After the flood of piercing desire eased into waves of pulsating emotion, Mari whispered, "I am yours."

How had it happened? How could she let herself come with such abandon to this faceless stranger. She had never allowed herself to take so much of everything she wanted. Would it stop now? Would she be free to cover her own nakedness, squeeze her legs together to shelter her sex? She wanted to be held, to be untied. She wanted to be embraced tenderly and to know for sure. As if reading her mind, the stranger came and lay next to her silently. Mari felt the nude heat of another woman's body and drifted to sleep.

In the haze of a sleep that was a dream and so much more, Mari heard the doorbell and felt the warmth that had been pressed against her rise and leave the room. Slowly she opened her eyes and fixed her gaze on the vase of irises bursting with purple and yellow vulvas. Realizing that she could see again she closed her lids, and felt the tingling blue ache of her body. She stretched her limbs, curled into herself again, and waited. After several moments of padded steps in the hall, murmured voices, and the folding of crisp bills, a beautiful smiling woman breezed into the fading autumn light of Mari's bedroom. Rosita. Her own black dressing gown flapping behind her as she came closer to the bed carrying two lacquered boxes, and chopsticks.

Rosita sat softly at the edge of the bed, crossing her long graceful legs. Her ebony lashes opened and closed languidly, carefully studying the prize before her. She lifted the lid of the shining black box and revealed a colorful cluster of *sushi* and *sashimi* wonders to Mari's questioning eyes. Expertly she dabbed her chopsticks into the green puddy on the plate and swirled it into the waiting sweet dark pool of liquid. Rosa lifted a tender morsel of pink flesh between the wooden vice held between her fingertips and raised her eyes to meet her lover's gaze. It had been much too long. "*Wasabi?*" she asked, and her lover surrendered again.

Karla E. Rosales

Erotic Reflection IX
translated by Carmen Chavez

Mujer	Woman
extrano el toque conocido	I miss that familiar touch
de tus manos fuertes	your strong hands
sobre mi peil	caressing my skin
acariciandome	
	Woman
Mujer	I remember nights
recuerdo las noches de tequila	filled with tequila
mi cuerpo	your tongue
la sal	in search of my salt
que tu lengua buscaba	my body
Mujer	Woman
tengo tu imagen	your image
pintado sobre mi ser.	is painted
	in my soul.

CAROL CAMPER

Gaia

Sleek she is
Sinew teases under taut bright skin of ebony.
Those breasts of hers like grapes
Black, round, glossy
Tipped by gleaming nipples
Black pearls.
Black silk satin beauty
Red silk gliding easily down moonlit shoulders.

Firm and pleasing
Her buttocks moulded as if by my own hands.
See how they move
As she walks they undulate.
I appreciate.
And when she dances
Oh, when she dances!

Her lovely face
Regal, smiling in my fortunate direction.
Glittering black eyes
Black opals' liquid mystery and depth.
Sloping, sensuous nose
Nostrils flared in anticipation
Velvety chocolate lips
Shaped by the fingertips - of some African goddess.

She is Gaia
Brown like the earth.
Round, firm, strong.
I long to plunge into her ocean depths,
Send waves crashing to her shores.
Her blackness like the vaulted sky
Of night - leaves me breathless,
Gazing helpless into the matchless heaven of her.

CAROL CAMPER

Untitled

Don't you just love to have your pussy sucked!
I mean, doesn't it just bring it on home
That your cunt is the centre of your being
(I mean the exact middle).
Physically and sensationally.
Don't you just love her tongue so paradoxical
Hard and insistent or
Dainty so dainty flitting crazily across your clit
Don't you just love it?
Don't you just!

Donayle L. Hammond

Tell Me

her legs parted easily
willing
inviting
I knew what she wanted
needed
had to have
and I was prepared to give it
but not right away
I wanted it to last
I wanted her to beg

as we kissed
my hand moved along her slightly rounded stomach
and down her thighs
her moans increased
the movement of her tongue quickened
my lips travelled up her cheek to her ear
I whispered
tell me what you want
she moved
that wasn't good enough
I had to hear it

I moved on top of her
the way her hands grabbed my ass
told me that she liked me there
I moved to a rhythm
I felt her quiver
I wanted her
She wanted me

but I had to hear it
tell me what you want
still no reply
she thought her reaction was good enough
But I had to hear it

my lips
found that place on her neck
her back arched
as my mouth made an excursion down her body
her hands were in my hair
pushing my head lower
as though I wouldn't be able
to find the way myself
my hands gripped her hips
my mouth stayed on her thighs
lingering there for a while
licking and nibbling
letting her know what was in store for her
believe me I wanted it
but I had to hear it,
i knew she couldn't take any more of my teasing
neither could I

softly she said
I want you to make me cum
at first I didn't hear her
she said it
over and over again
I buried my face between her legs
her body shook
sweet obscenities came from her mouth
telling me all the things she wanted
her words hot as her pussy

she shivered uncontrollably
as she came
she lifted my face
gently placing her lips on mine
she reached down to my cunt
a moan escaped from my throat
softly she took my ear lobe into her mouth
and with great pleasure
she said
tell me what you want
and I did just that.

LELETI TAMU

Wrap Around Joy

One finger maybe two
buried knuckle deep sticky sweet in you my
wrap around joy

Finger tips slip in easily as you wrap around me
Open again my love to three fingers maybe four
Knuckle deep sticky sweet inside you
I will take you there
We linger and begin again
Breath in slowly exhale now
Four fingers maybe more
Open again just a little bit more my love
Take me
buried knuckle deep sticky sweet inside you
my wrap around joy

LELETI TAMU

Expectations
One Snowy November Night

Lover so reserved
so intent on gauging
how much you give

When we dance your lips cuddle
my arms in secrecy
I follow -
like J'Ouvert morning
wanting more
wanting more
Eyes cool as copper
hard to read
Watch me
as you take my shape
I could wait
But hunger keeps me unsteady
You keep your soul away and
I follow like night
needing more
Your eyes open as I make
you promises
I cannot blame you for leaving
water in my eyes as you uncover me
peel back my skin without even knowing

How much is too much
what you know scares you
things I cannot ask
keep me silent

Expectations
My lover so reserved
one of us is lying

CHERYL CLARKE

Living as a lesbian on the make

Straight bars ain't so bad
though filled with men
cigarette smoke
and juke noises.
A martini straight up and jazz
can take me beyond their static.
Alone she came in denim and a
magenta tee
hair cut to a duck tail
ordered Miller's and smoked two
kinds of cigarettes
sat at a table close but distant
was pretty and I was lonely
and knew she was looking for a woman.
All through the set I looked at her
until she split in the middle of it.
I almost followed her out but was too
horny to leave the easy man talking
loud shit to me for a seduction I'd
have to work at.
The music sounding tasty
saxophone flugelhorn bass and drums
hitting familiar riffs
the titles escaping me.

VICTORIA LENA MANYARROWS

visionary woman

you move with such power
while my body holds you close
surrounding you with warmth
caressing you with passion
we are lovers without warning
as the evening sun begins its descent
marking time with a shine and a glow, leaving shadows
to fall across your face, gently now as the sun's heat
fades

i call to you with silent words, my eyes searching thru
your smiles
the lightness that you carry is a happiness ready to share
you are smiling as your eyes close, taking me with your
power deep
into your quiet places where the light always shines

visionary woman keep holding me close & within your
gaze
while the moon rises in the sky
and the sun sets
and we melt into this sky of everlasting memory
remembering these touches, these kisses
these never-dying passions...

RITZ CHOW

a moon to waves

my shiny new old lover gleams from the edge of the futon where
she has cradled the pillow against her closed breaths. her bare
back, brown in the thin light that has curved around the dark
paper blinds, approaches and recedes with each unconscious
second.

beyond this traced territory, our blood and bones rest. there is
greenery, a sun to feed our dark bodies, and wind and rain to
sweep our hair. skin and conversation make way into thick
cotton, in nights becoming dawn becoming. all the stories of
before in the here and now of this waking room. the rug on the
floor is coloured by steps. if shaken, the sheets release anger
and laughter into the still air.

my hand reaches out, opens softly down on inches of air above her
back. heat rises from her, leaves her cooler than october sand.
the skin breathes lungless.

watching her back, naked down to the sheet-covered hips, i play
the possibilities of touch. a move closer. tracing the flow of
hair and the spine line up, then down. her head moves, crushes
the moment in black hair. her left cheek leans toward me, its
thin vessels dance red with oxygen. the early colour of her arms
and legs in my snapping eyes. a seed in an over-turned mind. with
closed eyes, i water blackness.

the clock turns its electricity. the end table is cluttered with
issues: earrings and pamphlets and a glass half-filled. in the
night, bubbles have woven through the liquid, left it less pure.
a sigh surrenders her lips. her breasts break from the rhythm of
heart and lungs, and tear the soft light of the peeking sun.
nipples: diffuse as darkness, or brightness. inclusive moves.
warmth lures my face to her shoulder.

with measured seconds, i draw my hand up along her stomach, over her right breast, touching the edges of the nipple. her eyes flicker, acknowledging. her arms, tanned and sturdy, remove the distance. our breasts meet on a line of heat.

Coming Into Our Own Power

C. Allyson Lee

Hands

"Working in this prison is the most tranquil part of my life because the rest of my life is like riding white water without a raft." I used to say this to the nurses I worked with at the hospital unit, and this always managed to elicit some sort of response, whether it involved them shaking their heads in perplexity or knitting their eyebrows together in motherly concern for the state of my mental health.

But it was tranquil, working as a dental assistant in this maximum security environment. Surrounded by officers with brown uniforms and demented senses of humour, I worked on reluctant patients who wore green outfits and suspicious expressions. Some of these lovely specimens of the human race hadn't brushed their teeth for several months. Although some of them would be on the inside charged with breaking and entering, assault or murder, they would cower at the sight of a little dental needle. And here I was, an Asian lesbian working in an all-male prison, immune to all the cat-calls and come-ons by prisoners and officers alike.

Often I would wonder if I had been placed on Earth to do bizarre or peculiar jobs. Hearing the continuous sound of slamming steel doors, I would flit from room to room, carrying instruments, joking with the nurses and psychologists. My greatest fear while working in the slammer was that I would make my patients laugh so hard that they would spit out their rubber dams or that I would have to listen to the latest joke of the day from the dentist who, thankfully, was a good friend of mine.

My personal life on the outside was tumultuous and complicated, to say the least. Relationships with my previous lovers had always been draining and bewildering. So much that I often wondered what it would feel like to be bored, to be able to sit back and relax, contemplate life and get acquainted with myself. Everything in my life was intense. Even playing the guitar, sitting on the stage in front of a predominantly lesbian audience at a coffee house benefit was unsettling. It was the first time I ever played in public, and it was enough to make my fingernails sweat.

But here it was, the beginning of summer, and I was happily alone. Without a significant other. I didn't need to need anyone. I was on my way towards healing a bruised and broken psyche, and had decided to make a fresh start on my personal life. Out with the stale stuff. Get a new outlook on things. Be more positive. Look out, world.

Going to work at 0800 that particular Friday morning wasn't supposed to be any different from setting out on my regular routine on any other Friday. So how was I to know that from that point onwards life would take a different turn for me?

As I walked towards the shelf where I picked up my office keys, I passed by a new guard. I'd never seen this one before. Hands clasped behind her back, she faced a bulletin board, her back towards me. Somehow I knew that inside that brown androgynous uniform was a woman. A couple of inches taller than I was, medium build, strong-looking shoulders and short, black hair. She had Chinese hair! All this was churning around abruptly in my mind, in the space of about 3 seconds, as I walked on by her and caught a fleeting, peripheral glance at her from the corner of my eye.

I had always noticed whenever a new crop of guards arrived, especially if any of them happened to include women. After all, what kind of woman would want to work in an all-male prison? But this one threw me for a loop. Why would a woman of Asian heritage even think of doing this for a living? Totally unconventional, nontraditional. Not the usual occupation for a nice Chinese girl. Far out!

I didn't wait to find out the answer to my silent question, so, with some haste, proceeded to go upstairs to the clinic to begin working as usual. After a few minutes, when I had finished setting everything up, I heard a voice in the hall. It was Mr. Sooter, our regular unit officer. He was giving an informational talk to his new charge: that same Chinese woman! After telling her that we would be bringing in dental patients soon, he left. And there she stood, alone in the hall, with no one else around except for me. Then followed an awkward silence, as I looked down at the floor.

She took a couple of steps towards me, and said "Hi. My name's Julie." This was the first time we made eye contact. My mind raced. She talked with confidence and forthrightness. No accent. Obviously Canadian-born. And cute. A baby face. Bright and responsive.

My neurons fired wildly, trying to cluster together something intelligent to say, and all I could do was mutter "Hi." She waited a couple of seconds (which seemed like years), then cocked her head slightly and asked, "And you're . . .?" Whereupon I jolted myself into momentary lucidity and answered, "I'm Erika." She persisted with "And your last name?" Taken aback somewhat, I replied "Lee." While I pondered why she would be wanting to know my last name, she contemplated this last bit of information and then asked with disconcerting alertness, "Are you a guitarist?" At that, a million volts of electricity shot through me and stopped my breathing just long enough for me to realize that the only way she would know I played a guitar would be if she was at that coffee house in which the audience was full of gay women. Was she one of us, or merely a straight spectator in the company of lesbian friends? I had to know.

"How do you know that?" I asked her, probably a little too anxiously. And, as though she regretted asking me that question and thereby pronouncing herself guilty by association, she closed up. Didn't answer me. With a little embarrassed look in her face, she turned away from me and looked down at the floor. I challenged her, "Were you at that coffee concert at La Casa?" Again, no answer. She was looking away from me completely now, and seemed to be wanting to forget this line of conversation altogether. She turned away and walked out into another room, with her hands clasped behind her back, just like I'd seen her do downstairs.

But after some time, she came back and faced me, saying casually, "You're a dental assistant and you play the guitar. Does that mean you're good with your hands?" This was too much to bear. I couldn't look at her. My bewildered brain shot out two possible conclusions: She was a cheeky, flirtatious little sleaze, or she was an innocent, naive, friendly little person wishing to pay me a compliment. The shock of the moment refused to allow me to believe that either one was true.

Usually my mind runs about three miles ahead of my mouth, and it was fortunate that I did not choose to reply with: "I'll bet you say that to all the girls," or "Why don't you come over here and find out?" Instead, I managed to blurt out "Oh, I'd never admit anything like that in front of Mr. Sooter!", as he reappeared in the room.

By now, we were both shuffling our feet, and, thankfully, Mr. Sooter took her away to duties away from our floor. That was by far the most moronic non-conversation I'd ever managed to have with any human being. How could I suddenly become so brain-dead upon meeting someone I thought was attractive? I left a message on my closest friend Paulette's answering machine that I'd just met a new officer who was just too cute for words, and that I wouldn't mind being handcuffed by that one.

I wasn't used to becoming unsettled by anyone new, especially after I'd barely survived three serial relationships with three very different women. I was far too old (in the riper portion of my third decade in life) and mature (often wearing an orange construction helmet to protect myself against arguments with the Xray machine) to be swept off my feet or be rendered speechless. Well, anyway, someone who looked like that probably had dozens of little dykes running after her, dragging her off to coffee houses. Who was I kidding anyway?

A couple of days passed, and what do you know: she came up to my floor again, and this time went into the psychologist's office. She said a friendly hello, and seemed more relaxed this time. She told me that she'd been asked to come up and interpret for our Dr. Freisen (who had a beard and a penchant for rubber gloves). Apparently one of our prisoners had an appointment but could only speak Cantonese. She asked me why I wasn't doing the interpreting, and I told her that the last time I tried to speak Chinese, the waiter asked if I was Japanese. We had a chuckle over that.

I had to get back to work and didn't see her again that day. But I knew that I would eventually see her again, here and there, in this room or that, where her training would take her. I also felt that our second meeting was much easier than our first, and obviously she didn't think I was too much of a mental midget, because she talked to me again. I had to find out more about her. I went downstairs to the officer's central room to see Mr. Sooter, who, incidentally, was gay as Paree.

"Hey, Benny. How ya doing?" We talked a bit, exchanging small pleasantries, and then I got straight to the point. Asked him to find out if Julie was married. He gave me a reassuring wink, then told me "No problem." Then he turned over to another officer in the room, and very matter-of-factly asked "Hey, Art. You know that new officer, Miss Wong? Do you know if she's married or living with anyone?" Art, really rather sweet, straight and unsuspecting, replied, "Well, I think she lives at home, because I called her once and her mother answered."

Benny asked me quietly if I wanted Julie's phone number, and I said thanks but no thanks. That would be intruding on her, I thought. But, what to do now? She lives at home? How old is this person? Maybe she isn't a little dyke after all. Looks can be quite deceiving. But she was so cute...

Self-help books tell you that you should seize opportunities, not let them go. Don't sit around and build up a lifetime of regrets. Do something! Listen you, if you don't do something now, this little chance meeting may never progress beyond just that.

So, with all the courage I could muster, I got a pen and paper and wrote down: "Hi. Congratulations on your promotion to official interpreter for shrinks. If you'd like to meet for lunch sometime, I'm here every Friday." I scratched down my phone number then placed the note in her mail slot.

Ha. Perfect. Now the onus is on her to make the connection, if she wants to. If she never calls, we won't have lost anything. If she never wants to get to know me, she doesn't have to. And she'd never have to explain it to me. So be it.

Told my good fried Colleen about the note, and she gave me her congratulations for my bravery. I soon began to admire myself for having done something I'd never done in my life: being bold.

What followed after that day was about three weeks of agony. Not one call. I would see her on unit, fleetingly, and run away into another room so that we wouldn't have to have a conversation about anything at all. I felt a little silly, humiliated and ridiculous, having hoped for something that was never meant to be.

Then one Friday I was leaving early, wearing my volunteer T-shirt, on my way to the music festival. Julie was on the unit again, and exchanged civil hellos. But there was an obvious awkwardness on both of our parts. I, of course, felt the fool, having put her on the spot by leaving her that note. She probably felt embarrassed, not having called me at all, and not having acknowledged the note. I left in a hurry, not wishing to prolong the strangeness of the situation.

The music festival was (and always had been) an exhilarating event for me. I spent that weekend in the sanctity of gentle music, friendly faces and fresh air. The atmosphere and ambience was so trusting that you could leave your backpack on your blanket on the grass all day, and it would still be there when you returned to it. Those three days left me relaxed, happy and optimistic.

Then, the next morning, I came back home to a message on my answering machine: "Hi, Erika. It's Julie. I get off work at noon today, if you'd like to do something. You can call me at home. The number is 242-7345."

I had to play that message over again twice, to make sure I wasn't hallucinating. I began to panic. What now? Does this mean she wants to be friends? Is she calling only because we saw each other that last time and somehow I made her feel guilty? Is she wanting an innocent meeting? Is she a dyke? Does she know that I'm a dyke? Would that make a difference to her?

It was 11:30 and I didn't want to wait to call her when she got home. So I called the jail. Chased her down through several phone lines and finally got her. I asked her if she wanted to go bike riding around the seawall. She said "Great. See ya later."

Waiting for her call was like waiting for Godot. But she finally did call, and asked "So, where are ya? I'm at a phone booth downtown." She was close to my place and didn't have my address, so I told her how to get here. And when she arrived, all huffing and puffing from cycling down here and then running up 3 flights of stairs, she went straight to my fridge, opened it up and asked if I had anything cold to drink. I liked the fact that she felt comfortable enough to help herself to my fridge.

After a sip of juice, we decided to head out. I figured, what a good idea to go biking. It's something physical, and we won't have to worry about awkward silences or gaps in the conversation.

I took the lead, whisking us by breathtaking scenery that I was virtually ignoring. And then she wanted to know: "Do you mesh with the officers?" Trying to negotiate a turn with no visibility of oncoming traffic along the ocean wall while analyzing the intent of this question was for me quite the challenge. Now what? Is she asking an innocent question, using very unusual language indeed, or was she getting personal, using innuendos and double-edged phrases?

"Do you mean, do I socialize with the people at work?"

"Yes."

"Well, no, I don't."

Was this going to be another inane non-conversation? What followed was simply a little discussion about whether people at our workplace saw each other outside of work. Julie was new to the scene, and wanted to know what the common practices were. I told her that I kept to myself mostly, and that I had my own life outside of my workplace.

We got to talking about our backgrounds. Found out that she was born here, and that her mother had not assimilated into Canadian culture very much. Because we were both Chinese, I asked what year in the Chinese astrological calendar she was born in (which would give me a large hint about how old she was). She told me she was born in the Year of the Tiger. This time, I managed to swerve my bike on a perfectly straight, even stretch of the bike path. Born in the Year of the Tiger? So was I. Since I knew she couldn't be as old as I was, she had to be 12 years younger. When we both realized this, both of us laughed a bit, and then kept quiet for a little while.

She's a baby! Twelve years younger than I! I've never even been casual friends with anyone that much younger than I, let alone lovers. Was she a baby dyke? Or simply an innocent little creature waking up to life with wide-eyed anticipation? I had to know. I had to find out if we could possibly relate on the same wavelength, or was I wasting my time? I suggested that we stop at the beach, get a cold drink, and sit on the sand.

I decided that we needed to get into the topic of being gay, even if it meant taking a great risk. I asked her if she told her mother anything about her personal life. She told me that she kept her mother pretty well in the dark about her life, then asked about me. I told her that my brother and sister both knew I was gay, but that my father did not, and I hadn't any intention of telling him. Then I decided to talk to her, assuming she was gay, and then see. So I asked her if her mother knew she was gay. She replied easily that no, she did not.

And that was enough for me. Like a barrier had been lifted between us. It was now firmly established between us, and we proceeded to talk about previous relationships, crushes and the like. It was wonderful. I deduced from the way she was talking that she'd never actually been physically involved with another woman, but that she had had a number of "close calls", a lot of intense emotional relationships with and crushes on women.

We decided to get something to eat at a little Chinese restaurant around the corner from the beach, and we continued our conversation, easily and without effort. Hours later, when she decided to cycle back home, she said, "Well, little girl. Maybe I'll buy a guitar and get you to teach me to play sometime." A little taken aback at being called "little girl", I let her know that I generally had no patience teaching people how to play the guitar, but that she would be most welcome to come over to listen to music at my place, anytime. At that, I told her I would be going out of town on the weekend to my brother's wedding, and we agreed to get together after that.

We did get together, a few times, mostly as a result of spontaneous, unplanned ideas. We went to a play, but sat awkwardly in the theatre during intermission, throwing in disjointed fragments of conversation between long periods of disquieting silence. We went to an all-women's dance, and sat most of the night at a huge table, about three yards apart, talking about our personal lives and experiences. As she let me into her life, I watched her shred the bun she got with her soup into tiny little bits that looked like snowflakes, then gather them into a neat little pile for the bewildered waitress to take away. We never even danced one dance, much to the relief of both of us, I'm sure. We decided to leave the dance and go to a small restaurant in the gay section of town, to get a sandwich. We talked some more.

We found out that we both liked to go to the nude beach, and when I walked her to her car that night, she told me to come up and say hello, next time I was at that beach. I asked, "How will I recognize you?" She said, "Look for my necklace." We both acknowledged that we had a good time, and that we'd see each other soon.

Well. So she likes to go to the beach. Takes her clothes off in public? What kind of behaviour is that for a nice Chinese girl? I phoned her early the next morning and asked her to go to the beach. She agreed, although rather sleepily, to have me pick her up.

We arrived on the sand, and just as we decided where we'd stop, she'd taken off her T-shirt before I'd even laid the blanket on the ground. Well, I'm thinking, she's so easy and comfortable with all this. Like she's done this a zillion times before. Hmm. Maybe she's not as innocent as all that. And she's even more interesting to look at, with all her clothes off. Hmm . . .

We lay on our blankets, about two yards apart, each of us wearing earphones for our separate walkmans. We didn't talk much, just soaked up the sun, pretending not to look at each other through our sunglasses.

It's a funny feeling, lying naked beside someone you don't know very well but whom you'd like to get to know better. We continued this strange activity, sharing cookies and fruit, until too many men began to surround us. They sat on their blankets the size of dishcloths, keeping most of their clothes on.

She asked me into her house, showed me her bedroom right away. Then we quickly went into her living room, and I met her mother who invited me to dinner. Then Julie and I were alone.

We sat on the couch, about a yard apart, sipping orange juice and talking about our personal lives. But she was edgy. Fidgety and nervous. I asked her why she was pacing the floor. She said that she was not pacing, then stopped and sat on the floor. I was delighted that she had been pacing. Somehow I had gotten to know her better, and had made her nervous in the process. I left her there, satisfied in knowing that we'd established some sort of a personal friendship, some kind of a bond. I could even be content with just that, because it was so intriguing just getting to know her.

Spending time with my good friends became a strange ritual, consisting of their laughing in amusement at my frantic attempts to make some sense out of my squirrelly, schoolgirl behaviour. That someone my age could be turned upside-down at the very mention of the object of my affections was invigorating to me and disconcerting to my friends. Good ol' Georgette told me that she hoped that something would happen soon (i.e. would we please just get down to business and hit the sheets), because I was to her, in my present state of mind, impossible to be around.

I knew that there was a powerful chemistry happening between Julie and me, and I'd be damned if I was going to be the one to make the first move. It was just too scary thinking that I could get blamed for leading an innocent person astray. Besides, if there was a chance I'd be rejected, forget the whole thing! The first move would have to come from her.

She started calling me up, asking if I'd like some company, and we'd listen to music and plunk around on my guitar. I told her to feel free to drop by my place any time after work.

One weekend I had an out-of-town guest, Phil, who was a good, casual friend. He knew all about my interests, including my current one, and I told him that the next time Julie would come over, we'd want some privacy. So, just after she'd arrived one afternoon, Phil took my bike out for a spin. He'd left the pull-out sofa bed out on the livingroom floor. Julie and I sat on it, about one yard apart, having snacks and listening to Motown.

And then, after we'd finished eating, she took both of my hands in hers, looked down at them and said, "Such graceful hands. You should have been a doctor!" I issued no reply during that tender moment, and we stayed there for a little while, just holding hands. Then I asked her if she'd like me to file her nails so that she could learn how to play the guitar a little easier. I carefully and soundlessly sculpted her nails into works of art, but it had to have been the slowest manicure in history (anything to keep holding her hand).

Our quiet, yet electrifying little interlude was suddenly interrupted, however, by Phil's return. He was wringing his hands frantically, telling us that the chain fell off the bike as he ventured along on his ride. He was covered in black oil and didn't want to touch anything. So, I got up from the sofa, took him to the bathroom and helped him wash his hands (otherwise he'd have taken years to clean himself up). When we'd finished, I told him enthusiastically that there was a good movie playing a few blocks away, and if he left now he could make the first show. Thankfully, he finally did leave, promising not to come back early.

Julie and I laughed about the intrusion, then started to talk again on the sofa. We got into a discussion about familial obligations, and she leaned up against the back of the couch, with one leg bent. I remember admiring her strong, tanned, muscular thighs under those multicolored shorts. She wore a soft pink flannel shirt while I had on a red tank top and shorts.

She asked me why I didn't like Christmas, and I muttered some inaudible reply. "I can't hear you," she said, and, with a little growl, reached over, grabbed my hand and pulled me towards her. As I tried to keep my composure while talking about my least favourite subject, she sat right next to me and started to run her index finger slowly up and down my bare biceps. My voice tapered down to nothing while she placed her hand down on my solar plexus, just above my belly-button.

Well, this was all the sign I needed to proceed with confidence that she wanted to fool around just as much as I. I drew her to me, wrapping my arms around her, feeling her solid, well-built body under that soft flannel.

I started to brush my lips softly across her ear and cheek, and could see that her eyes were big as saucers. Was she shocked at what was happening to us? Surely she knew where this was leading. Was she not yet ready to explore something that she'd been curious about for so many years? When I lightly kissed her lips, I got my answer. She responded with openness and warmth.

Not wishing to be interrupted again by Phil, I suggested that we move along to my bedroom, where we could close the door. She thought that it was a good idea. I pulled back the covers, threw off my clothes, then helped her get rid of hers. It didn't take long for us to get locked together in passionate ecstasy, enjoying and exploring each other's bodies.

The night began to melt away into a splendour that was precious and fragile. She turned towards me, face just inches away, and asked, "So how come I had to make the first move?" We laughed together, confessing that we were waiting for signs from each other, not wanting to make a wrong, untimely move. We held each other gently, rolling around, talking some more. It felt like we didn't sleep at all.

Then, after we had dozed off for a little while, she suddenly turned and looked at me, leaped out of bed and crashed into the wall beside the door. She stood there for a moment, stark naked, and finally realized that, although she was not at home, she hadn't been sleeping beside a total stranger or burglar. Then she laughed and crawled right back into the warm safety of my bed.

We clasped our hands together and drifted off to sleep again, cozily wrapped around each other. Little did we know that we would be spending the next few years together laughing and crashing about in each other's lives.

SUSAN BEAVER

English and Biology

i will teach you to say

First Nations

i will demand respect
for my rules
and for myself

you will look closely
study
the grammar
both of injustice
and dignity

not to defend your innocence
in the canon of lies known as
canada's history
but to more eloquently pronounce

Justice

you will look into my eyes
"indian" comes to your mouth
comes to your mind

i come with my lover

who knows my skin is soft at night
hard by day

i will teach you
the anatomy of a people
that if you flood the Piegan
i will choke and sputter
my lungs filled with water
if you drill for oil in the Lubicon territory
the wind blows through
the holes left in my heart
point a gun at the Mohawk
and we
as a people
all see the barrel

you will look at a body
a people
learn the differences

not separate its parts
but to more fully understand
the whole
to be considered educated
you must learn to identify
Tlingit and Algonquin
pronounce Huron and Beothuk

I will sit down with you
I will whisper it gently in your ear
I may stand up against you
I will raise a flag and shout it

you will learn to say

I will teach you my language
not Mohawk or Cree

not Ojibway or Micmac
I will teach you to say

Nation

FIRST Nation

SDIANE A. BOGUS

The Joys and Power in Celibacy

Doing nothing sexy with nobody is torture
It makes for workaholism, unrelievable stress, and
    invites substance abuse
Do something with yourself, at least, and find out
    what I found out

You can have the bed to yourself
You can sprawl or you can curl up into a knot
You won't get no complaints about taking up all the
    space nor about having your knees in somebody's
    back.

You can sleep naked or with your clothes on
It won't have to be a signal that you're ready
Or that you don't care to

Three more things:
You don't have to cut your toe nails, unless you sleep
with your legs crossed at the ankles
You can slobber in your sleep and be your own witness
And you don't have to apologize for every random pass
of gas because someone's lying next to you

Now here's the good part:
You can experiment:
You can see how long you can hold out before true
horniness sets in
You can look and see what exactly makes you horny
You can wait and see exactly what you do and how

you act when you are horny
You can notice your cycles of horniness
Like do you feel the urge to hug/be hugged, kiss/be
    kissed, do it/have it
    done-once a month, once a week?

After that, you can find or let yourself be found by a
lover
Or, surprisingly, you can become your own —
Providing you have a sex drive
If you have no sex drive, celibacy is like indifference,
    hardly worth mentioning

Now, about being your own lover,
It takes courage and practice.
You have to start slow then go for the hidden
Simple masturbation can become mistressbathing
An innocent bath can become the delicious wet inside
    an imaginary
    woman's sweet stuff
Your own nakedness in the mirror invites you to call
    yourself something sexy, like "Sweetmeat," or
    "Honeymama."

In bed alone,
you have (1) your head, (2) your closed eyes, (3) your
desire, (4) your hands and (5) if desired, any props
    you wish
Give yourself the pleasure that expectation with
    another denies
Forget that there is such a thing as love-making with
    any but yourself

I guess it's fair to tell you about me in the interest of
the promotion of celibacy.

I have a baby bottle, a feather, a candlestick, and a
tube of KY
I have Prince, Whoopi, Tina and Aretha,
I have naked gay boys
I have motorcycle dykes and sweet young things
I have Prynne and Dimmsdale in the forest
I have rough fantasies of submission and the love of
ex-lovers
I have the safety of my room and great orgasms.

In celibacy
I learn my body, my rhythms, my wants, my
expectations,
my fantasies,
my need,
In celibacy I seek myself and find myself
What joy, what power - what endless discovery.

CAROLINA PESQUEIRA

De Limon y Nardo

En una vida de armonía
la mujer, descalza,
anda con pasos ligeros,
con el poder de la rosa
entre sus piernas
y el conocimiento de la espina
en su corazón.
Con tantas espinas y rosas
la mujer se acomoda
llegando a su trabajo
de hacerse una espada.
Detrás de los rosales,
con su martillo de roca y seda
la mujer hace del hierro
una espada,
un barco del mar
lleno de pajaros,
una taza azul que se llama cielo.
Entre su carne tierna
me bajé un rato
y ella con su saber de ondas,
de limón y nardo,
encuanto me paré
me encontró de sonrisa
en los brazos del poder.

CAROLINA PESQUEIRA

Of Limes & Pungent Flowers

In a life of harmony
the woman, barefoot,
goes with light steps
with the power of the rose
between her legs
& the knowledge of the thorn
in her heart.
The woman gets used to
so many roses & thorns
& begins her work
making her sword.
Behind the rose bushes
with her hammer of rock & silk
the woman makes of iron
a sword,
a ship of the sea
full of birds,
a blue cup that we call sky.
There within her tender flesh
I came down for a moment
& she with her knowledge of waves
& limes & pungent flowers
as i stopped
she found me smiling
in the arms of power.

MICHELE CHAI

We People, We Women

I can feel you moving inside me
fingers - two . . . four edging inward
lips linger on my breast,
I gasp   grasp
your body glistening with sexual heat
the swift movement of your hips
feel your desire stroking my thigh,
building - creating euphoria together.
Sliding , stroking - Out in - Out in.
Our pace escalates.
Lips part and contract in unison.
We rise and fall in rhythmic passion
move swiftly past seasons of pain,
hate and oppression -
to an end , our end.
To LIBERATION.

KIT YEE CHAN

Strategy Journal Excerpts

February . . .

It's really hectic all this running around, thinking of moving, running away from all this stress, myself (or a few of me). I'm in a whirlwind as i get caught up with friends, hoping to establish firm ground so i won't forget them or they, me. It's really exciting being with Gita. I really enjoy her company, feeling less nervous around her and not that same embarrassment or fear of her anger and how she expresses it. She would get into a cab, order the male cab driver to drive us around, put him down openly for thinking of cheating us, call him all these names . . . misogynist, rapist . . . and when i chuckle, try to laugh off the seriousness of what she is saying, i would try to engage her in conversation so as to stop the tension. Well, i don't do that any more. Sometimes, i laugh because the guy is so stunned by these two gorgeous women who are so deadly right and we tell him we won't play his game. We won't be polite and nice. So there.

Kat called me and i realized how much i love her. But it is really strange this love because i always have to take care of her feelings. We identify as survivors together, trying to make our worlds easier on us. I've tried so hard to take responsibility for her child, but it never worked out. I was trying to keep myself so busy that i wouldn't have to deal with me. The many me's. And Kat, she never became responsible for herself, either. I guess i have learned that this way doesn't help either of us. I have to keep on moving.

Meeting Someone New.

I went to the university with Gita today. She had organized a women of colour meeting at the women's centre. There were some recognizable faces but some new ones as well. The talk was usual. Check in: I am here coz i feel that... and we (the ones experienced with this kinda stuff) nodded, acknowledged the feelings, the frustrations... names were pulled out like Audre Lorde, bell hooks, Angela Davis, etc., words like ideology, colonial, feminist, woman of colour, all these terms... i kept looking around and found myself staring at a young black woman who had her head tilted, eyes exploring the space she was in. It was a scene that i knew too well. One of isolation, of loss, do i really belong here? What are they all saying?.. There was no recognition of her space in the room and that frustrated me. I caught her eyes, smiled and rolled my eyes around. A "wow, this meeting... " She let out a chuckle, i moved next to her to ask her name. Tissa. My name is Donna. I hated using this name but i keep spitting it out, like a bad habit. I told her i didn't go to this university so i felt a bit lost in the meeting, like i shouldn't be there. She told me her major (science). She came to this school but didn't know why she was here. It's just that she wanted to find out. I was completely excited, tingling. Maybe because i felt attracted to her... i would not ask her out though. I have never asked a woman out. Too shy. But i knew i wanted to see her again. But i am leaving in a week!!! We kept talking, she told me that she knew nothing of what the meeting was coz she didn't know Audre Lorde, bell hooks, etc. Then it struck me, "you know, if you want, i could lend you my books while i am gone." She was excited. Great, i told her to call me, gave her my number coz i wanted to make sure she wanted to do this and if she was being polite by saying "great!" then she could opt out and not call. Of course, i wished dearly for her call. One and a half days. Tissa did not call. Finally, Friday night and she calls me up, "Hey, Donna."

There is No Where to Go But Inside My Skull. or I Want Out of This White World.

I am sitting in Kat's room with Gwendolyn the seventeen year old "witch" as she calls herself. And Marlene. Marlene is my safety net right now, so i don't feel so gross with Gwendolyn. My anger and intolerance for Kat and Gwen's whiteness is growing and i like the fact that i am understanding this about myself. I am getting clearer so i can articulate it much more. Sitting with Marlene, by my side, while conversations fly around us, crashing against our Other skin - our yellow skin. It's so different for them who are so privileged with space. Gwen thinks she owns the room, dominates it with her incessant questions: so where are you from? Are you lesbian, too? Do you love the Goddess? I am a witch... i study Wicca, see my crystals? my books? my... my. my. my. my. my.

Do you have a problem with Wicca, she asks me - intruding on my limited space on the corner of the bed - Is it not obvious that i need some privacy? Stop invading my personal space!!! I was hunched over, with pen, in my book but she kept invading. Marlene decided to leave, so i left too.

I need some space to write. To think or not think. To be safe. So I go to a cafe. Now i am at Cafe whatever... This place is frequented by artists, three hour coffee drinkers, chess players. Catch the mood? It's the bastion of white privilege trying desperately to be "unique" - that cool mentality. Coolness being accepted amongst an elite - the alternative clique. I see it as another form of dominating culture. Privilege. I can count the number of people of colour here - me. I am isolated.

Kat is disappointed that Gwen and i do not get along. I see Gwen - I see through her shit. Gwen is the epitome of young/ignorant/privileged/white/rich... the privileged of taking on the "poor" look. She was bragging about looking like Evangelista from the George Michael Fashion/Beauty video... yah, Gwen, you are an evangelist for the Goddess crashing on my existence as a woman of colour. YOUR GODDESS DOES NOT REMEMBER RACISM, KNOWS HOW TO APPROPRIATE, HAS A SWISS BANK ACCOUNT!!! Dear, you try so hard you are tacky! Fuck off, coz i don't have any time to educate you. Do it yourself.

I realize i needed Marlene to stay with me for a while longer coz i can not face this isolation right now. I should have asked her out but i felt mediated by Kat. Kat would not have liked us to get together without her. I feel really awkward about it. Strange that ownership of friends game. I always experience it with Kat. I wanted to get Marlene's phone number, hug her, tell her that i appreciated her company in spite of Kat and Gwen. Especially those knowing looks she gave me. And the simultaneous glance away... I want to be around for her when she feels isolated, listen to her rant, rage at decolonizing ourselves, our bodies, our silences, our tolerance for whiteness.

The cafe is playing the Rolling Stones. It leaves stinging echoes of feedback in my skull - splits it open - blood dripping, maps out North America. Am i here? I am in North America - not of my will. I want to be amongst women of colour. That glance of solidarity -

of knowledge - of acknowledgement. "Yah, i caught that ." "Hold on." We know what you white validators want from us - we know what you colonizers have done to us - you cannot escape my sisters' blood and tears. We circle, whirl around you until you feel the fear - the danger - the isolated - the loss of power and control. You been brought up to believe you are worthwhile and you play it up to your ears. Now we fly around you - dance to your loss of power. We decolonize ourselves.

KAREN AUGUSTINE

JOE/Rape Poem

Your white hand shoved
up my raw
bleeding cunt
creates gashes
in my endometrium
I a womon gone mad from the repulsion
am bruised
to the deepest blues
at the central point
of my swollen uterus

Rammed through the ache
and the groan and the grunt
Between the scream
in my jugular veins
Above the tear on the
pupil of my eye
Caught in this core of pain
I am witness

straddled on your bed
legs forced apart
arms held down: your
      fucking hand
      fucking violently
between brown vaginal folds
to
the palest pink
ripped apart

one long evening in November

You remain with me
in the circumference of
my vaginal discharge
in the crimson paste
dried
on the palm of your hand

Your male attempt
  to confuse me with images
  in fashion magazines

Your male attempt
  to use my sexuality
  as a device to jerk off

Your male attempt
  to measure your self worth
  through
humiliation/degradation/violation
within your perverted orgasm
of sexual violence
called rape

MISOGYNIST don't define me by your status/race/class

Here
on this very dark pinch of skin
directly beneath the spit
  her warm tongue
defines me as
lesbian
  her strong voice

defines me as survivor
>   her pulse
thumping against
the weight of our struggle
shoves through
your self-defined systems
your destructive institutions
blood-staining me in a
vocal muscular chord
>   stronger than ever

INDIGO SOM

Euphemism

You say
I have almond eyes.

I say to you
look at these eyes.
You cannot use them for marzipan
Grinding sightless stones into paste
for your delicate sweets/filled croissants.
You cannot take my eyes
and shell them/slice them with your
Swiss kitchen knives/food processors
Let them eat desserts/decorated with
thin white slivers. Almond cookies
in pink Chinatown bakery boxes
are not exotic.
Look at these eyes/yours do not see them/
they see through your adjectives/nouns/verbs/My eyes
understand the shapes of eyelids
The importance of iris color/these eyes
can take the heat/can see
the blue in shadows

I know
that I have
eye-shaped eyes

visionary

Now
I have an adjective
for yours.

HEATHER D. CLARK

Untitled

We don't have to talk
    all I want is to be with you.
We can listen to music
      we could lay next to each other holding hands,
          look at the ceiling, letting the music play.
            When it stops we'll play it again,
as long as the music plays
         the night never ends.

Victoria Lena Manyarrows

fire of chance

gazing into the flame
i pass thru your candlelight
my mind racing thru the darkness
into the night
where magic transpires
and the darkness gives way to two bodies
aglow and together
awake to the sounds of the ocean's movements
wind in the trees
my hand in your hair
stroking thru the heat of the moment
and darkly, your eyes are shining
calling to me with a gaze of expectation
i am here and not turning back
your candle burns brighter
and deeper is your gaze

carry me away with your shining eyes
i am a woman waiting
eager to melt into your heat
fire of chance
fire of change

Victoria Lena Manyarrows

we are one

i find myself coming to you, sinking into your smile
flowing into the fire of your longing
with a desire to dance
i offer you my magic
embracing you with fever and calm
the power within us dissolving all boundaries
making alliances, forming bonds
joining together
in this time of need.

NILA GUPTA

Love Poem
for Sharmini

on our island
our bodies
are laughing
together
gentle waves
lapping
rolling

i taste the sea
on your lips
where the three seas meet
on your gentle mound
and cave

you, Sinhalese woman
black as the night
and i,
Kashmiri woman,
blue as the Kashmiri sky
blue as the Himalayas
in the distance
we meet
where the three seas meet
and braid hair
at *Kanniyakumari**
where we are
our bodies
laughing
together

gentle waves
lapping
rolling

Kanniyakumari: southernmost tip of India where the three seas meet—Indian
Ocean, Bay of Bengal, Arabian Sea.

NORIKO OKA

the portrait

i have in my room
    a picture
japanese womyn in a bath
    imagine: steam
permeates these four walls

    one womyn
yes, her back is always turned/
    want to run
    my hand slowly
    down the fine curves of her spine.
another, breast-deep in water
    hair in a bundle
    watches her own reflection.
other misty shadows drift
    in the corners.
    yearning
to join these womyn
to sweat profusely among them
    washing each other's back

but the Frame is not large
    enough for me/to enter
and i am terrified
of three dimensional surfaces
    that suddenly turn
    flat as i approach

i imagine: steam
permeates these four walls
making it easier to breathe
i inhale deeply.

CHERYL CLARKE

Great expectations

questing a lesbian adventure one splendid night
of furtive, fixed stars and fully intending to have you suck my breast and fuck me
til dawn called raunchy elizabeth to the window
of your brooklyn apartment saxophone and dolphin-
song muting the rudeness of engines

dreaming the encounter intense as engines
first me then you oh what a night
of rapture and risk and dolphin
acrobatics after years of intend-
ing to find my lesbian sources in the window
of longing wide open in me

fearing failing and wanting to do it again faked me
out - anxious wanting revved like 500 engines
inside your brooklyn apartment window
my body a pillar yours a furnace that curious night
of lesbian lore and fully intend-
ing to play an easy rider to your dolphin-

song. instead of asking you to dive on me dolphin-
like, butch stories hushed the lesbian lust in me
across that expanse of sofa and fully intending to make you make me like diesel engines
and taking you back over and over into the night
across your expanse of ass in front of the window.

trading passionate conquest tales and at your window
cobalt night grew pink in the stink, the dolphin
wearying wary of heroics asking for clarity all night
instead of covering face with cunt and entering me
low then spectacularly like rocket engines
you panicked the funky passion i fully intend-

ed. yeah, yeah, a funky passion i fully intended all over the floors walls to the cobalt window
of your brooklyn bedroom til the whine of cold engines
muted the saxophone and called the dolphin
back to sea and your lesbian wetness drying sticky on me
night of furtive, fixed stars oh venus in taurus night.

fully intending to have my way but having no dolphin-
like clarity and the window sticking in me —
a sounding fire engine gridlocked on a windy night.

MONA OIKAWA

Origins

When I think of you
I become a geisha
waiting to serve you
o-cha and *nori* —
wrapped morsels
on a cold winter day.

When my eye catches
your beauty
after long days absence,
your laughter is like
the first bursting *sakura* —
sweet fragrant colour —
swelling rivers in me
to rise deep with
ancient memory.

When we talk story
our black leather toughness
fades away,
and we don our grandmothers'
silken garments
cool against the raging heat
of our angry tears.

When we compare notes
on how it feels to be
the colonized daughters
of daughters of
Japanese mothers,
I want to brandish
the sharpest samurai sword
and slice off the head
of the latest racist
who caused you pain.

When we smile and say,
we too are Japanese women,
I slowly move toward you
finger loose your binding *obi*,
and uncover and rediscover
our origins in each
groaning embrace.

nori: seaweed
sakura: cherry blossoms
obi: sash

Biographies

KARIN AGUILAR-SAN JUAN

Is the editor of an anthology on contemporary Asian American activism (forthcoming from South End Press). When she is not working with books, she practices and competes in the martial arts.

LANUOLA ASIASIGA

I am a Samoan lesbian feminist 38 year old mother of three children. I was born in Aotearoa (New Zealand). At the moment I am enjoying peace and quiet because my children are in Samoa. I work full-time and study part-time and would love a holiday. Holidays seem to be something that everybody else does!

KAREN AUGUSTINE

Born in Toronto of Dominican parents. Writer and mixed media artist. Currently: working on a series of photo-text murals and installations dealing with black women and mental health, she is also developing a journal for women artists of African descent to be published early next year.

SUSAN BEAVER

She is a Mohawk, from Grand River Territory, Wolf Clan. She is currently president of Two-Spirited Peoples of the First Nations in Toronto, Canada. Her interests and priorities are in the area of A.I.D.S. education and sex. She is currently working on a novel entitled *Pow Wow*.

S. RENEE BESS

I am a professional educator, and I write whenever I have the time and the inspiration. I owe my love of reading and writing to my parents, who filled our home with books, music and love. I owe my desire to be creative to my lifetime companion who helps me clear away the trivia so that I may write. And I thank the valiant women of Sister Vision Press.

SDIANE BOGUS

SDiane Bogus is a poet, writer, publisher, teacher and scholar who has published in numerous journals and magazines. Her own books include *I'm Off to See the Goddamn Wizard, Alright! Woman in the Moon, Her Poems, Sapphire's Sampler, Dyke Hands,* and the soon to be released *The Chant of the Women of Magdelena.* Bogus is also the owner of the small lesbian-feminist press, WIM publications.

DIONNE BRAND

She is a Toronto writer, born in Trinidad. She has lived in Toronto for the past 20 years. She studied English and Philosophy at the University of Toronto, has an M.A. in Philosophy of Education and is working on a Ph.D. in Women's History.

Brand has published six books of poetry, *'Fore day morning, Earth Magic* (children's poetry), *Winter Epigrams and Epigrams to Ernesto Cardenal in Defense of Claudia, Primitive Offensive, Chronicles of the Hostile Sun* and *No Language is Neutral.* Her poems and other writings have appeared in Fireweed, Prism, This Magazine, Canadian Women's Studies, Fuse, and Poetry Canada.

She is the associate director and writer of the NFB Studio D documentaries *Older, Stronger, Wiser* and *Sisters in the Struggle.* She is currently working on her third film.

BETH BRANT

She is a Bay of Quinte Mohawk from Tyendinaga Mohawk Territory in Ontario. She is a mother and grandmother, a Taurus with Scorpio rising, a working-class woman who grew up with the sound of the factory whistle regulating the lives of her family. She is the author of *Mohawk Trail* (Women's Press), editor of *A Gathering of Spirit* (Women's Press/Firebrand Books) and *Food Spirits* (Press Gang). The story "Home Coming" is from *Food Spirits*, a collection of short fiction.

CAROL CAMPER

She is a Black Lesbian Mother, a visual artist, writer and womyn's health worker. She journeys seeking her true name.

MICHELE CHAI

I am a callaloo mix-up 1/2 Asian woman hailing from Port-of-Spain, Trinidad. I arrived in Canada in 1986 on a Foreign Students Visa. Having completed my 3rd year of study at York University, I hope to graduate with a degree in Women's Studies and Anthropology someday. I try to be as politically active as a student, part-time worker can be and my spare time is spent reading. Thanks to my bestest buddy Lori (I never used to read before I met her).

KIT YEE CHAN

Kit Yee Chan is a travelling woman. She writes, lives and loves in many parts of Canada. She will settle down one day.

LING HUA CHEN
She is a hapa Chinese middle-class dyke who loves the sensual pleasures of life. She co-founded Pacifica/Asian Lesbians Networking - Chicago, is active in her many communities in Seattle, and currently works as a social services aide. Her heroines include Han Suyin, Sawagi Taiko and her grandmother.

RITZ CHOW
She is an Asian Lesbian living in Toronto. She has published in the Toronto-based magazine Matriart and has been involved in the "Women Rising" Festivals. She says: "On the periphery of text, I stroke words by the sins of a slow-dragging sun. On yellow pages of skin are hooks for everything wordless raging through my numbered, tumbling selves. I write what I can & love what I must."

CHRYSTOS
She is a Native American, born in 1946 and raised in San Francisco. A political activist and speaker, as well as an artist and writer, she is self-educated. Her tireless momentum is directed at better understanding how issues of colonialism, genocide, class and gender affect the lives of women and Native people.

HEATHER D. CLARK
I am a woman of Afrikan descent, who is dedicated to paying homage to the women who have came before me and passing down the legacy to the women who will come after me.
I am 21 years old and was born and raised in Seattle, Washington State.

CHERYL CLARKE is an accomplished poet and writer whose works have appeared in numerous publications. Her books include *Narratives: poems in the tradition of black women* and *Living as a Lesbian*.

ANNETTE CLOUGH
She was born and grew up in Jamaica. She has spent most of her adult life in Canada. She now lives in Toronto with her beloved family, her partner of 12 years, and their daughter. Canada has treated her well but part of her heart is still in the Caribbean.

COLECTIVO PALABRAS ATREVIDAS
Colectivo Palabras Atrevidas is a San Francisco/Bay Area Latina Lesbian writers group which dares to speak our many truths. Members include Maria Cora, Sabrina D. Hernandez, Karla E. Rosales.

MARIA CORA

She is a lesbian feminist Puerto Rican of African heritage who has lived in the San Francisco Bay area for the last ten years. She is a writer of poetry, fiction and essays; she is also a member of the Palabras Atrevidas writer's collective. She is lead vocalist with Different Touch and Los Pleneros de la 24, and recently received the 1990 Prisma Award for Achievement in Performing Arts. She is a founding member of the Nia Collective, a Black lesbian organizing group, and of Mujerio, the northern California latina lesbian organization. She holds a BA from Radcliffe College and is currently employed by the Department of Public Health as an educator of adolescents. Her work has appeared in publications such as Ache, Mujerio Newsletter and Matrix.

DEBBIE DOUGLAS

Lively, lovely and lusty, Debbie Douglas, a Grenadian woman lives in Toronto with her lover and daughter. They are actively involved in filmmaking.

RUTH ELLIS

She is a 90 year old lesbian, our oldest contributor. She lives in Detroit, Michigan.

SHARON FERNANDEZ

Born in Kuala Lumpur, Malaya, she lives in Toronto and is always in serious pursuit of the "perfect" relationship.

CONNIE FIFE

She is a writer-in-residence at the En'Owkin International School of Writing, where she is in her third year there. Her book of poems, *Beneath the Naked Sun*, is upcoming from Write-On Press (Vancouver) in the fall of 1991. "I am a Cree woman who writes in the hope that my words find their mark. I offer with them healing, pain, and ways of making radical change in a confused world. Meegwetch to my sisters. They know who they are."

JEWELLE L. GOMEZ

She has written for numerous publications including The New York Times, The Village Voice, Essence and Belle Lettres. She is the author of two collections of poetry. Her novel, *The Gilda Stories* has been recently published by Firebrand Books.

NILA GUPTA
She is a South Asian lesbian writer who lives with her lover of seven years in Toronto. She is starting to paint and will soon be doing film.

DONAYLE HAMMOND
She is an Afro-Caribbean lesbian who lives in Toronto. She is a member of Young Ebony Sisters (YES), a Toronto-based lesbian group for young Black women.

DORIS HARRIS
She is a writer of poetry and prose, living in Seattle, Washington. Doris is the proud recipient of the 1988 Nikki Giovanni Poetry Award. Her work has appeared in diverse publications: *Gathering Ground*, a Northwest women of Color anthology; *Leading Edge:* lesbian erotica; ESSENCE magazine; and *Changing Power* a University of Washington textbook, etc. She has also completed her first book of poetry *God Takes Care of Fools and Babies*, a book filled with the voices and the vision of women - of today, yesterday, and tomorrow.

SABRINA HERNANDEZ
She is a chicana lesbian born and raised in San Francisco. Earns a living as a local union electrician, but if given the opportunity would prefer to involve herself in writing and community activism. Currently a member of Mujerio, the San Francisco based latina/chicana lesbian organization. Works in assistance to the San Francisco Women's Building in areas of events production. Former member of the Victoria Mercado Brigade, first lesbian and gay work brigade to Nicaragua. Current member of Colectivo Palabras Atrevidas, a latina lesbian writing collective.

TERRI L. JEWELL
Born October 4, 1954 in Louisville, Kentucky, USA, Terri is a Black Lesbian Feminist poet and writer. The Black elderwomen of the world belong to all of us and we must listen to their stories. We must not forget that these women carry the word from Africa - this planet's largest continent from which ALL of us arose.

MARIA AMPARO JIMENEZ
Born in Mexico in 1949. At a young age she moved to Havana, Cuba, where she lived until 1961. In the United States she has lived on the West Coast and more recently, in Chicago.

Although a veterinarian by profession, Jimenez has worked actively for feminist causes all her life. She was instrumental in establishing and directed, the Latino Program of STOP-AIDS in Chicago. She also created "Encuentro latino", a Hispanic-oriented page in a local gay and lesbian newspaper, Outlines. Since her move to Central America, she has founded Confidencial, a newspaper of gay and lesbian interest.

In 1990 she published her first book of poetry, *bajo mi relieve*, which has received a warm and enthusiastic response not only in the USA but throughout Hispanic America as well.

JOANNA KADI
She is a writer and activist with a BA in women's studies and an MA in feminist ethics. She is becoming more and more aware of how absolutely crucial a sense of humour is.

TAMAI KOBAYASHI
Born in Japan and raised Canada, she lives in Toronto. A recluse by nature, she is prone to smashing her hands and knees during drumming and collisions on the basketball court. A double Capricorn, born in the year of the snake. Approach with caution.

C. ALLYSON LEE
She is a West Coast transplant from Alberta, has published pieces in: *Awakening Thunder* - Fireweed Issue #30, Kinesis, Angles, Journal for the Canadian Dental Association and Phoenix Rising. She has an affinity for guitars and primates.

PATRICE LEUNG
Patrice works in film production and hopes one day to write and direct her own films. Trinidad born, Vancouver bred and Chinese to the soul.

SHARON LIM-HING
Sharon is a Chinese Jamaican lesbian. She is co-editing an anthology of writings by Asian Pacific lesbians.

AUDRE LORDE
Black woman, poet, essayist, lesbian, feminist, mother, activist, daughter of Grenadian immigrants and cancer survivor. Her poetry has appeared in numerous periodicals and anthologies both in the United States and abroad, and has been translated into many languages. She is the author of 13 books and lives in St. Croix, Virgin Islands, U.S.

VICTORIA LENA MANYARROWS
I am Native (Eastern Cherokee), mixed-blood and lesbian. Much of my childhood was spent close to the Canadian border in North Dakota, and from an early age I developed an interest in Canadian affairs and problems, particularly as they affect Native people.

My goal as a writer and artist is to use written and visual images to convey and promote a positive, indigenous, native-based world-view... a view that is generally ignored, overlooked, and usually not even thought of in this European-oriented USA and Canada.

DENISE MARIE hails from Ludington, Michigan.

RAYMINA MAYS
Raymina Mays is a writer. She has had stories published in Feminary and *Home Girls: A Black Feminist Anthology.*

MICHELLE MOHABEER is a Guyana born, independent filmmaker, programmer and writer living and working in Toronto. She graduated with a B.A. honours degree in Film Studies from Carleton University, Ottawa. Her most recent film, *Exposure* was screened in film festivals within Canada, the U.S.A. and Europe. She has worked in film as a sound recordist and art director.

JUDITH NICHOLSON
She is a freelance English editor and a poet. Originally from Jamaica, she now lives in Montreal.

MONA OIKAWA
Mona was born in Toronto and has lived in this city most of her life. She is a Sansei (third generation Japanese Canadian). She is a founding member of Asian Lesbians of Toronto. Her writing has been published in Fireweed, *Riding Desire* (Banned Books, 1991), Gay Community News, *The Poetry of Sex* (Banned Books, forthcoming). She is one of the editors of *Awakening Thunder*, issue 30 of Fireweed, the first anthology of creative work by Asian Canadian women.

NORIKO OKA
Currently she is working in clay and says her hands are always gooey with something.

MIDI ONODERA is a filmmaker living in Toronto.

MILAGROS PAREDES
I am Mestiza, Philipina-Spanish born in the Philippines and raised in Asia and North America. I'm a cosmic time traveller and through my writing I try to connect and separate my experiences of the past with the present.

VASHTI PERSAD
She is an Indo-Caribbean woman born in Trinidad. She's active within the Women of Colour, Immigrant Women's and anti-racist movement in Toronto. She returns often to Trinidad where she nurtures herself with the spirit of her people and the land, and to strengthen her soul so she can return with the balance needed to move forward.

CAROLINA PESQUEIRA
I am a Chicana born in Tucson, Arizona. My sangre es Mexicana of the Great Sonoran Desert. Walking my path through many places, I was married for 16 years and had seven children. Now I work here in Tucson and am a daughter, a mother, a sister and a lover of women.

NICE RODRIGUEZ
A certified public accountant in the Philippines, Nice's first writings were stock market, trade and corporate reports published in Manila's top business newspapers. When union busting efforts closed The Financial Times of Manila, the editor next door gave Nice her first feature writing break in Manila's People Magazine. Describing her country's business climate as homophobic, she changed beat and wrote instead articles on the Philippines' leading stars, artists and celebrities. Before she migrated to Canada in 1988, she was the assistant section editor at the Philippine Daily Globe. She now works as production artist in Toronto's NOW Magazine.

CARIDAD RODRIQUEZ
I am a Cubana artist, working with Rumbera and Salsera. I am the daughter of Ochun. The work that appears is my first piece of fiction.

KARLA E. ROSALES
I am a Latina lesbian, 27 years old, born and raised in San Francisco, California. I am a member of the Latina Lesbian writing group, Colectivo Palabras Atrevidas, teacher to be and a warrior. I try to speak and write truth.

JAISNE BLUE SEXTON
Jaisne Blue Sexton lives in Toronto. She says simply: "I offer my sisters these poems."

MAKEDA SILVERA
"I am an extraordinary woman, filled with silent power. When they made me, they unfortunately threw away the mould. I wish there was more of me to go around."

NALINI SINGH
Nalini is an Indo-Caribbean woman who hails from Guyana. Toronto has been her home for over eighteen years. She says: "For most of my life, I've had a close and stormy relationship with words."

BARBARA SMITH
Barbara Smith is one of the leading activists in the feminist movement and editor/author of numerous writings. Her literary criticism, reviews and essays have appeared in scores of publications including The New York Times. She edited *Home Girls: A Black Feminist Anthology* and is co-founder and publisher of Kitchen Table: Women of Color Press.

INDIGO SOM
garlic-chopping, silver-sawing, shuttle-throwing bitchy buddha. i am a cancer & fire horse born, raised & planning to die in the san francisco bay area where i belong. i am a woman-of-color-identified woman of color (specifically: abc - american born chinese) & bisexual-identified bisexual. my work has been published in various journals, including smell this from women of color in coalition and matrix women's newsmagazine.

i want to caution my sisters to maintain integrity; always check yourself to see that you are motivated by love for your community (however you might define it). if you are doing it from your ego you will eventually jam up your sisters, the movement & yourself as well. you know what i'm talking about. now let's go out & fight the good fight!

CHRISTINA SPRINGER
She is an African-American lesbian mother and filmmaker. She is the co-founder of Back Porch Productions: a women's media collective whose second film Creation of Destiny is currently in production. Her work is seen in numerous periodicals and *Riding Desire* edited by Tee Corinne.

SHENAZ STRI

Shenaz Stri is twenty two years old. She was born in India and came to Canada in 1976. She says: "My writing is a reflection of my experiences in Canada... And I love women."

LELETI TAMU

A soft butch with a craving for romance, Leleti spends many nights with Rose and together, the days with Jonathan.

SKYE WARD

Skye Ward is an afrofemcentric lesbian activist residing in Oakland, California. She is an original core group member of Ache: A Journal for Lesbians of African Descent and continues to work as the Outreach/Public Affairs Coordinator for the Ache Project. Meditation on LOC Sisterhood is dedicated to playwright, mentor, and sister-friend Cherrie Moraga "one of the most COURAGEOUS writers I know."

LAURA IRENE WAYNE

Laura Irene Wayne is a commercial artist, printer, writer and poet. She was born and raised in Detroit, Michigan. Wayne has attended and received a bachelor's of arts degree from Michigan State University. She and her lover reside in San Diego, California where they operate a graphic arts company.

Canadian Women (Fireweed Feminist Journal, Toronto, Canada, 1990).
Reprinted with permission of the author.
We Will Not Be Invisible
Jimenez, Maria Amparo, "Diosa/Goddess" (© 1990 Maria Amparo Jimenez). Reprinted with the permission of the author.
Aguilar-San Juan, Karin, "Exploding Myths, Creating Consciousness: Some First Steps Toward Pan-Asian Unity," (Sojourner: The Women's Forum, Vol. 16, No. 5, Boston, MA, 1991). Reprinted with permission of Sojourner: Women's Forum.
Clarke, Cheryl, "Saying the Least Said, Telling the Least Told: The Voices of Black Lesbian Writers" (Lesbian and Gay Studies Newsletter, Vol 17, No. 1, March 1990). Reprinted with permission of the author.
Pain and Betrayal
Brant, Beth, "Home Coming", from *Food and Spirits,* (Press Gang Publishers, Vancouver, Canada, 1991). Reprinted with permission of the author.
Cravings
Chrystos, "I just picked the first ripe" from *Dream On,* (Press Gang Publishers, Vancouver, Canada, 1991) Reprinted with permission of the publisher.
Chrystos, "Poem for lettuce" from *Not Vanishing,* (Press Gang Publishers, Vancouver, Canada, 1991) Reprinted with permission of the publisher.
Wayne, Layra Irene, "I too like to eat out" from *Black Lace,* No 1, Spring 1991,(Los Angeles, CA).
Wanting and Passion
Chrystos, "Dream Lesbian Lover", from *Dream On* (Press Gang Publishers, Vancouver, Canada, 1991). Reprinted with permission of the publisher.
Chrystos, "Sestina for Ilene" *Dream On* (Press Gang Publishers, Vancouver, Canada, 1991). Reprinted with permission of the publisher.
Clarke, Cheryl, "Living As a Lesbian On the Make". From *Living As a Lesbian: Poetry by Cheryl Clarke* (Firebrand Books, Ithaca, New York, 1986).
Coming Into Our Own Power
Bogus, SDiane, "The Joys and Power in Celibacy", from *Black Lace,* No 1, Spring 1991, (Los Angeles, CA).
Gupta, Nila, "Love Poem", from *Awakening Thunder: Asian Canadian Women* (Fireweed Feminist Journal, Toronto, Canada, 1990). Reprinted with permission of the author.
Oka, Noriko, "the portrait", from *Awakening Thunder: Asian Canadian Women* (Fireweed Feminist Journal, Toronto, Canada, 1990). Reprinted with permission of the author.

Clarke, Cheryl, "Great Expectations", from *Living As a Lesbian: Poetry by Cheryl Clarke* (Firebrand Books, Ithaca, New York, 1986).

The following are presses and periodicals which have published work by some of the contributors to *Piece of My Heart.*

Between The Lines
394 Euclid Ave. Suite 203
Toronto, Ontario
M6G 2S9
Canada

Black Lace
Box 83912
Los Angeles, CA
90083-0912
U.S.A.

Coach House Press
401 (rear) Huron St.
Toronto, Ontario
M5S 2G5
Canada

Firebrand Books
141 The Commons
Ithaca, New York
14850
U.S.A.

Fireweed Feminist Journal
P.O. Box 279
Station B
Toronto, Ontario
M5T 2W2
Canada

Kitchen Table
Womenof Colour Press
P.O. Box 908
Latham, N.Y. 2110
U.S.A.

Press Gang Publishers
603 Powell St.
Vancouver, B.C.
V6A 1H2
Canada

The Seal Press Feminist Publishers
3131 Western Ave. #410
Seattle, WA
98121-1028
U.S.A.

Sojourner: Women's Forum
42 Seaverns Ave.
Boston, MA
02130
U.S.A.

South End Press
116 St. Botoph St.
Boston, MA
02115
U.S.A.